Praise for bel...
Be...

"Neels is especially good at painting her scenes with choice words, and this adds to the charm of the story."
—*USATODAY.com*'s *Happy Ever After* blog on *Tulips for Augusta*

"Betty Neels surpasses herself with an excellent storyline, a hearty conflict and pleasing characters."
—*RT Book Reviews* on *The Right Kind of Girl*

"Once again Betty Neels delights readers with a sweet tale in which love conquers all."
—*RT Book Reviews* on *Fate Takes a Hand*

"One of the first Harlequin authors I remember reading. I was completely enthralled by the exotic locales… Her books will always be some of my favorites to re-read."
—*Goodreads* on *A Valentine for Daisy*

"I just love Betty Neels!… If you like a good old-fashioned romance…you can't go wrong with this author."
—*Goodreads* on *Caroline's Waterloo*

Romance readers around the world were sad to note the passing of **Betty Neels** in June 2001. Her career spanned thirty years, and she continued to write into her ninetieth year. To her millions of fans, Betty epitomized the romance writer, and yet she began writing almost by accident. She had retired from nursing, but her inquiring mind still sought stimulation. Her new career was born when she heard a lady in her local library bemoaning the lack of good romance novels. Betty's first book, *Sister Peters in Amsterdam*, was published in 1969, and she eventually completed 134 books. Her novels offer a reassuring warmth that was very much a part of her own personality. She was a wonderful writer, and she is greatly missed. Her spirit and genuine talent live on in all her stories.

BETTY NEELS

Stormy Springtime
& The Bachelor's Wedding

HHARLEQUIN SPECIAL RELEASE

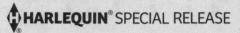

HARLEQUIN® SPECIAL RELEASE

PLEASE RECYCLE
THIS PRODUCT IS RECYCLABLE

ISBN-13: 978-1-335-00823-7

Recycling programs for this product may not exist in your area.

Stormy Springtime & The Bachelor's Wedding

Copyright © 2020 by Harlequin Books S.A.

Stormy Springtime
First published in 1986. This edition published in 2020.
Copyright © 1986 by Betty Neels

The Bachelor's Wedding
First published in 1995. This edition published in 2020.
Copyright © 1995 by Betty Neels

This edition published by arrangement with Harlequin Books S.A.

For questions and comments about the quality of this book, please contact us at CustomerService@Harlequin.com.

Harlequin Enterprises ULC
22 Adelaide St. West, 40th Floor
Toronto, Ontario M5H 4E3, Canada
www.Harlequin.com

Printed in U.S.A.

CONTENTS

STORMY SPRINGTIME

Chapter 1

The January afternoon was already darkening and a mean wind was driving rain against the windows of a room which, in its cheerful comfort, defied the evil weather outside. It was of a fair size, with a log fire blazing in its old-fashioned chimney-piece, lighted by several table lamps and furnished tastefully if somewhat shabbily. Its three occupants were seated close to the fire: three girls, sisters, deep in discussion.

'It's absolutely certain that the house will sell at once—it's got everything the estate agents like to boast about—modernised Georgian, adequate bathrooms, a tennis court—you name it, we've got it. It should fetch a good price.'

The speaker was a handsome young woman, older than the other two but still worth a second and third glance. She was very fair, with hair cut short and meticulous make-up. She was dressed expensively but without much imagination. She glanced at her two companions and went on, 'Charles says it would be downright foolish not to sell. We should each get a share...we shall invest ours, of course, so that James and Henry will have the proper schooling...'

The girl sitting opposite her stretched her long legs and yawned. 'Thank heaven I can please myself! I shall buy a flat near the hospital and give myself a super holiday.' She added smugly, 'I've been promised a Sister's post in a couple of months.' She was sunk in pleased thought for a few moments. 'Where will you send the boys?'

The third girl sat between them, curled up in an easy chair. She hadn't contributed to the conversation so far, but no one had expected her to. Ever since she could remember, she, the middle sister, had been ignored in a kindly fashion. As a child she had been very much in their shadows; that they were fond of her there was no doubt, the fondness strongly mixed with kindly indifference, but from earliest childhood she had been the one who had needed to be helped over hedges and gates, who fell out of trees, who hung back behind her sisters when people called. And the ease with which she passed her O and A levels at school was quite eclipsed by their brilliance at sports and theatricals. Besides, she was small and plump, with a face which was only redeemed from plainness by large grey eyes, heavily fringed, and a wide, gentle mouth. And now, with Cora married to a young accountant with ambition and the mother of two small sons, and Doreen embarked on a career in hospital—but only until such time as she could catch the eye of some eminent doctor—she had to admit to herself that she had nothing much to show for the last few years. True, she had stayed at home, largely because everyone took it for granted that she wanted to do so, and she had looked after her mother and after a year, she had taken over the housekeeping as well. She had, of necessity, become an excellent cook and a splendid housewife, helped by Betsy, who should have retired years ago but stubbornly refused, and by Mrs Griffiths, who popped in three times a week to do the rough work.

But now their mother was dead, her pension no longer paid, and there was precious little money save what their home would fetch. Cora and Doreen had never bothered overmuch about the pension—they had taken it for granted that it was enough for their mother and Meg to live on and pay their way. In their fashion they had been generous—dressing gowns and slippers and hampers at Christmas—but neither of them had suggested that Meg might like a holiday or even an evening out at a theatre… Meg bore them no grudge; Cora had her own life to lead and her own home and family, and besides, she lived in Kent and came home but rarely. And as for Doreen, everyone who knew her said what a splendid nurse she was and what a brilliant future she had before her. Besides, being such a handsome young woman, she could pick and choose from among her men friends and their invitations to dine and dance and go to the theatre, which left her little time to go to Hertfordshire.

Meg had been content enough; Hertingfordbury, where they had lived all their lives, was a charming village, the main roads bypassing it so that it was left in comparative peace with its church standing in the steep churchyard, its pub, the White Horse, still doing good business since the sixteenth century, and the equally ancient cottages. There were larger houses too—Georgian, built of rose brick, standing in roomy grounds, well cared for, handed on from one generation to the next. Meg's home was perhaps not as well cared for as other similar houses—there hadn't been the money during the last few years—but she had kept the garden in good order, and even if the outside paintwork wasn't as fresh as she might wish, she had done wonders with the lofty, well-proportioned rooms. Her sisters had good-naturedly dismissed her hours of careful painting and wallpapering as a pleasant little hobby to keep her occupied—to their credit, they had never realised that she had enough to occupy her without any hobbies. Their mother had had a worsening heart condition which, for the last few months of her life, had confined her to bed and couch, which meant a good deal of running to and fro and disturbed nights for Meg. And Meg, being Meg, had never complained. Not that she had ever felt downtrodden or put upon; she was a girl of common sense, and it was obvious to her that, since Cora had a home and family to look after, and Doreen had set her ambitious sights on becoming the wife of some eminent doctor, it was perfectly natural for them to pursue their own interests, since she had never exhibited any ambitions of her own.

She had those, of course, hidden away deep inside her—to marry and have a home of her own, a clutch of children, animals around the place and a garden—and a husband, of course. She was a little vague about him, but he would have to love her dearly for ever... At the moment, at any rate, there was no likelihood of meeting him. She had friends enough in the village, mostly elderly, and the young men she had grown up with had either got married or were engaged; besides, she had had very little time for the leisurely pursuits of her friends, and now that she was alone with time on her hands, she felt disinclined to join the activities in the village. Mrs Collins had died two months previously and Meg missed her sorely, more so because she had nursed her so devotedly for so long. She had gone on living alone save for Betsy, polishing the furniture, doing the flowers, tending the garden, taking it for granted that she would go on doing that for the foreseeable future. After all, it was her home, somewhere for Doreen to come when she wanted to, somewhere for Cora to send the boys to during the school holidays. She had a small annuity from her grandmother, just enough to live on and to pay Betsy and Mrs Griffiths.

She sat quietly now, filled with cold surprise and uncertainty. When Cora had finished explaining where the boys were to go to school, she asked, 'What about me—and Betsy?'

They turned to look at her, smiling reassuringly. 'Why, darling, you'll have your share, enough to buy a little flat somewhere—you could get a job—you'd like that after the quiet life you've been leading.'

It would be a waste of breath to ask what job; she wasn't trained for anything and it was a bit late to start at twenty-three. 'And Betsy?'

'Remember there was something in the will about those shares Mother had? They were for Betsy. They'll top up her state pension nicely.'

'Where will she live?'

Doreen said lightly, 'There must be any number of people in the village who'd be glad to let her have a room—she knows everyone for miles around.'

She got up and sat on the edge of Meg's chair and flung an arm around her shoulders. 'I'll get everyone looking for a flat for you, darling. You'll love London, and you'll make heaps of friends. You must be lonely here in this big place.'

Meg said in a wooden voice, 'No. I miss Mother, but it's still home, and there's plenty to keep me busy—and the garden even in winter.'

'We'll find you a basement flat with a paved area; you can fill it with pot plants.'

Meg let that pass. She said in her matter-of-fact way, 'I'll have to train for something,' and then, 'I suppose I *have* to leave here?' Neither of her sisters heard the wistfulness in her voice.

'Shorthand and typing,' said Cora, '—jobs going all the time for shorthand typists...'

'Receptionist?' suggested Doreen vaguely. She didn't say what for. 'Anyway, that's settled, isn't it? Let's get the estate agents on to it, Cora—there's a flat near the hospital which I rather like. There is no point in waiting, is there?'

'What about the furniture?' Meg had a quiet voice, but it brought them up short.

'Sell it?' essayed Cora.

'Put it in store? I could use it—some of it—in my new flat when I get it.'

Meg said slowly, 'Why not sell it with the house?' At the back of her mind there was an idea taking slow shape. She wasn't quite sure of it at the moment, but it would need thinking about later.

Cora looked at her approvingly. 'That's not a bad idea. We'll see what the agents say. I must fly—the boys will be back and Natasha—the au pair—is no good at all. I'll have to find someone else.'

They kissed Meg goodbye, went out to their cars, and

got in and drove away, and Meg went back into the house and sat down in the gathering gloom to think. If it were humanly possible, she didn't intend to leave her home, and certainly not to leave old Betsy to live out her days in a poky bedsitter. Presently Betsy came in with the teat-ray and Silky, the rather battered tomcat Meg had found skulking round the back door, had fed and sheltered and, since he had obviously made up his mind to become one of the family, had adopted. He got on to Meg's lap now, and Betsy put the tray down and said, 'Well, they've gone, then?' There was a question mark behind the words which couldn't be ignored.

'Cora and Doreen want to sell the house,' said Meg. 'And everything in it. But don't worry, Betsy, I've an idea…so that we can stay here.'

'Marry a millionaire, like as not, Miss Meg.' Betsy's cockney voice sounded cheerfully derisive. 'What's to happen to us, then?'

Meg said hearteningly, 'It takes weeks—months—to sell a house. I'll do something about it, I promise you.'

Betsy was only too willingly reassured; she trotted back to the kitchen and Meg sat drinking her tea, thinking about the future. Of course it would be marvellous if a very rich man came along and bought the house and fell in love with her at the same time, but that only happened in books… What was needed was someone elderly who needed a housekeeper or companion and a good plain cook and who didn't object to an elderly tomcat. Meg, who was a practical girl, thought it unlikely, though there was no harm in hoping.

Her sisters wasted no time. Within a week a pleasant young man from a London estate agent came to inspect the property. He walked round, with Meg beside him explaining about the old-fashioned bathrooms, the central heating, the Aga stove and why the large drawing-room was icy cold.

'There's only me,' she pointed out, 'there's no point in having a fire there just for one—my sisters are seldom here. We switch on the central heating twice a week, though, because of the furniture—Hepplewhite, you know.'

He nodded, rather at sea; he knew a lot about houses but not much about furniture. He felt vaguely sorry for the rather mouselike girl who was showing him round with such a self-possessed air. He spared a moment to wonder where she would go when the house was sold, for sold it would be, he could see that. Fine old Georgian houses with a generous spread of garden were much sought after. He accepted the coffee she offered him, agreed with her that people wishing to view the house might do so only with an appointment, and took his leave.

The first couple came within three days. In the morning, because Meg was on the committee which organised the Church Bazaar and that would take the whole afternoon.

Mr and Mrs Thorngood arrived in a splendid Mercedes and Meg, rarely given to criticising anyone, disliked them on sight. She led them round her home, listening with a calm face to their loud-voiced remarks about old-fashioned bathrooms, no fitted cupboards and a kitchen which must have come out of the Ark. They didn't like the garden, either: no swimming pool, all those trees and outbuildings which were of no use to anyone...

'We use the end one as a garage,' Meg pointed out.

'Well, that wouldn't do for us—we've three cars—we'd need to build a decent garage.' The man looked at her angrily as though it were her fault, and presently the pair of them drove away.

The next day a middle-aged woman with an overbearing manner came. She was looking for suitable premises for a school, she explained, but it took her only a short time to decide that the house wouldn't do at all. 'Most unsuitable,' she observed to Meg, who was politely standing on the doorstep to see her off. 'All those plastered ceilings, and none of the bedrooms would take more than five beds.'

Meg liked the next couple. They were young and friendly and admired everything wholeheartedly. It wasn't until they were drinking coffee with her in the sitting-room that the girl said suddenly, 'We can't possibly buy this place; actually we live in a poky little flat in Fulham, but when Mike's between jobs, we go around inspecting houses—it's fun, seeing how the other half live. I hope you don't mind.' She sighed. 'It must be nice to be rich and live in a lovely old house like this one.'

'Well', began Meg and decided not to go on. 'I'm glad you like it, anyway. It's been in the family for a fairly long time.'

There were quite a few viewers during the next week, but none of them came back a second time, although one man made an offer of slightly less than the price the agents had set. Instantly rejected, of course.

Then no one came at all for four days. Meg breathed a sigh of relief; perhaps no one would want to live in her home and she would be able to stay on there. She knew it was silly to think that; she would have to go sooner or later to some tiny basement flat unless she could find something to do locally. That wouldn't be easy, since she had no skills.

As each day passed she felt more and more lulled into false hopes; she ceased listening for the phone, put in hours of work in the garden and went for long walks. The weather had turned nasty—perhaps that was why no one came, but it made no difference to her. On the afternoon of the fourth day she came home from a muddy wet walk, kicked her sensible boots off at the back door and was met by an agitated Betsy.

'There's a gentleman,' said the old lady, all agog. 'The estate agent rang just after you'd gone and said he was on his way. I had to let him in... He's in the drawing-room.'

'Is he now? Well, he'll have to wait a bit longer, won't he, while I get tidied up? Bother the man!'

She had sat down on the floor of the back lobby, the better to pull off the old socks she wore inside her boots, and at a kind of gulping sound from Betsy, she turned her head. There was a man standing in the lobby doorway. A towering, wide-shouldered giant with black hair and even blacker eyes. Very good-looking too, thought Meg, and frowned fiercely at him. He had her at a disadvantage, and the nasty little smile on his thin mouth made that apparent.

'I must apologise,' he said in a voice which held no apology at all, and waited for her to speak. She sat there looking up at him. There was not much point in getting up until she had the socks off; for one thing she guessed that he must be over six feet and she was a mere five foot three; he would still look down on her. She disposed of the socks, stood up and pushed her feet into a shabby pair of slippers and flung off her wet raincoat, dragged off the scarf she had tied round her hair and addressed him coolly. 'No need,' she told him. 'You weren't to know that I wasn't at home.' She tossed back her damp hair, hanging untidily round her damp face, rosy from the wind and rain. 'You would like to see round the house?'

'You are right, that was my object in coming,' he informed her.

Oh, very stuffy, decided Meg, and led the way to the front hall which was, after all, the starting point. She had the patter off by heart now: the Adam fireplace in the drawing-room, the strap work on the dining-room ceiling, the rather special Serpentine scroll balustrade on the staircase, and as they wandered in and out of the bedrooms on the first floor she pointed out the quite ugly cast-iron fireplace—writhing forms, a mid-Victorian addition which her companion pronounced in a cold voice as frankly hideous. But other than that, he had little to say. She thought it very likely that the sight of the old-fashioned bathrooms with pipes all over the place and great cast-iron baths sitting on clawed feet in the middle of the rooms left him bereft of words. She was quite sure that it was a waste of time taking him round; she took his final comment—'A most interesting house'—as a polite way of getting himself out of the door. Not that she considered him a polite man; he should have stayed where Betsy put him, in the drawing-room, until he could have been fetched at the proper time and with suitable dignity.

She stood with him on the steps outside the front door, waiting for him to go. Only he didn't. 'You live here alone?' he asked.

'No—Betsy lives here with me.'

He glanced at her ringless, rather grubby hands. For a moment she thought that he was going to say something more, but he didn't. His, 'Thank you, Miss Collins,' was brisk and impersonal as he trod down the steps and got into the dark grey Rolls-Royce parked on the sweep before the house. He didn't look round either, but drove away without so much as a backward glance.

''andsome man,' remarked Betsy, coming into the hall as Meg closed the door. 'Nicely spoken, too. P'raps 'e'll buy…'

Meg said quite vehemently, 'I found him a rude man, and I hope never to see him again, Betsy.' Whereupon she flew upstairs and took a good look at herself in the pier glass in what had been her mother's room. Her reflection hardly reassured her; her nose shone, her hair was still damp and wispy and the serviceable guernsey and elderly tweed skirt she wore when she was gardening hardly enhanced her appearance. The slippers completed a decidedly unfashionable appearance. She wondered what he had thought of her, and then forgot him; he had joined all the house-hunters whom she would never see again. She wasn't even sure of his name—he had given it to her, but she hadn't paid attention. She could, of course, have asked Betsy, but she didn't; for some reason she wanted to forget him.

January slipped away into February and it turned cold and snowed. Cora and Doreen phoned each week, wanting to know if anyone had made a bid for the house and giving excellent reasons why they couldn't get down to see her. Meg, accepting them without rancour, none the less wished for more sisterly support. She was happy as things were, but there all the time at the back of her mind was the thought that sooner or later she would have to give up her home and live in some poky flat in an endless row of equally poky flats… Indeed, Doreen had told her only the evening before that she had heard of a semi-basement on the fringes of Highgate; two rooms and bathroom and kitchen—there wouldn't be much money over by the time Meg had bought it with her share, but then Meg would get a job easily enough.

'What at?' asked Meg of Betsy, who shook her head and said nothing at all.

No one could come until the snow had gone. Meg pottered round the house, polished the silver and got in Betsy's way in the kitchen. It was something of a shock when the estate agents phoned to say that there was a Mrs Culver on her way.

Meg, who had been in the kitchen making marmalade with Betsy, went to her room and tidied herself, re-did her hair, ran a powder puff over her face, changed into the cashmere sweater she kept for special occasions, and went downstairs just in time to watch an elderly but beautifully kept Daimler draw up before the door. She skipped into the drawing-room and picked up a book; it would never do to be caught snooping.

The doorbell rang and Betsy, in a clean apron, but smelling delightfully of marmalade on the boil, answered it and presently ushered Mrs Culver into the room.

'You're making marmalade,' observed that lady as she advanced across the wide expanse of Moorfields carpet. 'One of the most delightful aromas there is.' She smiled at Meg. 'How do you do? You will be Miss Collins? You must forgive me for coming at such an awkward time and at such short notice; I am only just back in England.'

Meg murmured politely; she hadn't met anyone like Mrs Culver before. She was a small, rather plump woman, well into middle age, but so well dressed and exquisitely made-up that she gave the lie to that. Not pretty but with a delightful smile and twinkling eyes so that one was forced to smile back at her.

'It's quite convenient,' Meg assured her. 'Would you

like to sit and rest for a few minutes or would you like to look round now?'

'May I look round?' Mrs Culver studied her surroundings. 'This is a charming room.'

Meg found herself liking the little lady. She led the way back into the hall and started her tour, and found for once an appreciative companion. What was more, Mrs Culver didn't seem at all put off by the bathroom pipes, and remarked upon the elegance of the Adam fireplace before Meg could even mention it.

'I like this house,' observed Mrs Culver as they returned to the drawing-room. 'I shall buy it.'

Meg said rather faintly, 'Oh, will you? Would you like some coffee?'

'Indeed I would,' and when Meg returned from the kitchen, 'Tell me, has it been in your family for a long time?'

'Ages. It was built in 1810, but of course it's had things done to it since then.'

'But not very recently,' remarked Mrs Culver drily, 'therein lies its charm. I promise you that if I do do anything at all it will be done so well that you wouldn't even notice it.'

Meg poured the coffee, wrestling with a variety of feelings. It was splendid news for Cora and Doreen, of course, but not for her and Betsy. The poky flat loomed large, and how was she going to bear leaving her home? She stifled these feelings with the common sense she had cultivated since she was a child; the house had to be sold, and who better to buy it than this nice elderly lady who liked the making of marmalade and knew an Adam fireplace when she saw one? She said, 'You'll be very happy here,' and meant it. 'Do you want the name of our solicitor or would you like to think about it first?'

'I've thought, my dear. I shall go straight to the estate agents and then instruct my solicitor.' She paused and frowned. 'There is just one thing.'

Meg waited for Mrs Culver to go on. Problems sometimes turned into insurmountable snags—it would be the bathrooms and those pipes. She herself had grown up with them, but every single person who had inspected the house had remarked upon them. She assumed a sympathetically listening face and looked across at her companion.

'My housekeeper,' began that lady, 'has been waiting for some months for an operation—something to do with her toes—and only this morning she told me that there was a bed for her at last. She offered to put the whole thing off, bless her, until it was convenient for me, but I can't have that—it isn't an emergency, you understand, but it will take time before she can come back to me— nasty little pins in her toes to straighten them, so I'm told, and when she does return she must have someone to do the lion's share of the work until she can cope once again. I'm told that when she has got over whatever it is that they intend to do to her, her feet will be like new. She has been with me for more than twenty years and is a treasure as well as a friend.' She stopped to take a breath. 'Very like that nice woman who opened the door to me.'

'Betsy—she's been with me since I was a baby.'

Mrs Culver eyed Meg thoughtfully. 'It's scarcely my business to ask, but when you leave here, will she go with you? If not, would she consider staying on until my Kate is well enough again? Two months at least…and I suppose you wouldn't know of a good cook? Someone to work with her—it's a big house and I'm not allowed to be energetic. I dare say I could get someone from the village to help with the rough work.' She smiled at Meg. 'I'm an impertinent old woman, aren't I? And you're at liberty to say so if you wish.'

'I wouldn't dream of it, and I don't think you are anyway,' declared Meg. 'It's a most sensible idea. As a matter of fact, my sisters want me to go and live in London in a flat and find a job, and they thought Betsy could find a room in the village.' She felt a strong urge to tell Mrs Culver all about her sisters' arrangements and plans, but of course that was out of the question.

Mrs Culver nodded and gave Meg a sharp glance, sensing that there was a lot left unsaid. 'What work will you do?' she asked.

'I have no idea. I'm not trained for anything; our mother was ill for a long time so I took over the housekeeping, and Betsy taught me to cook…' She stopped suddenly and stared at her companion, who stared back.

'It's as plain as the nose on my face,' said Mrs Culver. 'I suspect that we're being unbusinesslike and impulsive, but I've always relied on my female intuition, and it tells me that I can't go wrong. Will you stay on as housekeeper and have your Betsy to help you? It would give you time to settle your future; I dare say you're in no hurry to go and live in a London flat. And dear old Kate can have her feet put right without worrying about getting back to me until she's quite fit and well. Would you mind being a housekeeper, my dear?'

Meg hadn't felt so happy for months; the dreaded London flat could be abrogated at least for a month or two, she could stay in her home, doing exactly what she had been doing for some years, and Betsy would have time to get used to changes. Her vague idea had become reality.

'I wouldn't mind at all, Mrs Culver. I'd like it very much and I know Betsy would too, and if you want someone for the rough work, Mrs Griffiths, the postman's wife, has been coming here for years.'

They beamed at each other, and Mrs Culver asked, 'The garden? Is there a man...?'

'Well, no, I've been doing the gardening, though you could do with someone for the hedges and the digging—I've had to leave a good bit.'

'Well, you find someone, my dear; I'm sure I can safely leave it to you—and more help in the house if you need it. I suppose it will take the solicitors weeks to get things settled—I've been mystified as to why. But in the meantime, will you go on as you have been doing? I'll write to you as soon as things are settled, and we must have a talk before I move in.' She looked round the pleasant room. 'Would you consider selling the furniture? There must be treasured pieces you would want to keep so that you can furnish your flat eventually, but the rest?'

'I'll have to ask my sisters,' said Meg. 'They did suggest that I had some of it and my younger sister might want some things—she hopes to buy a flat near the hospital and live out.'

'And you have another sister?'

'Yes, older than me—she's married and doesn't want anything here.'

Mrs Culver got up to go. 'Well, we can settle that when you have seen them, can't we? You're sure that you are happy about our little arrangement?'

Meg smiled widely. 'Oh, yes—very happy. I—I really am not too keen on living in London.' They walked unhurriedly to the door, pleased with each other's company. 'Would you like a word with Betsy?'

'A very good idea. Shall we go to the kitchen, if she's there?'

Betsy's elderly face crumpled into dozens of wrinkles at the news; she looked as though she might cry, but she chuckled instead. 'There, Miss Meg—yer never know, do yer? What's round the corner, I mean. I'm sure I'll bide 'ere and 'appy ter do so just as long as I'm needed.'

'I'm so glad,' said Mrs Culver, and shook Betsy's hand. 'I look forward to living here in this nice old house.'

Meg saw her out to the car and gave the solid-looking man who opened the car door a guilty look. He understood at once. 'Your cook kindly gave me a coffee, miss,' he told her. 'Thank you.'

'Oh, good—I'm sorry I forgot—as long as Betsy saw to your comfort.'

She put her head through the still-open door. 'I'm glad it's you,' she told Mrs Culver, who was being cosily tucked in with rugs by the chauffeur. 'Mother and Father would have liked to have met you.'

'Why, thank you, my dear—what a nice thing to say. You shall hear from me very shortly. Goodbye.'

Over their midday snack Meg and Betsy talked over the morning. They found it difficult to believe that it had all happened. 'It's like a fairy tale,' said Meg. 'I can't believe it... I know it's not going to last, but it does give us another month or so. We'll be here when the daffodils are out.' She cut a wedge of cheese. 'You're to have your wages, Betsy, and so am I—nice to be paid for something I've been doing for nothing for years!'

She fell silent, her busy mind exploring the chances of getting a job as housekeeper when she finally left—

if Mrs Culver would give her a reference she might be lucky—then there would be no need to live in London. Presently she said, 'I must let Cora and Doreen know,' and went to the telephone in what had been her father's study.

Of course they were both delighted.

'Now we can get the boys' names down for school,' said Cora.

'I'll make a firm offer for that flat,' Doreen decided and added as an afterthought, 'once it's all dealt with, Meg, I'll look out for something for you—you'd better take a course in shorthand and typing.'

It seemed hardly the time to tell them that Mrs Culver had plans of her own; Meg put down the receiver without having said a word about herself and Betsy, but then, neither of them had asked.

There was purpose in the days now: the house to clean and polish, cupboards to turn out, the silver to polish, wrap up and stow away, curtains to be cleaned... Mrs Griffiths, when approached, was glad enough to continue coming three times a week, and what was more, she had an out-of-work nephew who would be glad to see to the garden.

There were letters too, learned ones from the solicitor, triumphant ones from the estate agents and a steady flow of instructions from Cora and Doreen. What was more important was that there was a letter from Mrs Culver, stating that she would be glad to employ both Meg and Betsy, and setting out their wages in black and white. She had urged the solicitors to make haste, she had written, and hoped to move in in about three weeks' time.

'A nice letter,' said Meg, putting it back neatly into

its envelope. 'I wonder where I've heard the name Culver before?'

She discovered the very next day. It was a lovely day, clear and frosty and with a brief sunshine which held no warmth but gave the illusion of spring. She was perched on a window-seat in the drawing-room, carefully mending one of the old, but still beautiful, brocade curtains, when a car drew up and a man got out. She remembered him at once—who could forget him, being the size and height he was anyway? She watched him walk unhurriedly to the door and pull the old-fashioned bell, and then listened to Betsy's feet trotting across the hall to open the door.

If he had had second thoughts, decided Meg with satisfaction, he was going to be disappointed. She remembered the look he had given the bathroom pipes and the Victorian fireplace; he would make an offer, perhaps, far below the one asked, and she would find great satisfaction in refusing it.

It wasn't like that at all. Betsy ushered him in. 'Mr Culver to see you, Miss Meg.' She winked as she went out.

Meg got up and said uncertainly, 'Have you come about the house? It's sold—' and at the same instant said, 'Culver—you aren't by any chance related to Mrs Culver?'

'Her son. I suggested that she should come and see the place; I knew she'd like it.' He raised dark eyebrows. 'You're disconcerted, Miss Collins?'

Meg eyed him cautiously, for he sounded cross. 'Not that,' she explained politely, 'just surprised. I'd forgotten your name, you see.'

'You're to remain here as my mother's housekeeper?

Oh, don't look alarmed—I have no intention of interfering with her plans. It seems a most suitable arrangement. But you do understand that when Kate, her own housekeeper, returns, you and your servant will have to go.'

'Betsy isn't a servant,' said Meg clearly, 'she's been with my family for a very long time. She's our friend and helper.'

The eyebrows rose once more. 'I stand corrected! May I sit down?'

She flushed. 'I'm sorry, please do. Why have you come, Mr Culver? And you had no need to remind me that we're only here temporarily.'

'I came to tell you that within the week there will be some furniture delivered, and to ask you to remove whatever you wish to keep for yourself. Presumably there are attics?'

'Three large ones, and yes, I'll do that.'

'A cheque for the furniture, which will be valued, will be paid to your solicitor in due course. Tell me, Miss Collins, don't your sisters want to discuss this with you?'

'No—my elder sister is married and my younger sister is too busy—she's a staff nurse in London...'

'And you?' For once his voice was friendly, and she responded to it without thinking.

'Me? I can't do anything except look after a house and cook; that's why I'm so happy to stay on here for a little while.'

She studied his bland face for a while. 'You don't mind?' she asked.

'Why should I mind?' He got to his feet. 'I won't keep you any longer. Let your solicitor know if there's anything which worries you.'

Meg went with him to the door, and because he looked

somehow put out about something, she said gently, 'I'm sorry you don't like me staying here, Mr Culver, but it won't be for long.'

He took her hand in his. 'That's what I'm afraid of, Miss Collins,' he told her gravely. 'Goodbye.'

Chapter 2

Meg shut the door firmly behind Mr Culver and then stood looking at the painted panelling in the hall. She wondered what he had meant; it was a strange remark to make, and it made no sense. She dismissed it from her mind and wandered off to the kitchen to tell Betsy about the furniture. 'So we'd better go round the house and pick out what we want,' she ended. 'I'll try and get Doreen to come down and sort out what she wants.'

Doreen came two days later, full of plans for herself and for Meg. 'You'll have to go into a bedsitter or digs for a while,' she told her. 'I'll ask around…'

'There's no need; I'm staying on here as housekeeper, and Betsy's staying too,' she said, and before an astonished Doreen could utter a word, added, 'I'll explain.'

When she had finished, Doreen said, 'Well, I don't know—housekeeper in your own home—it's a bit demeaning, and such hard work!'

'But I've been housekeeping for years,' Meg pointed out, 'and besides, I'm going to be paid for it now.'

Doreen was a bit huffy; she had been telling Meg what to do and how to do it since they were children, and until now Meg had meekly followed her lead. 'Oh, well,' she said grudgingly, 'I suppose you know your own mind best, though I think it's a mistake. Cora won't like it...'

'Why not?' asked Meg placidly. 'I should have thought you'd have both been pleased that I'm settled for a month or two.' She added cunningly, 'You'll be able to concentrate on your new flat.'

A remark which caused her sister to subside, still grumbling but resigned. Moreover, she declared that she would be down the following weekend to choose furniture. 'I don't want much,' she said. 'I'm going to buy very simple modern stuff.' She added, 'Cora doesn't want anything, only those paintings of the ancestors in the hall and the silver tea and coffee sets.'

As she got into her car she asked carelessly, 'What's this son like?'

Meg paused to think. 'Well, he's very tall—about six feet four inches—and broad. He's dark and his eyes look black, though I don't suppose they are...he's—he's arrogant and—off-hand.'

Doreen gave her a kindly, pitying look. 'Out of your depth, were you?' she asked. 'He sounds quite a dish.' She started the engine. 'What does he do?'

Meg stared at her. 'I haven't the faintest idea. We only talked about the house and the furniture.'

Doreen grinned. 'I can well believe that! When I've settled you in that semi-basement, Meg, I'm going to find you an unambitious curate.'

She shot away, and instead of going indoors Meg wandered along the path which circumvented the house. She had no wish to marry a curate, she was certain on that point, nor did she want to marry a man like her brother-in-law—something in the city and rising fast, and already pompous. She would like to marry, of course, but although she had a very clear idea of the home she would like and the children in it, not to mention dogs and cats and a donkey and perhaps a pony, the man who would provide her with all this was a vague nonentity. But she wanted to be loved and cherished, she was sure of that.

She went back into the house and sat at the kitchen table eating the little cakes Betsy had made for tea and which Doreen hadn't eaten because of her figure. 'Do you suppose I could have the furniture in my room, Betsy?' she asked at length. 'I could put a few chairs and tables in there before Mrs Culver comes, then it would be easy when we move out. I won't need much in a small flat...'

Betsy was beating eggs. 'Likely not,' she agreed. 'Poky places they are, them semi-basements—lived in one myself 'fore I came to yer ma. Can't see why yer 'ave ter live in one, meself.'

Meg ate another cake. 'No—well, I've been thinking. If I can get Mrs Culver to give us good references we might try for jobs in some large country house, the pair of us. I was looking through the advertisements in *The Lady*, Betsy, and there are dozens of jobs.'

'Yer ma and pa would turn in their graves if yer was ter do that, Miss Meg—housework indeed—and you a lady born and bred. I never 'eard such nonsense!'

Meg got up and flung an arm round her old friend's shoulders. 'I think I'd rather do anything than live in a basement flat in London,' she declared. 'Let's go round the house and choose what I'll take with me.'

Small pieces for the most part: her mother's papier
mâché work table, encrusted with mother-of-pearl and
inlaid with metal foil, a serpentine table in mahogany
with a pierced gallery, and a Martha Washington chair
reputed to be Chippendale and lastly a little rosewood
desk where her mother had been in the habit of writing
her letters. She added two standard chairs with sabre
legs, very early nineteenth century, and a sofa table on
capstan base with splayed feet which went very well with
the chairs and wouldn't take up too much room.

They went back to the kitchen and Meg made a neat
list. 'And now you, Betsy; of course you'll have the furniture which is already in your room, but you'll need
some bits and pieces.'

So they went round again, adding a rather shabby armchair Betsy had always liked, and the small, stoutly built
wooden table in the scullery with its two equally stout
chairs. Meg added a bookcase standing neglected in one
of the many small rooms at the back of the house, and
a standard lamp which had been by the bookcase for as
long as she could remember. No one was going to miss
it, and it would please Betsy mightily.

She got the butcher's boy from the village to come up
to the house and move the furniture into her and Betsy's
rooms. Doreen would see to her own things once she
had chosen them.

This was something which she did at the end of the
week, arriving at the house a bare five minutes after Mr
Culver's second totally unexpected visit. Getting no answer from the front doorbell, he had wandered round
the house and found Meg in an old sweater and slacks
covered by a sacking apron, intent on arranging seed potatoes on the shelves of the potting shed. She turned to

see who it was as he trod towards her, and said, rather crossly, 'Oh, it's you—you didn't say you were coming!'

He ignored that. 'It's careless of you to leave your front door open when you're not in the house, Miss Collins. You should be more careful.'

She gave him a long, considered look. He doubtless meant to be helpful, but it seemed that each time they met he said something to annoy her.

'This isn't London,' she said with some asperity, and then added in a kindly tone, 'though I dare say you mean well.'

He stood looking down his handsome nose at her. 'Naturally I have an interest in this house...'

'Premature,' Meg observed matter-of-factly. 'I haven't—that is, we haven't sold it to your mother yet.'

She wished the words unsaid at once: supposing that he took umbrage and advised his mother to withdraw from the sale? What would her sisters say? And she would have to start all over again, and next time she might not be as lucky as regards her future. She met his eyes and saw that he was smiling nastily.

'Exactly, Miss Collins, it behoves you to mind your words, does it not?' He added unwillingly, 'Your face is like an open book—you must learn to conceal your thoughts before you embark on a career in London!'

He looked over his shoulder as he spoke, in time to see Doreen coming towards them, and Meg, watching him saw that he was impressed. Her sister was looking particularly pretty in a wide tweed coat, draped dramatically over her shoulders, allowing a glimpse of a narrow cashmere dress in a blue to match her eyes. She fetched up beside him, cast him a smiling glance and said, 'Hello, Meg—darling, must you root around like a farm labourer?' She peered at the potatoes. 'Such a dirty job!'

Meg said 'Hello,' and waved a grubby hand at Mr Culver. 'This is Mr Culver, Mrs Culver's son—my sister, Doreen; she's come to choose her furniture before the valuers get here.'

Mr Culver, it seemed, could make himself very agreeable if he so wished, and Doreen, of course, had always been considered a charming girl. They fell at once into the kind of light talk which Meg had never learnt to master. She carefully arranged another row of potatoes, listening admiringly to Doreen's witty chatter, and when there was a pause asked, 'Why did you come, Mr Culver?'

Not the happiest way of putting it—Doreen's look told her that—so she added, 'Is there anything we can do.'

He glanced between the pair of them, and Meg caught the glance. Wondering how on earth we could possibly be sisters, she thought, and suddenly wished that she wasn't plain and could talk like Doreen.

'My mother asked me to call in—I'm on my way home and it isn't out of my way. She wants you to order coal and logs—a ton of each, I would suggest—and also, if you know of a young boy who would do odd jobs, would you hire him?'

'What to do?' asked Meg, ever practical. 'Not full time, I imagine?'

'I believe she was thinking of someone to carry in coal and so on. Perhaps on his way to school, or in the afternoon...'

'Well, there's Willy Wright—he's fifteen and looking for work. He goes to school still, but I dare say he'd be glad of the money.'

Mr Culver nodded carelessly. 'I'll leave it in your capable hands.'

'Oh, she's capable all right, our Meg,' put in Doreen. 'Always has been. You live near here, Mr Culver?' She was at her most charming.

He gave the kind of answer Meg would have expected of him. 'I work in London for most of the time. And you?'

Doreen told him, making the telling amusing and self-effacing at the same time. 'Come into the house and have a cup of tea—I know Meg is dying for us to go so that she can finish her potatoes.' She smiled at her sister. 'Finished in ten minutes or so, Meg? I'll have the tea made.'

She led the way back to the house, leaving Meg in the potting shed, quite happy to be left on her own once more. Doreen had never made a secret of the fact that she intended to marry and marry well. She thought it very likely that before Mr Culver left Doreen would have found out what he did, whether he was engaged or even married, and where he lived. She chuckled as she started on the last row of potatoes; Mr Culver had met his match.

It was half an hour before she joined them in the sitting-room, wearing a neat shirt blouse and a pleated skirt, her small waist cinched by a wide soft leather belt. Mr Culver was on the point of going, which was what she had been hoping; anyway, she wished him a coolly polite goodbye, leaving Doreen to see him to the door, assuring him that she would do as Mrs Culver asked. The moment they were in the hall, she picked up the tea-tray and whisked herself off to the kitchen to make a fresh pot. Doreen would want another cup before she started on the furniture.

'What a man!' observed that young lady as she sank into a chair. 'Is that fresh tea? I could do with a cup. Be-

lieve it or not, Meg, I couldn't get a thing out of him—
he's a real charmer, no doubt of that, but as close as an
oyster. I bet he's not married.' She took the cup Meg
was offering. 'I wonder what he does? Perhaps you can
find out…?'

'Why?' Meg sounded reasonable. 'He's nothing to
do with us; we're not likely to see him—he only called
with a message.'

Doreen looked thoughtful. 'Yes, well, we'll see. That's
a nice car, and unless I'm very mistaken, his shoes are
hand-made…'

'Perhaps he's got awkward feet,' suggested Meg, quite
seriously.

Doreen looked at her to see if she was joking and saw
that she wasn't, so she didn't reply. 'When's Mrs Culver
due to arrive?' she asked instead. 'I'd better decide on the
things I want and get them away. Have you got yours?'

Meg nodded. 'Yes, I got Willy to come up and move
them. Most of it's in my room; the rest is in the attic.
Betsy's got some bits and pieces, too—in her room and
some in the attic.'

'Well, I'll get it over with and have it taken up to town
and stored until I want it. Does Mrs Culver want everything else? How much will she pay for it?'

'I've no idea. There's a valuer coming… I'll let you
know as soon as he's been and she's agreed to his esti-
mate.'

Doreen wandered off and came back presently with
a scribbled list. Mostly portraits, a rent table which
wouldn't really be missed in the drawing-room, a little
button-backed Victorian chair from one of the bedrooms
and a corner cupboard. 'Not much,' she commented. 'I'd
rather have the money, anyway. Cora and I don't really

like the idea of you staying on here as housekeeper, you know. It's only for a few weeks, isn't it? Let me know in good time so that I can find somewhere for you, Meg.'

It seemed as good a time as any to talk about her future. Meg said quietly, 'Doreen, I'd like to go on housekeeping; if Mrs Culver will give me a reference I could get a job in some country house—and take Betsy with me—I'd probably get a cottage or a flat, and I'd much rather do that than live in London...'

Doreen looked at her with kindly tolerance. 'Don't be daft, love. Just you leave everything to Cora and me—we really know what's best for you. You've lived here too long; it's time you went into the world and had a look around.'

'I don't think it's my sort of world,' protested Meg doggedly. 'I like the country and keeping house and looking after people...'

'Nonsense,' said Doreen firmly. 'How can you be certain of that before you've lived somewhere else?' She added coaxingly, 'Cora and I do want you to be happy, darling; I know there wasn't much we could do about it while Mother was alive, but now we intend to see that you have some fun.'

There had been a lot they could have done, but Meg didn't say so; she loved her two pretty sisters and she wasn't a girl to bear a grudge.

All she said was, mildly, 'Well, Betsy and I will be here for two months—plenty of time to make plans.'

Doreen nodded her pretty head; she was looking thoughtful again. 'I don't suppose Mrs Culver will mind if I pop down to see you now and again?' And at Meg's look of surprise, 'Just to make sure that everything is OK...' She gave herself away completely by adding, 'I

wonder where he lives and what he does? I might be able
to find out…'

'Did you like him?' asked Meg.

'My dear Meg—grow up, do! He's got everything:
looks—my goodness, he's got those all right—obviously
a good job—probably chairman of something or other—
and money. He's every girl's dream, ducky.'

'Oh, is he? I don't much care for him. Besides, he may
be married.'

'But it's worth finding out. I must be off. I'll let you
know when to expect the carrier to collect my furniture.'
Doreen dropped a kiss on Meg's cheek. 'Be seeing you,
darling. Has Cora phoned?'

'Last week. I expect she's busy; the boys have half
term.'

Getting into the car, Doreen said, 'I'm broke—this
cashmere dress, but it's worth every penny. You must
get yourself some decent clothes, love. You look—well—
dowdy!'

She sped away with a wave and Meg stood in the
porch, shivering a little in the cold wind, aware that her
sister was quite right. A housekeeper should be decently
but soberly dressed, and she would need a couple of overalls.

She would go into Hertford in the morning; she had a
little money she had been hanging on to for emergencies,
and since she was to be paid, she could safely spend it.

It took her some time to find what she wanted. Sober
dresses suitable for a housekeeper seemed to be made for
very large, tall women and she was size ten. She found
something at last: dark grey with white collars and a
little black bow; it did nothing for her whatsoever, but
then it wasn't supposed to. She bought overalls too, blue

and white checks with a white collar and neat belts, and
since she had a little money over she bought Betsy two
new aprons, old-fashioned with bibs which crossed over
at the back and fastened with giant safety pins. Nothing
would convince Betsy that nylon overalls saved time and
labour; she had never fancied them, and she wasn't prepared to change her ideas at her time of life.

Another week went by. The solicitors, at last satisfied that all the parties concerned were not up to something unlawful, cautiously exchanged contracts and then,
doubtless egged on by Mrs Culver, allowed them to be
signed. The house was Mrs Culver's. All three of them
had had to sign; Doreen had fetched Meg and had driven
into Hertford, annoyed at what she called the waste of her
precious time, but excited too, and Cora had driven herself from Kent, excited in a controlled way, anxious to get
the business over and get back to her modern, split-level
house with its well-kept garden and the double garage.

The whole business took only a very few minutes;
they stood on the pavement outside the solicitor's office
and looked at each other. 'I'd better come back to the
house and get the pictures and silver,' said Cora. 'You
heard what Mr Dutton said, Meg? The money will be
paid into my account and I'll send you a cheque for your
share, and Doreen, of course.' She looked at her younger
sister. 'I expect you want to get back to the hospital. I'll
take Meg back, collect my things and go home—I've a
bridge party this afternoon.'

She tucked her arm into Meg's. 'Lovely to have it all
settled. What a difference it's going to make.'

Meg said nothing at all. Doreen and Cora might be
over the moon but she had just lost her home. She would
rather have gone on living there until it fell in ruins about

her ears; what use was the money to her if she had to use it to buy some ghastly basement flat? She swallowed back tears and got into Cora's car.

A week later Mrs Culver moved in. There had been a small van load of furniture first with instructions as to where it was to be put and at ten o'clock in the morning the Rolls-Royce had come to a quiet halt in front of the door and the new owner had stepped out, helped, Meg was annoyed to see, by her son, massive and calm and for some reason faintly amused. That the amusement had been engendered by her own sober appearance never entered her head. She welcomed Mrs Culver with shy dignity, and led the way to the drawing-room.

'I expect you'd like coffee. I'll bring it.' She glanced at Mr Culver. 'You'll have a cup, Mr Culver?'

'Thank you, yes.' He glanced round the room. 'I see you've had the time to arrange my mother's things.'

And when she said yes, he asked, 'The valuer has been?'

'Yes. He'll write to Mrs Culver.'

That lady was sitting back comfortably, taking no part in the conversation. Meg suspected that she was in the habit of leaving business matters to her son. She got herself out of the room and hurried to the kitchen to get the coffee tray.

'They're 'ere,' said Betsy, unnecessarily. ''E's 'ere too. A proper gent.'

Meg had her own ideas about that, but there was no time to discuss the man. She whipped up the tray and went back with it, and set it down on the lamp table by Mrs Culver's chair.

'Where's your cup?' asked the older woman.

'My cup?' Meg echoed.

'Yes, dear. Go and fetch it. Ralph hasn't much time, and he wants to be sure that there are no loose ends.'

Meg fetched another cup and saucer and sat down on a little chair as far from Mr Culver as she dared without being rude. He gave her a hooded glance.

'I wish merely to thank you for the help you've given my mother. Without you, she would have been unable to settle in so quickly. We're grateful. Do we owe you anything? Are there any outstanding bills?'

Meg said that, no, there weren't. 'Willy will be up tomorrow morning on his way to school and will fill the coal scuttles, and he'll come again in the afternoon on his way back home. The gardener starts on Monday.'

Mr Culver finished his coffee and got up. 'I think you'll be happy here, Mother. You know where I am if you need me, my dear.' He crossed the room and kissed her cheek, and nodded austerely to Meg. 'I'll see myself out.'

Meg poured more coffee, and Mrs Culver said, 'Such a good son—never interferes, you know, but always there when I want him. So convenient. He's just like his father.'

Meg looked at her companion with something like respect. If his father had been like him, then she must have had her work cut out—but perhaps he had loved her very much and never let her see the cold mockery and impatience—or perhaps it was Meg herself who induced those. She thought that probably it was; she had had no practice in turning a man up sweet. She murmured suitably and asked what Mrs Culver would like for lunch.

It took only a few days to settle into a routine. Mrs Culver liked her breakfast in bed, which meant that Meg and Betsy could eat their own meal and get on with the household chores. Even with Mrs Griffith's help there was plenty of work to be got through, and they did the bulk of it in the early mornings. Mrs Culver's own car had arrived with her chauffeur and she was out a good deal, which gave Meg time to see to the washing and ironing and help Betsy with the meals, so that tasks such as arranging the flowers and setting the table for meals could be done when that lady was at home, tasks which Meg concluded were quite suitable for a housekeeper. She had no doubt that Mrs Culver had little idea of what went on behind the scenes; she was charming, easy and very kind, and had very likely grown up and lived all her life with people to do her bidding.

But it had been a surprise to Meg when Mrs Culver had insisted on her taking her meals with her. And when she had demurred, she had insisted, 'Nonsense, child. You've sat at this table all your life; you will continue to do so or upset me very much.'

So Meg sat at the table she had laid so carefully, getting up to clear the dishes and fetch the food from the kitchen, for Betsy had enough to do and her legs hurt in any case, and she entirely approved of the arrangement. The dear soul still thought of her as the lady of the house. Mrs Culver was a nice enough lady, indeed, one couldn't wish for a better, but there had been Collinses living there for a long time, and she didn't take easily to change.

Meg was happy; she was still in her own home, she enjoyed the work even though her days were long and there was little time to get into the garden. Cora had phoned to say that her share of the money was paid into her account and to ask, rather casually, if she were happy. And when she had a satisfactory answer, 'Then I'll not bother you, Meg; let me know when you leave and I'll help in any way I can.'

She had a much longer call from Doreen, who wasted little time on questions but plunged at once into her news. She had discovered who Mr Culver was—a Professor, a consultant radiologist, based at one of the big teaching hospitals but with a large area to cover. 'He's well known,' said Doreen, 'goes to any number of hospitals for consultations—one of the best men in his field—Europe too. When is he going to visit his mother, Meg?'

'I've no idea. Did you want to see him about something? Shall I ask Mrs Culver?'

'I wish you'd grow up, Meg! Of course I want to see him, but only to get to know him. He's not married…'

Meg tried to imagine him as a future brother-in-law. 'He's quite old,' she pointed out in her practical manner.

'Rubbish—thirty-eight at the most. Quite brilliant at his work, too—he'll end up with a knighthood.'

'I thought you were keen on that registrar…'

'Oh, him! Listen, darling, if you hear that he's coming down to see his mother, give me a ring, will you?'

'Why?' asked Meg, being deliberately dim. She heard her sister's exasperated sigh as she hung up.

As it happened she had no chance to do that, and she was glad, for it smacked of disloyalty to Mrs Culver and to him. After all, she was in Mrs Culver's employ. The Professor walked in as they sat at lunch a day or two later. He had a dirty, half-starved dog under one arm which was cringing away from the sight of them, and Meg got up at once and said, 'Oh, the poor beast, let me have him. Have you come to lunch? There's plenty…'

It was a quiche Lorraine and she had just begun to cut it.

'Take it back to keep warm, Meg,' said Mrs Culver, 'it

won't spoil for ten minutes or so. Bring a towel or something with you to put that dog on.'

The Professor stood, the animal still in his arms, waiting for Meg to come back. 'Found him in the road—been knocked down and left. Not hurt, I fancy, and, by the look of him, lost or abandoned.'

His mother rose to the occasion. 'Just what we could do with here—a guard dog. What is he?'

'Difficult to say. Ah, there you are—if you will put the towel on that table I'll take a look at him. A little warm milk perhaps?' Meg went off to the kitchen again and came back with a bowl of milk, standing patiently while he examined the beast with gentle hands. 'Nothing broken.' He glanced at her and smiled. 'Just worn out, hungry and frightened. He'll be a splendid addition to the household.'

Meg proffered the milk; it disappeared with the speed of dust into a vacuum cleaner. 'There's a big box and some old blankets. I'll fetch them.'

'A nice child,' observed Mrs Culver when she had gone, 'and so sensible.'

'And a good housekeeper, I hope?'

'Excellent. I've been to visit Kate; she's doing well, but it will be a month at least…'

'No need to hurry her,' said the Professor easily, 'since Meg suits you so well. No problems?'

'None, my dear. And she is so happy to be here. It must be dreadful for her having to give up her home to strangers.'

'Do you see anything of her sisters?' He glanced at his mother. 'I met her younger sister—a very pretty girl; she's at the Royal—staff nurse hoping to be made a Sister. She had no regrets leaving here, nor, I understand, had her elder sister.'

'The married one—I believe she's just as handsome. Are you on your way home, dear, or are you going back to town?'

'Back to town. I've a dinner date. But may I have lunch?'

Meg came back with the box and blankets and the dog was laid gently down and promptly went to sleep. Which left her free to fetch the quiche back and lay another place. She put the plates before Mrs Culver and said in her calm way, 'If you wanted to talk together I'll go away...'

'No need,' said the Professor before his mother could speak. 'Besides, we have to plan this animal's future. I'll phone the vet if I may, Mother, and if he's not injured, presumably he may stay?'

'Of course, my dear.' Mrs Culver turned to Meg. 'You know about dogs, Meg?'

'Oh, yes, Mrs Culver.' Nothing in her quiet voice betrayed the fact that she would have to get up earlier than ever to take him for a walk, that he would have to be groomed, fed and generally looked after. Not that she minded; she liked animals, and he would be company for Silky.

'Then that settles the matter. If you're not already engaged, Mother, I'll come over after church on Sunday and take you back for lunch.'

So he can't live far away, thought Meg, collecting plates and piling them tidily on a tray and carrying it out to the kitchen, where she loaded it up again with light-as-air castle puddings and hot jam sauce.

'Your cook is excellent,' observed the Professor, accepting a second helping.

'Oh, but Meg made these, didn't you, dear?'

His look of polite astonishment annoyed Meg; he could have no opinion of her at all! She said, 'Yes, as a matter of fact, I did,' in a tart voice and went to fetch the coffee.

'Don't you like her, dear?' asked his mother.

The look on his face gave her food for thought. 'I hardly know her,' he said at length. 'I dare say she might grow on one—missed when she's no longer there...'

'Such a waste,' said Mrs Culver vaguely, watching him. 'And so easily overlooked, especially when her sisters are with her.'

As Meg came back in with the tray the Professor got up to close the door behind her and watched her pour the coffee. She was wearing the severe grey dress and she had pinned up her pale brown hair into a tidy bun, under the impression that it made her look like a housekeeper. She was really nothing to look at; he was at a loss to understand why the thought of her crossed his mind from time to time. She handed him his cup and looked at him with her lovely grey eyes. They were cool and clear, like a child's. She said, 'It was kind of you to rescue the dog. I'll take great care of him.'

'Yes, I know. That's why I brought him here.' He smiled, and his severe expression melted into a charm which took her by surprise. She didn't like him, but just for a moment she glimpsed another man entirely.

She slipped away presently, pleading some household duty which kept her occupied until she heard the Rolls sigh its way down the drive. By then she had helped Betsy with the washing up, rubbed up the silver and got the tea tray ready. It was Betsy's hour or so of peace and quiet, and Mrs Culver would doubtless be dozing. Meg went to look at the dog and found him awake, cringing in his box. She fed him, bathed some of the dirt and dust from him, tended his pathetically cracked paws and went to let the vet in.

They knew each other vaguely; years ago when her father had been alive there had been dogs and cats and ponies. He was a grouchy old man but a splendid vet. He examined the dog carefully, pronounced him half starved, in need of rest and bruised from his accident. 'But he'll live,' he said. 'God alone knows what breed he is, but he's a nice enough beast. You're looking after him?' He looked at her enquiringly. 'Professor Culver said that he would be here with you... He would have taken him to his home but he's only there at the weekends; a London flat is no place for dogs.'

Meg longed to ask where the Professor lived, but she didn't. At least she had learned something; that he had a flat in London. She listened carefully to the vet's instructions, offered him tea, which he refused, and saw him out to his car. By the time she had settled the dog again it was tea time.

A busy day, she reflected, getting ready for bed at the end of the day. It struck her that she earned every penny of the money Mrs Culver paid her, for she had little time to call her own. She set her alarm clock half an hour earlier than usual because she would have to take the dog out and feed him before starting on the morning's chores, and she found herself wondering what the Professor was doing. Lolling in an easy chair in a comfortable sitting-room, waited on hand and foot, she decided. Despite his kindness over the dog, her opinion of him was low.

He arrived on Sunday, expressed satisfaction at the dog's appearance, refused refreshment and ushered his mother out to the car. He settled her in the front seat and then turned back to speak to Meg, who was standing sedately by the front door. 'What will you call him?' he asked.

'Well, nothing at the moment. I thought that Mrs Culver or you…'

'We leave it to you.' He smiled his charming smile once more. 'Enjoy your afternoon, Meg.'

Meg, indeed! she thought indignantly, though of course she was employed by his mother and he had every right to address her in such a fashion. Perhaps he thought it might keep her in her place. She went indoors and made up the fire in the sitting-room, gave the dog a meal, took him for a short run in the garden, and went along to the kitchen. She and Betsy had their afternoon planned; lunch on a tray for Meg and a peaceful hour or so for Betsy in her chair by the Aga. They would have an early tea too, and there might even be time to potter in the garden. It was a miserably grey day, but Meg never let the weather bother her.

The afternoon was all that she had hoped for; accompanied by the now devoted animal, she repaired to the potting shed and, tied in her sacking apron, pricked out seedlings and transplanted wallflowers. Then she went to her tea, sitting at the kitchen table with Betsy opposite her and Silky and the dog sitting in a guarded friendship on the rug before the Aga. Betsy had made a cake that morning; the mixture had been too much for the cake tin, she explained guilelessly, so that there was a plate of little cakes as well as hot buttered toast and Meg's strawberry jam and strong tea in the brown earthenware pot which Betsy favoured.

They cleared away together; Meg fed the animals and then got into her old duffle coat and took the dog for a gentle walk. 'You'll have to have a name,' she told him, suiting her pace to his still painful paws. 'How about Lucky? Because that's what you are, you know!'

Then she stopped to rub the rough fur on the top of his head, and he gave her a devoted look. He was beginning to look happy and he had stopped cringing. Back in the house, she settled him in the kitchen with a bone and went to tidy herself. It was time to be the housekeeper again.

The sitting-room looked charming as she went into it; she had made a good fire, there were flowers and pot plants scattered around the tables, and shaded lamps. She began to draw the curtains and saw the lights of the Rolls-Royce sweep up the drive, and she went into the hall and opened the door.

'Oh, how nice it all looks!' declared Mrs Culver. 'Meg, you have no idea how happy I am to be living here—to have found such a delightful home, and you with it, too!'

She slid off her fur coat and Meg took it from her, thinking that she had done just that so many times for her mother when she had been alive and well. She glanced up and found Professor Culver's dark eyes on her, his thoughtful look disturbing. She turned away and suggested coffee, and, 'There's a fire in the sitting-room,' she pointed out.

'No coffee, Meg—we'll have a drink. You'll stay a few minutes, Ralph?'

He had taken off his car coat and thrown it on to the oak settle against a wall. 'Yes, of course.' His eyes were still on Meg. He asked, 'Have you named the dog?'

'Yes, I'd like to call him Lucky. It was lucky for him when you met him...'

'An appropriate name. I've never believed in luck, but I think that perhaps I have been mistaken about that. You've had a pleasant afternoon?'

She looked surprised. 'Yes, thank you.' She sought feverishly for an excuse to get away from his stare. 'I must take Lucky out... Unless you need me for anything, Mrs Culver?'

'No, my dear, off you go. Wrap up warmly; it's a chilly evening.'

Meg nipped off to the kitchen, thinking that sometimes her employer talked to her as though she were her daughter. She put on the duffle coat again and encountered Betsy's surprised look. 'You've just been out with the beast,' she pointed out, ''ad yer forgotten, Miss Meg?'

Meg opened the kitchen door and started off down the stone passage leading to the garden. Lucky, anxious to please, even if reluctant, trotted beside her.

'No—it's all right, Betsy, it's only until the Professor's gone.'

The remark puzzled Betsy; it puzzled Meg too. Just because one didn't like a person it didn't mean to say that one had to run away from them, and wasn't she being a bit silly, trudging round the garden on such a beastly evening just because Professor Culver was ill-mannered enough to stare so?

Chapter 3

Two or three days passed. The weather was what was to be expected for the time of year: rain and a flurry of snow, and then a lovely day with a blue sky and an icy wind; Mrs Culver kept to the house for the first two days and then decided to accept a lunch invitation with friends in Ware. Meg phoned Noakes, the chauffeur, who now lived in the village with his wife, and watched her employer borne away before calling to Lucky and taking him for a brisk walk. It had certainly turned cold; she settled him with Silky before the kitchen fire, had bread and cheese and a great pot of tea with Betsy sitting at the kitchen table, and then went away to make up the fires and get the tea tray ready; Mrs Culver would probably be cold and tired when she got back, and a few scones might be a good idea. She returned to the kitchen and made a batch while Betsy sat by the Aga, having what she called a bit of a shut-eye.

Mrs Culver arrived back rather sooner than Meg had expected, and she didn't look very well.

'I'm cold,' she complained. 'I mean cold inside; I'd like a cup of tea…'

'It's quite ready, Mrs Culver,' said Meg soothingly, 'and there's a lovely fire in the drawing-room. I'll bring the tray in there.' She drew a chair to the fire. 'I made some scones—you'll enjoy those.'

Only Mrs Culver didn't; she drank several cups of tea, her nice face becoming more and more flushed, and when Meg suggested that she might like to go to her bed, she agreed without a fuss.

'Well, you stay there for a few minutes; I'll see to the electric blanket and warm your nightie. I won't be long.'

She was barely ten minutes, and when she got back it was to find Mrs Culver shivering and reluctant to leave her chair. It took a good deal of coaxing to get her up the stairs and into her room, and once there Meg helped her undress and tucked her up in bed, and then proceeded to sponge off Mrs Culver's carefully applied make-up and comb her hair.

'I feel awful,' said Mrs Culver.

Meg refrained from telling her that she looked awful and worse every minute. 'A chill,' she said bracingly. 'I'm going to get you a warm drink and phone Doctor Woods. He'll give you something to make you feel better.'

She had known Doctor Woods all her life, and he had been in and out of the house for weeks before her mother died. She liked his forthright, gruff manner, and he for his part knew that she wasn't a girl to panic.

By the time he arrived, some twenty minutes later, Mrs Culver was looking decidedly worse.

''Flu,' said Doctor Woods. 'There's a lot of it about. Got anyone to fetch a prescription?'

'No. Willy has gone and there's only Betsy. I'll have to phone Noakes; he's the chauffeur and lives in the village. He'll have to come here and get the car...'

'Tell you what, I'll leave enough of these to last until tomorrow; let the chauffeur get the rest in the morning. I'll be in again tomorrow some time; you're sensible enough to let me know if you get worried.'

He closed his bag and started getting into his coat. 'Any family?'

'A son—Professor Culver...'

'You don't say? Brilliant man in his field. You'd better let him know. No danger as far as I can see, but all the same...'

'I'll go and do it right away,' promised Meg.

'You look a bit peaked yourself, Meg. Working too hard, are you? You could do with a holiday. Where are those sisters of yours?'

'Well, Cora has her own home and family, as you know, and Doreen's at the hospital still.'

He grunted, which could have meant anything, patted her on the shoulder and went out to his car, muttering.

Mrs Culver was dozing; she looked ill, but no worse. Meg went downstairs and went to the study and picked up the telephone. The Professor's number was written neatly on a card beside it, and she dialled it. A London number—and a rather severe voice told her that it was Professor Culver's residence. 'Is the Professor there?' Meg asked. 'And if he is, will you tell him it's his mother's housekeeper?'

'Be good enough to wait,' said the voice, and she glanced at the clock. It was getting on for seven o'clock;

he might be changing for the evening, in the shower, tossing down a sherry with some blonde beauty before going out to dine…

'Yes?' said the Professor's voice in her ear. Very calm and unhurried.

Terse, thought Meg. Well, two could be that. 'Mrs Culver came back from a visit this afternoon not feeling well. I've put her to bed and Doctor Woods has been to see her. He says she has 'flu. He thought that you should be told. She's on an antibiotic, and at present she's dozing.'

His voice was still calm and unhurried. 'I'll be with you within the hour. Give me Doctor Woods' telephone number, will you?'

Unfeeling monster, thought Meg, and gave it before hanging up with a speed which gave him no chance to say anything else.

She went to have another look at Mrs Culver, who was still asleep. and then went to the kitchen to tell Betsy. 'So there'll be no need to have dinner in the dining-room,' she concluded, 'we'll have it here when Professor Culver has gone.'

'Such a nice fish soufflé we've planned, too. I've got it all ready to cook.'

'Well, we'll still have it later on. The soup won't spoil, will it, and I made that upside-down pudding—is it already in the oven?'

'Yes, Miss Meg, but it'll come to no 'arm.'

'I'll make a jug of lemonade for Mrs Culver and beat up an egg in milk and put a pinch of nutmeg with it…' Her eye lighted on Lucky, watching her from his bed by the Aga. 'I'd better take Lucky out now.'

Lucky had no taste for a cold evening; perhaps he had too many of them. Ten minutes was enough for him, and

Meg saw to his and Silky's suppers and made the lemonade, adding ice and taking it upstairs.

Mrs Culver was awake and inclined to be peevish, but she allowed Meg to turn her pillows and sit her up with a gossamer wool shawl around her, and she obediently drank her lemonade. 'And presently I'll bring you egg and milk. I make it rather nicely; Mother loved it… Here's the bell, Mrs Culver; ring if you want me. I'll be in the kitchen, but I'll leave the doors open so that I'll be able to hear.'

Mrs Culver nodded and murmured and closed her eyes again; she really looked poorly and it would be a little while before the antibiotics did their work. Meg sped downstairs again, rearranging the running of the house to fit in with nursing the invalid. No difficult task for her, for she had had experience enough with her mother. She was crossing the hall when she saw the lights of a car coming up the drive. Professor Culver had made good time. she opened the door and he got out and gave her a civil good evening.

He threw off his coat, took her arm and walked her into the sitting-room. 'I've telephoned Doctor Woods. Before I see my mother I should like to know what you think, Meg.' He added brusquely, 'You've had experience of elderly ladies. Are you worried?'

She said coldly, 'Don't imagine, Professor, that because I nursed my mother for several months I'm an expert on such matters. My mother died of congestive heart failure; as far as I can remember, she never had 'flu.'

She was quite unprepared for his contrition. He turned her round to face him, still holding her arm. 'I'm sorry— that was unpardonable of me. I think what I meant to say was that you must have an understanding of elderly ladies and can perhaps set my mind at rest. My mother is a volatile little lady; I'm never quite sure…'

She said at once, 'I don't think you have need to worry, Professor. Mrs Culver is in good hands, I assure you. Doctor Woods is a splendid man; he's coming again in the morning. I'll take good care of her, but if you would like to have a nurse for her…'

'The idea hadn't entered my head. You're a most capable young woman, and very sensible. I'm going up to see her now.'

He left her standing there, fuming. To be taken so for granted; she was to run the house as usual, presumably, as well as look after his mother, and, unless she was very much mistaken, she wouldn't get much sleep for the next night or two. She went along to the kitchen, her colour so high that Betsy wanted to know if she had the 'flu as well.

She was beating egg and milk when the Professor came in. He stood for a moment, watching her. 'That's for my mother. Good. Something smells delicious.'

And when Betsy looked round he smiled with such charm at her that she said, 'Leek soup—me own make, an' fish soufflé an' as nice an upside-down pudding as ever Miss Meg made. Dab 'and at it, she is.'

'May I stay to supper?'

Meg didn't trust that humble voice one little bit, but before she could say anything, Betsy observed, 'Plenty for three!'

Meg went to the door with the egg and milk. 'I'll stay for a while with Mrs Culver…'

The little tray was whisked from her. 'No, I'll see that she drinks this while you dish up.'

He was gone before she could frame an answer.

He was back in ten minutes. 'She's dozed off again;

she drank it all—it looked revolting.' He smiled suddenly at Meg. 'Would you like me to stay overnight?'

She ladled soup. 'Heavens, no. If you're quite happy about your mother there's no need for you to stay. I guarantee I can get Doctor Woods if I'm worried.'

'I'm a doctor too,' he pointed out.

'Oh, are you? Doreen said you were a radiologist.' She blushed, because it must seem to him that they had been discussing him.

He watched the blush with interest. 'I am, but I was a doctor first, if you see what I mean.'

He sat down at the table and Lucky went to sit beside him, resting his woolly head on his knee. The Professor stroked it gently. 'Have you found a flat yet?' he asked idly.

Meg gave him an exasperated look. 'I haven't been up to London to look for one.'

'From choice, or has my mother overlooked the fact that you should have a day to yourself each week?'

'The question hasn't arisen,' she told him coldly. 'I'm very happy as matters stand.'

His eyes narrowed. 'But you do realise that once Kate returns you are to leave?'

They were sitting opposite to each other at the scrubbed table with Betsy at its head, half-way through their soup.

'Naturally I know that. Mrs Culver told me that Kate will be coming here in three weeks or so. I'm sure that Doreen will find me something—somewhere to live until I can buy a flat.'

'They're not very thick on the ground in London, nor are they cheap. What are you going to do?'

Meg collected up the soup plates. 'I can't see that that is any concern of yours, Professor Culver,' she said frostily.

'Which means that you have no idea.' He accepted the fish soufflé from Betsy, and when they had eaten it, collected the plates and took them over to the sink.

'Now there 'ain't no call fer yer to do that,' cried Betsy. 'Just you sit down while I dish that pudding, sir.' She trotted over to the Aga, tutting indignantly and secretly delighted with his help. She gave him the lion's share of the pudding, and when they had eaten it offered a cup of tea.

He accepted with alacrity, complimented them on the delicious meal, sat back comfortably in his chair and, to Meg's utter surprise, when they had drunk it, declared his intention of washing up.

'You won't know 'ow, sir!' said Betsy.

'Then you can sit there by the stove and instruct me while Meg does whatever needs doing for my mother.'

Meg wished most fervently that she was a statuesque beauty, so that she could have swept out of the kitchen with style. Instead she took her small person out of the room with something of a flounce, unaware of the amusement in the Professor's eyes.

'The nerve!' she muttered, going upstairs. 'Coming here and eating our supper and telling me what to do! He's insufferable!'

But the face which she presented to Mrs Culver was kind and smiling. She spent some time making her comfortable, took her temperature, sponged her face and hands, gave her a drink, assured her that she was getting better already and straightened the bed.

Surely the Professor would be gone by now, she thought as she went downstairs, but he wasn't. He was at the sink, making heavy weather of the cleaning of the saucepans and enjoying a chat with Betsy.

'If you want to see Mrs Culver...' Meg began severely.

'I must go now,' he finished with a meekness she didn't believe. He wiped out the last saucepan, washing his hands and then putting on his jacket. When he had left the kitchen Betsy said comfortably, 'Now there's a nice gent for yer, Miss Meg. Never washed dishes in his life before, I dare swear, and did them well enough too.'

'Any fool can wash up,' said Meg loftily. 'I hope he goes soon; we've got to plan...' She stopped, because Betsy was looking uncomfortable.

The Professor was standing just behind her, his hands in his pockets, listening with interest.

'Mother is asleep already. I'm going now.' He spoke pleasantly. 'If it doesn't disturb your plans, I should like to visit her tomorrow morning.'

He bade Betsy an affable goodnight and walked out of the kitchen, and Meg went after him. In the hall she said, 'I'm sorry I was rude, Professor Culver. You must come whenever you want.'

'Of course. Be good enough to ring me if you're worried—and thank you for my supper. Not quite the evening I had intended, but none the less a good deal more interesting. And I leave my mother in good hands.'

He stood towering over her, staring down at her upturned face. Probably a very nice man, she thought illogically, if one happened to like him. The last thing she expected was his sudden swoop and his kiss on her cheek. 'Thank you, little Meg,' he said softly, and let himself out of the house.

An action which left her with a head full of mixed emotions.

Mrs Culver, already feverish, became more so as the evening wore on, and Meg saw that it would make more sense if she were to get ready for bed and then curl up on one of the easy chairs in Mrs Culver's room. At least she was able to doze off each time her patient did; all the same, she was glad enough when morning came and Mrs Culver, refreshed with a cool drink, her bed smoothed and her pillows turned, dropped off into real sleep at last. Too late for Meg to go to her own bed; she had a shower and dressed, yawning her head off as she did so, and then went down to join Betsy in a cup of tea before putting on the duffle coat and taking Lucky for his walk. Mrs Culver was still sleeping peacefully when she got back, so she obediently ate the breakfast Betsy had ready and then, leaving the dear soul to clear the kitchen and start preparations for the day's meals, went along to set the fires going.

There was no point in lighting the drawing-room fire, but there had better be one in the sitting-room, she thought. She was arranging coals on the wood and paper when Professor Culver came quietly into the room to startle her with his 'Good morning, Meg.'

She was kneeling before the grate, and turned an un-made-up face to him. It was a tired, pale face too, framed by a rather untidy head of hair, and there was a smear of coal dust on one cheek. 'My goodness, don't you get up early?' she exclaimed.

He said softly, 'At least I went to bed. From the look of you, you didn't. How is my mother?'

'Sleeping. She had a restless night, just dozing now and then, but she dropped off soundly after I'd tidied her up and she's had a drink. She's still asleep.' She got to her feet. 'You'd like to go up…?'

He didn't answer her, but got his lighter from a pocket and bent down to light the fire. When he was sure that it was well and truly alight, he said, 'Yes, I should.' To her surprise he added, 'Will you be able to catch up on your sleep during the day?'

Meg lied briskly, 'Oh, yes, thank you,' and watched him go up the stairs before telephoning to Noakes, who arrived with commendable swiftness to take the prescription for Mrs Culver's pills and who accepted the shopping list Meg had made out without demur. 'Can you manage, Miss?' he asked kindly. 'Anything I can do to help out?'

He was a kindly man as well as being an excellent chauffeur. 'Well, no, thank you, Noakes,' said Meg. 'Mrs Griffiths comes today, so we can manage very well, but I dare say I might have to ask you to do some more shopping until Mrs Culver is well again.'

She took him along to the kitchen and Betsy made him a cup of tea while Meg went back to the sitting-room to see how the fire was doing. She found the Professor there, putting on coals.

'Mother is decidedly better,' he informed her. 'She'll have to stay in bed for a few days, though. Can you manage? Do you need help of any sort?'

She was surprised for the second time. 'Mrs Griffiths is coming today—she comes three times a week to do the rough,' and at his puzzled look, 'floors and scrubbing and windows,' she explained. 'Betsy and I can manage the rest easily enough.'

He eyed her small person thoughtfully. 'You're rather small,' he observed. 'Quality not quantity, no doubt. Couldn't one of your sisters come over to help out for a day or so?'

She turned a look of amazement on him. 'They

couldn't spare the time; besides, I think you're making a fuss about nothing, Professor Culver; I ran this house and nursed my mother for almost a year...'

'I stand corrected.' He was laughing at her, and she felt annoyed.

When he added that he would have to go, she offered him coffee in such a stiff voice that he refused at once. 'Will you ask Doctor Woods to give me a ring? He knows my number. I'll telephone you this evening. In the meantime, if you're worried, don't hesitate to ring my home—you have the number. Good morning, Meg—I'll see myself out.'

The day was filled with small, tiresome tasks which had to be done as well as a visit from Doctor Woods, who pronounced himself satisfied with his patient's progress, advised two or three days in bed and a light diet, gave instructions about pills and promised to call the following day.

'And you look as though you could do with a good sleep,' he informed Meg. 'See that you get one.'

Meg said that she would, knowing that it wasn't very likely; Mrs Culver, charming though she was in good health, was a bad patient.

The day drew to a close with a call from Professor Culver, full of searching questions. He thanked her austerely, told her that he would be along in the morning, and rang off. Meg, peevish after a day that had held no quiet moment for her, removed the frown from her face and eventually went to tell Mrs Culver that her son would visit her the following morning and to persuade her to take just a little of the dainty supper she had prepared.

But at least Mrs Culver slept for most of the night. Meg, after several hours' sleep, was quite her usual calm self by the time Professor Culver arrived. He took a good look at her as he came through the door.

'That's better,' he observed. 'I take it my mother had a good night and so did you?'

He was in no hurry to go; he accepted Meg's polite offer of coffee and said that since he was there he might as well stay and see Doctor Woods. Meg offered him the daily papers and excused herself on the grounds of jobs to do around the house. There was a nice fire burning, and he looked comfortable enough sitting beside it—thoroughly at home, in fact. But of course, she reminded herself, it was his home, or at least his mother's.

Doctor Woods came early just as Meg had made her patient comfortable for the morning. Mrs Culver was sitting up against her pillows, nicely wrapped in a pretty bed jacket, her hair tied back with a ribbon, still pale but decidedly better.

'No need to come for a couple of days,' said Doctor Woods, 'unless you want me, Meg. An hour or two out of bed tomorrow and then try going downstairs on the following day. I'll see you then.'

He bustled downstairs again, and Meg took in a fresh tray of coffee, heaving a sigh of relief when the two men left together, the Professor in his gleaming Rolls, Doctor Woods in his elderly Rover.

Professor Culver had paused at the door to tell her that he had to go to Edinburgh that afternoon and would telephone from there. 'I shall be away for three days,' he told her austerely. His goodbye was equally austere.

'And as far as I'm concerned,' declared Meg to Lucky, who was standing beside her as she watched him drive away, 'he may go for three years. It'll be nice to get back to normal again.'

It may have been nice, but she had to confess that it was unexpectedly dull; the Professor, tiresome though he was, had supplied an interest in her days. He had left her feeling unsettled, and it was a relief when Doctor Woods pronounced Mrs Culver well enough to resume normal life as long as she took care not to go out until the cold, wet spell was over. Which meant that Meg spent a good deal of time playing cribbage and two-handed patience with her while still contriving to do her usual household chores. Of the Professor there was no sign, although he telephoned his mother each day.

The wet February weather suddenly became a premature spring; it wouldn't last, but Mrs Culver took advantage of the mild, sunny days to visit friends in London and, since she felt no ill effects from that, another visit to see how Kate was getting on. She came back from that in the best of spirits, to tell Meg that her housekeeper would be able to return in two weeks' time.

'She won't be able to do a great deal, of course, but if Betsy would stay…do you suppose she would, Meg? And if you could persuade Mrs Griffiths to come for an extra day?' She smiled kindly at Meg. 'So now you'll be able to go to London and live nearer your sister. Has she found a flat for you yet?'

Somehow Meg had allowed her future to become vague; anything could happen, she had told herself, and the weeks had slipped by almost unnoticed. Doreen had phoned once or twice, but she had been more concerned with her new flat and whether or not Meg had seen any more of Professor Culver than with Meg's future. She had been living in cloud cuckoo land, and the sooner she returned to more realistic plans for the future the better.

She answered her companion in her usual calm manner. 'That's good news, Mrs Culver; shall I ask Betsy to come and see you tomorrow morning? I'm sure she'll be very glad to stay here. I'll ask Mrs Griffiths…'

She phoned Doreen that evening and was barely given time to tell her news. 'Couldn't be better, Meg—there's a basement flat for sale in a quite decent side street off Stamford Street—that's just behind Waterloo Station—very handy if you get a job in the City. I'll go to the agent's in the morning and I'll ring up tomorrow…' she hung up.

Meg sat down quietly to think. It was all very well for Doreen to find her somewhere to live; she had no job and no idea what to do, anyway. It would be far better for her to find something out of London; it would have to be domestic, for that was all she could do. She took herself off to bed, feeling worried.

Doreen phoned again the next day. Meg was to get a day off; the flat was just what she needed. It wouldn't need much done to it, and her share of the money from the house would be enough to pay for it and leave a little nest egg over.

'But I'll need to get a job,' said Meg, and was swamped by Doreen's brisk, 'Of course you will, but let's get this flat settled first. Let me know which day you're coming and I'll meet you.'

Mrs Culver thought it a splendid idea. 'You have a day in town, dear,' she said. 'I'm quite well again, and Betsy can look after me. Noakes shall drive you up and fetch you when you're ready; just let him know when and where.'

So Meg made her plans; she rang Doreen again and got the address of the flat, arranged with Noakes to take her there and fetch her again in the afternoon, and combed her rather scanty wardrobe for something to wear. Her jersey shirtwaister—by no means new, but it went well with her brown tweed coat. She had her wages in her purse and she would have liked to have done some shopping, but the flat wasn't anywhere near the shopping streets.

At the last minute Doreen telephoned to tell her to meet her at the hospital at midday. 'Wait in the entrance hall, love; I'll be off duty until four o'clock. We'll have a snack somewhere and then inspect the flat. The agent will meet us there and come back for the keys later.'

Meg had to wait for Doreen at the hospital; Noakes had deposited her at the entrance exactly at midday, promised to go to the flat at four to pick her up again, and had driven off. Meg whiled away the time wandering round the entrance hall, a vast, forbidding place, its walls hung with portraits of dead and gone medical men and with absolutely nowhere to sit.

Doreen was wearing the cashmere dress again, with a short suede jacket over it. She looked stunning, and there was a young man with her who eyed Meg in some astonishment. When introduced as Doctor Willis, he said, 'I say, are you really Doreen's sister? You're not a bit alike,' he added hastily.

It seemed that he was going to drive them to the flat. He had half an hour to spare and nothing better to do, and it wasn't very far.

All the streets looked alike to Meg, and when he turned off Stamford Street into a narrow side street lined with shabby houses, each with area steps leading to the basements, she glanced around her with something like horror. There wasn't a tree in sight, and not so much as a laurel bush growing.

Doctor Willis drew up with a flourish with a cheerful, 'Here you are—out you get, girls. See you, Doreen.' He nodded to Meg and drove off, and Doreen opened the iron gate of the area behind them and led the way down the steps.

The area was small, damp and cluttered with a variety of bottles, and the door needed a coat of paint urgently. It was opened as they reached it and the clerk from the estate agents ushered them inside. He opened the inner door at the same time; if he hadn't there wouldn't have been room for the three of them in the lobby.

'Not kept you waiting?' asked Doreen breezily. The man said no, certainly not; the half hour he had had to stand around would be worth it if he could pull off the sale. 'Quite a few people after this place,' he observed heartily. 'I'll take you round and then leave you and collect the key some time around four o'clock.'

The living-room was on the dark side, since the only window looked out on to the area. It had a small fireplace, what the clerk erroneously described as fitted bookshelves on either side and which were in fact planks put up by some DIY enthusiast, and a pipe running up one wall which he dismissed with a wave of the hand. A door at the side led to a tiny kitchen with no window, which led in turn to the bedroom overlooking a forlorn garden with a row of dustbins along one wall and a tangle of grass. The bathroom had been built on at some time; the bath was stained by a continuously dripping tap and the washbasin was cracked; Meg didn't dare look at the toilet. The man said brightly, 'The fixtures are included in the price, of course,' and waved a hand at a small wall cupboard. Meg, feeling that she should show some interest, opened it. Inside there was a used tube of toothpaste, a piece of very old soap and a half-filled bottle of brilliantine. She closed the door again without saying anything and watched a very large spider disappear down the waste pipe of the bath. It was a depressing little room, and the previous owner—a man, decided Meg because of the brilliantine—had obviously thought the same, for one wall had been painted shrimp pink. He had either run out of paint or lost heart, for the other walls were white…

'Well, I'll leave you ladies to inspect the flat thoroughly—' the man gave them a bright smile, '—redecorated and furnished, this place could be a little gem.'

They watched him go and went back to the living-room. It surprised Meg when Doreen said, 'He's right, you know. And you'll have enough money to have the place painted and papered.'

'Doreen, I don't think I could live here—not after home…there'd never by any sun, and it smells damp.'

Doreen took her arm. 'Look, love, you'll have a dear little home of your own and you're sure to get a job pretty soon. We're going down the road for something to eat—I saw a café in that row of shops on the corner—and then we'll come back and go over the place yard by yard.'

The café was small, with plastic tables and vinegar and tomato sauce arranged on each one. They had egg and chips and coffee, and Doreen pointed out that the shops on either side would provide day-to-day necessities without Meg having to walk miles.

They went back presently and went round the flat slowly. Meg tried hard to imagine living there and she couldn't. 'It's no good, Doreen,' she declared. 'I couldn't be happy here. I'm awfully grateful to you for finding it, but it's a kind of prison, isn't it? Is your flat like this?'

Doreen dealt with her with her usual briskness. 'No,

love—it's in a modern block and of course it's…' She
paused. 'You see, I've got a good job and I could afford
to pay more—besides I got a mortgage. You must come
and see it some time.' She frowned. 'What happens when
you leave Mrs Culver, though—you'll have nowhere to
go? I suppose Cora would have you for a little while, but
you would have no hope of getting a job if you stayed
there. It's much more sensible for you to snap this little
place up and settle in—there'll be enough money for you
to look round for a bit.' She glanced at her watch. 'I must
go; I'm on duty in half an hour. I'll go to the corner and
get a cab.' She kissed Meg. 'The clerk will be back for
the key—when is Noakes coming for you?'

'About four o'clock.'

'Oh, good. Cheer up, love; Cora and I are quite sure
that this is the best thing for you to do.' She gave Meg an
affectionate pat on the shoulder and hurried away. Watching her go, Meg reflected that she really knew nothing
of her two sisters' lives; they had lived away from home
for several years now and they didn't regret leaving the
pleasant old house and the peace and quiet of the country.

She fetched an empty tea chest from the kitchen, up-
ended it and sat down. She would have liked a cup of
tea, but the man from the estate agent's would be calling
shortly for the key, and after that she wouldn't dare go to
the café in case she missed Noakes. She would have to
wait in the area, she supposed, and so she got up and went
on another tour of inspection. It left her more convinced
than ever that she couldn't possibly live there. When she
got back she would look for a job as a housekeeper, au
pair—anything rather than live in London.

The sky had clouded over, and it would be dark earlier
than usual. The electricity had been cut off, naturally,

and although she found the dark of the country quite unfrightening, she winced away from the idea of sitting there in the dusk. It was still barely four o'clock, she told herself; the key would be fetched very soon and she could wait outside for Noakes. In the meantime she thought about her future: Betsy was safe, which was a blessing; and Meg herself had quite a sum of money now that she had her share of the house sale. A cottage in some small town or village would cost far less than even the pokiest of flats in London, and she could surely find a job— anything that would bring in enough to feed and clothe her! She become so engrossed in her planning that she failed to hear a car draw up and a measured tread on the area steps. The thump of the door knocker brought her to her feet. It would be the man from the estate agent's. She went to the door and opened it, and Professor Culver strode past her to come to a halt in the living-room. 'Good God!' he said, and then, 'You aren't going to live here?'

The very sight of him, large and assured and unexpected, acted upon Meg in a surprising manner. She burst into tears.

The Professor didn't say a word, merely scooped her against his massive shoulder and waited patiently while she sniffed and snorted and hiccupped.

When she finally heaved the last sobs, he offered a handkerchief and asked in a matter-of-fact voice, 'As bad as that, is it?'

'They want me to live here, but I can't—it's awful; there's a spider in the bath and there's no sun and all you can see out of the window are people's feet. They say I can have it done up and get a job, but I can't do any of the things people do in London—type and sell things, only they won't listen...'

'They?'

'Doreen and Cora. I know they think it's the best thing for me and I've always done what they suggested—they're clever, you see, but I really can't…'

He flung an arm round her shoulder. 'Let's look round?' he suggested.

When they were back in the living-room he said, 'I see what you mean—that's a frightful pink wall in the bathroom, and there's wood rot.'

'Oh, is that the smell in the kitchen?'

'Yes.' He left her to answer the knock on the door and came back with the clerk. 'Ready to go?' he asked her, and handed the man the key. 'The lady won't be buying this flat,' he observed pleasantly. 'Good day to you.'

He took Meg's arm and went ahead up the area steps on to the pavement. The Rolls was parked there, and the Professor opened the door and stowed her inside then got in beside her. Events had moved rather fast; Meg asked, 'Noakes is coming—how did you know where I was?'

'He told me. It seemed foolish for him to come back to town when I would be leaving at the same time.'

He drove off and turned into Stamford Street, and she thought about it before she said, 'Please don't tell Mrs Culver. She's so kind; I'll tell her that I have other plans, that I've got a job outside London.'

'Where?'

She said sharply, 'How should I know that until I've found something? But I'm good at housework and looking after people and shopping—there's bound to be something…' They stopped at traffic lights and she added, 'I'm sorry I made such a fuss just now. Only I didn't expect you, and somehow you made the flat look so dreadful…

I can't explain.' She put a gloved hand up to her face. 'I must look awful.'

'You look like anyone else who's just had a good howl. Have you finished crying?'

She felt suddenly cross. 'Yes. If you hadn't been there I wouldn't have cried; I practically never do.'

'Good. Now that you're in a sensible frame of mind you will listen to what I have to say; and don't interrupt. I don't like to be interrupted.'

Meg glanced sideways at his profile. He looked stern and she could hardly blame him; she had made a fine fool of herself. She folded her hands on her lap and looked at them. She wouldn't say a word, whatever it was he was going to say to her.

Chapter 4

The professor slid the Rolls smoothly past an articulated lorry, making his way towards the A10.

'You have to find a home and a job,' he said austerely. 'I can offer you both.' If he heard Meg's surprised gasp he took no notice of it. 'You probably know that I'm a radiologist. Most of my work is done at Maud's, but I have a private practice just off Wigmore Street and I travel a good deal to other hospitals. I live here in London during the week; I have a small house here, but my home is at Much Hadham; I go there whenever possible and at the weekends. I have a secretary at my rooms and a receptionist to answer the phone, make appointments and so forth—not an arduous job, but it does, however, require someone with a pleasant voice and manner, who is a hard worker and willing to undertake errands and make the tea. There's a caretaker living in the basement and a small flatlet on the top floor which goes with the job. And since your heart is set on the country, there's no reason why you shouldn't spend the weekends there. There's an empty gardener's cottage in the grounds; until I can find a suitable man to live there and work for me you're welcome to go there whenever you want—there's plenty of gardening for you if you feel inclined.'

It seemed that he had no more to say. There was a lot of traffic—they were on the A10 by now, on the outskirts of the sprawling city. After a silence which Meg felt had lasted long enough, she asked, 'What's happened to the receptionist?'

He laughed. 'Any other girl would have asked how much money she was being offered and what the hours would be! She's leaving to get married.'

'Why me? I might not do! I can't type or do shorthand; I've never been inside an office.' A sudden thought struck her. 'You haven't offered me a job because I was silly just now?' She was being foolish—she was just beginning to realise what a marvellous job it would be. Wigmore Street was a far cry from the side street behind Waterloo Station. And there would be weekends to look forward to, but if all these delights were being offered out of pity she would have to refuse.

Her doubts were put at rest in no uncertain manner. 'Now you are being silly,' said the Professor. 'You're right for the job—a hard worker, a pleasant voice, patience— and by heavens, you'll need that sometimes—no young men to distract you, a real need to earn your own living and make a home for yourself. And I need someone to air the cottage until it's required for a gardener. A very convenient arrangement for us both.' He told her the salary. 'And that's the basic, of course; you'll get an increase

every year. The hours are irregular at times—that's why
the flat is rent free. The phone will be switched through
each evening so that you can take messages. If you want
to go out—but I don't imagine you will—the caretaker
will take over.'

So she wouldn't want to go out! The nerve, thought
Meg peevishly; how is he to know that I shan't meet
someone—a young man who'll fall in love with me and
sweep me off my feet? She spent half a minute pursuing
this pleasant daydream and was brought down to earth
by his, 'Well, will you consider it? Yes or no?'

Meg heard herself say yes, although she wasn't sure
that she had meant to.

They were off the A10 now, on a secondary road going
to Much Hadham, and Meg suddenly realised the fact.
'But I'm going to Hertingfordbury!' she exclaimed.

'I'll take you there shortly. You'd better see the cottage. I'll give you a lift at weekends. Of course, you may
not like it.'

But she did. They went through the village, past the
Elizabethan cottages and the rather grand gentlemen's
houses, past the Bishop's Palace, until he slowed the car
and turned into an open gateway with a very small plaster and timber cottage tucked beside it.

If Meg had had any doubts about accepting the Professor's offer, they disappeared now. The cottage stood in a
small garden, protected by iron railings, and it had an important porch which dwarfed the rest of the lodge. Even
now, in the dusk of a late February evening, it looked
enchanting. Meg couldn't get out fast enough to have a
closer look at it.

Professor Culver produced a key, opened the stout
door and switched on a light. The door opened on to the

living-room, sparsely furnished although the table and chairs and dresser were old and well cared for. The fire-place was large, almost an inglenook, and the walls were white plaster. There was a small kitchen with a boiler for hot water, a bathroom in a pleasing shade of cream and a quite large bedroom, nicely furnished with a brass bed-stead and an applewood dressing table and wardrobe.

Meg revolved slowly, taking it all in. 'And I can come here each weekend?' She wanted to make sure of that. 'That is, until you find a gardener. I can't believe it's true!'

He was standing leaning against a wall, watching her. 'I doubt if I'll find a man before the spring,' he said care-lessly. 'Get Noakes to bring over anything of yours, and that applies to the London flat equally. I think perhaps it might be a good idea if we collect Lucky at the week-ends and he can stay here with you. We can drop him off on our way back on Monday mornings.' He paused to think. 'Better still, supposing I have him over here per-manently? I've two dogs; another one won't make any difference. He can come here whenever you're staying the night.'

'Oh, could he? I shall miss him, but I'm sure he'd be happy with you.'

'You flatter me.' The mockery in his voice sent the colour into her cheeks; he watched it fade before saying, 'That's settled. I'll take you back.'

She could think of nothing to say once they were back in the car. She sensed that chatter about her new job would irritate him; as far as he was concerned the whole business was cut and dried and there was no need to mull it over. Only, as he stopped the car outside her old home, he suggested, 'I'll send you a letter confirming the job, and give you dates and so on.'

She had no chance to do more than nod as they went into the house and Mrs Culver opened the drawing-room door. 'Ralph—how nice! Come in, dear, and have a drink—stay to dinner if you can.' She smiled at Meg. 'I'm sure Meg can do something about that.'

'Yes, of course, Mrs Culver.' She went, still in her outdoor things, to the kitchen, where she found Betsy putting the finishing touches to duckling and black cherry sauce.

'You look as though you could do with a cup of tea, Miss Meg. Just you wait a jiffy—the kettle's on the boil.' Betsy bustled around making the tea. 'I can see you're bursting with news, love, but I'll 'ave ter wait, won't I?'

Meg sipped the tea, stooped to fondle Lucky and Silky and took off her coat. 'Oh, I've lots to tell you, Betsy! But I think the Professor's staying for dinner—can we manage or shall I open a tin or two?' She looked up as one of the old-fashioned bells on the kitchen wall jangled. 'That's the drawing-room; I'll see what's wanted.'

When she went in Mrs Culver was sitting in her usual chair and the Professor was standing with an arm on the mantelpiece, staring into the fire. He put his glass down as she crossed the room. 'I'm not staying for dinner, Meg.' He gave his mother an apologetic smile. 'I've a date this evening, my dear.'

'Is she very beautiful?' Mrs Culver chuckled.

'Very. And she doesn't like to be kept waiting.' He put down his glass, kissed her and went to the door. 'I'll send you the details, Meg. Don't bother to see me out.'

The rest of the evening was spent in discussing the details of Meg's new job. 'Really—it's providential!' declared Mrs Culver. 'Tell me, dear, what was this London flat like? Ralph thought nothing of it...'

Presently, on the plea of helping Betsy wash up and prepare for the morning, Meg told her old friend what had happened.

Betsy nodded her head. 'As was to be expected,' she observed. 'I'ad a feeling that all would come right. A pity as 'ow yer've got to work in London, but yer'll be near enough at the weekends—we'll see each other now and then, I've no doubt. 'Ave yer told yer sisters, Miss Meg?'

'Not yet. It's a bit late to do it now; I'll phone them in the morning.'

She rang Cora first and found little opposition, 'Well, if that's what you want to do, Meg. I suppose you can buy a place later on. I must say it'll be a relief to have you settled at last, at least for a time. What's the flat like that you'll take over?'

'I haven't seen it...'

Cora sounded huffy. 'Well, you know your own business best, I suppose. If you choose to ignore Doreen and me that's your affair.'

Meg agreed quietly that it was and then hung up. Doreen answered the phone with something of a snap. 'Meg, you know I don't like you ringing up when I'm on duty. If it's something to do with the flat...'

Meg told her and then listened to Doreen's voice pointing out all the drawbacks. 'What's come over you?' she wanted to know. 'You've always done what Cora and I have suggested, and now here you are going off on a wild-goose chase... Well, I suppose you'll do what you want.' She added, 'Once you're settled in I'll come and see you. Does Professor Culver live over his rooms?'

'No, there's only a caretaker and his wife. I don't know where he lives.'

Doreen said thoughtfully, 'You'll be able to find out. We got on rather well together when we met...' She rang off and Meg, relieved that her sisters had been only mildly annoyed, looked for Lucky and took him for a walk and then cycled into Hertingfordbury to give Mrs Grimes the weekly order; Mrs Culver believed in supporting the local tradespeople.

She received a letter from the Professor the following day—very businesslike, setting out her duties and the conditions concerning her job, and directing that she was to go to town with Noakes in three days' time so that she might see the flat and be taken over the consulting rooms and meet his secretary and the receptionist whose place she was to take.

She showed the letter to Mrs Culver, who read it through and then observed comfortably that Ralph would see to everything and she was to do as he suggested. 'And when you want to go over to the cottage at Much Hadham, just let me know, dear, so that Noakes can take you.' She glanced at the letter again. 'Ralph suggests that you start work in two weeks. That fits very nicely; Kate comes here two days earlier and you'll be able to show her the house and see that she knows where everything is. Were your sisters pleased?'

Meg folded her letter carefully. 'Rather surprised, but—well, relieved that I would be settled. I only hope I'll be satisfactory.'

Mrs Culver smiled. 'Ralph never makes mistakes; if he decided that you'll be good in the job, then you will be.' She spoke with a firm conviction which bolstered up Meg's dubious second thoughts.

It was teeming with rain as Noakes and Meg left three days later. There had been no help for it but to wear her elderly Burberry and tie a scarf over her hair. Hardly what she would have chosen to wear on a trip to London, but she assumed that once she had paid her visit to the consulting rooms and seen the flat she would have to find her way to the station and take a train back. No one had said anything about the return journey, and she could hardly ask Noakes. Perhaps he would mention it on the way.

He didn't; she got out, a bundle of nerves, when he drew up before an elegant, narrow house in a terrace of similar houses in a tree-lined street, bade him goodbye, and rang the highly polished bell by the front door.

It opened and she went inside to find a surprisingly roomy hall with several handsome mahogany doors and a graceful staircase ahead of her. The door nearest her had 'Reception' written above it, so she opened it and went in. It was a pleasant room and she had the impression of neutral shades tinged with amber as she crossed the thick carpet to the desk in one corner.

The young woman sitting behind it was pretty, and she had a nice smile. She said now, 'You're Meg Collins, aren't you? Professor Culver told us you would be coming. He's not here at present—it's his morning at Maud's—but I'm to show you round. Miss Standish, his secretary, will come in here while I'm away. Would you like a cup of coffee? There won't be any patients until two o'clock.' She got up, and Meg saw that she was quite tall and slim and elegantly dressed; she would have to buy clothes, she thought worriedly, very conscious of the Burberry.

'I'm Rosalind Adams,' the girl added. 'Do sit down and I'll get the coffee.'

She disappeared through a door behind the desk and reappeared almost at once with a tray with cups and saucers and a percolator.

Meg took a heartening sip from the cup handed to her. 'I'm scared,' she admitted. 'I've never worked in an office before.'

'Well, this isn't quite like an office. Professor Culver believes that people who come here for consultation need to feel reassured, so it's more like paying a visit, if you see what I mean. The work's easy: making appointments, writing them up, checking patients as they come, going to the Post Office, making tea and coffee and doing odd jobs. The difficult part is knowing what to say to the patients; you know, being sympathetic, or bracing, or impersonal. It's a kind of instinct, and if the Professor offered you the job you'll have got it, so you've no need to worry.' Rosalind sounded quite sure about it, and Meg began to feel better. Presently Miss Standish, cosily middle-aged and not at all the kind of secretary Meg would have supposed the Professor to have, came in, made a few kindly remarks and sat down at the desk as Rosalind ushered Meg back into the hall and up the stairs. The first floor was given over to treatment rooms, a cloakroom, a miniature kitchen for making tea and a second consulting room, and the floor above that was the flat. It had its own front door, opening on to a lobby with three doors. 'Sitting-room,' said Rosalind, flinging open one of them and disclosing a pleasant room with a small window at the front and glass doors leading to a balcony at the back. It was nicely furnished with a couple of easy chairs in cretonne covers, matching curtains, a small table and two chairs, bookshelves on either side of a small gas fire, and a television in one corner.

Rosalind whisked back into the lobby and opened the door opposite. 'Bedroom—a bit small.'

It had a sloping roof and window at the front. Small it might be, but it was pretty too, with a flowery wallpaper and a white-painted bed and furniture, and a door in the far wall opened into a very small bathroom, tiled in pale pink.

'Kitchen,' said Rosalind, back in the lobby, and opened the last door. Another small room with a door leading to a balcony, with everything in it that one might need.

Meg breathed a deep sigh. 'It's super; I had no idea... do you mean to say that I can live here?'

'Goes with the job. Mind you, you'll get disturbed by the phone and have to pass messages on and so on—not everyone's cup of tea, but I've been here for years and loved it. If I hadn't been going to marry I dare say I'd have gone on for ever. As you know, there's a caretaker and his wife—they live in the basement, and he'll do little jobs for you if you need help. Come down and see the consulting room; I'll show you where everything is so that you won't feel too lost.'

It was behind the reception room with a wide window overlooking a narrow walled garden at the back of the house. It had a massive desk covered untidily with papers and folders, two or three comfortable chairs and heavy silk curtains at the windows. There was a little rosewood wall table opposite the desk with a bowl of pink chrysanthemums on it, and the carpet was thick and soft. A door at one side led to Miss Standish's office. 'Of course, you don't come in here often,' explained Rosalind, 'just to collect the post or take a message or usher in a patient. I'll be here for a couple of days when you start, and you'll pick everything up quickly enough.'

'I do hope so. I'll have to buy the right kind of clothes.'
Meg looked at her companion's plain blue dress, well cut
and elegant.

'Yes—well, the Professor's against overalls and so on.
He has a nurse, of course—she's in uniform and comes
for consulting hours—but I wear navy blue or grey, either a dress or a skirt and plain blouse.'

They went back to the reception room and Miss
Standish trotted off with the remark that she was looking forward to having Meg working with her. 'Oh, and
Professor Culver telephoned—you're to be here at four
o'clock and he'll drive you back.' She glanced at her
watch. 'Lots of time for you to do some shopping if you
want to.'

'Why not?' thought Meg, suddenly light-hearted.
Armed with useful information about buses and a suitable café for a snack lunch, she bade a temporary goodbye and went to the nearest bus stop.

She was back just before four o'clock with a carrier
bag containing a navy blue dress in wool crêpe with a
white collar and a demure bow. It had cost quite a lot of
money, but nothing less would have done for the quiet
luxury of the consulting rooms. It was practical too, for
the collar was detachable and she had bought several
more in different colours. She had bought shoes—plain
black courts—and sheer stockings, and once she was
living in the flat she would add to her wardrobe and see
that it was adequate; she hadn't realised until now just
how dowdy she had become.

Rosalind gave her a cup of tea and took one in to Miss
Standish, and they were tidying the cups and saucers
away when the Professor arrived. He gave her a brief

nod, gave Rosalind a handful of envelopes and went to his consulting room.

'I post these on the way home,' said Rosalind. 'If he's got patients here we usually work until five or six o'clock, and most Saturday mornings too. Miss Standish and I take it in turns to take a few hours off to make up for that.'

The Professor came out of his room then, wished Miss Standish and Rosalind a good day, and swept Meg before him out to the car.

She was still feeling light-hearted. She said shyly, 'The flat is lovely, Professor Culver.' And when he grunted in reply, she added, 'I think I shall like working for you; I hope… I'll do my best.'

'You won't stay long if you don't!' He sounded so unfriendly that she decided not to say another word until he did. Only he didn't; not a word was said until he stopped outside his mother's front door. 'Thank you for the lift, Professor Culver,' said Meg clearly; her voice held a volume of feeling and his stern mouth relaxed. If he had been going to say anything, she didn't give him the chance; she darted indoors, whisked into the drawing-room to tell Mrs Culver that she was back and went to the kitchen, where she shed her coat, kicked off her shoes and sat down at the table where Betsy was rolling pastry.

'Well?' said her old friend. 'Everything nicely settled, Miss Meg?'

'Oh, yes, Betsy. It's a lovely flat, and the place where I'm to work is very upper crust. I wish I'd never said I'd take the job…'

Betsy finished putting little dabs of butter on her pastry and folding it carefully before she observed, 'You're tired, love, and think of that lovely little cottage; if I can manage it, I'll come over on me Sunday, 'alf day.'

'Oh, Betsy, will you? I'll love that.' Meg twiddled Lucky's ears. 'I'll have him, too.' She got up. 'I'd better tidy myself and go to Mrs Culver. I must let Doreen and Cora know when I'm moving.'

When she went to the drawing-room ten minutes later, Professor Culver had gone. 'He couldn't stay,' said Mrs Culver with regret. 'He has two consultations this evening. Do you feel you can be happy in that little flat, Meg?'

'Oh, yes, it's lovely.' It struck Meg that the Professor hadn't asked her if she had liked it, nor, to give him his due, had he evinced any desire for gratitude on her part. 'I think I shall be very happy there.'

'I do hope so, my dear. I shall miss you… Kate comes tomorrow; I shall leave you to show her round and settle her in and of course you must come and see me whenever you can—and see Betsy too. She will miss you so.'

'Yes, but at least she's not being uprooted—she's been here for such a long time, I think it would have killed her…'

'Well, dear, you may be sure that she will stay here for the rest of her days. She'll be such a support for Kate.'

'You think they'll get on?'

'I'm sure they will.'

When Kate arrived, Meg thought that probably Mrs Culver was right. Kate was tall, thin and unassuming. Her voice was quiet and her manner retiring, and she professed herself delighted with the house, her room and Betsy. Moreover, she took instantly to the elderly and cunning Silky, who lost no time in ingratiating himself. Meg left the two women gossiping happily over a pot

of tea in the kitchen and went upstairs to pack her trea-
sures in the boxes Noakes would take to the flat for her.
While she did it she mulled over her sisters' reactions.
Cora was annoyed because she hadn't taken her advice,
but all the same she was relieved. 'You can always come
here when you get your holidays,' she had invited. 'I only
hope the job lasts.'

Doreen had been even more annoyed, largely because
Meg had taken such an important step without relying
on her sister's considered advice. But that annoyance too
had been tempered with a thinly veiled curiosity about
Professor Culver. 'I dare say I shall see more of him, for
of course I shall keep an eye on you, darling.' She could
almost hear Doreen thinking. 'And that dear little cottage
for the weekends—how very kind he is—I must thank
him when I see him!'

'I've done that,' said Meg with unwonted tartness.

Noakes took her over the next day to the cottage, with
her bits of furniture sticking out of the boot, and helped
her to carry them in and arrange them; there wasn't
much: a little work table of her mother's, a few pictures
and a little prayer chair, and a few books. The rest were
to go to the flat in London, and the village carrier had
undertaken to deliver those before she got there. She had
been careful to arrange for their delivery in the evening
after everyone had gone home, when only the caretaker
was there.

She spent the next two days showing Kate around and
initiating her into the daily routine. 'Though I dare say
you'll alter things to suit yourself,' said Meg politely.
'You'll find Betsy a great help, and there's Mrs Griffiths
who comes in from the village and is very good—she's
been coming for years.' She cast a quick glance and saw

Kate's feet in roomy felt slippers. 'You're sure you feel well enough to manage? Mrs Griffiths is going to do an extra day each week…'

'Bless you, miss; I'll be all right. That Betsy knows the place back to front, and I'm sure we're going to like each other. And the house almost runs itself, doesn't it? Nice place it is too, after that flat in Amsterdam.'

'Amsterdam?' queried Meg.

'Well, Mrs Culver's mother is Dutch—when her husband died she went back there to live and naturally Mrs Culver pays her long visits, especially now she's lost her own husband. It's a lovely flat, mind you, far too large for the old lady, but there, it was her home when she was a child and she refuses to leave it. Verging on ninety, too—the Professor's very fond of her.'

The idea of Professor Culver having a granny struck Meg as surprising, somehow he didn't seem much of a family man. She murmured a suitable reply to this interesting bit of information and offered to show Kate the stock of jams and bottled fruit, kept in a chilly little room leading off the kitchen. 'Pickled apricots,' said Kate admiringly, 'spiced oranges you're a good house-wife, if I may say so, miss. The Professor's granny would take to you—a great one she is with jams and pickles, or she was when she was younger. She'd spend hours bottling fruit and such…mind you, there was always someone to clear up afterwards.'

The two days went pleasantly, and on the third morning Meg bade everyone farewell, got into the car beside Noakes and was whisked away to London. She had hated leaving Lucky. Noakes was taking him over to Much Hadham that evening and she would see him at the weekend. But before that there was almost a whole week to get through…

Four days later she had to admit that she had enjoyed every moment of them. She had seen practically nothing of Professor Culver; for a good bit of the day he wasn't there, anyway, and when he was, she only glimpsed him at his desk as she ushered his patients in or took in his tea or coffee. He had paused once on his way out to ask if she had settled in, and when she had told him yes, he had nodded and gone away without a word. Rosalind had been very kind, nudging her into doing the right thing, explaining good-temperedly about the patients, writing out a timetable of her work, going with her to the Post Office, showing her where the spare keys were kept and how to manage the intercom and the small switchboard. The Professor had been right; there was nothing complicated about the job. All one needed was a willingness to work hard, and not watch the clock, and the ability to make tea or coffee at a moment's notice. She hadn't a great deal to do with the patients yet, but now that Rosalind had gone, she would see rather more of them, although Miss Standish dealt with all the major enquiries.

She had enjoyed making herself at home in the flat. With her own small possessions scattered around, it took on a cosy familiarity which was most satisfying to return to at the end of the day's work. And on Saturday she would be going to the cottage and would see Lucky again.

Doreen had phoned; she would come and see Meg one evening the following week, she said, and she asked casually if the Professor was ever there in the evenings. 'Never,' said Meg. 'I've a number I switch calls to; I suppose it's his home or the hospital.' Doreen had seemed disappointed.

It was quiet once everyone had gone; Meg had been sorry to see Rosalind's elegant back disappearing through the street door. She called good night to the caretaker, shut the door and went up to her flat. It looked delightful in the soft light of a table lamp, the curtains drawn against the dusk outside and the gas fire glowing. She went into the kitchen and put a lamb chop under the grill; she used her lunch hour in which to shop and made do with coffee and a sandwich, for cooking in the evenings gave her something to do. In a few days when she was thoroughly at home, she would go for a brisk walk before she got her supper, and of course in the summer she would be able to sit on the balcony.

Supper eaten, she wrote a letter to Mrs Culver and another one to Betsy, and since her kitchen bin was full and the caretaker wouldn't be along to empty it until the end of the week, she tied the plastic bag neatly, took her key and went downstairs to the side door on the ground floor which opened on to the square of paving stones where the bins were kept. There were four of them; she put her bag into the last of them and was on the point of going back indoors when something caught her eye. A bedraggled cat, sitting uneasily against the brick wall, watching her. The light over the door shone on to his face; he was one-eyed and had tattered ears. He sat and made no sound, and Meg went slowly towards him and picked him up. He was feather-light, skin and bones, and she exclaimed in pity. Without stopping to consider the matter, she carried him up to her flat where she sat him down in front of the fire and fetched a saucer of milk. He lapped it up with pathetic speed and she gave him more, this time with bread soaked in it. He scoffed that too, and crept nervously back towards the fire, to turn and slink under her chair as she arranged a cushion on the floor. 'Well, it was a bit lonely,' she told him, 'and if you care to stay, you're more than welcome, for I'm sure you've no home of your own.'

She sat down and kept quite still until presently he crept out again and sat down on the cushion. 'It'll be nice to have someone to talk to.' Meg went on, 'but you'll have to fit in with me—no going out, just the balcony, but if you're good I'll take you to the cottage each weekend.'

The cat stared at her with his one eye and presently went to sleep, which gave her the chance to go downstairs to the caretaker and beg an old wooden box from him. There was a flower bed in the back garden, and she shovelled earth and went back upstairs and put the box on the balcony, and then went back to look at the cat. He was awake again, watching her warily, and she offered more food, and this time he purred wheezily.

By the time she had showered and got ready for bed he had explored the flat, investigated the balcony and returned to his cushion. She put yet another saucer of milk down on the kitchen floor, wished him a good night and got into bed. She hadn't shut her bedroom door; she was almost asleep when he crept on to the bed and arranged himself on her feet. He was grubby, to say the least, but she was grateful for his company.

He got up when she did, ate the breakfast she gave him and sat down on the cushion and began rather half-heartedly to wash himself. Meg left the door on to the balcony open and went down to the consulting rooms to begin her day's work. The cat had given her a worried look when she had gone to the door, and she had told him hearteningly that she would be back in an hour or two. Tomorrow, she thought happily, I'll be going to the cottage; he can come too. He could travel in a cardboard box—there were plenty in the basement—but she would have to ask the Professor if he minded. She thrust the thought to the back of her mind and started on her chores, making sure that the waiting-room was just so, arranging the daily papers and magazines on the two or three tables, getting out the coffee percolator, freshening the flowers, opening the windows and lastly getting out the case notes. There weren't very many; the Professor always went to Maud's at half past eleven on Friday mornings and didn't get back until his first afternoon appointment.

She had remembered everything. Miss Standish, arriving half an hour later, expressed her satisfaction, rearranged her stylish hairdo and drank the tea Meg had made for her. Five minutes later the Professor arrived, gave her an austere good morning and went into his consulting room. Meg, going in with his coffee, saw that he was already deep in his post, with Miss Standish, enviably efficient, sitting close by, notebook and pencil at the ready.

There was a brief wait for the first patient; Meg drank the rest of Miss Standish's tea and arranged herself at the desk. At least she looked the part in her blue dress.

The first two patients were elderly, come for their regular check-ups, and they were familiar with the procedure and knew what was expected of them without being told. The nurse, with a cheerful nod at Meg, had fetched them in their turn, and after short intervals they returned to make appointments for their next visits. Meg ushered them out with suitable murmurs and looked at the appointments book. One more: a Mrs Denver.

The girl who walked in didn't look old enough to be Mrs anyone. She was tall and slim, exquisitely dressed and made-up; she was in the kind of clothes models wore.

Meg smiled at her as she crossed to the desk and saw
then that the girl was shaking with fright. With luck the
nurse would come quickly, thought Meg, being politely
welcoming and asking the girl to take a seat. She looked
so wretched that Meg began on a mild chat about the
weather, to be interrupted by her companion.

'I don't believe it,' she declared in a voice squeaky
with nerves. 'They make mistakes, don't they? These
clever professors think they know everything! I don't
feel ill, and I don't see why I should have to come here—
they said I might have to go to hospital!' She shuddered
strongly. 'Well, I won't and no one can make me. I told
my husband so.' She looked as though she was going
to cry. 'He couldn't come with me. What's he like, this
Professor Culver?'

'You'll like him,' said Meg promptly. 'He's kind, very
clever and everyone likes him.' She wasn't sure if she
should discuss him with a patient, but Rosalind hadn't
said anything about it. It was a relief when the nurse came
to fetch Mrs Denver.

She was in the consulting room for a long time, and
half-way through Meg was asked on the intercom to take
in a cup of coffee for the patient. Mrs Denver was white
under her make-up; she was sitting in the chair facing
Professor Culver's desk, and the nurse was standing beside her. The Professor said, 'Thank you, Meg,' without
looking at her, and she went back to the waiting-room,
tidied it and got out the case sheets for the afternoon
patients. It struck her forcibly that she would have to
learn something of the Professor's work; she read the
case sheets and made little or no sense of them. To understand them, she would have to get hold of a book about
radiology and what it was all about. There were lots of

books in the consulting room; when everyone had gone home she would take her pick and study the subject. Mrs Denver, escorted by the nurse, came back presently.

'You were quite right,' she told Meg. 'He is awfully kind.' She looked as though she was going to cry. 'I'm going into Maud's and he'll look after me.' She turned to leave. 'You've got a nice little face,' she told an astounded Meg. 'Motherly, if you know what I mean.'

The nurse came back, smiling. 'We haven't met,' she said. 'I'm Mary Giles, and you're Meg, aren't you? I'm not always here—I'm going off now as soon as the Professor's gone—but I come in again this afternoon. Do you think you're going to like it here?'

'Yes,' said Meg, and she meant it.

She went upstairs for her snack lunch later, locking up carefully before she went. The cat was sitting on the balcony; he looked cleaner but he was woefully thin. She gave him a heaped saucer of food—cheese and bits of bacon and bread in milk—and he gobbled the lot. There was no time to go to the shops for cat food; she would ask the caretaker if he would get it for her. She hadn't quite got her shopping organised yet. She made coffee and sandwiches for herself, loaded the saucer again and went to see the caretaker. A fat little man—always cheerful. 'Got a cat, 'ave you?' He beamed at her. 'Make a bit of company evenings, like, won't it? I'll put the stuff outside yer door, 'fore I go down to the pub for 'arf an hour.'

The afternoon went smoothly. The last patient had gone by four o'clock, and the Professor followed him almost at once. Beyond telling Meg to phone him at the number he'd left, and wishing her a cool good afternoon, he had nothing to say. Miss Standish went shortly afterwards, and Meg, left on her own, wondered if he had forgotten his offer of a lift the next day. But she didn't waste time worrying about that; she went to the consulting room, chose what she hoped was a suitable book on radiology, locked up, and then went up to her flat. She fed the cat, made tea, and with him curled up beside her on her chair, began to read. It was all way above her head but absorbing; she had quite forgotten where she was. When there was a knock on the door she called 'Come in,' without even taking her eyes off the book.

Chapter 5

It was Professor Culver who came in and paused in the open door of the sitting-room. He began politely, 'I'm sorry to disturb you, Meg, I came back to fetch a book from my consulting room but it isn't on its usual shelf. Perhaps you've seen it? Miss Standish may have had it.'

Meg had got to her feet, the book in her hand, one finger marking the open page. 'Is this it?' she asked helpfully.

He strode towards her, bringing with him such a circumjacence of rage that she took a step backwards.

'Ah, so you have it—I wasn't aware that I'd made you free of the books in my consulting room.' He spoke softly, but she would rather that he had shouted at her; he had the look of an angry man.

He took the book from her and at the same time saw the cat, staring at him one-eyed from her chair. He said in the same soft voice, 'And what is that bedraggled crea-

ture doing here, filthy dirty and no doubt flea-ridden?'
His black eyes narrowed and his mouth had a nasty curl
to it. 'Have you not got a little above yourself, my girl?
Helping yourself to my books, bringing verminous animals into this house...' He was getting really cross; it was
time to stop him before he was in a real rage.

'One animal,' she corrected him in a reasonable voice,
'and although he's starved and dirty he is not verminous.
I dare say if you had to live from hand to mouth among
the dustbins you would be dirty and probably flea-ridden
too. I shall take good care of him, and in a few weeks'
time you won't know him.' She returned his dark look
with an almost motherly smile. 'And there's really no
need to be so cross,' and at his outraged snort, 'well,
you are, you know—it can't be good for you. I'm sorry I
took the book without asking you first, but you see, now
that I've been working here for a few days it seems to
me that I don't know a thing about your work—that Mrs
Denver who came this morning, she was so frightened
and I couldn't comfort her because I didn't understand
what was wrong with her—I mean, she could have had a
broken rib or TB or something, couldn't she? And you're
a radiologist, and that's X-rays, isn't it?' She looked at
him hopefully. 'You see what I mean, Professor Culver?'

'Your grammar is deplorable, but I get the gist of your
remarks. I must tell you that TB is seldom encountered
these days, and I don't have much to do with broken
bones. I work with radium, either as X-rays or radioac-
tive substances; they're used for the treatment or cure
of malignant diseases, either on their own or combined
with surgery. I have no intention of going into the matter
deeply with you, but since you're interested I'll let you

have a book which explains the work we do. If you'll come with me I'll get it for you.'

'And may I keep the cat?' she added with unconscious wistfulness. 'He's company, you know. Someone to talk to.'

He turned away to open the door. 'Provided that he stays here. What do you intend to do with him at weekends?'

'If I may put him in a box…would you mind if he came in the car with me?'

'And supposing that I mind?'

'Well, you didn't mind about Lucky?'

'Hoist with my own petard! I've no option, have I? Bring the beast.'

'Thank you.' Meg preceded him down to the consulting room and waited quietly while he found the book which she was to have. He made no attempt at any further conversation, merely gave it to her and wished her an indifferent good night.

It wasn't that he disliked her, thought Meg, going slowly upstairs again, it was complete indifference. She doubted if he had looked at her for more than a couple of seconds. In the flat she delivered a short lecture to the cat on the subject of behaving himself in the car.

His behaviour was excellent; he sat in his box, not moving, his eye on the road ahead. After a little while Meg, in the front beside the Professor, stopped sitting with her head over one shoulder anxiously watching his every move, and relaxed. It was an unexpectedly spring-like day, and the country, once they reached it, was giving a hint of better weather to come. The Professor hardly spoke, but by now Meg had reconciled herself to his lack of interest; she had so much to be thankful for, she reminded herself robustly: a job, a cosy little home in the best part of London and the bonus of a weekend cottage in the country. She didn't think that that would last long, but while it did she was going to enjoy it.

They were going through Much Hadham before the Professor said, 'I shall be driving back tomorrow evening. Please be ready by half past six. I'll stop outside the lodge.'

He slowed the car, and she was surprised when he got out and carried the cat's box into the cottage for her. 'Lucky will be brought down very shortly,' he told her, and got back into the car and drove on. Her thanks, half said, died on her lips.

'Rude,' said Meg, and forgot him in the pleasure of being at the cottage. She had brought food and milk and tea with her, and presently she would walk into Much Hadham and stock up with something of everything. There was a small fridge in the kitchen, and an old-fashioned pantry. She fed the cat and allowed him to roam through the little place, although he showed no wish to go outside. There hadn't been time to eat lunch before they left, so she made tea and cut a hunk of bread from the loaf and munched and swallowed as she put the little place to rights. There were logs outside the back door; she laid a fire in the sitting-room and, with the cat sitting on the open window sill, went into the garden. As soon as Lucky came, she could go to the shops; in the meantime she was happy enough to inspect the flower beds.

She was crouching on her heels admiring a clump of primroses half hidden by the hedge when she heard a car. The professor, going the other way with Lucky sitting in the back.

Meg went to the little wooden gate and opened the car

door. Lucky shot out, overjoyed to see her, and the Professor said, 'I'll fetch him back before we leave tomorrow,' and raised a hand as he drove off.

The animals didn't object to each other; beyond a few minutes of wary scrutiny, they seemed prepared to accept the situation. Meg found a length of rope to tie to Lucky's collar, shut the doors and windows and set off with her shopping basket and the dog.

It was marvellous to be in the country again, and after a week of wearing her sober navy dress, it was a nice change to wear a tweed skirt and a thick sweater. She walked briskly, towed by Lucky, did her shopping and started off home again. She was almost there when the Rolls passed her, and this time there was a girl sitting beside the Professor. Meg, who had splendid eyesight, could see that she was very pretty; she was laughing at the Professor too, tossing golden hair off her shoulders. She glanced at Meg as they went by, an indifferent look which took in the elderly sweater and sensible shoes. The Professor raised his hand again but he didn't look at her. The girl looked back, and Meg guessed she had wanted to know who she was. 'Well, she needn't worry,' she told Lucky, 'there's absolutely no competition.'

Which set her thinking. It would be nice to provide that competition, but how? How to attract the Professor's attention, get him to be interested in her, even to fall for her? She was quite shocked at the idea, for she was hopelessly out-of-date in her views. She liked the idea of getting married and having children; she even believed it was possible to live happily ever after. The Professor was hardly the man she would choose to fulfil these hopes. On the other hand, he could do with a lesson; just because she was plain and a nonentity it didn't mean that she had to stay that way.

She reached the cottage, fed the animals and sat down to think. He was a tiresome man, accustomed to having his own way and ill-tempered when he didn't get it. On the other hand he was kind. A good wife could turn him into something quite different.

She made tea, lit the fire and presently busied herself getting supper. When she had eaten it, she sat down by the fire again with Lucky at her feet and the cat squashed between them. 'I must give you a name,' she told him. 'Something rather splendid to make up for only having one eye.' She reflected for a few minutes. 'Nelson,' she declared.

She slept dreamlessly, lulled by the quiet around the cottage, and then spent a happy day poking round the garden; there was a lot to be done, for it had been neglected throughout the winter. None the less there were green shoots poking up amongst the weeds and dead leaves. After her lunch she left Nelson in front of the fire and took Lucky for a walk. She had tea early and packed her bag and set the cottage to rights. She was bringing in logs, ready for the following weekend, when the Rolls went whispering past with Professor Culver and his pretty companion. She was cleaning the grate ready for laying a fire when he returned and stopped outside, this time alone. She whistled to Lucky and went out to the gate. 'He's had his tea,' she observed, and popped him into the back of the car. She gave the Professor a pleasant smile. 'I'm quite ready when you want to go.'

He said slowly, 'Have you had tea? Come up to the house and have it with me.'

She said gently, 'Thank you, but I've had my tea.' Then added kindly, 'Besides, I expect you've had it already.'

He looked surprised as he drove off.

Meg was ready and waiting for him when he came back, standing at the gate with Nelson dozing in his box, and she got into the car without fuss while he saw to the bag and the cat. They had passed Much Hadham and were on the main road before he spoke.

'You've enjoyed your weekend, Meg?'

'Yes, thank you. Very much.'

He glanced sideways at her, expecting her to say more. 'You have all you need in the cottage?'

'Yes, thank you.'

His firm mouth twitched with amusement. 'Has the cat got your tongue, Meg?'

'Certainly not.' She sounded matter-of-fact. 'I can't think of anything interesting to talk about, and I think you dislike chatter.'

He drove in silence for a while. 'Now what have I done or said to deserve such severity? Are you disliking the idea of going back to work?'

'Not a bit—I'm quite looking forward to it. I read the book you lent me and now I'm reading it again, just to make sure that I understood it.'

'What else do you do, Meg? Besides reading and gardening and rescuing animals? Theatre? Concerts? Dancing, dining out...?'

'Well, I haven't been out much; I expect I like all those things, though.'

He glanced at her serene little face again but didn't say anything. The rest of the journey was passed in silence, and when they got to the consulting rooms, although he carried Nelson upstairs for her and waited while she unlocked the door, he merely wished her good night, ignoring her thanks.

Meg settled Nelson before the fire and went to get their supper. She hoped she hadn't been too offhand with the Professor, but at least she had startled him a bit. This week, she decided, she would speak when spoken to, do her work to perfection and take great care not to annoy him in any way. Of course, he might not even notice, and she would fade into even greater obscurity but what would that matter? Right at the back of her head was the nagging thought that he wasn't as happy as he ought to be; he had money, work he obviously enjoyed, he was good-looking and doubtless had any number of friends and could take his pick of pretty girls, so what else did he want? A wife, said Meg to Nelson, who winked back at her. 'Someone like me.' The idea was so preposterous that she burst out laughing.

All the same, she went down to start work on Monday morning determined to keep to her plan. She was sitting demurely at her desk by the time the Professor arrived; she had done all her small chores, given Miss Standish her tea and had the coffee ready to pour. She wished him good morning and gave him the sort of smile she imagined a receptionist would give a distinguished consultant. Presently she went into his room and put his coffee down on the desk beside him and slipped out again soundlessly. He looked up from his letter to watch her disappear through the door, a faint frown between his eyes. He frowned several times during the day too. Meg seemed different; she had become a shadow of herself, so self-effacing that he found himself watching her, something he hadn't done before. He had begun, unconsciously, to expect her direct way of talking, her matter-of-fact manner, her flashes of temper, just as he had taken for granted the rather dull life she led. He still didn't know why he had offered her a job and the lodge; he had done it on the spur of the moment and had been sorry about it afterwards, although he had been agreeably surprised to find that she was everything that he expected of someone working for him.

At the end of a busy afternoon, on his way out, he stopped to ask her if she felt all right.

'Oh, I'm very well, thank you Professor Culver.' She smiled, 'Good night.'

After he had gone, she took the post, locked up and went upstairs to get her outdoor things. The Post Office was five minutes' walk away, and she enjoyed the short trip each evening. There were quite a few people about, going home or going out for the evening; she wouldn't admit to herself that she was lonely, but she felt less so with people hurrying to and fro around her. It could have been far worse, she told herself; she could have been living in that dreadful flat behind Waterloo Station with some dreary job and no lovely weekends at Much Hadham. She stopped to talk to Percy the caretaker as she went indoors, and let herself into her flat, feeling cheerful again. Quite a bit of the evening was taken up cooking her supper, and twice she had to switch the phone through to the Professor's house. She was getting ready for bed when Doreen rang to say that she would be round on the following evening. 'About seven o'clock,' she said. 'Will Professor Culver be there?'

'He goes about five o'clock, sometimes later if there's a patient, but tomorrow he's at Maud's in the afternoon and he doesn't come back.'

Doreen sounded disappointed. 'Oh, well, I'll come just

the same,' she told Meg tactlessly, and rang off without asking her how she was getting on.

She arrived punctually and was instantly aggrieved because Meg wouldn't unlock the waiting-room door and let her look round. 'You are silly!' she said, half angrily. 'As though it matters! There's nobody there—I only want to look.'

'I'll ask Professor Culver if he minds, and next time you come perhaps we can go in. But not now. Come upstairs: I've got supper ready.'

Doreen was impressed by the flat. 'Why, it's delightful—you lucky girl!' She saw Nelson in his box. 'What on earth have you got there?'

Meg explained and Doreen laughed. 'You always were a funny little thing, finding animals and persuading half the village to give them homes. You like looking after people too, don't you? You coped with Mother beautifully.'

Meg didn't answer that. 'Sit down, Doreen. I've got some sherry—we'll have it before I dish up.'

'When do you shop?' asked Doreen.

'Well, there's just about time during the lunch hour, only I have to look sharp about it.'

'Did you go to this marvellous cottage you were telling us about?'

'Yes, it was so lovely—I had Lucky with me and Nelson came down too.'

'Did Professor Culver give you a lift?'

'Yes. He has to pass the door to get to his home.'

'What's it like, his home?'

'I don't know…'

'Meg, you're hopeless! Didn't you go and explore?'

'I never thought about it. Anyway it would be a bit

rude, wouldn't it? I didn't see it the first time we went down to the cottage.'

Over supper Doreen asked, 'Do you get on with him well, Meg?'

'I work for him.' said Meg soberly. 'We don't—don't socialise.'

Doreen laughed. 'Any other girl would be making the most of her chances,' she observed. 'He'd be quite a catch.'

'Well, I think he's caught. There was a very pretty girl there this weekend. Just the kind of girl one would imagine he would marry...'

'So you think about him?' Doreen observed slyly.

Meg passed the vegetables. 'As an employer, yes—I expect you think about the doctors you work for? I don't know anything about him—his private life—and I don't particularly want to.' Which wasn't quite true. Moreover, she didn't want to talk about him.

Doreen's flat proved a splendid red herring; she described it at length, saying rather casually that when Meg was free she must come and spend an evening with her. 'Though I go out a great deal and I suppose you like to have a bit of peace and quiet at the end of the day.'

Meg got to up to switch a call through to the Professor's house. 'Yes, I do, and I have to be here to take phone calls, though the caretaker will do it if I want to go out. As long as it's not too often.'

'Well, you don't know anyone, do you?' Doreen accepted ice cream. 'I must say Cora and I are surprised that you've fallen on your feet. We don't need to worry about you any more, thank goodness.'

Meg didn't say anything to that. She loved her sisters, but there was no getting away from the fact that when their mother had become ill, they had taken it for granted that she should be the one to stay at home and nurse her. In all fairness, she supposed that if she had been one or other of them, she might have done the same. She would have liked to explain to Doreen that even though she had this good job and a little home to go with it, she would have preferred to have stayed in Hertingfordbury. But that would have sounded ungrateful. She was very grateful; she had only to remember the horrid basement flat to be awash with gratitude.

Wednesday already, she thought happily as she got her breakfast the next morning, three more days and she would be at the lodge again. She washed up, saw to Nelson, tidied the flat and skipped downstairs and un-locked the waiting-room door, pulled the curtains back, opened the windows and went to unlock the consulting room. The door wasn't locked; after a second of hesita-tion, she opened it wide. Professor Culver was at his desk, writing. He looked up briefly, said irritably, 'Well, don't gape like that—make me some coffee, will you? I'll be gone in ten minutes or so, but until then I don't want to be disturbed.'

Meg prudently said nothing but left him there to get out the percolator and his cup and saucer. He was wear-ing a sweater and he needed a shave—she was an ob-servant girl—he'd been up all night, or at least part of it, and she could forgive him for being testy.

She went back within a few minutes with the coffee, hot and milky and sweet, put it on the desk and skimmed silently to the door.

'Had your breakfast?' enquired the Professor as he flung down his pen.

'Yes, thank you.' She opened the door wide enough

to go through and was halted by his, 'Get yourself some coffee and come back here. Please,' he added, in such a mild voice that she did as she was bid, fetched a mug and sat down in Miss Standish's chair, the one she used when she was taking letters. She did it soundlessly and with composure. If he wanted company he should have it. She didn't think he would want to chat and she had no intention of starting a conversation.

He sat back in his chair, the mug in his hand. 'Mrs James and her small daughter Nancy are coming at half past nine. I've given Miss Standish the morning off. Mrs James is young and, for want of a better word, frivolous. Nancy has a sarcoma which I'm almost certain can be cured, but her mother is going to take the news badly. I shall want you to cope with her—you have phlegm and common sense...'

Meg took a sip of coffee. Compliments, if one could call them that, were flying. She said quietly, 'Very well, Professor Culver. Would you like some more coffee?'

When she had fetched it he asked, 'Are you happy here, Meg?'

'Yes, thank you.' She finished her own coffee and sat without fidgeting, ready to answer politely if questioned. It was quiet in the room and their silence lasted rather too long. The Professor put down his cup and she heard his sigh.

'Will you tell Nurse that I'll be back at nine-twenty?'

She collected the mugs and went back to the little kitchen, and soon heard him leave. She dearly wanted to know why he had been up during the night. She would find out from Miss Standish after their dinner hour; meanwhile there was nothing to do until Mary Giles arrived.

She received the news of the Professor's disturbed

night with a shake of her head. 'He's a consultant, love, and a lecturer too, travels the world…and he's an expert if ever there was one, yet if there is a hitch he'll think nothing of spending hours at the hospital. There are Mrs James and Nancy coming too, they were here just before you came and he told her then that there would be tests on the child and it might be necessary for her to have some hospital treatment. She wouldn't listen, of course. The child's as good as gold, but the mother…'

Mrs Giles rolled her eyes upwards. 'And Miss Standish at the dentist!'

'Yes, well, the Professor said I was to look after Mrs James.'

'Rather you than me, love!'

The Professor arrived soon afterwards, immaculate in his dark grey suit and Italian silk tie and looking none the worse for his sleepless night. Hard on his heels came Mrs James and Nancy.

Reflecting later upon her morning while she ate her sandwiches and fed Nelson, Meg hoped there would never be another one like it. Nancy had been a model patient, but her mother had at first refused to listen to the Professor, and after a patient ten minutes or so on his part, had declared roundly that no one in her family or her husband's had ever had cancer and she wasn't going to believe him. 'Nancy will be a cripple—you say it's one of her legs.' She burst into angry tears.

The Professor said sternly, 'There is no reason to suppose that radiotherapy will turn Nancy into a *cripple*, Mrs James.'

It was then that Meg was summoned to bring tea. Which she did, and was told to stay. She poured out for Mrs James, murmured soothingly and melted into a corner. 'I'll simply not believe it,' said Mrs James, and sipped her tea.

The Professor examined his nails. 'It's the child's life, Mrs James. Perhaps I could have a word with your husband?'

Mrs James held her cup out for more tea. 'Well, I suppose you know what you're talking about,' she said rudely. 'You'd better come and see him, I suppose.'

Meg had to admire his bland silkiness. 'Meg, fetch my appointments book, if you will,' and when he had it, 'I can spare fifteen minutes this evening, Mrs James. If your husband would be good enough to come here at half past six? He will be back in London by then?'

He gave Meg the book. 'Tell Nurse that Mrs James is ready to leave, please. She's upstairs with Nancy.'

There had been twenty minutes or so before the next patient; she had taken in his coffee and marvelled at his calm after all that hassle. She and Mrs Giles, snatching a quick cup of tea, agreed that even allowing for overwrought feelings, Mrs James had been awful.

The Professor would be at Maud's all that afternoon and Mrs Giles would go home as soon as she had set the examination room to rights and got things ready for the next day, which gave Meg a chance to take a little time off after her lunch and do some shopping. She came back with a laden basket, saw Mrs Giles away and set about putting the reception room in a state of pristine order. She tidied the consulting room too, being very careful to arrange the muddle on the desk in exactly the way it had been before, and by then it was time to lock up for the evening. She hadn't forgotten that the Professor would be back, but he could let himself in. She took the keys with her and went upstairs.

She had fed Nelson, done a few small chores and was contemplating the contents of the fridge with a view to making supper when the doorbell rang. It would be Percy to collect her rubbish; she opened the door and was met by the Professor's austere, 'Never open the door without first putting up the chain, Meg.'

She opened the door wide and invited him in, prudently forbearing from answering him back. Once inside, he stood in the centre of the room, towering over everything, dwarfing the table and chairs. He had the look of a man who needed soothing, but she wasn't sure how to set about it.

'Will you sit down?'

He ignored that. 'I have the urge to talk,' he said testily, 'and for some reason I find you a good listener. Come back to my house and have dinner with me, Meg?'

If he had told her to jump off the balcony she couldn't have been more surprised. Surely there were half a dozen girls who would fit the bill far better than she. He saw her hesitation and added blandly, 'Never timid, Meg? I shouldn't have thought it of you.'

'Certainly not,' she said sharply, quite forgetting to be self-effacing. She remembered just in time to add meekly, 'I was a little surprised, Professor.' She looked so demure that he gave her a second glance. 'But of course I'll come.' She made it sound as though he had asked her to run an errand in her free time, and he frowned.

She gave him a kind smile. 'I'll fetch my coat.'

She had changed into a skirt and sweater after work and she was hardly dressed for an evening out, but that couldn't be helped. She put on some more lipstick, ran a comb through her hair and went back to the sitting-room. The Professor was standing where she had left him, studying Nelson, who was sitting very erect in his box, watching him.

'He looks more like a cat,' commented the Professor laconically. Meg opened her mouth to make the obvious answer to that and then closed it again; she said with her new-found meekness, 'Yes, doesn't he? I'm ready, Professor Culver.'

She switched off all but one table lamp and opened the door, stopping to make sure that she had the key.

The Rolls was at the kerb and she got in without fuss. She had no idea where he lived and she longed to ask, but she wasn't going to. Before her father and mother died they had visited London often enough; he drove towards Regent's Park, past Gloucester Gate and turned in the direction of the Grand Union Canal.

Little Venice, Meg reflected silently; she had a vague recollection of it, tucked away, a much sought-after spot. The Professor drove past the row of handsome houses overlooking the canal and a hundred yards further on stopped before a brick house standing on its own. It was older than the other dwellings there and while not large, was built in a higgledy-piggledy style which suggested that from time to time its owners had added a room here and there, a hooded iron balcony jutting out over the street and an oriel window and what Meg took to be an Adam doorway.

There was a narrow strip of grass between the house and the pavement and a short flagstone path to the front door. Light streamed from the downstairs windows and from the fanlight over the door, and when the Professor unlocked it, Meg found herself in a square hall lit by a cut-glass chandelier. There were thin silky rugs on the

polished wooden floor and a porter's chair in one corner
with a marble-topped console table against either wall.

The Professor was behind her, urging her on, and coming towards them from the door beside the gracefully
curved staircase was a tall and very stout middle-aged
woman, dressed severely in black.

The Professor addressed her in a genial voice. 'Rosie,
I've brought Miss Collins from the consulting rooms to
keep me company at dinner. Show her where she can
leave her coat, will you?' He glanced at Meg. 'Rosie is
an old family friend; she housekeeps for me.'

Meg offered a hand and looked up into Rosie's face.
Unlike the rest of her appearance, it wasn't severe at all.
She found herself smiling at the shrewd blue eyes twin-
kling at her.

She regretted the plainness of her appearance; in the
small, elegant cloakroom she did the best she could with
her hair and her face, feeling quite inadequate in such a
splendid house. Not that it mattered, she consoled herself; the Professor never looked at her for long enough to
know if she was wearing a sack or a ballgown.

He stuck his head round a door as she went back into
the hall, and then opened it wide for her to go in. The
room was facing the canal, and the long velvet curtains
were still undrawn over the wide windows. There was a
brisk fire in the grate facing them and a deep couch and
chairs arranged around it. Meg took the chair he offered
her and glanced around her, trying not to appear too in-
quisitive. The colours were charming, a mixture of tawny
browns and rich cream with a hint of apricot lamps and
cushions, mingling nicely with the maple lamp tables
and the rosewood rent table by the windows. There was
a magnificent walnut and yew wood escritoire against

the end wall with spoonbacked buttoned velvet chairs on either side of it, and bowls of spring flowers here and there. A truly lovely room, comfortable to the point of luxury but lived-in too.

She accepted the sherry she was offered and sat quietly, answering her companion's desultory remarks politely without offering any of her own. Presently, across the hall in the dining-room, sitting opposite him at the oval mahogany table, she took care to agree with whatever he said, even though once or twice her wish to argue was very great.

The meal was delicious: artichoke soup, fillets of sole with lobster sauce, a winter salad and to finish, a hot chocolate soufflé served with whipped cream. They went back to the sitting-room for coffee, and not until then did Meg remind him, 'You wanted to talk, Professor...'

He was sitting back, his long legs stretched out to the fire, his face in shadow. 'You're a restful companion, Meg; you don't wear jangling bracelets, nor do you whip out a mirror and stare at your face every half-hour or so.'

'I expect if I had bracelets to jangle and a face to admire I'd do that too.'

She couldn't see his smile. 'I was beginning to wonder what had come over you—not a single waspish remark for two days! I feared that you were sickening for something.'

'I had no intention of being waspish.' Her voice achieved meekness once more. 'I'm sorry.'

She sat back in her chair, her hands in her lap, so self-effacing that she might not have been there. Presently she said, 'I'm listening...'

He gave a little laugh. 'Determined to sing for your

supper, aren't you, Meg? What did you think of little Nancy this morning?'

'A dear little girl—she has no idea that she's ill, I imagine?'

'Perhaps she knows a little—you see, she has pain from time to time—not bad at the moment. Thanks to an observant nanny, we can deal with that and, with God's good grace, cure her. And her mother?'

Meg said carefully, 'It's harder for some people—I mean when they get bad news or things go wrong.'

'I had a talk with Nancy's father.' The Professor suddenly sounded tired. 'Sometimes I almost lose faith in my fellow beings, Meg.'

'Well, you mustn't. Where would we all be without clever men like you?'

He said in a surprised voice, 'You really mean that, don't you?'

'Of course I do!' She had forgotten about being meek. 'You're tired, you need to go to bed early and sleep soundly.' She stirred in her chair. 'I'm going back now so that you can do just that.'

It was silly to feel disappointed when he said quietly, 'Why, that's a good idea, Meg,' for it meant that she had to get to her feet with every appearance of satisfaction; she could have sat there in the peace of the lovely room for hours, just listening. Only he hadn't wanted a listener, just someone to keep him company for an hour while he unwound from a difficult day. She got her coat and wished Rosie a civil good night, then followed him out to the door and into the car, sitting quietly beside him as he drove the short distance back to the consulting rooms. At the door she undid her seat belt and reached for the handle, but his hand came down on hers. 'Wait.' So she waited while he got out and ushered her out and took the door key from her and, rather to her surprise, went upstairs with her. He opened the flat door too, and went in with her without having been invited. Nelson was still in his box, asleep, and the room was warm and welcoming in the lamplight. He went to the kitchen and opened the kitchen door, and glanced along the balcony before shutting it and locking it again. When he was standing beside her again, Meg said, 'Thank you for my dinner, Professor; I do hope you have a good night's sleep.'

'So do I—I'm taking a very glamorous young lady out for the evening tomorrow—I shall be needing all my energy.'

'But you'll enjoy it,' observed Meg in a motherly voice. Then she asked, 'Is she very pretty?'

'Delightfully so. She collects men in the same way as you collect down-and-out animals.' He gave her a mocking smile and she went pink. It had been a mistake to have spent the evening with him. He hadn't wanted her company; she had been the first thing at hand to occupy his mind and take his thoughts from his day's work. She went to the door. 'Good night, Professor.' Her voice was quite without expression, and she smiled nicely as he went through the door.

She was shutting it quickly on his broad back when he turned suddenly and she had to open it again. He said slowly, 'I don't know why it should be, but you bring out the worst in me, Meg. I wonder why?' He bent and kissed her swiftly on one cheek. 'It's a situation which requires some thought,' he told her in a silky voice which disturbed her.

It continued disturbing her while she got ready for bed. 'Anyone would think that he'd been drinking,' she told Nelson, 'but we only had sherry and wine at dinner. Perhaps he's so tired he doesn't know what he's saying.'

A silly remark, she had to admit; the Professor was a man who would always know what he was saying.

Chapter 6

There was no sign of tiredness or drunkenness in Professor Culver when he arrived in the morning. Indeed, in his sober, superbly cut suit he gave Meg the impression that neither of these conditions would dare to intrude upon him. He gave her a suave good morning as he went into his consulting room, and when she went in with his coffee he was already deep in his post, with the faithful Miss Standish taking notes. Meg was left with the supposition that he had made a subtle joke she hadn't understood. As for kissing her, well, everyone kissed everyone these days. She went back to her desk and assumed the mantle of the perfect receptionist.

She was getting rather good at it. All the same, it was a delight to wake up on Saturday morning with the prospect of the weekend at the lodge. That it was pelting with rain did nothing to dampen her spirits; she rose early, got everything ready and went to her morning's work with a light heart.

It was still raining when they left and the Professor, beyond a few remarks about the weather, had nothing to say. But nothing could dampen her pleasure at the prospect of a weekend at the lodge. She gave a quick sigh of contentment as the Professor swept the car through the gates, which changed to a soundless 'Oh!' as he continued past it. She said nothing, and when he leaned across her and undid the door she got out and stood on the sweep before his house. It was surprisingly close to the lodge, but well screened by trees and shrubs, a fair-sized house with fine pargeting and black and white timber cladding. A small manor house, beautifully maintained. Its mullioned windows and stout front door gave it the cosy look of a much smaller place and Meg, studying it, sighed with unconscious envy. To live in such a delightful home must be everyone's dear dream...

'Come inside,' invited the Professor. 'Nelson will be all right for a few minutes. I'd like you to meet Mr and Mrs Trugg, who look after the house... In case you should ever need to come here while I'm not at home,' he added blandly.

Trugg advanced to meet them as they went inside— a man of about the Professor's age, already going a little bald and on the stout side. He greeted his employer with grave pleasure, acknowledged Meg's smile, and with dignity took her old Burberry as though it were Russian sable.

The Professor led the way into a long, low room with windows at either end and a magnificent strapwork ceiling, furnished mostly with William and Mary period pieces, blending nicely with the great wing-back armchairs on either side of the William Cheave fireplace. The leaded windows were small and curtained with mulberry satin. Quite perfect, reflected Meg, taking it all in without saying a word.

'Such a miserable day,' commented her companion. 'Have you had lunch?' He didn't give her a chance to answer. 'Of course you haven't—there was no time.' He tugged an old-fashioned bell rope by the fireplace, and when Trugg came, he asked for coffee and sandwiches.

He was about to sit down when three dogs nosed their way past Trugg and rushed across the room. The first two were bull terriers, the third was Lucky. He made for Meg, greeted her with a good deal of excitement and then went to the Professor's chair, reared up to look into his face and then returned to sit by her.

'Ben and Polly,' said the Professor, and at a wave of his hand they went obediently to her. She patted their heads, careful to keep a hand on Lucky. 'Don't worry, they get on well,' he said. 'We'll walk them back to the lodge presently and they can meet Nelson—then if he happens to stray this way they won't do anything, if they've made friends.'

The coffee and sandwiches came, and Meg allowed the Professor to make conversation, giving polite answers from time to time but making no effort to attract his attention with any remarks of her own. Soon, when they got up to go, she caught him looking at her with a puzzled frown. Really looking, she was pleased to see, not just a hasty glance. She accepted her old mac from Trugg, waited while the Professor got her bag and Nelson in his box from the car, and walked beside him down the drive and round the curve which hid the house from the lodge. She was a bit apprehensive for Nelson, who was watching the dogs with a watchful eye, but when they got to the lodge, the Professor set the box down in the porch, spoke to his dogs, who merely sniffed at Nelson, and opened the door. He put her bag down on the floor, lifted Nelson's box on to the table, bade her a pleasant goodbye and with the dogs at his heels started back along the drive.

Meg just had time to thank him for her lunch. He nodded vaguely. 'My pleasure—we'll leave tomorrow about six o'clock.'

Meg, trotting round doing her small chores and lighting the fire, wondered if the girl was going to join him again and, without actually being aware of doing so, listened out for his car to pass the lodge. But it didn't; she did her shopping with Lucky, had tea round the fire, found the tapestry work she had taken up when her mother was ill, and spent a blissful evening with no sounds but the radio and Lucky and Nelson's snores.

It was still raining when she got up the next morning. She took Lucky for a walk, got her dinner ready and then went into the garden; there was a lot to do, whatever the weather. She was happily grubbing up weeds on either side of the little gate when two cars went past. The girl was in the first one, sitting beside the driver, and there were people in the back. The second car was full too, and they had hardly disappeared round the curve when Mrs Culver's old-fashioned car appeared. Mrs Culver was sitting in the back and the car slowed and stopped at the gate.

'Ralph said you would be here,' began Mrs Culver. 'How delightful to see you, my dear; aren't you getting rather wet?'

'It's nice to be out of doors, and I quite like the rain. How are you, Mrs Culver?'

'Splendid. I must tell Betsy I've seen you. You're happy, Meg?'

'Very happy, Mrs Culver.'

'You're not coming up to the house for lunch?'

'Oh, my goodness, no!' And then, in case Mrs Culver should be offended, 'There's so much that I want to do here.' She looked down at her small untidy person. 'Besides, I'm hardly dressed for it…'

Mrs Culver beamed at her. 'Perhaps not, dear, but you look rather nice all the same—wholesome is the word.' She sat back and Noakes started the car again, and Meg went back to her weeding; she wasn't quite sure if she liked being called wholesome—it sounded like a wholemeal loaf.

She was washing up after her lunch when she heard the cars going past, but she resisted the temptation to peep from the sitting-room window.

It was going to rain all day; she got into the Burberry again, got Lucky's lead and went for another walk. The hedges were drenched, but here and there were primroses tucked away under the trees. She picked a small bunch to take back with her to the flat and went back to make tea, feed the animals and get ready to leave. It was almost six o'clock when the Professor thumped on the door, and when Meg opened it he came in with Ben and Polly, who, obedient to his quiet command, sat down and stared inscrutably at the opposite wall.

His enquiry as to whether she had enjoyed her weekend was perfunctory, but all the same she answered it with enthusiasm, nicely damped down to a wooden politeness.

'Well, it's more than I have.' His eye fell on the primroses, neatly wrapped in damp paper. 'You went walking?'

'Oh, yes. I don't mind the rain. You'd like to take Lucky now?'

She bade the faithful beast goodbye, and the Professor turned on his heel, whistled to his own dogs and strode off.

He came back again presently, loaded Nelson into the car, waited while she locked the door and then shut the car door on her with something of a snap. It seemed prudent to remain silent, and not a word was uttered until they were within five minutes of the consulting rooms.

'In two weeks' time I shall be taking my mother over to Amsterdam. We shall be there a week. Remind me to check the appointments book with you in the morning.'

'Very well, Professor.' Meg had been taken by surprise, but she didn't allow it to show.

He drew up and got out of the car, accompanied her to the flat, waited until she had lighted a table lamp, stalked to the balcony and looked around and then with a brief good night, went away.

'Very upset,' said Meg to Nelson. 'Perhaps he's had a tiff with that girl. A holiday will do him good. Do you suppose we'll be able to spend a week at the lodge or stay here with nothing to do?'

But in fact the week was to be spent quite differently, as she discovered in the morning.

The morning patients were all for check-ups and the first one wouldn't come until ten o'clock; in the afternoon the Professor would be at the hospital presiding over his outpatients' clinic. Meg, her chores done and the coffee percolating, gave him a cheerful good morning when he arrived, but instead of going into his consulting room he crossed to the desk.

'Those appointments,' he began. 'The check-ups for the week when I shall be away can be fitted in on the week following; there are several new patients—get them on the phone, please, and make appointments for the week before I go. Fit them in where you can; if necessary we can work until six o'clock.'

He sat down on the edge of the desk. 'Now listen to me, Meg. While my mother is away, Kate is to have a holiday, Betsy will stay and Noakes and his wife will move in to keep her company. We shall be staying with my grandmother, whose elderly housekeeper could do with a few days' rest. My mother hopes that you will consider coming with us and acting as housekeeper in her stead.'

Meg didn't say anything for a long moment; such a wealth of delight and excitement had engulfed her that she couldn't have uttered anyway. Outwardly serene, she looked at him, while she pondered the astounding fact that she had fallen in love; this then was what poets since the world began had been writing about, this delightful bubbly feeling which made her want to sing and shout, this wild desire to fling herself into the Professor's arms. The remnant of good sense left in her neat head reminded her that he was hardly likely to welcome that; a more unsuitable man with whom to fall in love was surely not to be found.

She said in a quiet voice which gave none of her feelings away, 'I can't speak or understand Dutch. And what about Nelson?' Then after a pause for thought, 'I have no passport.' He was watching her closely.

'My grandmother's household is bilingual. Nelson can go to Much Hadham; he'll be quite safe there. You can get a visitor's passport at the nearest Post Office.' He smiled at her and her heart turned over. 'Just for a week, Meg?'

He could have asked for a lifetime. 'Very well, Professor Culver.'

He got off the desk. 'My mother will be deeply grateful,' he told her. An answer which gave her no satisfaction at all. She watched him leave the room, aware that life would never be the same again and perhaps would not be very happy either.

The week passed: Meg found herself living for the moment when the Professor arrived in the mornings, and that was something which would have to stop, she told herself repeatedly. As soon as she could, she would look for another job where she wouldn't see him and in time, would forget him. This, she had to admit to herself, was wishful thinking; the tiresome man had taken root in her heart and head. She busied herself with plans for her week in Amsterdam; the housekeeper's grey dress, of course, but she had a little money to spend now, a new coat and perhaps a knitted dress to go under it. A pair of boots would also be nice.

Towards the end of the week the Professor went to Birmingham for an afternoon, lecturing, and Meg, offered a couple of hours off after her lunch, took herself out to do some shopping.

She found a tweed coat, beautifully cut, at Jaeger's, and since there was a matching skirt she bought that too, as well as a couple of sweaters to go with it. She had already spent all the money she had planned to, but she was feeling reckless; she hadn't needed much of the money she had earned and there was her share of the house in the bank. She made a beeline for Harrods and bought a knitted dress in a pleasing shade of amber and a silk jersey two-piece in several shades of old rose. She thought it unlikely that she would wear it, but she would feel happier if she had something pretty with her. One never knew… She left the thought hanging in the air and wandered into the shoe department.

She had intended buying boots and she did, but she bought a pair of high-heeled pumps too and, since she still had time to spare, she stocked up on undies and on more make-up. Then, to round off her afternoon, she had a taxi home.

She had phoned Cora the day before and told her about her week in Amsterdam. Cora had observed that it sounded very nice and added crossly that she couldn't think what had got into Meg, adding that both boys had the measles. She sounded as though it was Meg's fault.

She would have to let Doreen know, but before she had a chance to phone after she got back to the flat, her sister rang.

'What's all this about you going to Amsterdam? As a housekeeper, too—aren't you satisfactory at the consulting rooms? Have you got the sack already?'

Then, before Meg could get a word in edgeways, 'This really won't do, you know, Meg. I blame myself for not insisting on you buying that flat and training as a shorthand typist. You would have got a good steady job in another month or two; now here you are, not trained for anything and heaven knows where you'll end up. That's what comes of letting you have your own way!'

'But I've got a good steady job. I'm perfectly satisfactory; I'm going to Amsterdam to help out Mrs Culver's mother so that her own housekeeper can have a rest—the one who had her feet done, you know. I'm looking forward to it. I can't think why you and Cora are making such a fuss. I'm very happy and I really like the job.'

'Is Professor Culver going?'

'I believe so. Have you settled into your flat?'

'Just about. I'm going to give a housewarming party. You must come and bring Professor Culver—after all, we have met.'

'You can always invite him. Miss Standish, his secretary, says that he has a very busy life.'

'Well, I dare say he might not come unless I asked him myself—you don't hit it off together, do you? I shall ring him up.'

There was one thing about Doreen, Meg reflected as she hung up—she had plenty of self-confidence. She thought it doubtful that the Professor would go. He had his own friends, and by the look of things, the girl she had seen him with most likely occupied most of his leisure. The thought hurt, but stronger than the hurt was the conviction that given the chance she could make the Professor happy. True, he was dictatorial at times and positively testy if he was tired, but if he had a loving wife to go home to, that could be changed. She had little hope of him falling in love with her, but there was no harm in trying…

She crossed the room and studied her face in the mirror above the fireplace. It gave her little encouragement; she had experimented with a more elaborate make-up and then discarded it. Hers wasn't that kind of face. Her eyes were all right, she supposed, and the lashes curled long and thick, but not everyone admired grey eyes and her hair, long and fine and silky, was a pale brown which a more enterprising girl would have tinted years ago. She reminded herself that beauty was only skin deep and went to cook her supper. She gave the matter some thought during the evening; there wasn't much she could do except keep a curb on her tongue and present him with a picture of serenity and meekness. The meekness would come hard, but she noticed that it puzzled him; at least it had made him aware of her.

She saw the Professor only briefly on the following day, and on the Saturday, contrary to his usual practice, he had several patients. Two of them had come for a first consultation and took up a great deal of the morning; he was unhurried in his work, deeming, quite rightly, that anyone threatened with a possibility of serious illness had the right to talk about it from every angle. Meg made appointments for them, made tea for them both and said all the right things; now she knew a little about the Professor's work she found it easier to talk to them. With very few exceptions they reacted well to the Professor's pleasant, reassuring manner. They drank their tea, convinced that he would cure them, and since Meg lent a kindly ear, they discussed their treatment, their domestic worries and occasionally their fears.

Tidying the waiting-room when the last patient had gone, Meg reflected that there was nothing sad about her work; it was like fighting an enemy and mostly winning. She supposed the Professor felt like that too.

She was just finished when he came into the room. Miss Standish had gone and she could hear Percy in the yard clashing the dustbin lids.

'We're late,' observed the Professor, stating the obvious. 'I'll be back for you in half an hour. Can you get yourself a sandwich by then and be ready to leave? I've guests coming for the weekend and I want to get home before they arrive.'

He barely waited for her answer; she heard the car leave as she skipped up to the flat, drank some milk, fed Nelson, gobbled a slice of bread and butter and tore out of her dress and into a tweed skirt and pullover. She flung on her Burberry and, snatching up her bag and Nelson's box, got to the front door just as the Rolls slid to a silent halt before it.

'You had your lunch?' enquired the Professor, stuffing Nelson and her bag on to the back seat.

'Yes, thank you.' Her quiet voice implied contentment, while her hungry insides started to rumble. Their ideas of lunch would hardly be the same. She sat beside him, planning supper to make up for it: steak and tomatoes and courgettes and creamed potatoes, and, since she would have all the time in the world to cook that evening, an egg custard with cream and coffee afterwards.

'You're very quiet,' observed her companion, and then before she could reply, 'you smell like a country garden.'

So the wildly expensive bottle of Anaïs-Anaïs she had bought at Harrods had paid dividends! She thought it prudent to ignore the second part of his remark. 'I'm planning my weekend,' she told him pleasantly.

'What are your plans?' He sounded very faintly bored.

'Walking with Lucky, gardening, shopping.'

He said silkily, 'Sometimes you sound too good to be true, Meg.'

She bit back the retort she had on her tongue. If she said anything else she would sound like a prig. 'The country is beginning to look delightful,' she observed gently.

He mumbled something and drove fast and in silence until they were going through Much Hadham. 'I'll send Lucky down with Trugg.' He stopped the car by the lodge, unloaded Nelson and put her bag in the porch before getting back into the car. 'Enjoy your weekend, such as it is,' he told her. There was mockery in his smile.

The little cottage welcomed her; she saw to Nelson and then, since the shops would close at four o'clock, she put Lucky, handed over by a friendly Trugg, on his lead and walked into Much Hadham. The high street was full of late shoppers, and she enjoyed pottering in and out of the butcher's and the greengrocer's. She bought doughnuts for tea and decided to bake her own bread.

The days were lengthening, but she lit the fire and turned on the lamps when she got back. She had bought a paper and now she sat, eating her doughnuts and drinking cup after cup of tea, the curtains drawn against the dusk, listening to Radio Three. She wasn't happy—she wasn't sure if she would ever be quite happy again—but for the moment she was content.

It was a couple of hours later that she heard voices and the creak of the gate. She was in the kitchen; the steak was under the grill, smelling delicious, the vegetables were on the stove and she was taking two loaves from the oven. When there was a knock on the door she laid them carefully on the kitchen table and went to open it.

The girl was outside, with a tall young man, his face hidden behind a beard and a moustache.

They walked past Meg into the sitting-room and the girl said, 'Hello—we wanted Ralph to bring us but he wouldn't, said you needed privacy or some such nonsense.' She gave a little fluting laugh. 'We escaped while he took those dogs of his for a walk.'

Meg stood in the centre of the little room and looked at them. The girl was every bit as pretty as she had thought, and dressed in the height of fashion, her hair pulled off her face and wound into a strange lop-sided topknot. The man she dismissed as someone she didn't like on sight.

She said politely, 'Good evening,' and then, 'why did you come?'

'We thought we'd do a bit of slumming, my dear.' The girl smiled widely, showing beautiful teeth.

Capped, thought Meg waspishly, and out loud said, 'I'm cooking—you will have to excuse me for a moment...'

'My God, can you cook too?' The girl added deliberately, 'Ralph said you were a pre-war paragon with no ambition. Domesticated too...'

She looked round her. 'We'll sit down while you slave over your hot stove.' She took one of the armchairs and raised her eyebrows at Lucky and Nelson, sitting, very much on guard, before the fire. 'I don't think much of your taste in pets,' she said, and laughed at the young man.

None of them heard the Professor coming through the open gate. Ben and Polly nosed their way in the door which had been left ajar, with their master on their heels. He said without preamble, 'I'm so sorry about this, Meg; I must apologise for my guests, they must have misunderstood me. I know you cherish your privacy.' He stared blandly round. 'We'll go at once.'

He opened the door wide and stood by it as the girl swept past him and the young man followed.

'You've been making bread,' declared the Professor as he followed them. 'And I smell something delicious— steak?'

Meg nodded. She was too near tears of rage to speak, and to her shame, two of them trickled down her cheeks before she could swallow them back.

The Professor watched them with an expressionless face. 'Don't worry, this won't happen again,' he told her, and took a step back into the cottage and kissed her gently.

He shut the door quietly behind him and she turned the key, not caring if he heard or not. But she wasn't going to let it spoil her weekend; she finished cooking her supper, fed the animals, laid the plates and glasses and silver she had brought with her from her old home, and turned up the radio. Crying wouldn't help—she knew that; she was more determined than ever that the Professor shouldn't marry that truly awful girl.

Sunday passed twice as fast as any other day in the week. The morning was fine and cold and she and Lucky walked their fill before going back to the casserole she had put in the oven. There wasn't much of the afternoon left by the time she had washed the dishes and tidied up. The garden was repaying her labours; there were daffodils in bud and grape hyacinths already out as well as the primroses and violets under the hedges. She grubbed round happily and presently went to put the kettle on for tea, thus missing the car, with the bearded man at the wheel, speeding past.

The Professor came to fetch Lucky while she was on her knees emptying ashes from the grate. He frowned when he saw her and asked, 'Do you have to do that?'

Meg thought of several pert answers and said matter-of-factly 'Well, yes, I do.' She got up and fetched Lucky's lead. She bent to fondle him and said briskly, 'Off you go, see you next week. Be a good fellow.'

She assured the Professor with equal briskness that she would be ready when he came, and got down on her knees once again. She had managed to say almost nothing to him, and she had barely glanced at him. She supposed it was because she loved him so much that she could forgive him calling her a domesticated pre-war paragon with no ambition; all the same, it rankled.

The cottage was locked up and she was standing by the gate with Nelson beside her in his box when the Professor came. He said sharply, 'There's no need for you to stand around as though you were waiting for a bus. Stay indoors in future.'

Her 'Very well, Professor,' was uttered in a soothing voice, and he added testily, 'And don't be so damned meek about it!'

They were half-way back to London when he said, 'About next week; we shall leave on Sunday evening. I'll take you down to the lodge as usual on Saturday, and Nelson can go from there to the house. We'll leave in the afternoon and pick up my mother on the way. We shall be going by sea; she doesn't care for flying. Have you got your passport? Good, pack at the flat then, and bring your things with you.'

Meg just stopped herself in time from saying, 'Very well, Professor.'

It was a good thing that she had already done her shopping, for there was no time during the week; the appointments book was full and the Professor worked until six o'clock each evening. What was more, he went to Maud's earlier each morning, so that Meg had to be ready for him well before nine o'clock. In a way she was glad, for it meant that she had little time to reflect on her own problems. She washed and ironed and packed a case and an overnight bag, did her hair and her nails and phoned her sisters, and all the while she was aware of steadily mounting excitement. She would be busy enough in Am-

sterdam, she supposed, cooking the kind of meals Mrs
Culver, and presumably her mother and son, expected
would occupy her time and there would be household
chores. All the same she would be in the same house as
he; it was the last thing she thought of before she went
to sleep each night.

Saturday came and it was almost one o'clock when the
last patient went away. Meg started to clear up, thinking
of all the little jobs she still had to do before she would
be finished. Any moment now the Professor would put
his head round the door and tell her to be ready in some
impossibly short time.

Sure enough, she was putting the final touches to her
desk when he appeared. 'I'll be back in half an hour. Be
ready with Nelson and your case and don't bother about
lunch. We'll have a quick snack at my place.'

She said, 'Very well, Professor,' before she could stop
herself, and added a brisk, 'I'll be quite ready.'

It was chilling to be told that she had better be because
he had no intention of waiting for her.

She longed to tell him that he was the rudest man she
had ever met, but that would spoil her image.

She had prudently left everything ready in the flat.
With five minutes in hand she went down to the hall,
wearing the new coat, her overnight bag slung over one
shoulder, Nelson, nicely full with his dinner, already
snoozing in his box. She had already told Percy that she
would be away, and he shouted up a cheerful goodbye
from his semi-basement. The house would be quiet with
none of them there. Meg sat down on the stairs to wait
and took a last look in her handbag to make sure that she
had her passport as well as her money. When the street
door opened she was sitting, the picture of serenity, one

hand on Nelson's battered head. The Professor paused in the doorway to look at her. 'Did I ever tell you that you're too good to be true?' he wanted to know.

'Oh, yes.' She got to her feet and picked up the box, giving him a gentle smile, noting at the same time that he had changed from his sober grey suit to well-worn, beautifully cut tweeds. They made him look approachable and much younger. Her smile widened and, surprisingly he smiled back, but all he said, puzzling her, was, 'Granny will like you.'

Rosie was waiting for them with soup and omelettes and hot coffee, and they made short work of their meal, with just enough conversation to ensure politeness. Meg would have liked to have lingered a while, but her host made it plain that there was to be no hanging around. They were away again in half an hour or so, travelling fast. Perhaps the girl was going to be at Much Hadham; perhaps, heaven forbid, she was going with them to Holland. Meg hadn't thought of that, and it quite spoilt the drive.

At the lodge the Professor offloaded Nelson and her case, unlocked the door and ushered her inside. 'You've had a busy week,' he said surprising her, 'and doubtless you'll have an even busier one after tomorrow. Don't go for a ten-mile walk or dig the garden.' He was at the door. 'I'll be along tomorrow afternoon for Lucky—you'd better come up to the house then with Nelson, otherwise he might feel abandoned. Trugg will be down with Lucky in a few minutes.'

He had gone before she could answer him.

She settled Nelson, got her shopping basket, and when Trugg arrived with the devoted Lucky, she lost no time in going in to Much Hadham to buy food for the three of them. It was a dry, fine afternoon and she enjoyed the walk there and back again with the dog prancing along beside her. Back indoors, she lit the fire and made tea, all the time listening for a car to go past. There was nothing, however, and on Sunday the quiet morning was undisturbed. She pottered in the garden, with an apron over the new skirt and sweater, had an early lunch and settled down to wait for the Professor. He came earlier than she had expected, whistled to Lucky who had rushed off with Ben and Polly and strolled back to the house with Nelson's box under one arm, talking pleasantly about this and that as they went. At the house Trugg was waiting and led the way across the hall and through the door at one side of the wide staircase. The kitchen was beyond, a large, old-fashioned-seeming room, yet fitted out with every modern convenience. The floor was of flagstones with a rug before the Aga. There was an old-fashioned dresser too, with rows of dishes and plates and a vast scrubbed wooden table with a Windsor chair at each end. The sort of kitchen where one could feel at home, decided Meg, and smiled at Mrs Trugg, who beamed back at her.

'So here's the little old cat, miss. I'll take good care of him, don't you worry. He can sit here right by the stove; the dogs won't touch him and I'll see he doesn't stray far.'

Meg set the box down by the Aga and Nelson, sensing comfort and cosseting, purred throatily, curled up and closed his eye. 'I know you'll look after him,' she said a little anxiously, 'he's old and not awfully tough…'

Mrs Trugg said comfortably, 'He'll stay by the fire, miss, and we'll feed him up—don't you go worrying about him.'

Meg gave him a final pat and followed the Professor out to the car. Questions jostled around inside her head but she wasn't going to ask them. Presumably they would fetch Mrs Culver, then drive to the ferry. Which ferry? she wondered, and occupied the short drive to Herting-fordbury trying to guess.

It was lovely to see Betsy again; Meg, slipping back into her role of housekeeper, helped take in the tea be-cause Kate had already gone for a few days to her niece. Betsy was happy to be on her own, although Noakes and his wife would sleep in the house. 'I'll 'ave the day to me-self,' she explained happily to Meg as they got the tea-tray ready. 'I'll have a fair treat. Not that me and Kate don't get on—we do, like an 'ouse on fire.' She eyed Meg lov-ingly. 'You look smart, Miss Meg. You're happy, aren't you?' She busied herself making the tea. 'That Profes-sor's a nice man to work for, no doubt.'

'Very nice, Betsy, and I'm very happy.'

They left soon after they had had tea, with Mrs Culver in the back of the car. 'So that I can doze if I want to,' she observed. 'It's so very nice to see you again, Meg, and such a relief that you're coming with us. I'm sure you'll enjoy being in Amsterdam—there's a lot to see.'

Meg agreed politely and wondered if she would have a chance to see anything of the city. She rather doubted it. Just for the moment she was happy, true; the Professor had very little to say for himself, but just to sit beside him was a secret delight. She still didn't know which ferry they would travel on, but when he reached Bishop's Stortford and took the Braintree road she guessed that it would be Harwich.

She settled back in her seat, her head turned a little sideways so that she could watch the Professor's hand-some profile. For the moment she was content. The week ahead of her held she knew not what, but some of it must be good; her clothes were right, she had done her best with her hair and face and there was no sign of that girl. She sank into a kind of euphoria until the Professor's voice smoothly dispersed it.

'My grandmother is old, Meg. Eighty-four next birthday. She has a sharp tongue and there's nothing wrong with her intellect. She's also very outspoken. I hope you'll remember that and not let her upset you. She speaks English—she lived here most of her married life—her housekeeper is English, too—elderly; she could do with a few days' rest. There's a maid who lives in and a daily woman; all you'll need to do is to arrange the meals and cook and see that the house is run smoothly.'

He paused, waiting, no doubt, for Meg to make some tart rejoinder. She said merely, 'I shall do my best, Professor.' And listened to his sigh.

He drove in silence for some miles. From where she was sitting he looked cross, and without stopping to mind her tongue she said, 'You're annoyed—why?'

He shot her a sharp glance. 'Not annoyed—puzzled, Meg. You've changed—and don't ask me how because I don't know… You're hiding; the real you is tucked away out of reach.'

So he had noticed her, enough to remark upon it. A small triumph which warmed her. 'I'm just the same,' she pointed out quietly.

He frowned. 'When you're here I don't notice you, but when you're not I find myself wondering where you are and what you're doing.'

She tried to think of an answer to that and couldn't. Luckily Mrs Culver asked something or other of her son and he said nothing more. A good thing, because Meg had plenty to think about.

Chapter 7

At Harwich they embarked with little delay and were taken to their cabins. Meg was standing in the middle of hers, contemplating its comfort, when the stewardess came back with a message. She was to go to the bar by the restaurant as soon as she was ready. So she tidied her hair and did things to her face and found her way to the bar where Mrs Culver and her son were already sitting. They talked over their sherry, mostly of Holland and Amsterdam in particular; presently they had dinner, and then, when they had had their coffee, Meg excused herself and went to her cabin. They would dock quite early in the morning and she would be called with tea and toast, the Professor had told her; he made no effort to detain her.

She slept soundly and was up on deck in time to watch the ferry nose its way into the quay. There was no sign of either Mrs Culver or the Professor when a voice requested passengers to rejoin their cars. Meg went back to her cabin, picked up her overnight bag and made her way down to the car deck. She met the Professor on the way, coming to look for her. He said tersely, 'I've been all over the boat looking for you...'

'Good morning, Professor Culver.' She sounded tolerant of someone who wasn't in the best of tempers. 'I was on deck watching us dock. It was most interesting.'

To which he answered with a grunt.

Mrs Culver was already in the car, placidly waiting for whatever came next. She had slept well, she assured Meg, and wasn't it pleasant to be in Holland again? 'Such an easy journey,' she observed, 'since Ralph sees to everything.'

She settled herself more comfortably. 'Are you hungry, dear? It's about ninety kilometres to Amsterdam—only a little over an hour's driving, but I dare say Ralph will stop for coffee on the way.'

Which Meg knew from experience was that lady's way of making sure that they did.

They drove to Den Haag, the traffic already thick although it was still early enough, but the Professor wove his way through the city and on to the motorway to Amsterdam and presently pulled in at a roadside café. It was a cheerful spot, with rows of flags flying before it, and all its lights on. A great improvement on the service stations in England, Meg considered, following Mrs Culver into a room furnished with little tables and chairs surrounding a billiard table. There were several people there, drinking coffee, playing the fruit machines and talking among themselves. They exchanged good mornings and sat down at a table by the window. The coffee was rich and creamy, served in small cups, and they drank it slowly while Mrs Culver talked, her lively chatter covering her companion's silence.

They went on their way again, with the Professor pointing out the various towns they were bypassing. As they circumnavigated Schiphol he said, 'We shall be in the outskirts of Amsterdam in a few minutes. My grandmother lives in the heart of the city, just off the Herengracht.'

Meg had no idea where or what that was; she murmured and looked out of the window at the blocks of modern flats on either side. Very disappointing; she had expected old gabled houses and canals.

Both of which she very soon got. Without hesitation the Professor left the main road and drove in and out of narrow streets bisected by enough canals to satisfy the most demanding of sightseers. He stopped finally half-way down a cul-de-sac facing a canal and lined with the tall, gabled houses which Meg had expected to see. The houses, alike in age, were all different. Each had its own type of gable, and one or two had steep tiled roofs without gables. They leaned against each other, their massive doors firmly shut against the world outside, their large windows gleaming with highly polished glass. The Professor got out, helped his mother and turned to Meg. She was already on the narrow cobbled pavement, her eyes everywhere, trying to see everything at once.

Mrs Culver skipped up the worn stone steps before the door and tugged the old-fashioned bell. The door opened, although Meg couldn't see anyone there, and they went inside. The hall was long and narrow with an elaborate plaster ceiling and tiled floor. There was a staircase at the end, but half-way along the hall there was a lift, tucked away in the panelled wall. It took them to the second floor and opened on to another narrow hallway with a large mahogany door in its centre. That opened as they got out of the lift and a tall, bony woman advanced to welcome them. She was elderly with grey hair and bright blue eyes; she greeted Mrs Culver warmly and then turned to the Professor. 'Well, Ralph, it's a while since you were here; your grandmother will be so pleased...' She glanced at Meg and smiled. 'And you'll be the young lady who's to take my place, and indeed I'm grateful for a few days.'

She stood aside and they went into a wide lobby with a number of doors in it. Mrs Culver went straight to the double doors facing them and flung them open, breaking into a flood of Dutch as she did so.

'Come and meet my grandmother,' invited the Professor. He flung an arm around the housekeeper. 'You don't change, Nanny. It's good to see you again. I'll bring Meg to you as soon as she has met Grandmother.'

He gave Meg a prod between the shoulders and she went ahead of him into the room. It was high ceilinged and the walls were panelled. There was a good deal of dark, heavy furniture, all very old and beautifully polished, and an elaborate cast-iron stove with a great mantelshelf above it.

The dusting, thought Meg, making her way towards the old lady sitting in a high-backed chair near the window. There were china ornaments everywhere too and cabinets of silver against the walls. She came to a halt and stood quietly while the old lady inspected her.

'Small, but neat.' The voice was clear and surprisingly youthful. 'Nice face, too. I hope you will be happy here, my dear; I'm very glad to welcome you.'

Meg murmured suitably and wondered what to do next. The Professor came to her rescue. 'When we've had coffee I'll hand Meg over to Florence so that she can get her bearings.' He bent to kiss the old lady. 'As pretty as ever, I see, Granny.'

She chuckled. 'Save your pretty speeches for all the pretty girls you know,' she told him. 'Here's the coffee.'

Presently the Professor took Meg across the lobby and into the kitchen where Florence was waiting. There was a young woman there too, cleaning vegetables at the sink. 'Anna,' he explained, 'the housemaid. She doesn't speak English but that won't matter—she knows her work.'

He went away and Florence said kindly, 'A bit of an upheaval for you, miss, but Anna here is a good girl and there's Mevrouw Til who comes in to do the rough. Come and see your room. Anna's brought the bags up so you can unpack later on.'

The flat was a good deal larger than Meg had thought. Her room was at the end of a narrow passage and down three steps. At the back of the house, it overlooked a very narrow long garden and was most comfortably furnished. 'There's a shower room through that door,' Florence pointed out. 'Anna will sleep across the passage and call you each morning. We could sit down for a moment while I tell you how the place is run.'

Not so different from her own home, Meg decided. Meal times were earlier, and there would be very little cooking required until dinner in the evening. Shopping would be no difficulty: Florence would leave a list of the various things to buy, and besides, she had stocked up with as much as possible. 'Meat and fish mostly,' she said comfortably, 'and you can point out what you want. Do you understand the money?' Going over the various coins didn't take long, and the bank notes were straightforward. 'Now, as to the work around the flat...'

That didn't take long to explain either; what did take time were the small likes and dislikes of Professor Culver's grandmother. 'Not very active, but eyes like a hawk,' declared Florence. 'Enjoys her food and everything has to be just so. I'll show you the table silver and linen cupboard.'

Meg didn't go back to the drawing-room, but helped set the table in the sombre dining-room and went to the kitchen to watch the lunch being prepared. A variety of breads, cheeses and cold meats, a salad and omelettes to cook at the last minute. She was breaking eggs into a bowl when she was summoned to the drawing-room.

'You will have your meals with us, naturally,' said the old lady. 'Tell Nanny to set another place if she hasn't already done so.'

'Well, I set the table for three, and if you don't mind, I'd rather have my meals in the kitchen.'

'I do mind. You'll kindly do what I ask without arguing. When you have seen to the table, come back here—for a glass of sherry.'

Meg said, 'Very well,' and saw that the Professor was smiling. She gave him a cold look as she went out of the room. It was obvious that he had inherited a good slice of his grandmother's character as well as her black eyes.

It was a good thing that she had bought the pink dress; it couldn't compete with the old lady's black, high-necked, long-sleeved velvet, or with her daughter's blue crêpe, but at least it provided a suitable background. Both ladies were wearing pearls and several beautiful rings, and the elder also wore a tortoiseshell lorgnette on a gold chain through which she studied Meg at some length. The Professor studied Meg too, but with more discretion.

Florence went after breakfast the next day and Meg,

neat and businesslike in her sober grey dress, set about her duties. The Professor had driven Florence to the station and hadn't returned, and it wasn't until she had taken the coffee tray into the drawing-room that she learned that he wouldn't be back until the evening.

'This is supposed to be a break for him,' explained his mother, 'but I doubt if he has much free time. He'll be in Leiden all day, and tomorrow he's lecturing at one of the hospitals and I know he has at least two consultations. Of course he'll have his evenings, but he has friends here; he'll be out again after dinner or will be dining out.'

Meg went back to the kitchen, poured coffee for herself and Anna and sat down to drink it. The week she had been looking forward to didn't promise much after all. She had hoped that she would see something of the Professor at meals; he might have offered to show her something of Amsterdam, but she could see now that her modest expectations had left her in a fool's paradise. She finished her coffee, got the list Florence had given her, made sure that the two ladies were happily gossiping in the drawing-room, and took herself out to the shops.

They were ten minutes' walk away, and Florence had thoughtfully drawn a little street map for her. When she reached them, the shops were very like those at home. She enjoyed the little outing; no one seemed to mind that she couldn't speak Dutch, and indeed quite a few of the shop assistants spoke English. In a day or two, when she had some idea of the day's pattern, she would go and see the sights.

She certainly had no time to go sight-seeing on that first day; true, of course, Mrs Culver and her mother both took a nap after their lunch, but Meg, anxious to appear at her best, spent the afternoon in the kitchen preparing dinner, and by the time she had done that it was time to take in the tea-tray.

She wore the pink dress again that evening, and blushed faintly at the Professor's thoughtful stare. Well, he would see it each evening whether he liked it or not. She lifted her firm little chin, wished him a cool good evening and went to the kitchen to don an apron and dish up.

She had been quick to hear that when she wasn't with them, they all three spoke Dutch; once dinner was over and she brought in the coffee she excused herself and slipped out of the room. Anna had the evening off; the dining-room would have to be cleared and breakfast set for the morning. Meg trotted to and fro, making almost no noise, and finally shut the kitchen door, put on her apron once more and started the washing up. It was a double sink and there was a splendid plate rack above it. She decided to do the silver separately, and with the plates and dishes drying themselves, set to work on the silver, worn thin with age, and she guessed valuable.

She was polishing the spoons when the Professor said from the door, 'Oh, dear, oh, dear, Granny wants to know where you are. Why are you washing up?'

She swallowed a waspish reply. 'Anna has the evening off...'

'Well, leave it for her in the morning.'

She forgot about being unobtrusive and meek. 'Don't be silly; she has enough to do in the mornings and you want your breakfast at eight o'clock sharp and I'll be busy with the trays.'

He said softly, 'Perhaps this wasn't such a good idea after all...'

'It will be perfectly all right provided everyone remembers that I'm the housekeeper.'

He took the teacloth from her and embarked upon the forks. 'I for one,' he observed in his blandest voice, 'never think of you as that. I believe that my mother and Granny live in a world where the washing up does itself and food cooks itself too. They're rather too old to change their views, but I'll see what I can do to lighten your burden.'

Meg rounded on him. 'You'll do no such thing! I came here to housekeep and that's what I'm going to do.'

'Ah, that's more like you, Meg!'

She instantly assumed her mantle of meekness. 'It's very kind of you to offer to help, but it's quite unnecessary, Professor Culver.'

He went on drying the silver. 'What free time do you have, Meg?' He sounded casually friendly.

'Oh, I'm sure I shall get an hour or so in the afternoons.'

'Good, I'll take you to the Rijksmuseum and the Dam Palace—oh, and Rembrandt's museum, and of course, there's the canal trip—you mustn't miss that.'

He put down the last of the forks and, throwing down the cloth, sat on the edge of the table.

She started putting the silver in the baize-lined box. 'Well, that's very kind of you, but I couldn't spare the time for all that; there's dinner to prepare and cook.'

'There are four afternoons before we return. Each day we will try to visit one of the places I've told you about. Better still, one evening Anna can do the washing up and whatever else you do after dinner, and we'll stroll round the town.'

He got off the table. 'Now dry your hands and take off

that apron and come and make a fourth at bridge. I warn you that both my mother and Granny cheat if they can!'

Meg was up early the next morning, cooking bacon, eggs, fried bread and mushrooms for the Professor's breakfast. Beyond wishing him good morning, she said nothing, and she doubted if he was aware of who it was serving his breakfast. She went back to the kitchen and started to get the breakfast trays ready; once the Professor was out of the house, she and Anna would have their own meal and then get on with the chores. She heard the front door shut with a heavy thump and she whisked back to the dining-room with a tray, intent on clearing the table. The Professor was standing by the window, gazing idly at the street below.

'Oh, I heard the front door—I thought you'd gone! I'll come back,' she said hastily.

'Can't get rid of me fast enough, Meg? Don't worry, I'll not be back until this evening, I'm going to Groningen.'

Her heart sank; she was seeing even less of him than she did at home. 'I hope you have a pleasant day,' she told him. 'It must make a nice change for you…'

His smile mocked her. 'To lecture medical students in Dutch, exchange views with my colleagues at various hospitals, make small talk over drinks with pretty girls—I do all that in England, Meg—my idea of a nice change is hardly the same as yours!' He turned round to face her. 'Now that, for me, would be a quiet afternoon wandering round Amsterdam, showing you the sights. It's time you had a few hours to yourself. We'll do that tomorrow, after lunch. I'm sure you're quite capable of planning a meal which doesn't need your presence in the kitchen for the entire day.'

He strolled to the door. 'Will you spend the afternoon with me, Meg?'

Her heart leapt. 'If it can be arranged and Mrs Culver doesn't mind.' She couldn't stop the lilt of delight in her voice. 'I'd like that very much.'

He nodded. 'So will I.' He was gone, leaving her to dream.

But not for long; while she went round the flat she planned a meal that would need the very minimum of attention, and made sure that Anna would be on hand to get tea. When the old lady was nicely settled drinking her coffee, Meg asked rather diffidently if she had any objection to her grandson's plans.

'Object? Why should I object?' she demanded. 'He's done exactly what he wanted ever since he left his cradle—besides, you're a sensible young woman,' she shot a lightning glance at Meg, 'not likely to have silly ideas about him. You'll make a change from those witless girls he meets at parties.' She addressed herself to her daughter. 'It's time he got married.'

Mrs Culver looked amused. 'He will when he's ready,' was all she said, and then, 'You'll enjoy looking round Amsterdam, Meg, and I'm sure Ralph will be glad to get away from his lectures for an hour or so. Can Anna cope?'

There was no fault to be found with Meg's arrangements for the following afternoon. Both ladies advised her as to what she should see, which shops she should visit, and that on no account must she miss the trip round the canals. She thanked them nicely; it wasn't likely that she would see a fraction of the sights they suggested and she thought it unlikely that the Professor would give her the chance to shop.

He didn't return until long after she was in bed that night. She had left a thermos of coffee ready for him and a covered plate of sandwiches—probably a waste of time, since he would most certainly have dined out. Maybe with one of the witless girls his grandmother despised.

The weather had turned wintry again, so Meg wore the knitted dress and her good winter coat and, since it was so cold, tucked her hair into a beret. At least she looked passable; no one was going to look at her twice—by no one, of course, she meant the Professor—but he need not be ashamed of her either. She turned away from the looking glass, stifling a dreadful feeling that she looked like a housekeeper on her day off.

It was perhaps a blessing that the Professor hardly looked at her when she joined him in the hall. The ladies were already in their rooms having their postprandial nap, and Anna was hovering, ready to close the door behind them.

Outside on the pavement, he paused to look at her feet. 'You'll see more of the city if we walk; I see you're wearing sensible boots.'

She wondered what he would have said if she had teetered out on four-inch heels.

For a moment she was sorry that she had accepted his invitation, despite the delight of being with him, but within ten minutes she had forgotten that. The Professor was a splendid companion; he knew Amsterdam like the back of his hand, and led her through narrow streets and over high-arched bridges, pointing out the different types of houses as they went, and explaining the geography of the city to her. The Rijksmuseum was their first stopping place, and the half-hour they spent there wasn't nearly long enough. But he showed her the *Nachtwacht*, because it was something everyone went to see when they visited Amsterdam, and then led her into some of the smaller rooms where she was shown small paintings by Jan Vermeer, Pieter de Hoogh, Paulus Potter and Ruysdael. At length he dragged her away. 'A pity there's no more time, but there's so much for you to see.'

He walked her straight down the Nieuwe Spiegel Staat to the Munt Plein and the Munt tower with its clock and bells, and then into Kalverstraat. There were shops here, but he didn't linger, turning off instead into a peaceful little square with a church in its centre and ringed by quaint old alms-houses. 'The Begijnsteeg,' he told her, and here he allowed her to linger and peer inside the church. 'Given to the English Reformed Church three hundred years ago,' he told her, and waited patiently while she wandered around.

She went reluctantly, wanting to stay in the quiet place—it would have been nice to sit down with him and talk, but when he took her arm and asked, 'What about tea? There's a good place close by,' she agreed readily, worried that he might be getting impatient with what to him must be a dull afternoon.

He took her to the Sonesta Hotel and gave her a splendid tea, the waitress offering her a great tray of rich cream cakes which she eyed with a childish pleasure which her companion, did she but know it, found vaguely pathetic. He remembered the spoilt girl he had spent the previous evening with, how she had demanded champagne and caviar and fresh peaches and accepted them as her right, and here was Meg getting the maximum enjoyment out of cream cakes. He studied her face and noticed—not for the first time—the dark curling lashes resting on her healthy pink cheeks. He found that he had got into the habit of watching her when he was with her—because she was restful, he supposed, and didn't chatter all the time. Indeed, once or twice he wished she had more to say for herself. She had changed in the past few weeks, become quiet and meek, as though she didn't want him to notice her...

'We'll stroll as far as the Dam Palace,' he told her as they left the hotel, 'so that you can see the square and the War Memorial. We can take a taxi back from there. You're not tired?'

Meg turned a glowing face to him. 'Oh, no—it's been lovely. I've seen such a lot; you've been very kind.'

There was a great street organ playing by the palace; she stood listening to it until she caught sight of her companion's face. Bland indifference, she thought—I must be as tiresome to him as a child being taken to see the sights. She said, 'I'm sorry—you must find all this so tedious.'

He gave her a keen glance; she meant it, too. He signalled a taxi and carried on an undemanding conversation until they arrived back at the flat.

She thanked him again in the hall and saw the small frown of annoyance, although he replied civilly enough as he opened the drawing-room door for her.

She didn't stay long, only to say that she was back and to ask if either lady wanted anything before she started on the dinner. Within ten minutes, once more in her grey dress, she was in the kitchen, tying an apron round herself, putting the soup to warm, beating eggs for the jam soufflé, collecting things for a winter salad, and getting the salmon she had poached the day before while Anna finished setting the table.

Presently, when she had everything organised, she went back to her room and got into the pink dress once more. Mrs Culver's mother, with sublime indifference to the amount of work to be done in the kitchen, expected her to sit in the drawing-room and drink her sherry each evening.

The Professor wasn't at dinner. His grandmother, pecking daintily at the salmon, observed that she had seen very little of him. 'But I suppose he needs his pleasure—he works hard enough and she's a pretty girl.' She looked at her daughter. 'Do you suppose he's serious this time?'

Mrs Culver shook her head and gave a small, secret smile. 'No, not this time. I know he wanted to see Professor Tacx again—after all, he studied under him for several years—and I dare say he wants to see if Julie has grown into a pretty woman—she's been in America, you know.'

With which unsettling conversation Meg had to be satisfied. She lay awake a long time wondering about Julie. He'd have to settle down sooner or later, and somehow she sounded suitable.

She learnt a little more about her during dinner the following day; she had given the Professor his breakfast that morning, but beyond an exchange of good mornings they had had nothing to say to each other. But now he joined them for dinner wearing a dinner jacket.

'Did you have a good dinner?' enquired his grandmother.

'Excellent, my dear. Professor Tacx doesn't change—he must be getting on a bit, though.'

'Indeed, yes. And Julie? She was such a pretty child? I hear she loved the States.'

'She's become a beautiful young woman. I'm taking her dancing and out to supper.' He addressed the table at large, but his eyes were on Meg. She couldn't stop herself from looking at him, but encountered his hard stare, so she calmly looked away; he was comparing her in her familiar pink dress with the brilliant creature he would soon meet. She went pink with mortification.

She woke after a night broken with long periods of wakefulness. It was the last day. Tomorrow they would leave Amsterdam, and she was glad. She wasn't sure what she had expected, but she had been disappointed. She got up earlier than usual, anxious to have everything just so before Florence arrived back at midday, and on the pretext of having extra household chores asked Anna to take the Professor's breakfast. Although he didn't go out, she managed to avoid having her coffee as usual in the drawing-room with the excuse that she had some shopping to do.

Florence, fetched from the station by the Professor, declared everything to be perfect. While they saw to lunch together she said, 'Why don't you have a few hours off this afternoon? Go on the canal trip or do some shopping? I dare say no one thought to ask you if you wanted any time to yourself...'

'Professor Culver very kindly took me to the Rijksmuseum and the Dam and some other places one afternoon,' Meg told her. 'Do you suppose anyone would mind If I went out after lunch? Just for an hour or two? I've got dinner ready as far as possible, and all the shopping is done. Anna's been marvellous.'

'You go, miss. Mr Ralph will be going out after lunch, I'll be bound, and the two ladies will be resting. No need for you to come back before tea, either, though I'll be glad of a bit of help before dinner, I dare say.'

'I'll be back soon after five o'clock—would that be early enough?'

'That would do nicely. I don't like asking you really,

miss—it doesn't seem right, you being a housekeeper, somehow.' Florence added, 'You being a young lady used to better things.'

Meg flushed. 'Well, I'm not really trained for anything, Florence, and I'm really very happy; I have a good job helping at the Professor's consulting rooms in London with my own little flat.'

'There's nothing like a home of your own, miss. Now, this evening—what did you have in mind for dinner?'

At lunch the talk was of their departure on the next day; they were to go by Hovercraft from Calais, leaving Amsterdam directly after breakfast. They should be home by teatime, declared the Professor; he would take his mother home and go on to Much Hadham with Meg to collect Nelson and make sure that everything there was as it should be. 'Work on Monday, Meg,' he warned her, and she smilingly agreed. She had been working all week, but he probably hadn't noticed that.

The two ladies went to their rooms after they had had coffee and the Professor went to the library at the back of the hall to telephone. Meg helped to clear the lunch dishes and then skipped to her room, changed into her Jaeger coat over a skirt and jumper and sped out of the house. Lunch had been a leisurely affair and she had less than three hours, but she knew exactly what she was going to do. She had noted the way they had walked when she had gone out with the Professor. She didn't go as far as the Rijksmuseum but turned off towards the Munt Plein and presently found herself in Kalverstraat. At one time, the Professor had told her, it had been the fashionable shopping street, but nowadays the shops were mostly for teenagers' gear mixed in with bookshops, one or two dress shops and some rather dark, sinister sex shops. Meg went the length of the street and came out on the Dam Plein. She crossed its patterned stones and went into the Bijenkorf, a kind of miniature Selfridges where she felt sure she would find something for her sisters as well as Miss Standish and Mary Giles. She had spent no money, and there were guilders enough in her purse.

After a lengthy search, she bought Delft Blue pottery for Doreen and Cora, small beribboned boxes of chocolates for Mrs Giles and Miss Standish, and a carton of Dutch cigars for Percy. For Betsy she chose more chocolates and a silk scarf and then, well pleased with her purchases, she took herself off to the nearby Damrak, purchased a ticket and got on one of the canal boats about to leave. It wasn't the best of days for sightseeing; there was a raw wind blowing and the sky was a uniform grey, but the boats were covered and warm. Meg sat with a couple of dozen other people and listened to the guide pointing out the sights in three languages. She arrived back at the landing stage stuffed with facts and information which she hoped she would be able to remember. It had all been so quick—she had wanted to linger by the old houses, and get more than a hurried glimpse of the narrow canals branching away on every side—but it had been marvellous all the same. She had decided to have a cup of tea and take a taxi back, and sat down in one of the cafés close to the Dam Palace. Tea came in a glass with no milk, but the cake she had with it more than made up for that. She would have liked to have sat there for half an hour and watched the crowds surging past, but it was time to go. She paid her bill, found a taxi and arrived back with ten minutes to spare.

Anna opened the door to her, and as Meg went past her into the hall the Professor came out of the drawing-room. He stood in front of her so that she couldn't pass him. 'Where have you been?' he asked her in what she privately called his nasty voice. He was smiling a nasty smile, too.

'I had the afternoon off, Professor Culver.'

'In other words, mind my own business, eh?'

She didn't answer him, and after a moment he said half angrily, 'I thought we might do the canal trip this evening—I said I would take you.'

She said gently, 'I went this afternoon. It was most interesting.'

His eyes narrowed; they looked very black. He turned on his heel and went back into the drawing-room, and Meg went to her room and changed back into the grey dress trying to guess why he had suddenly looked so furiously angry.

There was plenty to do in the kitchen while Anna set the table and Florence put the finishing touches to the trifle. 'Mr Ralph always loved trifle,' she declared fondly. 'I always make him one when he comes to visit.'

'He comes often?' asked Meg.

'Bless you, yes. Seeing that he's such a busy gentleman, you'd been surprised at the times he pops over just to spend a night with his grandmother. Very fond of her, he is, like he is of his ma, too. Had his hands full, I reckon, since his grandfather and his father died; sees to all their business for them, and there's a lot of that, I can tell you, being that they're wealthy folk… And he's kind—he'll help anyone—does it unbeknownst, too— you'd be surprised at the jobs he's created just to give someone a chance to earn an honest living. There's that Percy in London and the gardener at Much Hadham and the men on the farm he owns in Friesland.'

You can add me to the list, thought Meg silently, and in a sudden spurt of rage decided there and then to start looking for another job as soon as they got back to London, although as the rage died she had to admit there were difficulties: where would she find a flat like the one she lived in now, and would she get a job such as the one she now had, and what about Nelson and the lodge and Lucky?

She changed into the pink dress and went along to the drawing-room to join everybody. The Professor was there, dispensing drinks. His politeness chilled her to the very marrow of her bones; there was no sign of his previous ill temper. The talk ranged from their journey on the morrow to comments upon Amsterdam and its charms. It was disconcerting when his grandmother said suddenly, 'You're a nice girl, Meg. You must come again, but of course you will, anyway.'

Probably she would, Meg agreed politely; she would like to see more of Holland and it was an easy journey—less than an hour's flying time. 'Not that I've ever flown,' she finished honestly.

Dinner was pleasant; the Professor exerted himself to be amicable and amusing. The food was delicious, and they sat over it in a leisurely way. It was as Meg was carrying the coffee tray into the drawing-room that Anna came to say that the Professor was wanted on the telephone. She was handing Mrs Culver her cup when he came back.

'Julie, asking if I'll go round for a drink and to say goodbye. You'll forgive me, Granny? I promise you I'll be back before you go to bed.'

He shook his head at Meg's offer of coffee, dropped a kiss on the old lady's cheek and went.

'I thought he said something about taking you on the canal trip this evening, dear?' remarked his mother.

'Nothing definite, Mrs Culver—and what a good thing we didn't go—he would have missed seeing his friends.' Meg's voice was as calm as usual. 'Besides, I went this afternoon; it was fascinating.'

They sat and talked until Mrs Culver said, 'Oh, I've still got my packing to do and I do so hate that.' She looked at Meg, who said at once, 'I'll do it for you, Mrs Culver. What do you want me to leave out for you to wear for the journey?'

She was glad to have something to do, so that she could shut her mind to Ralph. He wouldn't be back until late; the old lady went to bed at eleven o'clock each evening, but she didn't sleep until the small hours but sat up in bed and read. Meg knew that because she had taken hot drinks to her on two occasions. She finished Mrs Culver's packing and looked at her watch: it was eleven o'clock and the house was quiet. As she reached the door, Mrs Culver came in.

'Finished, dear? How kind you are! I'm going to bed, as we have to be away fairly early, don't we?'

They wished each other a good night and Meg went along to the drawing-room. The old lady would have gone to her room, too; she would just make sure the lights were out and the room fairly tidy before she went to the kitchen to see if Florence needed her help.

There was one small table lamp burning. The Professor was sitting in the dimness, doing nothing. He got to his feet as Meg stopped in surprise, and said, 'There you are—where have you been?'

'Packing for your mother, Professor. I came to turn

off the lights, but perhaps you would do that when you go to bed?'

She turned to go and found him beside her, staring down into her face. 'Prim,' he said nastily, and 'A poker down your back,' and kissed her hard.

Chapter 8

Meg rushed past him, quite forgetting that she had been going to help Florence in the kitchen, and once she was in her room she sat down on her bed, a prey to a multitude of strong feelings. Her head told her that she must ignore his kiss, although her heart denied that. She wasn't sure why he had kissed her. He could have had no pleasure from it; he had called her prim and poker-backed, and that was something she would always remember. She had been out of her mind to imagine he could become even a little interested in her.

She undressed like a whirlwind and jumped into bed, where she burst into tears; let Julie or that horrible girl in England get their dainty, devastating claws into him— he'd make a rotten husband anyway. She sniffed and snuffled for a long time before she went to sleep at last to wake early with a headache and a red nose from weeping.

She showered and dressed and did her best to disguise her nose, and went along to the kitchen where Florence was already busy.

'I'm sorry about last night,' began Meg. 'I really did mean to come and give you a hand, but I—I got delayed.'

Florence had taken a look at her face. 'Don't you worry, miss—Anna came in early and we had everything cleared up in no time. If you'd take in Mrs Culver's tea? I won't disturb the mistress for a bit but I'll get a tray ready for them both.' She glanced at the clock. 'There isn't all that much time, and Mr Ralph wants to leave not a minute after nine o'clock.'

Mrs Culver grumbled a little when Meg woke her. 'So early,' she moaned. 'I can't think why Ralph couldn't leave later in the day; surely he need not work on Monday.' She glanced at Meg and then looked again. 'My dear, are you all right? You look as though you haven't slept a wink. What a selfish woman I am; you must have been up hours ago!' She sat up in bed and said contritely, 'Tell me what I can do to help.' And then added helplessly, 'I'll never be ready to leave, and Ralph will be annoyed.'

Meg poured her tea. 'If you take your bath as soon as you've had your tea, I'll bring your breakfast tray, then all you have to do is to dress. I'll finish your packing.'

'You are a treasure! Tea and toast, dear, and some of that black cherry jam...'

Florence had set the table for two, and the idea of being at breakfast with the Professor gave Meg cold feet, but if she had absented herself from it he would know that she minded what he had said, and that was the last thing she wanted. He was already at table, but he got to his feet as she sat down, wished her a good morning in his usual rather cool manner, passed her the toast and offered the coffee pot.

She wasn't hungry, but she did her best, exchanging casual remarks with him with her usual calm until with a glance at her watch she excused herself.

'Escaping, Meg?' he asked blandly.

'No—I'm going to take Mrs Culver her breakfast. She's anxious not to keep you waiting.' She gave him a small, tolerant smile as she got up from the table, her lovely eyes wide and innocent. 'And what is there for me to escape from?'

She closed the door gently on his rumble of laughter.

They left at nine o'clock precisely. Meg had gone spare getting Mrs Culver into her hat and coat, finding her handbag, her passport and the pills she needed in case she felt queasy on the journey. She had packed the last of her cases and then gone to say goodbye to the Professor's grandmother, sitting up in bed, wrapped in a white cobweb shawl.

A small bony hand beckoned her to the bedside. 'You're a good girl, and a splendid housekeeper. You've not had the pleasure a young woman should have at your age, but it'll come—it'll come. You may kiss me.'

Which Meg, did, rather surprised, for she hadn't thought that the old lady had noticed her more than good manners expected of her.

'I'm glad Florence had her holiday and that I could help out', Meg smiled. 'She's a marvellous person, isn't she? I've enjoyed being here, and I shall think of you.' She kissed the soft old cheek.

'Send that grandson of mine in here, will you?' called the old lady after her as she left.

The Professor was loading the luggage into the boot.

In the early morning sunlight he looked remarkably handsome. Meg sighed with silent longing and gave him his grandmother's message, and then went to urge Mrs Culver to get into the car.

The Professor entered his grandparent's room quietly and went to sit on the edge of the bed. 'Not long enough, was it, Granny?' he asked cheerfully. 'I'll come over at Easter for a couple of days.'

The bright old eyes behind the gold-rimmed spectacles studied his impassive face. 'Do that, my dear; I enjoyed these few days. That girl of yours is a treasure.'

He agreed amiably. 'Yes, isn't she, but she's not my girl, Granny.'

She put her small hand in his large one. 'I look forward to seeing you, Ralph.' She chuckled gently. 'Wasn't Julie the one, my dear?'

'No, Granny. I think I'm impossible to please.'

'There's no such word as impossible. Don't forget to say goodbye to Nanny.'

The motorway was fairly empty, and the Rolls made light of the miles; they stopped for coffee and Meg was glad of the half-hour in the wayside café. She had been sitting in front and the Professor had proved difficult to talk to. In fact she had given up after a series of monosyllabic answers to her observations, and on the short way back to the car she had asked him if he would prefer to have his mother sitting beside him.

'Good God, no! Sitting in the back she can't see the speedometer; anything over fifty miles an hour gives her palpitations.'

They had more coffee and sandwiches on the Hovercraft once they had boarded it at Calais and, once free of Customs, they drove up the M2, through the Blackwall Tunnel and so northwards to Hertfordshire. He had said that they would be home by teatime, and they were.

Meg's old home looked charming as he stopped before its door. The garden had been restored to its former pristine condition and was a blaze of daffodils and early tulips. And there was Betsy, opening the door to them, and Kate coming forward to welcome them.

They had tea in the drawing-room, with a log fire blazing and Silky weaving his way from one to the other of them, but they didn't linger. Commenting that he would telephone his mother within the next day or so, the Professor urged Meg out to the car and drove to his own home.

Meg craned her neck as they went past the lodge. The garden looked lovely; the daffodils were out there too and the primroses she had cherished were a yellow carpet under the hedge. The window boxes and flower beds round the house were even more colourful. She paused to look at them as she got out of the car and was almost knocked flat on to her back by Lucky, who had raced out of the door Trugg was holding open. The bull terriers were more dignified, and they made for the Professor.

Mrs Trugg came into the hall as they went in, beaming at the sight of them, wanting to know if they would like a meal and if the journey had been a good one.

'No meal,' said the Professor, 'and we had tea at my mother's. We must be on our way.'

'Then you'll want Nelson—he's all ready, and won't he be pleased to see you? He's been so good, but he's missed you, miss. Trugg shall fetch him. You'll be down at the weekend, sir?'

The Professor was leafing through his post. 'Yes, Mrs Trugg. I may be coming down one evening during the week; I'll let you know.'

Nelson, dignified in his box, allowed Meg to hug him before he was stowed in the back of the car. Lucky wanted to get in too.

'Not now, Lucky!' Meg hated to leave him again. 'But I'll see you at the weekend.'

She got into the car and sat quietly while the Professor bade his dogs goodbye, told Lucky to be good and exchanged a few words with Trugg and then got in beside her and drove off.

Meg had plenty to think about; she would feed Nelson as soon as she got in, get herself a supper of sorts, unpack and put things ready for the morning. She would have to phone Doreen and Cora too; the evening wasn't going to be long enough. She was jolted out of her plans by the Professor's voice. 'I'll be in early in the morning, Meg. Be ready by half past eight, will you?'

'Yes, Professor.'

They lapsed into silence once again until they reached the consulting rooms.

'Thank you for fetching Nelson,' said Meg politely, 'and for bringing me back. I—I enjoyed my stay in Holland.'

The Professor said 'Ha,' in a fierce way and got out of the car. He undid his door and collected Nelson and her suitcase. 'Lead the way,' he said.

The flat felt cold and unlived-in. He closed its front door, put Nelson down, took her case through to the bedroom and bent to light the gas fire. Meg was trying to decide whether to ask him if he would like a cup of coffee when he said, 'If you give this animal his supper, we'll be on our way.'

Meg turned to look at him. 'Where to?' she asked.

'My house, of course—where else? Rosie will have a meal ready for us.'

Meg started to unbutton her coat. 'Professor Culver, I'm sure you mean to be kind, but I find you a little overbearing. I wasn't aware until this moment that I was to have my supper with you. I should have liked to have been asked.'

'So that you could think up some sensible reason why you shouldn't accept! Your opinion of me may be low, my girl, but I hope I still have a vestige of good manners left. Do you expect me to leave you here, opening baked beans and finding milkless tea?'

'Well, yes—I did rather. You've been in a bad temper all day,' she went on in a matter-of-fact voice, 'and I thought you'd want to be rid of me as soon as possible.'

He went past her into the kitchen and opened a cupboard, found a tin of cat food and started to open it. Only when Nelson had bowed his elderly head over his plate did he say, 'I'm sorry.' He didn't say why he was angry. 'Shall we cry pax for the rest of the evening?'

He loomed over her, his handsome face full of tired lines, and just for one moment her heart wasn't curbed by her cautious tongue. 'Oh, my dear, you're tired to death,' she said impulsively. 'How thoughtless I am—of course I'll come, you'll feel so much better when you've had a nice meal...all those miles and an early start this morning.'

She switched off the kitchen light and didn't see the look in his eyes as he watched her, her plain and earnest face tired too. She was still as neat as when they had set out that morning, only the tip of her small nose shone powderless now, and she had forgotten to put on more lipstick.

He smiled, and the tiredness was swept away. He turned the fire down low, switched off all but one table lamp, and then buttoned her coat again.

Meg stood like a small statue, her arms rigid in case she should throw them around his neck. Which would never do! She bade Nelson goodbye, told him to be a good boy and was swept downstairs again and into the car.

Rosie was waiting for them. If she was surprised to see Meg there was nothing in her face to show it; when the Professor had taken Meg's coat she led her away to tidy herself, shaking her head over the length of their journey. 'There's no stopping the Professor,' she confided to Meg. 'Always on the go, he is; he needs a wife to keep him at his own fireside and see that he eats proper meals.' She gave an indignant snort. 'And I don't mean those haughty types who swan in and out of the best restaurants. Bless the man, he deserves better than that.'

Meg, doing things to her face, agreed silently; what was more, she was going to work at it, hopeless though it seemed.

She sipped the sherry he gave her warily; her insides were empty and she wasn't sure what would happen if she tossed it back. She sat rather primly opposite him, watching him with his whisky and soda, striving to make light conversation.

He said rather impatiently, 'Mrs James and Nancy will be coming in the morning. The child's had her treatment, and now she's to stay at home for a couple of weeks before she goes to Maud's again.'

Meg perceived that his mind was already busy with the following day; small talk was the last thing he wanted. She asked, 'And was it successful, the treatment?'

He began to tell her about it, and she listened carefully; a good deal of what he was saying was way above her head but she did her best to understand. He stopped suddenly in mid-sentence. 'You've not understood the half of it, have you? I must beg your pardon for boring you.' He added with a surprised annoyance, 'I can't think why I should want to tell you all this.'

'Well,' said Meg sensibly, 'you need to talk about your work, and I'm here—I expect if I were your mother or one of your—your girl-friends you'd do just the same.'

'Good Lord, no! Certainly not my mother, and anyone else would be bored to tears.'

Which made her even more determined to rescue him from some selfish, uncaring wife. But to be determined wasn't enough...

'What are you plotting?' asked the Professor suddenly.

'Plotting? Me? Nothing. Would you explain exactly what high-speed neutrons and pi mesons are?'

He put down his drink and sat forward in his chair. 'You really want to know?'

When she nodded he told her, using simple language which she could understand, and he was only interrupted by Rosie coming to tell them that dinner was ready.

Meg was famished; she would have welcomed food of any sort to still the rumblings of her insides. The Tomates Suisses with which Rosie served them were delicious, but the tomatoes stuffed with cream cheese and chives, while absolutely delectable, did little more than take the edge off her appetite. She sighed with relieved delight when a deep earthenware dish of Boeuf Bourguignon was placed before the Professor, and her nose wrinkled appreciatively at the delicious aroma of steak and pork and onions and the tang of the red wine in which they had been cooking for hours.

The Professor gravely pressed her to a second helping and talked casually of nothing in particular while he watched her with a genuine gleam of amusement.

Chocolate orange mousse ended their meal, and Meg, who was no mean cook herself, observed seriously, 'Your housekeeper is a Cordon Bleu cook, isn't she? Would you mind if I told her how much I've enjoyed my dinner?' She added, 'I was so hungry!'

He said in a voice as bland as his face, 'Rosie will be delighted to hear it. I'm afraid I seldom remember to tell her how excellent her cooking is. Shall we have coffee in the drawing-room?'

Meg could have stayed for hours, sitting by the fire in the comfortable room over coffee, not talking much, utterly content just to be with the Professor. But she had seen the great pile of letters on the hall table as they had entered the house and he would want to read them in peace—and probably telephone that horrid girl to tell her that he was back again, whispered a small voice at the back of her head. After half an hour she said, 'I think I should go Professor— unpacking and Nelson and things…it's been lovely.'

'My pleasure, Meg.' All of a sudden he was coolly impassive and made no effort to keep her.

Nelson's ecstatic welcome couldn't disperse the loneliness of the flat once the Professor had dropped her there and gone. Meg unpacked, made ready for the morning, bustling around so that she had no chance to think too much, and then went to bed. In the morning she would see him again, but it wouldn't be at all the same thing.

He was punctual, but Miss Standish and Mrs Giles were ahead of him; Meg had time to give them her small presents and run down to the basement with the cigars for Percy. When he came he was pleasantly friendly to everyone, and a little remote. Certainly there was little warmth in his manner toward Meg; she had been treasuring the memory of their pleasant evening together, but apparently he had dismissed it as an obligatory invitation which good manners had compelled him to make. She assumed her self-effacing image without loss of time.

The day unwound itself briskly; Mrs James and Nancy were the first of the patients, and when they had gone and Meg was filing away the notes, she sneaked a look at them. The Professor's writing was atrocious, and it took her a minute or two to discover that he was satisfied with the child's progress and that she was to go back for further treatment in a few days' time. Mrs James had been tearful but quiet, and Nancy, unaware that the Professor was pitting his brilliant brain against her illness, skipped around the waiting-room, chattering happily to Meg.

It was a good beginning to the day; patients came and went and just before lunch the Professor left for the hospital. He wouldn't be back until three o'clock, so that Mrs Giles left soon after, and then Miss Standish for her lunch hour. Meg tidied up ready for the afternoon and went up to the flat to share a snack meal with Nelson, do her hand-washing and daydream. The phone interrupted her; Doreen, wanting to know why she hadn't telephoned as soon as she got back. Meg gave her a brief account of her stay in Amsterdam, not mentioning the dinner with the Professor, and on the plea of being busy rang off, with the promise that she would ring again later.

By the end of the day it was just as though she had never been away; she took up the reins of her uneventful days and the week went by. She could have counted on two hands the number of times the Professor had spoken to her, but she refused to be discouraged by that. She saw him each day, and there was the weekend to look forward to.

Towards the end of the week he went to Bristol to give

a lecture, and the three of them were more or less free until he returned in the late afternoon to see a patient. Meg, with a couple of hours to herself, took a bus to Harrods and bought a soft suede jacket to go with the Jaeger skirt. She bought shoes too, and then hurried back before she spent too much money.

She showed them to Miss Standish when she got back in and waltzed around the waiting-room, trying them on. But by the time the Professor got back, she was sitting at her desk, neat and demure, giving the strong impression that she didn't want anyone to notice her.

It wasn't until Friday evening that he stopped on his way out to say, 'You'd like to go to the lodge for the weekend, Meg? I'll pick you up just after one o'clock.'

It was a rush to be ready; the last patient had taken up a lot of time. Meg rushed upstairs to the flat, bolted cheese and biscuits while she flung a few things into her overnight bag, changed into the skirt and the new jacket and shoes, and popped Nelson in the new basket she had brought for him. She was closing the front door behind her as the Professor drew up, and a couple of minutes later, with her bag and Nelson in the back, she was sitting beside him as he started on the now familiar journey.

She sensed that he didn't want to talk. They were almost there when he said, 'You are the only woman I know who doesn't chatter, Meg.' He added in a voice which she didn't much care for, 'Sometimes I wonder what you're thinking about.'

A good thing he had no idea, she reflected silently. 'Oh, this and that,' he was told airily, and she lapsed into her usual self-imposed silence once more.

He got out at the lodge gate, opened the door for her and put Nelson and her bag inside. 'About six o'clock tomorrow evening?' he warned her, and drove off. She watched the car disappear round the corner of the drive; he had become remote during the past week and she couldn't help but notice that it was only with her. With Miss Standish and Mrs Giles he had been exactly as he always was. As far as she knew she had done her work well enough and she had been careful not to take advantage of his various kindnesses—on the contrary. She went back into the cottage and plunged into the pleasant business of putting it to rights before Lucky should arrive. It was Trugg who brought him, and he stayed to chat for a few minutes, letting fall the information that there would be weekend guests up at the house.

'Oh, that will be nice for Professor Culver; he needs to relax after a busy week.' Meg spoke lightly and smiled widely, mentally tearing the blonde girl limb from limb.

She had been to Much Hadham and done her shopping with Lucky, and was poking round the garden when a red sports car went past. The girl was driving and there was no one with her, and hard on her heels came a second car, a big BMW with four people in it. Meg went indoors and put the kettle on and presently sat down to her tea. She had lit the fire and she sat on long after she had finished, watching the flames and wondering what the Professor was doing.

He was entertaining his guests with his usual impeccable good manners and thinking about her.

It was almost light when Meg woke the next morning, but still early. Something had woken her, and she sat up in bed and listened; someone was trying to get a car to go, out in the road, near the gate, and she hopped out of bed, put on her dressing gown and slippers and went to look from the living-room window. Whoever it was sounded desperate, and above the banging and clanking she could hear a soft moaning. Nelson and Lucky were still more or less asleep by the fire; Meg unlocked the door and went round the corner of the drive to the road.

There was a down-at-heel car parked on the verge with its bonnet open and a man with his head and shoulders inside it. The moans were definitely coming from inside the car and Meg tapped him on the arm. 'What's wrong?'

He was a young man with a very worried face. 'My wife—I'm taking her to hospital at Bishop's Stortford, but the car's broken down and she's sure the baby's coming!'

Meg looked at his white face and poked her head through the car window. There was a young woman on the back seat, tears streaming down her cheeks. She said weakly, 'Do help me—I know the baby's almost here and I'm so cold!'

'Can you manage to walk just a few yards?' Meg turned to speak to the man, who had given up on the car and was standing beside her. A nice enough lad, she considered, but not very able to cope. 'Will you carry your wife into the lodge; it's just inside that entrance gate. I'll go and see to the bed.'

She didn't wait to see if he agreed but sped to the lodge, flung a sheet over the bedclothes and piled the blankets on a chair. Bed, she thought in a panic, seemed the best place. She shut the animals in the kitchen and held the door wide for the man to come in. The girl was terrified as well as cold. Meg took off the coat she was wearing on top of her dressing gown and nightie, piled blankets on to her, bade the man to stay and ran to the house. Six o'clock in the morning wasn't an ideal time to bang on people's doors, but she had to have help.

The house was quiet, just tinged by the light in the sky, a chilly little wind blowing through the trees surrounding it. Meg rushed to the door, rang the bell and banged on the big brass knocker. She kept her finger on the bell until she heard sounds of movement inside and almost fell into the hall, when Trugg, cosily wrapped in a dressing gown, opened the door.

He put out a hand to steady her, closed the door and asked anxiously, 'What's the matter, Miss Collins? Come into the sitting-room and sit down...'

'No time, Trugg, I want Professor Culver...'

'A matter of some urgency?' asked the Professor from the staircase.

Even in a dressing gown and pyjamas he looked capable of dealing with any situation, however outlandish.

'You must come at once,' said Meg, not mincing her words. 'There's a woman in the lodge—the car broke down, she's having a baby and I'm not sure what to do.' She added fiercely. 'You're a doctor...'

The Professor smiled faintly. It was quite some years since, as a medical student, he had delivered a baby. 'I'll get my bag,' he said calmly, and a moment later was striding down the drive with Meg trotting along beside him.

The next hour or so was so packed with action that Meg had no idea of what was happening. The Professor, exuding confidence and calm, reassured the girl, assessed the situation without fuss, suggested that the man should sit by the wife and hold her hand, and issued orders to Meg in an unhurried voice as though delivering babies in his lodge was something he was accustomed to do as a matter of course.

Presently Meg found herself holding out a folded blanket to receive a baby boy, yelling with gratifying vigour.

'Give him to his mother—hold those forceps,' the Professor demanded, and then with well-held impatience, 'hold them still...'

Meg resisted a desire to cast everything down and rush out of the cottage. She was icy cold, faintly queasy and she had just come through the fright of her life. She sniffed back tears and clenched her teeth.

'Right,' said the Professor, 'let go now. Will you make us all a cup of tea?'

She went without a word into the kitchen and put the kettle on, and while it was boiling gave Nelson and Lucky their breakfasts. When she took the tea-tray back into the bedroom the Professor was sitting on the side of the bed, discussing suitable names for the baby. She loved him to distraction, but just then she could have boxed his ears.

She poured tea for everyone, listening to the man and his wife's happy voices repeating their thanks over and over again. She finished her tea and became aware that the Professor was watching her.

'If you've finished, Meg, will you go to the house and get Trugg to phone for an ambulance? Tell him to say it's urgent, and then ring the hospital and tell them that Mrs Pitt is on the way with a newborn infant.' As she went out of the door, he added, 'And put on a coat or something—you'll catch your death of cold!'

A bit late in the day for that, she muttered, and flung an old mac she kept for Lucky's walk over her shoulders.

Trugg was hovering in the hall, and the door was opened before she could ring the bell. The ambulance was called and he got the hospital number for her and then handed her the telephone.

'Who's speaking?' asked the voice at the other end.

'Meg Collins on behalf of Professor Culver; the baby was born in his cottage. He delivered it.'

The voice warmed. 'Will you tell him that we'll be quite ready? Will he be coming with the patient?'

'I don't know. I'll ask him to phone you as soon as he can leave Mrs Pitt.'

Trugg looked at her with fatherly concern. 'You didn't ought to run around like that, miss—catch your death, you will! Come to the kitchen and Mrs Trugg will give you a nice hot drink.'

'I think the Professor expects me to go straight back, thank you, Trugg. I hope I didn't wake everyone?'

'Well, miss, there was a modicum of grumbling, but tea has been taken to everyone and I dare say that by now they're all sleeping.' His voice held no expression.

'Well, thank you, Trugg.' Meg went to the door and he pushed it open for her. 'Trugg,' she hesitated, 'the Professor will be cold and tired when he gets back—I can't suggest it to him, but he'll listen to you—if you could get him to put on some warm clothes and eat his breakfast?'

Trugg smiled all over his face. 'Don't worry, miss; Mrs Trugg and I'll see that he does just that.'

'Thank you, Trugg.'

'Thank *you*, miss, and if I might say so, you could do with the same treatment.'

The Professor was still sitting on Mrs Pitt's bed when she got back. The room showed signs of upheaval, and she thought unhappily of the work which lay ahead of her. She took off the mac and collected the mugs after assuring the Professor that the ambulance was on its way and the hospital had been warned. She was so cold that the mugs rattled on the tray as she carried it out to the kitchen.

When the ambulance men came she shook hands with Mr and Mrs Pitt and then retired to a corner out of everyone's way. The baby was still yelling; she had peered at him, wrapped in his blankets, and his small fist had unfolded and caught her finger and gripped it tightly. She had smiled widely and the Professor, watching her, smiled too.

The ambulance slid away and Meg fetched a plastic rubbish bag and started cramming it with the bed linen. It surprised her very much when the Professor took it from her and finished the job. 'I'll take this up to the house with me and send Winnie the housemaid down to give you a hand,' he said, and when she protested, 'Don't argue with me. And have a hot shower and get into some clothes.' He was going through the door when he paused to say, 'You did very well.' His voice held warmth. 'But then I wouldn't have expected otherwise.'

At the door of his house, Trugg, still hovering, took the plastic bag from him with an annoyed 'Tut tut,' and the Professor, who wasn't a man to laugh very often laughed now. 'Ask Winnie to go down to the lodge and give Miss Collins a hand, will you, Trugg?'

'At once, Mr Ralph. And the young lady told me to see that you had a good hot shower and dressed warmly and ate a good breakfast.'

His master stood staring at him. 'Did she indeed?' He smiled slowly. 'Trugg, tell Winnie to see that Miss Collins comes up here for her breakfast—do you suppose Mrs Trugg could give us a meal in say, half an hour? No one will be down for hours yet, will they?'

'Half an hour, sir, and I'll send Winnie down at once.'

Meg was putting clean sheets on the bed when Winnie arrived.

'What a thing to happen, miss, so early in the morning, too!

'Now you're to have your shower and dress and go up to the house for your breakfast. Half an hour, the master

said. I'll soon have this place put to rights—you must be
frozen to the bone. I'd have been scared...'

'Well, I was. Thank you, Winnie, but have you the
time to spare?'

'Lor' bless you, miss, there's Mary up at the house
to carry the trays to the rooms. I had my breakfast an
hour ago.'

Meg, warmer now and wearing the skirt and new
jacket over her sweater, warned Winnie to keep an eye
on the animals, and hurried up to the house a minute or
two late. The Professor opened the door to her, swept
her into the dining-room and sat her down at the table.
'That's better, though I must say you looked rather nice
en déshabillé, even if distraught.'

She went pink. 'I didn't have time to dress,' she began.

'No—I was glad of that.' He spoke with a gravity
which belied the gleam in his eyes, and went on briskly
as Trugg put a covered dish before him. 'Now, eggs,
bacon, mushrooms, tomatoes, fried bread... Mrs Trugg
seems to think we need feeding up!'

The food was delicious, as was the coffee, and they
didn't hurry. But a glance at the clock set Meg on her
feet. 'I must go—thank you for my lovely breakfast and
for sending Winnie.'

He went to the door with her. 'I'm going to Bishop's
Stortford this afternoon, just a follow-up visit—I'd like
you to come with me.'

'Your guests...?'

'They can come too if they wish, but I think it most
unlikely. I'll collect you just before two o'clock.' He bent
and kissed her cheek and said softly, 'Please, Meg?' So
that she said hastily,

'Yes, all right, I'll come.'

The lodge was in apple-pie order when she got back. She soothed Nelson's ruffled feelings, took Lucky for a walk and got herself lunch.

The Professor arrived five minutes early; he banged on the door and stalked in. 'I've got Ben and Polly with me, and there's no reason why Lucky shouldn't come too; we shall only be away for an hour.'

A remark which Meg received with regret.

It was barely four miles to Bishop Stortford. The Professor parked the car in the consultants' car park, and at Meg's look said, 'I've friends here.' He marched her in and up to the Maternity Unit.

Mrs Pitt was in a corner bed, and now that all the hassle was over, she looked a very pretty girl. Meg had picked a bunch of spring flowers from the garden; she offered them and then went to the foot of the bed to admire the infant Pitt in his cot, leaving the Professor to talk to Mrs Pitt, until Sister came rustling down the ward and he wandered off with her with a quick excuse. He wasn't gone for more than five minutes, and when he came back he suggested that Mr Pitt might like a stroll in the hospital grounds.

Which left Meg and Mrs Pitt quite happily discussing baby clothes and the best sort of pram. 'Not that we can buy one,' said Mrs Pitt. 'Ned's out of work and our landlord's putting up the rent next week.'

'What will you do?' asked Meg. Perhaps they would accept some money, a loan even; she could spare enough to keep them going for a time...

'Our luck is bound to change,' declared Mrs Pitt, uttering, if she did but know it, the truth.

They didn't stay long; the Professor seemed in a hurry

to get back home. He looked smug, thought Meg, studying his face when he wasn't looking.

She was getting out of the car at the lodge when the red sports car flashed past and she said, 'Oh, there's one of your guests...the girl.'

He got out too and opened the door for Lucky. 'She's leaving. We said goodbye. Come up for tea at half past four, Meg—I'd like you to meet my friends.'

'I'd rather not, if you don't mind.'

'But I do mind. You'll like them.'

He got back into the car and drove off without waiting for her to answer.

Meg took Lucky for a walk, made sure that the cottage was tidy and ready for the following week, and reluctantly went up to the house.

The Professor seemed determined to show his charming side; she was introduced to the four people in the drawing-room and skilfully put at her ease. Old friends, explained the Professor blandly; they had been students together. The wives were friendly, neither of them particularly pretty but both well dressed. The talk was easy and Meg found herself liking them, at the same time feeling surprised; they didn't seem at all the kind of young women the Professor would take to. She had a fleeting memory of the girl with the fair hair, so unlike his four other guests.

She didn't stay long, and shortly after she was back at the lodge she heard the car go past and got ready to leave. Trugg came for Lucky presently, and then minutes later the Professor arrived, still blandly friendly but thoughtful too.

At his consulting rooms he carried Nelson up to the flat and then stood in the middle of the room saying nothing, so that Meg asked him hesitantly if he would like a cup of coffee. And when he refused she said, 'I'm glad Mrs Pitt's all right. How lucky that the car broke down at your gateway.' She added, 'He's out of work and the landlord is putting up his rent. Did you know that?'

'Yes, we had a little chat.' He sat down and said, 'I'll have that coffee after all, Meg.'

She made good coffee; they emptied the pot between them and half an hour passed like lightning. The Professor put himself out to be charming and Meg felt happiness welling up inside her. She didn't only love him, she liked him too, and just for the moment he was giving her the impression that he liked her as well.

He got to his feet reluctantly. 'I've a mass of work to do,' he told her. 'I have no wish to go, but I must.'

She walked with him to the door, and hoped that he would kiss her again. He didn't, but as he turned to go he said casually, 'Pitt is a farm labourer; I've taken him on as a gardener. They can have the lodge to live in. I'll be free on Wednesday afternoon and I'll drive you down so that you can pack up your odds and ends. Trugg will store them for you in the attic.'

He lifted a casual hand and ran downstairs, leaving her with a very white face, staring into a suddenly disrupted future.

Chapter 9

Meg closed the door slowly and rather blindly collected the coffee tray and took it into the kitchen. She fed Nelson, washed the mugs and unpacked her bag, and only when she had done this did she sit down to think.

Of course it made sense. The Professor had offered her the cottage until such time as he should want it for a gardener; to him, with his delightful home in Little Venice and his still lovelier home at Much Hadham, it would seem a trivial enough matter. After all, her home was here. She caught her breath and sat up very straight; or was it? He could sack her any day he liked and she would have to move, find herself somewhere to live and get another job. He wouldn't do that; he was, under that chilly manner, a kind man. He hadn't been very kind to her, though... On the other hand he had given a much-needed helping hand to the Pitts; they needed a home and work and he had offered both. Something she had been trying not to think about persisted at the back of her head. Perhaps the girl had made him do it; perhaps if she was going to marry the Professor, she had objected to Meg being in the lodge. She was a beautiful girl, thought Meg wistfully, and the Professor had demonstrated only too clearly that she had no occasion to feel even a twinge of jealousy.

She sniffed back a threatening tear and addressed Nelson. 'And I actually thought I could do something about it! I thought I could compete with her, and look where it's got me… And if she doesn't like the idea of me spending the weekend at the lodge, she most certainly won't like me living here!'

Nelson climbed rather stiffly on to her lap and butted her with his elderly head, and she gave him a hug which he suffered with silent dignity. 'We'd better start looking at flats,' she told him, and went to get the supper she didn't want.

Monday proved to be like all other Mondays: a tight schedule of patients and hospitals and a great many phone calls. The Professor was no different; he greeted her with his normal cool affability, drank the coffee she took in to him and started on his day's work. There was no mention of the lodge and she hadn't expected it; possibly he had dismissed the whole matter from his mind. Once work was over for the day she repaired to her flat, made a pot of strong tea and worked her way through the 'To Let' advertisements in the evening paper. She had read through a whole page of convenient flats, described in rosy terms and offered at fabulous rents, when Doreen phoned.

She was a Ward Sister now and had a great deal to say about it, so beyond asking Meg if she was well she asked few questions, which was a good thing, for Meg had decided not to say a word to either of her sisters. She would wait and see what was to happen; she couldn't be turned out at a moment's notice. She would have time to find somewhere to live and a job of some sort. Besides, she would have a reference now, and that would help.

Of course the Professor might want her to stay; the weekends at the lodge had been a kindly gesture and she supposed she had taken it for granted that there would never be a gardener. It was ironic that in befriending the Pitts she had done herself a disservice. Self-pity would get her nowhere; she had a home, no financial worry and a job she enjoyed. And Nelson, of course. She would miss Lucky, but he had a good home and Ben and Polly for company and she could explore London each week-end—and there were the parks.

Tuesday was as busy as Monday, but when the last patient had gone on Wednesday morning and they were clearing up after the morning's consulting, the Professor put his head round the waiting-room door.

'I'll be back at half past one, Meg.' He didn't wait for an answer.

'Going out, dear?' asked Miss Standish, and looked coy.

Mrs Giles was there too, so it seemed a good opportunity to explain about the lodge.

'You'll miss it, Meg,' observed Mrs Giles. 'Luckily it's spring and the parks are beginning to look lovely— and you've got the dear little flat.'

'Oh, there's a lot of London I must see,' said Meg cheerfully. 'Sunday is a nice day for wandering about. Of course I shall miss the lodge, but it will be a perfect home for the Pitts. The Professor's going to his home this afternoon and he's giving me a lift so that I can collect my bits and pieces. The Pitts are moving in at the weekend.'

She closed the door on her colleagues and ran upstairs; there wasn't much time and the Professor hated to be kept waiting.

She was waiting on the doorstep as he drew up, armed with a large shopping basket; there would be things to bring back with her, although she intended leaving pots and pans and the cheap china she had bought for the cottage.

She asked in her sensible way, 'How long may I have to pack up? There isn't much…'

He said impatiently, 'A couple of hours at least. Trugg will fetch whatever you want to store—he can take the Range Rover. I suggest that you don't bring too much back to the flat.'

All her worried guesses came crowding back, but she said quietly, 'No, I won't—only some bits of china and silver.'

He grunted a reply and the rest of the journey was accomplished in silence.

It was a fine afternoon after a rainy morning; the cottage sparkled in the sunshine and its little garden had repaid all Meg's hard work with a display of tulips and daffodils and forget-me-nots. She got out of the car, silently shaking her head at the Professor's offer to go in with her, and then she turned the key in the door and went inside. The little room looked inviting, and the sun had warmed it. She stood a minute looking around her, filled with regret at having to leave it, then she took off her jacket, fetched a duster and started packing the small ornaments. It took no time at all; she put the basket on the table and took down the pictures she had brought with her from home. There were only the little work table and prayer chair to go into the attic. She dusted them lovingly, wondering if she could take them back with her to that flat; they would go in the boot…

Lucky's happy bark sent her to the door, to find Trugg there.

'Is this all, miss?' he wanted to know. 'No call for the Range Rover—leave them there, and I'll take them up this evening. I thought you'd like to have Lucky for an hour, miss, and Professor Culver says will you come up to the house for tea—half past four.'

It was already three o'clock and she hesitated. Trugg said, 'He'd be glad of the company, miss.'

'All right, Trugg. I'd love to come. I'll take Lucky for a walk and just make sure that everything's all right here.'

Left alone once more, and with Lucky in close attendance, she turned out drawers and cupboards, leaving anything Mrs Pitt might find useful; she left tea and sugar too and a tin of milk and a couple of tins of soup and a packet of biscuits. She wished she could have been there to see the Pitts' happy faces when they moved in.

She crossed the road presently and walked briskly along the bridle path which would take her to Penny Green; there wasn't time to go the whole way, and she turned regretfully and went back past the lodge to the house.

The Professor came out of his study as Trugg admitted her. He had Ben and Polly at his heels, and they came to greet her and then tangled happily with Lucky. 'Packed up?' asked the Professor in what Meg considered to be a heartless manner. 'Let's have tea.'

Mrs Trugg had old-fashioned ideas about afternoon tea. There were tiny sandwiches, toasted muffins swim-

ming in butter, a large fruit cake and a plate of little chocolate cakes. Meg, asked to pour out, did so and, being a
sensible girl, made a good tea. Love, she had discovered,
had made no difference to her appetite.

The Professor talked idly, mostly about her old home,
and presently she realised that he was questioning her
closely. Did she miss it? Would she rather live in the
country than in London? Would she enjoy living in London if she led a different life—theatres and dining out
and so on?

She answered him as honestly as she could. 'Well, I
should think it would be lovely if one could have a bit of
both. She added ingeniously, 'You have, haven't you?'

'Indeed, yes. I look forward to sharing my life with
someone who will appreciate it.'

There was a lead weight in Meg's chest. She said
inanely, 'Oh, how nice,' and mentally consigned the
blonde girl to the bottom of the sea. They had made it
up; perhaps the Professor liked to live in a constant state
of dispute and reconciliation, and probably the girl was
tender and loving towards him, although she found that
hard to stomach. She asked with false brightness, 'You're
getting married, Professor?'

'I do have that in mind. I suppose we should be going—I have a dinner date.'

She stopped herself in time from saying, 'How nice,'
again. Instead she jumped to her feet with eagerness
which made him lift his brows, said goodbye to the
dogs, lingering over Lucky, for she might never see him
again, and walked briskly into the hall where Trugg was
waiting. She said goodbye to him too, then got into the
car feeling as though her small world was falling apart
around her. Any minute now, she reflected, and he would

tell her in his cool way that he no longer required her services at his consulting rooms.

But he didn't; he carried on a desultory conversation
about gardening in general and the garden at Much Hadham in particular. They were back in London without
anything of significance having been said. Meg made
haste to get out of the car, fearful that he might deal her
a last-minute blow.

He got out too, carried her basket of odds and ends up
to the flat and bade her a pleasant good evening.

It seemed strange, when Saturday came round, not
being in a hurry to get ready to leave for the lodge. Meg
changed into her outdoor things and took the bus to the
Victoria and Albert Museum, but, interesting though
it was, it was a poor substitute for Much Hadham; she
wandered round for an hour and then went in search of a
tea shop. London on a Saturday afternoon had closed its
doors until Monday morning; she found a small down-
at-heel café finally, had a cup of tea, and then started to
walk back home. It was early evening by now, but the day
had been fine and she walked briskly, crossed Park Lane
and went the length of South Audley Street into Grosve-
nor Square, turned into Duke Street and then Wigmore
Street. There weren't many people about; it was too late
for the sightseers and too early for the theatre traffic to
have started. She got to the flat nicely tired, to be greeted
by Nelson who wanted his supper. She might as well have
her own, she decided, and go to bed early. Tomorrow she
would walk through St James's Park and into Green Park
and in the evening try to go to church. She could have
phoned Doreen, she supposed, but Doreen didn't like to
be rung up on duty, and when Meg had called her earlier in the week she had said that she simply hadn't the

time to see her. Next week, she suggested vaguely. And Cora was away, spending the weekend with her in-laws.

It was raining when she got up in the morning, but the prospect of a whole day indoors didn't appeal. Meg put on her raincoat, tied a scarf over her head, and went to St James's Park where she walked for an hour or more, stopping to have coffee at a stall before crossing Green Park into Mayfair and so finally back to the consulting rooms. She had sandwiches for lunch, sitting before the fire reading the Sunday papers with Nelson on her knee, and in the afternoon for something to do, she turned out the kitchen.

She took more trouble than usual over cooking her supper; it took time to grill the small trout and make pepper sauce, cream the potatoes and make a hot fennel salad, and also just as long to cook the *crème au choco-lat*. Such a waste of time, she reflected, laying the table with as much care as if she had guests. But it kept her occupied; she wasn't a girl to cook something out of a tin and eat it off a tray in front of the television.

She had finished her supper and was trying to decide whether to go to bed with a book or get on with her knitting when Doreen phoned.

'A party, love!' she cried loudly into Meg's ear. 'Next Tuesday, and you simply must come! You'll meet masses of new people and it'll be such fun. Half past eight, and wear something pretty.' Before Meg could say a word, she added breathlessly, 'Must go—see you Tuesday.'

It would be something to do, thought Meg, getting into bed; she didn't want to meet masses of people, but she had the good sense to know that to sit at home and brood over the Professor was going to do no good at all.

She got out of bed, causing Nelson, already asleep on

her feet, to grumble under his breath, and went to inspect her wardrobe. The black pleated crêpe-de-Chine skirt— she had had it for years but it didn't seem to date—and the oyster satin blouse which she had hardly worn. Not in the least exciting, but she would have no chance to buy anything before Tuesday, and no one was likely to give her more than a casual glance.

She could, of course, have worn the pink, but on reflection, she did decide that she never wanted to wear it again.

Monday was busy, and she had only a glimpse of the Professor arriving in the morning and leaving again in the evening, and on Tuesday he was at the hospital all day. She had her supper as usual, changed into the blouse and skirt, covered them with her winter coat since it was a chilly evening, and took the bus to her sister's hospital. Her flat was five minutes' walk away, and she had been told exactly where to go. It was in a modern block of flats on a pleasant enough street, and easy to find. Meg climbed the stairs to the third floor, and since the door was ajar she walked in. There was a good deal of noise coming from the room at the end of the hall, and an open door on her left revealed a pile of coats on chairs and the bed. She added hers to the pile and went to join the party.

The room was packed with people, and a splendid mixture they were too. The girls were dressed either in tight skirts with slits at the back and vivid silk tops or in rather peculiar loose draperies swathed in layers around them. The men too seemed equally varied: jeans and T-shirts, velvet jackets and pink shirts, one or two nicely cut dark suits and two young men in black leather. Meg stood just inside the door; she had no idea that Doreen was so modern, and knew instantly that her own clothes were, in such company, quite freakish. She caught a glimpse of her sister's handsome head at the end of the room and edged her way round to her.

Doreen was talking to several people and she didn't see Meg at once. She was wearing a slinky black dress with a cascade of beads round her neck, and anyone less like a Ward Sister was hard to imagine. Her eyes lighted on Meg eventually and she cried, 'Darling, there you are! Come and meet everyone!' She cast a worried look at the blouse and skirt, which Meg caught, but covered it at once with a smile. 'This is Tom—he's the surgical registrar—and this is Ned, he's one of the house physicians, and this is Marlene, she's a Theatre Sister...'

Meg shook hands and smiled as Doreen led her round the room and then, with a nod and a smile, left her. The small group who had been interrupted by Doreen smiled and said hello and went on talking together, pausing after a moment to ask her which hospital she was from.

'I'm not a nurse,' said Meg. 'I'm Doreen's sister.'

They smiled vaguely and presently drifted away. She wasn't alone for long; a youngish man, one of the T-shirt brigade, flung an arm round her shoulders. 'Hello, darling—all alone?' He studied her at some length. 'In fancy dress, are you? Or someone's nanny?'

'I'm Doreen's sister, and take your arm away, please.'

'Someone's nanny. This isn't quite your scene, is it, darling? What about a ride around and a drink somewhere quiet?'

They were hemmed in by uninterested people's backs. Meg tried to see where Doreen was by standing on tiptoe and peering round shoulders, all the time aware of the man's heavy arm. She was quite capable of squirming away from him, but for all she knew he might be a firm friend of Doreen's from the hospital; besides, one or two people had turned to look at her and were beginning to laugh—the young man's voice carried…

Then at the other side of the room the door opened and the Professor walked in.

He stood for a moment, looking about him, oblivious of the interest he had stirred up. Doreen abandoned the people she was talking to and went to meet him. Meg was too far away to hear what she was saying, but the Professor listened gravely, smiled and said something in his turn. If only he'd look this way, thought Meg. She could have spoken out loud, for he looked across the packed room and smiled faintly, said something else to Doreen and made his way towards her.

There was no need for her to say anything; her eyes told him everything. He said easily, 'Hello, there you are—if you're ready, we'll go.'

He took the young man's arm from her shoulder and took her hand.

'I say…hang on,' began the young man sullenly.

The Professor ignored him, tucked Meg's hand in his and made a leisurely progress to the door where Doreen was still standing. 'You'll forgive us if we leave? I should have telephoned to say that I wouldn't be able to come this evening, but as I was coming this way to an appointment I thought I'd call in.' He added smoothly, 'I'll see Meg home—I'll be going past the door.'

He barely gave Meg time to bid her sister a bewildered goodbye. In the hall he nodded to the open bedroom door. 'Your coat is there. Put it on, Meg and we'll go.'

Going down the stairs she exclaimed, 'I've only just come!'

He halted so abruptly that she almost overbalanced.

'You would like to go back? I could have sworn that you wanted me to rescue you…'

She looked up at his face. 'Oh, I did! I hated it—you see, I didn't look like any of the girls—that man—he asked me if I was in fancy dress and he thought I was someone's nanny.'

Her voice had become a little squeaky despite her best efforts.

The Professor's voice was casual in the extreme. 'My dear girl, you don't give credence to such hubris?'

'What's hubris?'

He laughed. 'Insolence, arrogance, cockiness—any of those.' He went on down the stairs, taking her with him. 'I promise you that you are dressed very nicely, and anything less like a nanny I have yet to meet.'

The very carelessness of his voice reassured her. 'I didn't know you'd been invited,' she remarked.

He didn't answer her but took her arm and marched her out of the house and across the pavement to the Rolls.

'There's a bus…'

He opened the car door and ushered her in. Getting in beside her, he said, 'Will you come and have a meal, Meg, I'm famished?'

'You have an appointment—you told Doreen…'

'A social lie. I hate eating alone.'

She found it impossible to say no, and anyway he didn't wait for her to answer; he was already driving away from the flat. He took her to the Capital Hotel Restaurant where she found, to her relief, that the other women were dressed with a quiet elegance with which her own appearance merged easily. She heaved a sigh of relief as they sat down at their table, and the Professor hid a smile.

'Champagne, I think,' he observed with an impersonal

friendliness she found comforting. 'Now, what shall we eat? The sardines with mustard sauce are excellent, and I can recommend the *caneton Père Léon...*'

Meg sipped her champagne and was lulled into peaceful content by her companion's gentle flow of talk. They were served with champagne sorbets before the main course and her eyes grew round with delight. Pressed to try the sherry trifle, she did so, and over it, her tongue loosened by the champagne, she talked and laughed as though he were an old friend. It wasn't until much later, when she was back in the flat getting ready for bed, that she recalled this—and still more vivid was the remembrance of his kiss. He had gone up to the flat with her, opened the door and switched on the light, and when she had thanked him for her lovely evening, he had caught her close and kissed her soundly and she had kissed him back, alight with the false euphoria engendered by the champagne and the delight of his company.

Her last waking thought as she fell into a troubled sleep was that she would never be able to face him in the morning.

Of course, she did, sitting self-effacing behind her desk, and his good morning was the usual coolly pleasant greeting without a flicker of warmth.

When the last of the morning's patients had gone, he put his head round the door on his way to the hospital.

'You'll be glad to know that the Pitts have settled in well and the baby's fine. Lucky spends a lot of time with them and they like him.'

Meg felt tears crowding her throat. No self-pity, she told herself sternly, and managed to say, 'How nice, I'm so glad.'

'I knew you would be.' His voice was silky. When he

had gone, she applied herself to tidying her desk and getting out the notes concerning the afternoon's patients. She was a fool to love anyone as unpleasant as the Professor. Not always unpleasant, she corrected herself, thinking of the previous evening.

The weekend came round once more and since it was dry even if overcast, Meg took herself off to Hampton Court, where she did everything the guide book suggested and then took the bus home again, warning Percy when she got in so that the phone could be switched through to her flat once more.

She was cooking her supper when it rang, and she went to answer it. She had a list of numbers where the Professor might be found in an emergency and, sensing the urgency of the voice from Maud's, promised instant help and started systematically on the numbers. His home first, although she thought that Maud's would already have phoned there. Rosie answered, 'He's been out of the house since tea time. Said you had the phone numbers if he was wanted.'

Meg went on down the list, chafing at the small delays while the phone was answered. It was her fourth call before she had success.

She recognised the voice which answered her—the girl. It was a London number, so he wasn't too far away, she thought thankfully, and when the girl said she would give him a message she insisted on speaking to him.

'Culver,' said the Professor in her ear. 'Who wants me, Meg?'

'Maud's. He said it was urgent and I told him that if I could find you you'd phone him. A Mr Wyatt.'

'My registrar. Thanks.' He hung up.

The girl would be furious, thought Meg naughtily.

She had just finished writing to Betsy when the doorbell rang. It was a bit late for anyone to call, but it could be Percy with an offer to empty her kitchen bin. She opened the door on the chain and the Professor said testily, 'Why the caution? You might have guessed it would be me.'

She opened the door and he went past her. 'No, I didn't guess, and it was you who told me never to answer the door unless the chain was up.' She added severely, 'There's no pleasing you, Professor.'

He muttered something and she asked politely, 'Would you like a cup of tea? I've just made some.'

'Tea? At this hour? Yes, yes, I'll have a cup.'

He sat himself down, and Nelson scrambled on to his knee in an elderly fashion.

Meg brought him the tea and offered him a biscuit and they sat munching their digestives, saying nothing, looking at each other. But presently the Professor said, 'I don't understand why you've disrupted my life—you're never the same girl for more than half an hour at a time! You scold me and infuriate me by turns and yet you're a splendid listener. You efface yourself so completely at times that I miss you, and yet you have the gall to foist stray animals into my household. Something must be done about it.'

He finished his tea, and Meg said in a matter-of-fact voice, 'Would you like another cup?'

'You see what I mean? I think you've not heard a word of what I've been saying, or worse, you heard it all and chose to ignore it?' He added bleakly. 'My life has always been an ordered one, but that's no longer the case.'

Meg didn't say anything. To a certain extent she had succeeded. At least he had noticed her—it was a pity that he didn't seem very pleased about that. All the same, it was something. She studied his frowning face, loving every line of it.

When the silence had been going on for too long she said kindly, 'You've been working too hard. Can you not take a holiday? I mean a real one, not lectures and things.'

'And now you presume to tell me what I am to do…'

'That's rubbish!' said Meg vigorously. 'You know as well as I do that you do exactly what you want. Why did you come here, Professor?'

'Do you know why they wanted me at Maud's this evening?' and when she shook her head, 'Nancy—you remember her? She collapsed. She's all right now; with luck she'll respond to treatment and in a little while she'll be able to go home. She'll have to come into hospital from time to time, but if we can keep her going…'

'You will,' said Meg firmly. 'It's a challenge, isn't it?'

He smiled with great charm and she smiled back, quite forgetting to be self-effacing.

'I'm going to Much Hadham tomorrow morning; would you like a lift to see Betsy? I'll pick you up again after tea.'

Her whole face lit up, but she said, 'That is kind of you, but it might not suit your mother.'

'She's lunching with me.' He got to his feet and put Nelson back in his box. 'I'll collect you about ten o'clock.' At the door he said, 'Thanks for the tea. Goodnight, Meg.'

This time he didn't kiss her.

Meg was ready and waiting in the morning; it would be a dull day for Nelson and she wondered if she should take him in his basket, a suggestion to which the Professor instantly agreed. Nelson wasn't a cat to run away, nor was he likely to fight with Silky; he was popped into his basket and settled on the back seat of the Rolls.

The Professor had little to say as he drove; Meg admired the countryside once they reached it, thanked him gravely when they arrived at her old home, spent a few minutes talking to Mrs Culver and went along to the kitchen, where she found Betsy waiting for her. Kate had gone to London to spend the day with a niece and they had the house to themselves. Meg was hugged and kissed and told to sit down while Betsy saw Mrs Culver safely into her son's car.

They spent the morning having a good gossip over their coffee while Nelson and Silky sat in armed neutrality before the stove. Betsy was happy; she liked Kate and Kate liked her, and between them they ran the house with the aid of Mrs Griffiths. The boy who came to see to the garden did outside jobs for them and there was always Noakes, willing to lend a hand. 'A bed of roses, Miss Meg, that's what it is! If you was here it 'ud be perfect.'

'We've both been lucky,' said Meg. 'I like my job and I've got the dearest little flat.'

'Do you see much of Miss Doreen or Miss Cora?'

'Well, they're both so busy… I went to a party at Doreen's new flat. She has a lot of friends…'

'You never was one for parties,' declared Betsy. 'Lucky you've got that nice little lodge to go to at weekends.'

'Yes, isn't it?' Meg spoke cheerfully; she had no intention of telling her devoted friend that that was all finished and done with.

She set the table while Betsy saw to their lunch and afterwards when they had washed up and Betsy had gone for what she described as 'a bit of a lay down', she went to the garden and roamed happily. The boy had worked

well. As well as the flower borders, the kitchen garden
was laid out in orderly rows. Meg went round identify-
ing the green shoots, nodding happily. For a moment she
allowed her thoughts to dwell on the little lodge garden.
Her careful weekend gardening would be paying dividends now; the tiny grass patch in the centre would be
just large enough to hold a pram. She sighed and went
back into the house and put the kettle on for tea.

It was the kind of tea she seldom had. Betsy was old-
fashioned; when Meg's parents had been alive, tea had
been sandwiches cut wafer-thin, thin bread and butter and
a cake to cut at, and the dear soul had never changed the
pleasant habit. Kate, she told Meg, had the same views, so
that Mrs Culver, even when alone, was served with some
dainty little meal. The kitchen was pleasantly warm, the
cats were already asleep, back to back, and Betsy, nicely
rested, was inclined to be even chattier than usual.

'It's time Miss Doreen got herself married,' she observed, 'and isn't it about time you found yourself a husband, Miss Meg?' She looked worried. 'Though I suppose
the Professor will keep you on after he's married. No call
to give you the push when all's said and done. Mrs Culver
told me she's delighted that he's found himself a wife—
very choosy, he's been, according to her.'

The delicious fruit cake Meg was eating suddenly
tasted like sawdust in her mouth. She asked casually, 'I
wonder if it's the girl I've seen over at Much Hadham—
fair-haired and so pretty...'

'No idea, Miss Meg. Mrs Culver didn't say. Why not
ask him?'

'I'm not all that interested,' said Meg mendaciously.

There was plenty of opportunity to ask him on their
way back to London presently. He was in a good mood;

he was never a talkative man, but now he had quite a lot to say about the Pitts. The baby was thriving and they were very happy. Pitt was proving a good worker, and Mrs Pitt was willing to help out up at the house if she was needed. 'It's all worked out splendidly!' observed the Professor, glancing sideways at Meg. 'You found Betsy well?'

He carried Nelson's basket up to the flat when they reached it, but beyond switching on the light and taking a quick look round, he didn't stay, but made some bracing remark about the busy morning which lay ahead of them, wished her good night and went away again.

Beyond a rather cross phone call from Doreen during the week, who declared that she had been disagreeably surprised at the way Meg had rushed away from her party and taken the Professor with her, and an equally cross one from Cora whose au pair had left without giving notice, the week went well. 'If you hadn't got this job,' Cora had grumbled, 'you could have come here. Why you had to go off like that I'll never know. Doreen and I would have got you settled in a good job…'

Minding Cora's children, thought Meg. 'I'm sorry about the au pair,' she had said, 'but I'm sure you'll find someone. And this is a good job, you know; besides, the flat is lovely…'

For how long? she wondered as she rang off. The Professor had said nothing to give her cause for alarm, but she wasn't happy about the future.

'I'm getting fanciful,' she told Nelson. 'I'm not sure that being in love is all that it's cracked up to be.'

She had reason to remember those words that very afternoon.

There were no patients until four o'clock; Miss

Standish was taking a couple of hours off and Mrs Giles wouldn't be in until later. Meg, tidying patients' cards in the filing cabinet, heard the Rolls, and a moment later the Professor walked in. He nodded as he crossed to his door and closed it gently behind him, and five minutes later called her over the intercom to go in.

She switched the phone through in case of urgent calls, knocked on the door and stood waiting. She had gone rather pale and she didn't smile as she took the chair he offered her without speaking.

The Professor didn't sit down but came round to lean against his desk, watching her. He said, 'Why do you look like that? As though I were going to sack you?'

Meg clasped her hands in her lap to keep them from shaking. Her insides were filled with an icy foreboding. 'I expect I look like that because you are, aren't you? Going to sack me?'

She peeped up at him and was affronted to see that he was smiling, although he said gravely enough, 'Yes, I am; a Mrs Loftus will be starting on Monday.' And when she was silent, 'Don't you want to know why I want you to leave?'

It was a pity that she had her eyes lowered because she couldn't bear to see him smiling; she missed the look on his face, a look which would have sent her straight into his arms. When she did look it was too late; the phone was ringing and he was answering it.

'Culver.' He listened intently, giving no sign of annoyance because he had been interrupted. 'My dear fellow—this is her second day—does she not understand that she has three more days to go? I thought I'd made it clear that she must remain supine for that length of time.' He listened again. 'Oh, we can't have that,' he ob-

served. 'I'll come over at once; she'll have to be sedated.'
He put down the receiver.

'Later,' he said to Meg as he went through the door.

He got back just after four o'clock, and Meg, who had
been keeping his first patient happy with tea and gentle gossip, ushered her in. She was still pale, but no one
looking at her composed face would have guessed at her
shattered heart.

The second patient came and went, and Mrs Giles and
Miss Standish, instead of staying for their usual little
chat, went too. Meg tidied up once more and checked the
list of patients for the morning, and when the Professor
put his head round the door and said, 'Come in, please,
Meg,' she did so.

He closed the door and stood leaning against it. 'Now,
where were we?' he asked affably.

'You'd just sacked me.'

'Ah, yes—and you've probably spent the last hour or
two wondering why?'

She said in an expressionless voice, 'Yes, of course I
have. I think it's because I vex you sometimes in some
way—I *have* tried not to…'

She didn't quite suppress a watery sniff; all her silly,
pathetic ideas about attracting his attention were so much
moonshine.

'You've never vexed me.' He had left the door and was
standing very close to her, looking down on to her neat,
downbent head. 'You intrigue me, humble me, delight me,
you've wormed your small person into my very heart, but
never once have you vexed me. My dearest little darling,
I've been in love with you since we first met, although I
didn't know it then; I only knew that when you weren't

here I missed you intolerably. I'll never be happy until you're my wife.'

He caught her close and held her gently. 'You're so beautiful and kind and loving. I love the way you laugh and grub in the garden and collect stray animals. Darling, would you consider collecting me?'

Meg looked up into his face and saw so much love there that she blinked. 'Oh yes, indeed I will—I can't think of anything I'd rather do!' She smiled radiantly at him. 'I love you, too...'

She wasn't given the chance to say more than that. He had kissed her before, but never like this. Presently she sighed happily and caught her breath. 'There are several things...' she began, remembering the girl with the golden hair.

'Not important.' He kissed her again.

'Yes, well... What shall we do, Ralph?'

'Why not go upstairs and tell Nelson, dear heart?'

'Yes, but what about...'

He kissed her quiet. 'Later—I've other plans for the moment.'

'Oh, well,' said Meg happily, 'if you say so.' She reached up and kissed him.

* * * * *

THE BACHELOR'S WEDDING

Chapter 1

The pale February sunshine shining through the window highlighted the pleasant room beyond: a room of restful colours, greens and blues and greys, chosen no doubt to dispel the unease of the patients who entered it. Such a one was on the point of leaving, escorted to the door by Professor Jason Lister, a large, very tall man, remarkably handsome with it. He shook hands now, gave the lady a reassuring smile, and handed her over to his receptionist before closing the door again and going back to his desk to pick up his pen and begin to write.

He had hardly done so when the door opened and the receptionist poked her head round it. The professor didn't lift his head. 'Later, Mrs Wells, I'm due at the hospital in half an hour…'

'Yes, I know, sir, but it's Mrs Gault on the outside line. She says she must speak to you at once.'

He took off his reading-glasses and sighed. 'Very well.' He smiled as he spoke, and Mrs Wells, a middle-aged widow with a sentimental heart, beamed at him.

The voice at the other end of the phone was urgent and agitated. 'Jason? Is that you?' The voice didn't wait for an answer. 'I've just had a phone call from that place in Chile where Tom is—he's ill, and they want me to go there as soon as possible. I'm packing now. The children have half-term tomorrow and my flight goes mid-morning. I can't leave them here alone...'

'Where is Patty?'

'She's gone home to nurse her mother—I've been managing without her. Jason, what shall I do?'

'The children can come here; I'll find someone to collect them and look after them while you're away. I can't get to your place, I'm afraid, but I'll arrange something and phone you back. Don't worry more than you must.'

He put down the receiver, switched on the intercom, and asked Mrs Wells to come in.

'We have a problem,' he told her, his placid voice giving no hint of the size of it. And when he had finished telling her, he asked, 'Do you know of an agency where I can get someone at a moment's notice?'

'Yes, I do, sir. There's a very good one—in Kingsway, I believe. I can look it up. Will you speak to them?'

'Please, and as soon as possible.'

The mellifluous voice at the agency assured him that a person suitable to his requirements would be sent immediately.

'After six o'clock,' he made the request, 'and this is the address. It must be someone who is prepared to travel down to Tisbury—that is a small town in Wiltshire—by the early-morning train.'

The professor put down the receiver, put his spectacles on again and resumed his writing, and presently took himself off to the hospital in his dark grey Rolls Royce.

When the phone rang, Araminta was peeling potatoes. She dried her hands and went to answer it, although her sister Alice was sitting within a foot of the instrument, but then Alice had been told two years ago that she had anaemia and must lead a quiet life, an instruction which she obeyed to the letter, encouraged by their father, who doted on her.

'Yes?' said Araminta, anxious to get back to the potatoes.

'Miss Smith? I have an urgent job for you. Short-term, I believe.'

The woman from the agency gave the details in a businesslike manner. 'After six o'clock, and Professor Lister is depending on you.'

She rang off prudently before Araminta could refuse to go.

'That's a job,' said Araminta. 'I'll finish the potatoes, but perhaps you could cook the supper. I may be gone for a few hours.'

Alice looked alarmed. 'But, Araminta, you know I'm supposed to take life easily...'

'I don't suppose it would harm you to grill the chops, love. We do need the money—Father borrowed the housekeeping. I don't know what for.'

Alice looked awkward. 'Well, I did mention that I needed another dressing-gown, and he bought me one.'

Araminta turned round at the door. She spoke cheerfully, for there was no point in voicing her hurt that their father loved Alice dearly and regarded herself as the housekeeper and occasional wage-earner. He was kind to her and sometimes, when he remembered, he told her how useful it was that she was so handy around the house, as well as getting the occasional job from the agency. 'There's plenty of food in the fridge if I'm not back in a day or two.'

She finished the potatoes, changed into her tweed jacket and skirt—suitable for the occasion, she hoped— made sure that her hair was neatly coiled and that her nose was powdered, found an umbrella and went to catch a bus.

It was a long bus ride from her home in a narrow street near Warren Street station to the address she had been given—a small street close to Cavendish Square—and it was already after five o'clock. Six o'clock had long since struck by the time she reached the house, one of a terrace of Regency houses, pristine in their gleaming paint and shining brasswork, and she paused a moment to take a good look before mounting the steps to its front door.

It was opened by an elderly, rotund man with a fringe of hair and an impassive face. When she stated her name he stood aside for her to go in, waved her to a chair in the hall, and begged her to wait.

It was a pleasant hall, not large but welcoming, with crimson wallpaper, a polished wood floor and ormolu wall-lights; there were no pictures on the walls, but on the small mahogany table there was a beautiful bowl full of early spring flowers. Araminta sniffed appreciatively.

She wasn't kept waiting; the rotund man came back within a few minutes and asked her to follow him to the end of the hall and through a door at its end. The room had a large bay window, its heavy velvet curtains not drawn; there would be a garden beyond, she supposed, as she crossed the carpeted floor to stand before the large desk in one corner of the room. The professor got slowly to his feet, the book he had been reading in his hand, a finger marking the page. He stood for a moment, looking at her over his spectacles.

'Miss Smith? Miss Araminta Smith?'

She took exception to the lifted eyebrow. 'Yes—Araminta because it makes up for Smith, if you see what I mean!'

He perceived that this rather dowdy girl with no looks worth mentioning might not be quite what she seemed. He put his book on the desk reluctantly—for he had been relaxing with the poems of Horace—in the original Latin, of course.

'Please sit down, Miss Smith. I was expecting someone of a rather more mature… That is, your charges are young teenagers and, if you will forgive me for saying so, you look—er—rather young yourself.'

'Twenty-three,' said Araminta matter-of-factly. 'Young enough to be able to understand them and old enough to be listened to.' Since he looked doubtful, she added kindly, 'Try me—if I don't do you can find someone else, but the agency said that you needed someone urgently, so perhaps I could be of help until you do.'

She wasn't suitable but she would have to do, at least for the moment.

'It will be necessary for you to catch an early-morning train from Paddington. My nephew and niece are to stay here with me while their mother goes to her husband, who is ill. I have a manservant and his wife who live in the house, but they are too elderly to cope with teenagers. That will be your task.'

'For how long, Mr Lister?' She paused. 'Should I have

said Doctor? The agency said you were in the medical profession.'

'Professor will do.' He smiled at her. She was nothing to look at, but he liked her sensible manner. 'Only for their half-term—a week. My sister has a splendid house-keeper, who has unfortunately gone to her home to nurse her mother. She should be back, and probably my sister will have returned by then.'

Everything quite satisfactory, thought Araminta; the problem of making arrangements for Alice and her father at a few hours' notice would be dealt with presently. She bade the professor a staid goodbye, and he called her back as she reached the door.

'You will need some money for fares and expenses,' he pointed out mildly, and took out his notecase. The amount he gave her was over-generous, and she said so.

'I shall expect an exact account of what you have spent,' he told her.

She flashed him a look from her dark eyes. 'Naturally,' she told him coldly.

He ignored the coldness. 'Mrs Buller will have every-thing ready; perhaps you will phone her as to what time you expect to arrive here. My sister has the number.'

Araminta nodded her tidy head. 'Very well, Profes-sor Lister. Good evening.' He had opened the door for her, and she went past him into the hall and found Buller there, ready to speed her on her way. He gave her a fa-therly smile.

'Quite an upheaval, Miss—the professor leads a very quiet life—but I daresay we shall manage.'

She hoped so, and then concentrated on her own prob-lems.

It was to be expected that Alice would be difficult.

Araminta had been working for the agency for some time now, but always on a daily basis; now she was actually going to leave Alice and her father on their own.

'How am I supposed to manage?' stormed Alice when Araminta arrived at home. 'You know how delicate I am—the doctor said I had to lead a quiet life. You're self-ish, Araminta, going off like this. You must say you can't go.' She lapsed into easy tears. 'You might think of me...'

'Well, I am,' said Araminta sensibly. 'There's almost no money in the house, there's the gas bill waiting to be paid and the TV licence, and Father's salary won't be paid into the bank for another week. If you want to eat, I'll have to take this job. There's plenty in the fridge, and you can go to the shops for anything you need. I dare say a little walk would do you good. Or Father can shop on his way home.'

'Who is to make the beds and cook and do the house-work?' wailed Alice.

'Well, I expect you could manage between you for a few days.'

'You're hard,' cried Alice. 'All you do is think of your-self.'

Araminta bit back the words on the tip of her tongue. She was, after all, a normal girl, wishing for pretty clothes and money in her pocket and a man to love her, and she saw no hope of getting any of these wishes. She went upstairs to her small bedroom in the little terraced house and packed a bag. Her wardrobe was meagre; she folded a sober grey dress—half-price in the sales and useful for her kind of job—a couple of sweaters, blouses and undies, dressing-gown and slippers, a tweed skirt and a rainproof jacket. Almost all she had, actually, and as she packed she could hear her father and sister talking in the sitting-room downstairs. She sighed a little, and made sure that she had all she needed in her handbag before going to join them.

It took the rest of that evening convincing her father that she really had to go. He was an easygoing man, spending money when he had it and borrowing when he hadn't, but even he had to admit that there was a shortage of cash in the house.

'Well,' he said easily, 'you go along and enjoy yourself, my dear. Alice and I will manage somehow. I'll use what money there is, for you'll bring your fees back with you, I suppose?' He smiled at her with vague affection. 'Our little wage-earner.' He got up. 'I'll make a pot of tea before we go to bed.'

'Not all the fees, Father,' said Araminta in a quiet voice. 'I need a new pair of shoes...'

She was up and dressed and eating a hasty breakfast when Alice came yawning into the kitchen. 'You might have brought me a cup,' she said plaintively.

'No time,' said Araminta, her mouth full. 'I'll phone you in a day or two when I know how things are going. Say goodbye to Father for me, will you?'

She dropped a kiss on her sister's cheek and flew out of the door with her case, intent on catching a bus to Paddington.

The train was half-empty and she sat in a window-seat, watching the wintry landscape, glad to have the next hour and a half to herself. She had few qualms about the job; she had been working for the agency for more than a year now, although this was the first time the job was expected to last as long as a week—perhaps not even that if Professor Lister found her unsatisfactory. She wasn't sure what to make of him; he hadn't approved of her, that was evident, but he had been pleasant enough in a rather absent-minded manner. Hopefully he would be out of the house for most of the day; she would only need to keep the children out of his way in the early mornings and the evenings.

When she got out of the train at Tisbury she was thankful to find an elderly taxi parked outside the station. The driver was pleasant and chatty and, when she gave him the address, said at once, 'Oh, Mrs Gault—poor lady. Worried sick, she is, with her husband ill on the other side of the world. Come to give a hand, have you? Half-term and all...'

The house was at the other end of the little town: a red-brick dwelling in a large garden. There was nothing elaborate about it; it was roomy, with large sash windows and a handsome front door with a splendid fanlight—what Araminta supposed one would describe as a gentleman's residence. She paid the taxi-driver, took her case and rang the bell, and then, since no one came, banged the brass knocker.

The door was flung open then by a youngish woman with untidy dark hair and Professor Lister's blue eyes. 'Oh, good, you're here. Do come in—you have no idea how glad I am to see you.' She held out a firm, friendly hand. 'I'm Lydia Gault...'

'Araminta Smith. What would you like me to do first?'

'You're heaven-sent, and sensible too. My taxi comes for me in just two hours. I'm trying to get the children organised—you've no idea... You'd like a cup of coffee, I expect?'

Araminta put down her case and took off her coat. She was wearing a tweed skirt and a blouse and cardigan, and the sensible shoes which needed replacing. 'I'd love one. If you will show me where the kitchen is, I'll make coffee for everyone, shall I? And, while we drink it, you can tell me what you want me to do.'

'Through here—everything's in the cupboard in the corner. I'll see how the children are getting on with their packing. It's only for a week...'

Mrs Gault disappeared and Araminta put on the kettle, found coffee, sugar and milk, assembled four mugs on the kitchen table and opened a tin of biscuits, and when that was done she got her notebook and pen from her handbag and laid them on the table too. She had a good memory, but she imagined that Mrs Gault would have a great many instructions to give her.

Mrs Gault came back again then, and the children with her. The boy, Jimmy, was tall and thin, with fair hair and a look of mischief about him; Gloria was younger, barely thirteen, but already very pretty. She was fair too, and she looked friendly. She was holding a large tabby cat in her arms and a Jack Russell trotted beside her, barking loudly.

She said at once, 'Tibs and Mutt are coming with us to Uncle Jason's.'

'Why not?' agreed Araminta, smiling. 'They couldn't possibly be left alone, could they?'

'He might mind,' said Jimmy.

'Well, if they are already there I don't suppose he'll object.' Araminta swallowed some coffee and picked up her pen. 'I assume there's a train this afternoon, Mrs Gault? We leave after you, I expect?'

'Yes, there's a train just after four o'clock. You'll need a taxi. Leave a note for the milkman, will you, and turn off the gas—I suppose we could leave the electricity on? Jimmy—what do you think?'

'Of course. Did you stop the papers? When is Patty coming back?'

His mother frowned. 'I phoned but there was no answer. Will you ring from Uncle Jason's?' She turned to Araminta. 'Will you leave the fridge and freezer on and be sure to lock up and see that all the windows are shut? Does Jason know what time you'll be back in London?'

'No, he asked me to ring his housekeeper as soon as I knew the train time.'

'Yes, of course. I'm sorry this is all such a muddle, but I suppose you're used to this kind of job.' Mrs Gault hesitated. 'I suppose you couldn't get some sort of meal for us all? Just anything,' she added vaguely. 'I've mislaid my sunglasses—I'm sure to need them. Gloria, finish your packing, darling, and, Jimmy, write a note for the milkman, will you?'

The three of them hurried away and Araminta, with Tibs and Mutt getting very much under her feet, flung open cupboards and fridge. Omelettes, oven chips and peas, she decided, since there wasn't time to cook anything elaborate. The animals needed to be fed too. She dealt with them first and, with them satisfied, set about getting the food ready.

She had the table in the kitchen laid after a fashion and the meal just ready when Mrs Gault and the children came back, and this time they were dressed ready to leave.

There was a great rush at the last minute: things missing, messages forgotten, and Mrs Gault, worried to death about her husband, hating to leave the children, spilling instructions until the final moment as she drove away in the taxi.

If Araminta had worked hard before Mrs Gault left, she found the rest of the afternoon even more arduous. Jimmy and Gloria were nice young people, but she was quick to see that they intended to reduce her to the level of a superior servant given half a chance. Only she didn't give them that; there was still a lot to do before they could leave. She toured the house with Jimmy, making sure that he watched her closing windows and locking doors before they all piled into the taxi.

The train was nearly empty. Mutt sat on Jimmy's knees and Tibby slept in her basket. The children didn't say much; now that the rush and bustle were over they were despondent, talking together quietly, ignoring her, and she for her part was glad to be left in peace, for she was tired now; her day had started early and was by no means over yet.

She had phoned the professor's house before they left Tisbury, and Buller had assured her that there would be an early supper and their rooms would be ready for them. 'Professor Lister will probably be late home, miss,' he had told her, and she hoped that that would be the case. She suspected that after a hard day's work at the hospital he relished his quiet evenings. It would be nice if she could get the children to bed before he returned.

It was quite a short journey from Paddington to his house, and Buller was waiting for them. The children treated him as an old friend and went at once to the kitchen to see Mrs Buller, leaving Araminta with the animals and the luggage. 'Now just you leave everything, miss,' said Buller kindly. 'There'll be a tray of tea in the sitting-room at the back of the hall in five minutes, and

I'll get the bags upstairs. The children are on the right at the top of the stairs, miss, and your room is on the opposite side, if you care to go up.'

The stairs opened on to a square landing, with doors on either side and a passage leading to the back of the house. There was another smaller staircase too, but she didn't stop to look around her but opened the door Buller had pointed out and went in.

The room was fair-sized, light and airy and charmingly furnished, and there was a bathroom leading from it. She registered a strong desire to tumble on to the bed and go to sleep, but she took off her outdoor things, tidied her hair and did her face, and went downstairs again.

Buller was in the hall. 'Jimmy came for Tibs and Mutt,' he told her. 'Tea is ready for you, miss.'

She thanked him. 'Do you suppose the professor will mind about the animals?' she asked.

'I think not, miss. We have two dogs—golden Labradors. They are at present being exercised by Maisie, the housemaid. They are mild-tempered animals, however, and I foresee no trouble.'

He led the way to the small cosy room where he had set the tea-tray. There was a bright fire in the steel grate and comfortable chairs drawn up to it.

'I'll send the children to you, miss,' said Buller.

They came presently, not over-friendly. Araminta handed round tea and buttered toast, sandwiches and little cakes, and said in her sensible voice, 'When we've had tea, perhaps you would unpack your things and put them away? I don't know what arrangements are to be made about Tibs and Mutt—perhaps you've already seen to that?' She looked at Jimmy. 'Your Uncle has two dogs, I believe.'

'They'll be OK. They've met Mutt and Tibs when Uncle Jason has been down to see us.'

'Oh, good, and we can take Mutt for a walk—Hyde Park isn't far away, is it? And Tibs—will she settle down nicely?'

'She's my cat,' said Gloria. 'She sleeps on my bed.' She sounded sulky. 'Mrs Buller says we may have our supper in the kitchen; Uncle won't be home for ages. I'll unpack in the morning.'

'We'll go upstairs and unpack now,' said Araminta, 'otherwise you'll have to waste the morning doing it, when you might want to be doing something more interesting.'

'You're awfully bossy,' said Gloria. 'I suppose you'll eat in the kitchen with Buller and Mrs Buller and Maisie?'

'I dare say,' said Araminta equably. 'Never mind about me—let's get our things put away.'

'Patty always saw to our things for us,' grumbled Jimmy, tumbling shirts into the elegant little tallboy in his room.

Araminta turned to look at him from the pile of socks she was sorting out. 'Did she?' She sounded surprised. 'But you're almost grown-up, Jimmy.'

He muttered a reply, and she went to see how Gloria was getting on.

She was on the bed, leafing through a magazine, clothes strewn around on the chairs and the floor. She looked up as Araminta went in.

'I can't be bothered to put everything away—Patty always does it.'

'Well, Patty's not here, and since I'm not your nanny I think you had better tidy things up, for no one else is going to do it for you.'

'I don't think I'm going to like you,' said Gloria.

'That's a pity, but it's only for a few days, and if I make you unhappy I'm sure your uncle will try and get someone else from the agency. You see, there wasn't time for him to pick and choose—he had to take the only person free, and that was me.'

'Haven't you got a home?'

'Oh, yes, and a father and sister.'

'Why do you go out to work, then?'

Araminta said bracingly, 'Let's not talk about me. I'm not a bit interesting.'

She sat down on one of the little armchairs by the window and Gloria got off the bed and began to push things into cupboards and drawers.

'I'm tired,' she grumbled, but she sounded more friendly now. 'We had to get up ever so early.'

'Well, I expect supper won't be too long. Then you can come to bed with a book—your uncle's not here, so you don't need to stay up unless you want to.'

'Oh.' She glanced sideways at Araminta. 'Don't you mind Tibs sleeping on my bed?'

'Mind? Why should I mind? I like cats—dogs too. How old is she?'

'Daddy gave her to me on my sixth birthday.'

'She's very pretty, and your constant companion, I dare say.'

Gloria raked a comb through her hair. 'I want my supper.'

'Then let's go and see if it's ready.'

'Jimmy and me, not you,' said Gloria. 'The kitchen staff eat later.'

'We'd better get Jimmy,' said Araminta mildly. She was used, after a year at the agency, to living in a kind of no man's land while she was at a job. She had minded at first, but now she accepted whatever status was offered her.

Supper was ready, and Buller led the children down to the basement kitchen and then came back to where Araminta stood uncertainly in the hall.

'The professor telephoned. He hopes you will dine with him if you are not too tired. In the meantime, once Jimmy and Gloria are in bed, perhaps you would care to sit in the drawing-room? There are the day's papers there and some magazines.'

Araminta said bluntly, 'Aren't I supposed to take my meals in the kitchen?'

Buller said in a shocked voice, 'Certainly not, Miss. I have my instructions from the professor.'

'Well, thank you. I'll sit in the room where we had tea, shall I, until the children are ready? Will Professor Lister be very late, do you think?'

'There's no telling, miss. But I should imagine within the next hour or so.'

So she went and sat by the fire and thought about her day and contemplated the week ahead of her. Jimmy and Gloria were nice young people, she was sure, but, she suspected, spoilt. They were of an age to be rude and thoughtless—she could remember being both at their age—but as long as she could keep them occupied and happy, and at the same time out of their uncle's way unless he wished for their company, it shouldn't be too bad.

They joined her presently and, when she suggested that they might go to bed since they had had a long day, they demurred.

Araminta made no attempt to change their minds; instead she suggested that they might write letters to their mother. 'It takes nearly a week by airmail to get to that part of the world,' she told them, hoping that she was right. 'Your mother would be glad to hear from you both before she returns.'

'We'll phone her tomorrow,' said Jimmy.

'Even better,' said Araminta. 'You have the number?'

He gave her a sulky look. 'No, of course not. Uncle Jason will know.'

'Then you must be sure and get it from him before he leaves in the morning.'

She embarked on a tedious conversation about museums, some of which she suggested that they might go and see during the next few days. She was boring herself and, as she had intended, Jimmy and Gloria as well. It wasn't long before they declared that they would go to bed. Gloria scooped up Tibs, wished Araminta a sullen goodnight, and went upstairs, and Jimmy, after taking Mutt to the kitchen, followed her. Araminta glanced at the little carriage-clock on the mantelpiece. Almost nine o'clock and no sign of Professor Lister. Her insides rumbled emptily; she would have liked to go to bed too, but not on an empty stomach.

It was very quiet in the house. Buller had suggested that she should sit in the drawing-room once the children were in bed, so she got up and went to the door. The hall was empty and softly lighted and she went a little way into it, wondering which door led to the drawing-room. When she had come to see the professor she had been shown into a room at the back of the house, but there were doors on either side as well. She went to the nearest, opened it, and poked her head round. The dining-room, the oval table laid for dinner, presumably, the silver and glass gleaming in the light of the wall-sconces. She shut the door and crossed the hall to open the one opposite. The library, and a very handsome one too, and, although there was no one there, there was a bright fire burning, and a reading-lamp lighted on one of the small tables drawn up beside the comfortable chairs.

The professor's voice, soft in her ear, caused her to withdraw her head smartly. 'Finding your way around, I hope, Miss Smith?'

She turned to face him, breathing rather hard. 'You should never creep up on people,' she advised him. 'They might have weak hearts or something! Buller told me to sit in the drawing-room, if I would like that, but I haven't found it yet.'

He towered over her, looking concerned and at the same time impatient.

'My dear Miss Smith, my apologies—I trust no harm has been done to your heart or—er—something. The drawing-room is over here.' He led the way across the hall and opened another door, and she went past him and stood waiting.

'Please sit down. I dare say you're starving, but do have a glass of sherry before we dine.'

'Thank you. There's another thing, Professor Lister. Buller gave me a message that I was to dine with you, but if I might put you right about that... I'm just some-one from an agency, not your guest. Usually I have my meals in the kitchen with the staff.'

'While you are in my house you will be so good as to take your meals with me and the children.'

He sounded annoyed, and she murmured, 'Very well, Professor,' in a placatory voice which he ignored.

'They are here, I presume?'

'Yes, there were no difficulties. They are upstairs in

their rooms, but I can't say they are asleep because I don't know.'

'Difficult, were they?' he wanted to know. 'Nice children, but spoilt. My sister got away on time? She's not much good at organising things.'

'I believe that everything went well. There's just one thing—Jimmy has brought his dog with him and Gloria has her cat.' She peeped at him to see how he was taking the news, but his face was impassive. 'Your two dogs were out with the housemaid when we arrived, and she took them straight to the kitchen. I think they are still there, and so is Mutt—the Jack Russell.'

'Yes, Buller told me when I phoned. You like dogs?'

'Yes, I do.'

'Good—they can join us then. They appear to have absorbed Jimmy's dog. They are very good-natured beasts.'

He glanced up as Buller came in. 'Dinner, Buller? Good—and let Goldie and Neptune out, will you?'

They were crossing the hall when the dogs came padding to meet them. They gave muffled barks as he greeted them, and then went to Araminta, looking up at her with liquid brown eyes, ready to be friends. She crouched down, the better to greet them, while their master stood patiently. She looked up, smiling, and saw the look on his face—impatience? Indifference? She wasn't sure which of the two, but she got to her feet at once, feeling vaguely foolish. He must find her and the children a tiresome hindrance in his busy life.

'You must wish me at Jericho,' she said, and instantly wished the words unsaid.

'My dear young lady, on the contrary. Much as I have an affection for my nephew and niece, the thought of overseeing their daily activities fills me with alarm. You are more than welcome in my house.'

He was smiling and his voice was kind, but she had the feeling that he was thinking about something else.

She was hungry and the food was delicious. Mrs Buller must be a cordon bleu cook: the parsnip soup with just a hint of garlic, the roast pheasant, followed by a treacle tart which melted in the mouth, were witnesses to that. Araminta, quite famished by now, did full justice to the lot, but when the professor suggested that they might have their coffee at the table, she excused herself on the grounds of tiredness. She bade him a cheerful goodnight and wished that she hadn't seen the quick look of relief on his face; she was aware that she had hardly added to his evening's enjoyment.

Chapter 2

Araminta slept soundly. She was far too sensible to lie awake and speculate about the following day. No doubt it would have its problems, more easily faced after a good night's sleep. Waking up to find a cheerful young woman with a tea-tray and the information that breakfast was in half an hour was a splendid start to it.

The knowledge that their uncle was at home and expecting to see them at breakfast got Jimmy and Gloria out of bed, dressed and downstairs, without any coaxing on Araminta's part.

He was already at the breakfast-table and he looked up from reading his post to wish them good morning, but as Araminta came into the room behind them he got out of his chair, enquired politely if she had slept well, and invited her to take a seat at the table.

It was Gloria who asked, 'Oh, is Araminta going to have her meals with us?'

He offered Araminta a dish of scrambled eggs. 'Naturally Miss Smith will do so—why do you ask, Gloria?' His glance was frosty. 'She has sole charge of both of you while you are here, and be good enough to remember that. I am delighted to have you here, but you will have to fit into my household. Mutt is in the garden with Goldie and Neptune. Jimmy, you will make yourself responsible for him, won't you? And you, Gloria, will do everything necessary for Tibs. She should be safe enough in the garden as long as you are with her. You will be going out this morning, I dare say?' He glanced at Araminta, who nodded. 'Will you take all three dogs with you? The park is only a short walk away. I should be home about five o'clock. We might take the dogs in the car up to Hampstead Heath and give them a good run. Miss Smith will be glad of an hour to herself, I have no doubt.'

He gathered up his post. 'I'll give myself a day off on Saturday,' he told them. 'Decide what you want to do and let me know.'

The pair of them munched in silence after he had gone, then Jimmy said, 'We're quite old enough to look after ourselves…'

'Well, of course you are,' said Araminta briskly, 'but perhaps as you are your uncle's guests it would be polite to do as he asks. When we've had breakfast I'll go and ask Mrs Buller what time she serves lunch, while you two see to Mutt and Tibs.'

They muttered an answer and she finished her breakfast without haste, talking cheerfully about this and that, ignoring their unfriendly faces, and presently went down to the kitchen, introduced herself to Mrs Buller and sat down at the kitchen table at that lady's request so that they might discuss the days ahead.

'Professor Lister don't come 'ome for 'is lunch, miss, just now and then, like.' Mrs Buller beamed at her and Araminta beamed back at the cosy little woman. 'Suppose we say one o'clock sharp and tea at four o'clock? Dinner's at half-past seven when 'e's 'ome—leastways when 'e isn't called away. 'E entertains off and on, you might say, got a lot of friends but no one in particular, if you get my meaning—not a ladies' man, more's the pity. 'E'd make a fine husband. Likes 'is books...' Mrs Buller shook her grey head. 'Now, as to lunch, 'ow about a nice cheese soufflé? And the children will want chips and I'll do some baby carrots and a chocolate pudding...'

'That sounds lovely. I hope we aren't giving you a lot of extra trouble, Mrs Buller.'

'Bless you, miss, of course not.'

'I'll let Buller know when we go out and where we are going, shall I?'

'Now that sounds like good sense, miss.'

The morning went rather better than she had expected; the three of them went to the park with the dogs as she had suggested and, although Gloria and Jimmy made no effort to be friendly, at least they fell in with her carefully worded suggestions, couched in a friendly no-nonsense voice. They gave the dogs a good run and got back with just enough time to tidy themselves for lunch. Over the chocolate pudding Araminta broached her suggestion for the afternoon. 'I don't know this part of London very well,' she observed casually. 'I wondered if we got on a bus and went somewhere—another park, perhaps? We could look around and have a cup of tea, and then bus back in time for your uncle's return.'

The idea went down well, but they weren't going to let her have it all her own way.

'I'd rather go to Richmond,' said Jimmy.

'Why not? Would you like to take Mutt?'

He gave her a surprised look and she said calmly, 'Well, he's small enough to be carried if he gets tired, isn't he? Perhaps Tibs ought to have a few minutes in the garden before we go. I'll go and tell Buller—I don't expect Goldie and Neptune will need to go out again until we get back.'

The afternoon was a success; they sat overlooking the river, admired the Thames and the country beyond, and found a tea-room before getting a bus back. It had been an expensive outing, reflected Araminta, sitting on her bed counting the change in her purse, but worth every penny. Any minute now the professor would be home, and he would take the children and the dogs on the promised trip to Hampstead Heath...

When she went downstairs he was at home, sitting in his chair by the fire with his dogs at his feet. He got up as she went in, and she said quickly, 'Oh, you're home,' and blushed because it had been a silly thing to say. 'The children will be down in a few minutes; they're tidying themselves for the evening.'

'Sit down, Miss Smith. No difficulties?'

'None, thank you, Professor.'

The children came then, and she sat quietly while they recounted their day to him. 'But we're still going out with you, aren't we, Uncle?' asked Gloria.

'Of course. I'm glad you enjoyed yourselves. Go and get your coats; we'll go now.' When they had gone he said, 'Let me know how much you paid out on my behalf, Miss Smith,' and when she murmured vaguely, he said, 'Now if you please.'

So she told him. 'It's rather a lot of money, but they did enjoy their tea.'

'A small price to pay for their enjoyment. Have they seemed worried about their mother and father?'

'They haven't said anything to me, but I wouldn't expect them to...'

The children came back then. 'Isn't Araminta coming with us?' asked Gloria.

'No—I believe Miss Smith may be glad of an hour or so to herself.' He smiled kindly at her and she gave a grateful murmur. She wished that he would stop calling her Miss Smith, it highlighted her mousy dullness.

Day followed day, and Gloria and Jimmy showed no sign of liking her any better. True, they did what she asked them to do, fell in with her suggestions as to how to spend their days and treated her with politeness at any meal when their uncle was present. They had, for some reason, made up their minds not to like her, and in a way she could understand that; she was a stranger, wished on them at a moment's notice and instantly to be forgotten the moment they returned home to their mother's and Patty's casual spoiling.

It was towards the end of the week when Professor Lister received a phone call from his sister. She had no idea when she would be coming home; her husband was still very ill and it was impossible for her to leave him. 'I know how awkward it is for you to have the children,' she told him. 'Send them back in time for school—Patty should be back by now; she can look after them. That girl—what's her name?—Araminta can take them back and hand them over.'

'Don't worry about them,' he told her, 'I'll see that

they get back home and settled in with Patty. I'm sorry Tom is still not fit, but stay as long as you need to—I'll drive down whenever I can and keep an eye on the children.'

'Bless you.' Lydia Gault rang off and he put the phone down and went to sit in his armchair. He would have to make time to drive the children back on Saturday and Araminta Smith would have to go with them. He could bring her back that same day and she could return home...

He got up presently and went to tell the three of them, who were playing a rather rowdy game of Monopoly in the sitting-room.

His news was received with mixed feelings by the children. They were troubled that their father was still ill and their mother wouldn't be coming home for a time; on the other hand they were pleased at the idea of going home again and returning to school and the loving care of Patty, who let them do exactly what they wanted. The professor watched their faces with a wry smile before he turned to Araminta.

'You will be kind enough to return with the children?' The question was a statement, politely put. 'I will drive you back in the evening.'

She agreed; she had telephoned Alice during the week and told her that she would be back at the weekend, listening patiently to the flood of complaints before putting the receiver down.

'I'll phone Patty,' said the professor. 'She's probably back by now—if not, I'll phone her at home.'

An urgent call from the hospital prevented him from doing that; it was only after his ward round that he remembered to do it. He pushed aside the notes he was writing in Theatre Sister's office and picked up the phone.

There was no reply from his sister's home, but he had Patty's home number with him. He phoned that, waiting patiently while it rang.

Patty's soft Scottish voice said, 'Hello?'

He said at once, 'Patty? Jason Lister here. I don't suppose you've heard from Mrs Gault. She won't be able to return at present—Mr Gault isn't so well. I'll bring the children back on Saturday—so could you come back as soon as you can and open up the house? I know it's short notice, but perhaps you could take the night sleeper or fly back to Bristol or Exeter. Take a car, and don't spare the expense. I'll see to that—'

'Professor Lister, I can't—my mother's desperately ill. I cannot leave her—you must understand that—I was going to phone Mrs Gault when she got back. What is to be done?'

'Don't worry, Patty, we'll brush through. The young lady who has been looking after Jimmy and Gloria is still with us. I'll get her to go back with them and stay until either you or Mrs Gault get back. You stay and look after your mother.'

'You're sure, sir? I'll come the moment I can.'

'Stay as long as you need to,' he told her, 'and let me know how you get on.' He hung up; it was providential that Araminta Smith was still with them. He would see her as soon as he got home.

Which was late that evening. The children were in bed and Araminta was sitting uneasily in the drawing-room when he got back. She didn't much like sitting there on her own but Buller had told her that the professor wanted her to make use of the room whenever she wished. One more day, she was thinking, then back home to a disgruntled Alice and the careless affection of her father, eager to know how much she had earned. The money had been hard-earned too; true, she had lived in the lap of luxury in this lovely house, but not for one moment had the children shown her any sign of friendliness.

As for Professor Lister, he treated her with an impersonal politeness which held no more warmth than when they had first met.

She got to her feet as he came in, the dogs at his heels. Her 'Good evening, Professor Lister,' was quietly said. 'I was just going to bed. You must be tired…'

'Yes, but please don't go for a moment. I have something to say to you.'

She sat down again and he sat in his chair opposite to her. She looked at his tired face. 'You should go to your bed,' she told him in her matter-of-fact way, 'but perhaps you are hungry too. Shall I go and see if Mrs Buller could warm up some soup?'

'I believe Buller has the matter in hand, but it is kind of you to bother. Perhaps you will have a drink with me first?'

He got up and poured her a glass of sherry and gave himself some whisky. 'We have a problem,' he told her, 'and I must rely on you to solve it.'

She listened without interruption, and when he had finished she said simply, 'How very unfortunate. Of course I will do as you ask, only I must go home and get some clothes—I only brought enough for a week with me.'

'Certainly. I'll drive you home tomorrow—I should be home round about four o'clock. That will give you time to pack whatever you need to take there and decide what you wish to take with you. I have no idea how long you may need to stay, but I would suggest that you think in terms of two weeks.' He saw the doubt in her face. 'That presents difficulties? Your family?'

'My sister isn't very used to running the house.'

'She is alone?'

'No. No—but my father is away all day.' She would have stopped there but the faint enquiry in his face forced her to go on. 'She's delicate.'

He said kindly, 'Well, suppose we go to your home and see what she says; if necessary I could arrange for her to have some help. May I ask in what way your sister is delicate?'

'Well, the doctor told her she would have to take things easy.'

'This was recent, this advice?'

Araminta wrinkled her forehead in thought. 'Well, no—about two years ago.'

'Has she been taking things easy since then? Does she see her doctor regularly?'

'Not since then.' Araminta glanced at him as she said it, and surprised a look on his face; she wasn't sure what the look was because it had gone at once. She must have imagined it.

The children were upset, looking at her as though it were all her fault. She was thankful when the professor came home the next afternoon, his calm, logical acceptance of the situation allowing them to take a more cheerful view of it.

'I'll phone each evening,' he promised them, 'and if I can manage it I'll come down at the weekend, and as soon as I have any news I'll let you know. I know you both want to help your mother and father, and the best way of doing that is to give them no cause to worry about you. Will you get your things packed up while I take Miss Smith to her home to get what she needs? We'll go after breakfast tomorrow—that will give us time to do any shopping and air the house. When your mother and father are back home, I promise we'll all have a marvellous celebration.'

He had nothing to say as he drove Araminta home; he wasn't a talkative man and his well-ordered life had been turned upside-down and, even though the three of them would be gone, he would still need to keep an eye on them from a distance, and that over and above his own busy life.

The contrast between his handsome house and her own home was cruel, but she didn't allow it to bother her. He stopped before its front door and she prepared to get out. She stopped halfway. 'I shall be about half an hour,' she told him. 'Would you like to come in, or perhaps you would rather come back?'

His mouth twitched. 'I'll come in, if I may.' It would be interesting to see how this unassuming girl, who had fitted into the quiet luxury of his home with unselfconscious naturalness, behaved in her own house. Besides, he had a wish to meet the delicate sister. As plain as her sister? he wondered.

Araminta put her key in the lock and opened the door, and stood aside to allow him to pass her into the narrow hall. It was a bit of a squeeze, for he was so very large, but she said nothing, only called softly, 'Alice? Alice, I'm back…'

Alice's voice came from the kitchen. 'And about time too, I'm sick of all this beastly housework…' Her voice got louder as she opened the door wider and came through, and then changed miraculously as she saw Pro-

fessor Lister. 'Oh, we weren't expecting you...' Her cross
face became wreathed in smiles.

'This is Professor Lister, Alice. My sister, Professor.
Alice, I shall be away for another week or ten days. I've
come to collect some more clothes. I've brought my case
with me...'

The professor had shaken hands and smiled but not
spoken; now he said, 'Ah, yes, I'll fetch it in for you.'
And he went out to the car again.

Alice clutched Araminta's arm. 'Why didn't you warn
me? I'd have had my hair done and put on a decent dress.
He's quite something.' She added peevishly, 'The house
is in a mess...'

'I doubt if he notices,' said Araminta prosaically. 'He's
a bit absent-minded.'

Alice tossed her head. 'I'll make him notice me...' She
turned to smile at him as he came back into the house.
'You run along, dear,' she said sweetly to Araminta. 'I
daresay Professor Lister would like a cup of coffee.'

Araminta climbed the stairs to her room and set about
the business of finding fresh clothes, stout shoes and an
all-enveloping overall, since it seemed likely that she
would be expected to do the housework as well as keep
an eye on Jimmy and Gloria. That done, she took a pile of
undies and blouses down to the kitchen, stuffed them into
the washing-machine and switched it on. Alice wasn't
likely to iron them, but at least they would be clean when
she got back. She could hear voices in the sitting-room,
and Alice's laugh, as she went back upstairs to collect
her writing-case and choose a book to take with her. She
thought that she might need soothing by bedtime each
day, and ran her hand along the row of books by her
bed. She chose *Vanity Fair* and Thackeray's *Ballads and*

Songs. She hesitated, her small, nicely kept hand hovering over *Jane Eyre*, but there wasn't room for it in her case. She closed the case, carried it downstairs, and went into the sitting-room. The professor was sitting in one of the shabby armchairs by the fireplace and he got up as she went in. Alice was sitting on the old-fashioned sofa. She looked prettier than ever, thought Araminta without envy, but it was a pity that the room was so untidy, more than untidy, grubby. Why did Alice look so cross, anyway?

She looked quickly at the professor, but he looked as he always did, pleasant and at the same time unconcerned, as though his mind were elsewhere. She could hardly blame him for that; she longed to get a duster and tidy up a bit. All the same, Alice was surely pretty enough to override her surroundings—something must have gone wrong...

'I'm ready, Professor,' she said briskly. 'I'll let you know as soon as possible when I'll be coming home,' she told her sister, and was rewarded by a pouting face.

'I suppose I'll have to manage. Lucky you, it'll be as good as a holiday.'

Alice got up and offered a hand to Professor Lister, looking at him in a little-girl-lost manner which Araminta found irritating, although probably, being a man, he liked it. He showed no signs of either liking or disliking it; she had never met a man who concealed his feelings so completely.

'I'm sure you must be relieved to know that, after all this time, whatever it was your doctor diagnosed has apparently cured itself. I must urge you to go and have a check-up. It isn't for me to say, but I feel sure that you have little reason to fear for your health.' He shook her hand firmly and stood aside while Araminta kissed her sister's cheek, but Alice was still peevish. She went over to the door with them and wished them a cold goodbye as they got into the car, shutting the door before they had driven away.

Araminta peeped at her companion's profile; he looked stern.

'As I said it is, of course, not for me to say, but I believe that your sister is in excellent health. I suggested that she should see her doctor so that he might reassure her. If she had needed medical care when she first went to him he would have advised her to see him regularly.'

'He told her that she had to take things easily.'

'But not for two years or more.'

'It's very kind of you to concern yourself, Professor Lister,' said Araminta frostily, 'but perhaps...' She paused, not quite sure how to put it. 'You're a surgeon,' she pointed out.

'I am also a doctor of medicine,' he told her blandly. 'Have you all that you require for the next week or so?'

She wondered if she had been rude. 'Yes, thank you. I'm sorry if I was rude; I didn't mean to be.'

'It is of no consequence. Indeed, I prefer outspokenness to mealy-mouthed deception.'

They were almost back at his house. 'We shall leave directly after breakfast,' he observed, with the cool courtesy which she found so daunting. 'Will you see that the children are ready by nine o'clock—and the animals, of course?' He drew up before his door and got out and opened her door for her. 'I expect you would like an hour or so in which to pack for yourself—I'll take the children out with the dogs.'

He stood in the hall looking down at her, unsmiling, while Buller fetched her bag from the car. He must find all this a most frightful nuisance, she reflected, his days turned upside-down and, even if he's fond of the children, he doesn't like me overmuch. A sudden wish to be as pretty as Alice swam into her head; it was the impersonal indifference which she found so hard to bear.

She thanked him in her quiet way, and went upstairs and began to pack her things before going to see if Jimmy and Gloria had made a start on theirs. They hadn't, and it would be too late by the time they got back and had had dinner; getting them up in the morning would be bad enough. She fetched their cases and began to pack for them as well.

The professor went to his study after dinner and Araminta, mindful of his placid, 'We shall leave directly after breakfast. Will you see that the children are ready by nine o'clock,' finished the packing, persuaded the children to go to their beds and went to her room, intent on a long hot bath and washing her hair, but she had got no further than taking the pins out when there was a tap on the door. There was Buller with a request that she would go at once to the study as the professor had been called away and wished to see her before he went.

'He'll have to wait while I get my hair up,' said Araminta.

'If I might venture to say so, miss, the professor is anxious to be gone—an urgent matter at the hospital, I believe. Could you not tie it back or plait it?'

'Well, all right, I expect I'd better.' She began with quick fingers to weave a tidy rope of hair over one shoulder; it hung almost to her waist, thick and mousy, and she was braiding the last inch or so when Buller knocked on the study door and held it open for her.

The professor was stuffing papers into his bag. He

looked up as she went in and, if he noticed the hair, he made no comment.

'Miss Smith, I have to return to the hospital, and I am not sure when I shall get back. There may not be time to discuss anything at our leisure before we leave. You will need money for household expenses—it is in this envelope, together with the telephone numbers you might need in an emergency. You will not hesitate to get in touch with me should you judge it necessary, or if you need more money. Does the agency pay you?'

'Yes, when I've finished the job.'

'You have enough money for yourself?'

She had very little, but she wasn't going to say so. 'Quite enough, thank you, Professor Lister.' She had spoken quickly and he gazed at her sharply. He didn't say anything, though, only nodded and gave her the envelope. 'I'll keep an account of what I spend,' she assured him.

'If you wish to do so.' He sounded uninterested. 'I'll see you in the morning. Breakfast at eight o'clock.' He went to open the door for her and, as she went past, he said softly, 'I like the hair. Why do you bundle it up out of sight?'

Araminta was annoyed to find herself blushing. 'It gets in the way,' she said and added, for no reason at all, 'I was going to wash it.'

She slid past him and away across the hall and up the staircase; halfway up she remembered that she hadn't wished him goodnight.

By some miracle Araminta managed to get the children and the animals ready and down to breakfast by eight o'clock. There was no sign of their uncle, and Jimmy was quick to point out that she need not have

chivvied them into such haste, but he had scarcely finished his grumbling when Professor Lister came in. He
was wearing casual clothes and greeted them in his usual
manner, but he looked tired, and Araminta wondered if
he had been up half the night. She had the good sense
not to ask, though, but ate her breakfast, saw to it that
Jimmy and Gloria ate theirs, and then excused the three
of them so that the animals could have last-minute attention. Obedient to his wish, she presented her small party
at nine o'clock precisely in the hall. The cases had already
been brought down and Buller had put them in the boot.
Goldie and Neptune were there too, and the professor
began to load the Rolls with its passengers.

'You will sit in front with me, Miss Smith,' he observed. 'If you will have Tibs and his basket on your
knee, Mutt can sit on Jimmy, and Goldie and Neptune
can sit on the floor.'

If they felt rebellious the children didn't say so, but got
into the car and settled down with room to spare, leaving
Araminta to settle herself in the comfort of the front seat.

Beyond enquiring as to everyone's comfort, the professor had little to say, and Araminta, guessing that he was
tired, kept silent. The children sounded happy enough
and the animals were giving no trouble; she sat back and
allowed her thoughts to wander.

They didn't wander far. She was very conscious of the
professor's vast silent bulk beside her; if he had a private
life—friends, girlfriends, a woman he loved—there had
been no sign of them during the week; as far as she had
seen, his days were wholly occupied by his work. He must
have a private life, she thought. I dare say he's tucked
it out of sight while we've been living in his house. She
began to think about the kind of woman he might love.

Beautiful, of course, exquisitely dressed, amusing and witty, knowing just how to soothe him when he got home from a busy day at the hospital...

She looked out of her window and saw that they were well away from London; the A303 wasn't far off. He wasn't wasting time.

She turned to see if everything was as it should be on the back seat and, since it was, settled back again.

'Comfortable?' asked the professor.

'Yes, thank you. Have you been up all night?'

He laughed a little. 'Am I driving so badly? Not all night; I got home just after two o'clock.'

'You would have time for a nap before you have to return.'

'I'm flattered by your concern, Miss Smith, but I am quite rested.'

Snubbed, thought Araminta, and looked out of the window again.

Halfway down the A303 he stopped at a Happy Eater, and everyone piled out except Tibs, asleep in her basket. The dogs on their leads were walked by Jimmy and his uncle while Araminta and Gloria went inside, in a hurry to get to the ladies', and then to find a table. They were joined shortly by Jimmy and the professor, who ordered coffee for all of them and a plate of buns. The coffee was hot and the children wolfed the buns as though they were starving, but no one wasted time in casual talk. In ten minutes they were back in the car and on their way. Tisbury wasn't far; Professor Lister took a left-hand turning into a side road and they were at once surrounded by rural Wiltshire. There was only one village on their way, Chilmark, then they were back running between high hedges and scattered farms. Araminta gave an appreciative sniff and the professor observed, 'Restful, isn't it? When we arrive I shall leave you to open up the house, make the beds and so on. I'll take the children into the village— you'll need bread and milk and so on, won't you?'

'Yes, do you want a list? I can take a quick look in the fridge and the freezer.'

'That would help. Do you feel up to cooking a meal?'

'Yes, of course.'

They lapsed into silence, but this time it seemed to her that the silence was friendly.

The children were glad to be home. They rushed inside as soon as the professor had unlocked the door and then, at his placid request, carried the bags indoors and upstairs. That done, he said, 'If you'll see to Tibs, Gloria, Jimmy can see to the dogs while Miss Smith and I make a list of the food we'll need. We'll go down to the village and do the shopping while she gets the place aired.'

Whatever made me think that he was absent-minded? reflected Araminta, busily writing a list of the food to be bought.

Once they were out of the house, leaving her with Tibs for company, she set about opening the windows, looking into the cupboards and peering into drawers. The linen-cupboard was nicely filled; she took the bedlinen off the beds and filled the washing-machine. The beds could be made up later. She laid the table for lunch, peeled the potatoes she found in the garden shed, and nipped round with a duster—not ideal, but all she had time for.

They came back laden. 'Sausages,' said the professor, emptying plastic bags all over the table, 'spring greens, carrots and turnips. Apples, oranges and lettuces. Jimmy has the rest and Gloria went to the baker's. We'll go into the garden while you get the lunch—do you want a hand?'

'No, thanks.' She glanced at the clock. 'Half an hour?'

All the same he stowed away the butter, milk and cheese before he went into the garden, the dogs trailing after him.

Araminta was a good cook: the sausages, grilled to a golden brown, lay on a mound of creamed potatoes, she had glazed the carrots with sugar and butter, and the spring greens, chopped fine, added a note of colour. Everything was eaten, as were the cheese and biscuits which followed. A pot of coffee washed everything down nicely and the professor sat back with a sigh.

'A delicious meal, Miss Smith,' he observed. 'We'll wash up while you do whatever you want to do. Gloria, don't forget to feed that cat of yours, and what about the dogs?'

Araminta left them to it, and sped upstairs to make beds, put out towels and tidy the rooms. There would be several loads of washing, but she could iron all day, if necessary, when the children had gone back to school.

When she got back to the kitchen everything had been tidily put away and she found the three of them in the hall by the open door.

'There you are,' said Professor Lister. 'I'm going back now—I'll phone you this evening and, if you need help or advice, don't hesitate to ring me. I'll do my best to come down.'

He nodded to her, said goodbye to Jimmy and Gloria, got into his car with the dogs and drove away. The three of them stood watching the car disappearing down the drive and into the lane, and even when it was out of sight they still stood there.

It was Araminta who said briskly, 'I expect you've heaps of things you want to do, but first will you let me have all your washing? I dare say there are some things you'll need for school on Monday.'

'Patty usually...' began Gloria, and thought better of it. 'All right, but then I want to go and see Jean down at the Rectory.'

'Why not?' agreed Araminta cheerfully. 'But please both be here for tea. Half-past four. We can discuss supper then.'

She was surprised that they didn't demur, but fetched their washing, put Mutt on his lead, and went off together—which gave her time to check the cupboards again, pick some flowers from the garden and unpack her own things; all the while, Professor Lister was never far from her thoughts.

Chapter 3

Araminta went to bed that night thankful that the day had gone so well. The children had returned for their tea and afterwards had helped her wash up, albeit grudgingly. They were still unfriendly but at least they did what she asked them to do with only a modicum of grumbling. The professor had telephoned as he had promised, a brief conversation undertaken against a background of voices—women's voices as well as men's. Probably he was relaxing with his friends; she pictured him in his lovely house, entertaining them. A mistake, of course. He was in Theatre Sister's office, drinking coffee after operating…

At breakfast the next morning Jimmy said reluctantly, 'Uncle Jason said we were to take you to church with us.'

'Why, thank you, Jimmy, I shall be glad to go. The morning service?'

'Yes—who's going to cook our dinner?'

'I shall. It can cook in the oven while we are away. What do you do with Mutt?'

'Shut him in the house; he doesn't mind as long as Tibs is there too.'

So they went to church, and when they got back the steak and kidney pie she had made from the contents of the freezer the night before was nicely cooked. She left it warm in the oven while the potatoes and the greens cooked. They had brought a carton of ice-cream back with them on the previous day; she scooped it out into three dishes, embellished it with some chocolate sauce she had found, and put it back in the freezer. Everything was ready by the time the children had fed Mutt and Tibs.

They both ate everything she put before them, although they didn't say if they liked it, and once they had finished they told her that they were going over to a friend's house. 'We'll probably stay for tea,' said Gloria airily.

'Why not? But please tell me where you are going, in case I should want you rather urgently.' And at their blank stares she added gently, 'Your mother might telephone, or your uncle, and do give me a ring if you're staying for tea, will you? Do you want to take Mutt?'

'Of course, and I wish you wouldn't make a fuss,' said Jimmy rudely.

'Well, of course I could wash my hands of the pair of you,' observed Araminta cheerfully, 'but your uncle asked me to be here until someone gets back and I said that I would. We'll all have to make the best of it, won't we?' She began to gather up the plates. 'Write it on the pad over there, will you, and please put the phone number. Tea at half-past four, if you decide to come home.'

She was prepared for them to ignore her request, and it was an agreeable surprise when Gloria phoned to say that they *were* staying for tea and would be home in time for supper. It gave her a chance to sit down for a bit with a pot of tea and a plate of scones while she jotted down menus for the week ahead.

It was while she was getting the supper that she realised that there was a problem she hadn't thought of—Mrs Gault had driven the children to their schools each day and either she or Patty had fetched them back. There was a car in the garage but that wouldn't be of much use since she couldn't drive. There would be a school bus, of course, but probably that served the comprehensive school and the other state schools in Salisbury. Gloria was at a private girls' school a few miles from Tisbury, and Jimmy at a minor public school lying in the other direction. Not far in a car, but they could be at the North Pole if there was no transport. She sat and wrestled with the problem for some time, and reluctantly decided to wait until the children came back to see if between them they could think of a way out of their dilemma.

Hire a car? she wondered. But would Professor Lister agree to that? Perhaps she could phone him and ask his advice.

She had no need to do so, for he phoned within the next half-hour.

Her, 'Hello,' was breathless with relief.

He said at once, 'Problems? You sound quietly desperate.'

'I am.' She explained with commendable brevity.

'I should have thought of that. Leave it with me. My sister has several friends in the village. I believe the doctor's sons go to Jimmy's school—he can give him a lift and drop Gloria off on his way. I'm sure that he will help. I'll ring you back, so don't worry.' He rang off with a quick goodbye and she went back to her cooking. It was all very well to tell her not to worry, but she wouldn't feel easy until he phoned again.

Which he did, shortly before the children came home. 'Mrs Sloane—Dr Sloane's wife—will collect Jimmy and Gloria at eight o'clock and bring them back after school.'

Araminta thanked him. 'I'm sorry I had to bother you.'

He said coolly, 'It was merely a question of picking up the telephone, Miss Smith.' His goodbye sounded like an afterthought.

As they sat down to supper presently, Jimmy said, 'We shan't be able to go to school—Mother always took us in the car—or Patty. I don't suppose you can drive a car.'

'No, I can't. Mrs Sloane is calling for you both each day and will give you a lift back in the afternoon. Your uncle has arranged it.' She smiled at him. 'Eight o'clock at the gate, so we'd better have everything ready before you go to bed. Do you take anything with you? Lunch or a snack?'

Gloria said prissily, 'We don't go to state schools, Araminta.'

A remark Araminta let pass. 'What about Mutt and Tibs? Will you let me know if they have to be fed and when—and does Mutt go for a walk during the day?'

'If you take him on his lead, and he has a biscuit at lunchtime.'

'Tibs has a meal then too,' said Gloria. 'Of course, you don't belong here so she might run away—then it'll be your fault.'

Araminta reminded herself silently that this was a job and she was being paid for it. She said equably, 'Oh, I like cats, but if you don't like to leave her in my care perhaps we could find a good cattery where she would be safe.'

Jimmy frowned at his sister. 'Tibs will be OK—you're being a bit silly.'

'And rude,' added Araminta mildly.

They weren't an easy pair to handle; they loitered over their breakfast, had a last-minute hunt for school-books, and their rooms, when she went upstairs to make the beds, were in a state of chaos. 'Patty must be an angel,' observed Araminta to Tibs, who was comfortably snoozing on Gloria's bed. At least she had the house to herself while she vacuumed and dusted, hung the washing on the line at the bottom of the garden and gave the kitchen a good clean. Jimmy had said something about a Mrs Pretty, who came twice a week, but perhaps Mrs Gault had told her not to come while she was away. Araminta, armed with a shopping-basket and the household purse and with Mutt on his lead, took herself off to the village to buy lettuce, cucumber and tomatoes. The children wanted baked beans for their supper; she intended to add bubble-and-squeak and a small salad. As for their demands for Coca-Cola, she had different ideas. Without conceit she knew that her home-made lemonade was perfection itself. She added lemons to her basket at the village stores and replied suitably to the proprietor's questions. Mr Moody was stout and bald and good-natured, and he liked a chat.

'A bit of a carry-on up at Mrs Gault's, eh? Poor lady, and then that Patty going off at a moment's notice—not that she could help that, poor soul.' He eyed Araminta. 'You're a young woman with your hands full, I've no doubt. Need their dad, do Jimmy and Gloria. Not but what Professor Lister don't do his best, and him a busy man. Coming down this weekend, no doubt?'

'I don't know; I expect that will depend on whether he can get away or not.'

Araminta smiled and Mr Moody decided that, plain though she might be, she had a lovely smile.

'Well, just you let me know if there is aught I can do,' he told her, 'and that'll be two pounds and sixty-three pence.' He handed over the change. 'Half a mo'—that Mutt usually has a bit of biscuit...'

'There's a Mrs Pretty,' began Araminta, 'but the children weren't sure if Mrs Gault had told her she would be away.'

'Bless your heart, love, Mrs Gault didn't need to tell her. Everyone knows everyone else's business here. She was in the shop this morning early, and mentioned that she'd be going up as usual.'

'Oh, good. When is that?'

'Tomorrow and Friday mornings—half-past eight till noon. Does the rough.'

'Oh, good,' said Araminta again, and wished him a cheerful good day.

There was plenty to do when she got back: more washing to hang out, ironing to do, a meal to get for herself and then tea to lay, ready for the children's return. She made a cake and some scones, and boiled the potatoes ready for the bubble-and-squeak and, after her own lunch, set about making the lemonade. It was an old recipe, involving the steeping of the lemons in boiling water and the sieving of the fruit and the careful adding of sugar and finally, when it was nicely cool, a few sprigs of mint.

The children came racing into the house, calling for

Tibs and Mutt, flinging down hat and cap and coats and demanding tea.

Araminta had come into the hall to meet them. She said in a firm voice, 'The kettle is boiling, and tea will be put on the table when you have picked your things off the floor and hung them up, changed your shoes and washed your hands.'

They stared at her. 'Patty always…' began Gloria, and thought better of it. She began to gather up her coat and hat, and after a moment Jimmy did the same. Under Araminta's eye they changed their shoes and washed their hands in the cloakroom and then went sulkily into the kitchen.

Araminta had taken pains with the tea; there were scones, split and buttered, strawberry jam, Marmite sandwiches and a fruitcake.

'You didn't make these, did you?' asked Jimmy, sitting down at the table.

'Yes. Now tell me, at what time do you have supper? After your homework and before bed?'

'We have supper when we feel like it,' Gloria said.

'Ah, I see—you get your own? That's all right, then.'

'Hold on,' said Jimmy, 'we can't cook—don't be stupid, Gloria.'

Araminta allowed them to bicker for a few minutes. Then she said, 'Homework after tea, then supper. That gives you time to do whatever you want before bed.'

'You're a tyrant—no, a martinet,' declared Gloria. 'We always do what we want.'

'So do I,' said Araminta calmly. 'Have another slice of cake?'

Much later that evening, when the professor phoned,

she told him everything was fine. 'Jimmy and Gloria will be sorry to have missed you...'

'It's late—I'm sorry. I'll ring earlier tomorrow.'

'You have no news?' asked Araminta.

'None. I think you must be prepared to remain for at least ten days. Do you wish me to contact your father?'

'Thank you, but there is no need. I told Alice I'd be away for a week or longer.'

He rang off then, after bidding her a civil goodnight.

Life settled down into a rather uneasy pattern; the children were no friendlier, but at least they did what she asked of them; she suspected that the telephone conversations with their uncle each evening had something to do with that. He was punctilious in his daily phone call but it was brief, and her report was just as brief. Sometimes, she reflected wistfully, he sounded as unfriendly as his young relations.

There was Mrs Pretty to brighten things two days a week, a lady whose appearance had nothing to do with her name; she was a big bony woman, nudging sixty, with a craggy face and a disconcerting squint. She had a powerful voice, smoked like a chimney, and had an elaborate hair-do which was tinted an unsuitable chestnut with highlights. She had marched up to the house on Tuesday morning, announced who she was, declared that Araminta didn't look fit to cope with the Gault youngsters and said that she intended to turn out the kitchen, but not before she had had her usual cup of tea. 'And I like it strong,' she had added.

She was a treasure, going through the house like a whirlwind, cigarette dangling from her lip and, over the snack lunch she shared with Araminta, making her familiar with those who lived in the village. 'Not a bad lot,' she concluded, 'and Mrs Gault's well-liked, though them kids of hers need a firm hand. A good thing when their dad's back again. That Patty's a good sort, but she spoils them rotten. A pity that uncle of theirs can't have 'em for a while—nice gent—bit absent-minded, likes to bury his 'andsome 'ead in a book, don't seem to notice the girls much—'as a way with 'im, though. Like him, do you, my lovely?'

Araminta blinked. No one had ever called her 'my lovely' before; she found it delightful. 'Yes, I like him,' she agreed, 'although, of course, I don't know him at all well. The children are very fond of him.'

'Let's hope 'e gets down here a bit then, and knocks some manners into the pair of them. Need to go away to school they do—well, Jimmy will be boarding next term, going to some posh place.' Mrs Pretty swallowed the rest of her tea and took herself off to clean the bathroom the children used. 'It needs a fair walloping,' she shouted over a massive shoulder as she left the kitchen.

Well-primed on her second visit, Araminta had a pot of tea, strong enough to knock out an elephant, ready on the kitchen table. Mrs Pretty drank the pot dry, recommended that Araminta should get on with the ironing while she gave the drawing-room the once-over, and took herself off until it was time for elevenses.

'Coming for the weekend, is 'e?' she asked, and bit into one of Araminta's cakes. 'Nice little cook you be.'

'I don't know; he hasn't said so—he is a very busy man.'

Mrs Pretty shrugged. 'Doctors—well, he's a surgeon, isn't he? Don't hold with them meself. Old miseries, telling me that a cig's bad for me. Smoked all me life I 'ave, and look at me.'

Araminta hoped that she was looking at the right eye;
it was difficult with the squint. 'I'm sure you're awfully
fit,' she agreed politely, 'but I don't think smoking does
much good…'

Mrs Pretty laughed; she had a loud, cheerful laugh.
'Me old granny always said, "A little of what you fancy
does you good", and I fancy a cig off and on. Got a young
man, have you, love?'

'No. I'm not pretty,' said Araminta, baldly and without self-pity.

'What's that got to do with it? Look at me, I'm no
beauty.' Mrs Pretty let out another laugh. ''Ad two
'usbands. Beauty's but skin-deep, ducks, and don't you
forget it.'

Which was all very well, reflected Araminta, but it
hardly weighed against a pretty face.

It was Saturday and there had been no word from
Mrs Gault or Patty. Araminta did her best to reassure
Jimmy and Gloria, and wished that their uncle would at
least telephone, something he hadn't done for the past
two days. She had written home and warned her father
that she might not be home for some days yet, but she
had had no reply and she didn't want to phone because
Alice would try to persuade her to return, something she
didn't intend to do until she was no longer needed. It was
a blessing that Gloria and Jimmy were asked out to tea
in the village on Saturday; it helped the day along. She
had suggested that they might like to show her something
of the countryside around the village, but the idea had
fallen flat and, since they so obviously didn't wish for
her company, she busied herself around the house and

about the garden. She hoped that they had plans of their own for Sunday, but she was too wise to ask.

It was a pity that they held her in such dislike, but she could understand that—in their eyes she wasn't much older than they were, besides being small and insignificant. Their comfortable world had been turned topsy-turvy, and they needed to take it out on somebody...

The professor hadn't phoned; she realised that she had been counting on his coming at the weekend. It would be nice to be given an idea of how much longer she was to stay at Tisbury. Not that she wasn't content; the village was delightful, its few shops surprisingly up-market, the people friendly, but she was uneasy about Alice and her father. Since her mother's death she had automatically taken over the housekeeping, managed the finances of their day-to-day living and looked after Alice. Even when she had worked for the agency she had taken jobs which had allowed her to go home each evening.

An afternoon in the garden did much to restore her to her usual sensible self, and after supper Jimmy and Gloria went up to their rooms with their record-players and then to the sitting-room to watch television, and very much to her surprise made no demur when she went along presently and suggested that they went to bed.

She got up early the next morning; she supposed that they would go to church, and if they were to eat the shoulder of lamb for their lunch she would have to have it ready to put into the oven before they went. It was a bright morning and Tibs wandered off into the garden, following Mutt. She filled their saucers and left the door open for them to come back in and went to put on the kettle. A cup of tea would be a good start to her day...

She had laid the table ready for breakfast the night before; now she got out bacon, mushrooms and eggs and put the bread ready for the toaster.

Neither of the children was a quick dresser and she would have to look sharp if they were to get off to church. She made a pot of tea, donned an apron over her dressing-gown, rolled up her sleeves, and began to peel the potatoes.

She didn't turn round from the sink when she heard Mutt's claws on the ceramic tiles. 'Your breakfast is in your saucer,' she told him, 'and is Tibs with you?'

She put her knife down and took a drink from the cup of tea beside her and turned round. Professor Lister was leaning against the door-jamb, Tibs under one arm. He had had plenty of time to study her—hair hanging in a long shining curtain, the useful dressing-gown which did nothing for her tied round her small waist, the cuffs turned back...

He said, pleasantly impersonal, 'Good morning, Miss Smith. Forgive me for arriving at such an awkward hour. It was a last-minute decision to come...'

She wiped her hands and fetched another mug. 'Good morning, Professor Lister. The children are going to be delighted. Have a mug of tea—would you like something to eat? I can easily...'

'I'll share your breakfast, if I may, but tea would be delightful. Don't stop whatever you are doing. I'm sure that you have your hands full. Is everything all right?'

'Yes, thank you. If we are going to church, I need to get lunch ready to put in the oven before we go...'

He drank his tea and refilled their mugs. 'You have too much to do?' he wanted to know. 'Does Mrs Pretty not come?'

'Oh, yes—she's marvellous, and I'm not in the least

overworked.' She tossed her hair over her shoulder and picked up another potato. 'You'll be here for lunch?'

'Certainly, and tea and supper if I may. I have had news from my sister—she phoned a few hours ago. The children will want to hear what she said.'

She put the potatoes into a saucepan and attacked a spring cabbage. 'Would you like me to call them now? They're not very quick at getting dressed.'

'Perhaps if I were to go up to their rooms and talk to them? That will give you a chance to get dressed...' His eyes swept over her person.

She suddenly went very red, and he wished he hadn't said that. He hadn't taken much notice of her, for the simple reason that there wasn't much to notice; now he hastened to make amends. 'I'll hurry them up a bit, shall I? If they are down before you are, they can make the toast and the tea.' He stood towering over her, smiling kindly, and a surge of rage swept through her.

What did he expect at seven o'clock in the morning? How dared he look at her like that, as though she were an object of pity? She said frostily, 'That seems a good idea, Professor.' She put the mugs tidily in the sink and went away without looking at him.

As she showered and dressed she could hear the children's excited voices from the other side of the landing and the rumble of their uncle's laughter. The news must be good, which meant that soon she would go home again. 'And a good thing too,' she told her reflection, as she pinned up her hair into a ruthless bun.

There was no one in the kitchen when she went downstairs; she put an apron on over her skirt and blouse and began to fry bacon.

They all came in together and Gloria said at once,

'You'll be able to go home soon, Araminta, our mother's coming home.'

'That's splendid news, and what a lovely surprise for you. Your father's better?'

She began to dish up eggs and mushrooms and bacon, and the professor came to take the plates from her. He switched on the toaster too, and told Gloria to pour the tea. 'My brother-in-law isn't well enough to come home yet, but he is making a good recovery and my sister feels able to return. He'll be flown back within the next week or so. Now it is just a question of Patty's return.'

'When Mother's back we shan't need Araminta,' said Jimmy.

The professor lifted his eyebrows. 'I think it very likely that your mother will be only too glad to have such a splendid helper. I do not dare to think how we would have managed without her help.'

Araminta, pecking at her bacon, didn't look up.

The talk was all of their mother's return and the prospect of seeing their father again, but breakfast was finished at last and the professor got up. 'Jimmy, take the plates over to the sink, will you? Gloria, put away the butter and the marmalade in the dresser. There are fifteen minutes before we need leave for church. Be ready in the hall, the pair of you, and see to Mutt and Tibs before we go, won't you?'

'Why didn't you bring Goldie and Neptune with you?' asked Gloria.

'I left home very early this morning. Buller will take them for a walk and I'll be home again this evening.'

He turned to Araminta. 'I'll wash the dishes if you want to get ready for church, Miss Smith.'

'Since you are here, do you mind if I stay at home? I'd be glad of an hour or two.'

'I upset you, didn't I? I'm sorry. You must be anxious to return to your own home, and I dare say the children have been difficult.'

She looked up at him. 'No, not at all. They have been very good, and I've been happy here.' She added tartly, 'I don't upset easily, Professor Lister.'

He said indifferently, 'Which, considering the work you do, must be a great advantage to you.'

With the place to herself she got the house tidied, made her own bed and, since neither Gloria nor Jimmy had done more than toss their duvets over the rumpled sheets, made theirs too, and then sped back to the kitchen to lay a tray for coffee before starting to prepare the lunch. She was usually a cheerful girl, but her thoughts were gloomy, and most of them centred on the professor. It was absurd that she should expect him to be more friendly; she was, after all, someone he had hired to do a job. He was invariably kind in an impersonal way, careful to treat her with courtesy, but all the same she was just Miss Smith to him, and that morning he had looked at her standing there in that old dressing-gown with her hair all over the place... She winced at what he must have thought. Anyway, she reminded herself, Mrs Gault would be home very soon now and that would be the end of it. The children would be glad to see her go— She heard them coming into the house and put the milk on to boil.

'Uncle Jason's gone back to the Manor for drinks and coffee—he'll be here for lunch.' They threw their outdoor things down. 'Isn't coffee ready?'

'It will be by the time you've hung up your things.' It was no good being sharp with them, they had had too many years of spoiling, but at least they did as she asked, albeit grudgingly.

'We're going out after lunch—Uncle's going to take us to Bulbarrow for tea.'

Araminta poured the coffee and fetched the tin of biscuits. 'Isn't that a hill somewhere near Sturminster Newton?'

They looked surprised. 'Have you been there?'

'No, but there's an article about it in a magazine in the sitting-room. You'll be able to take Mutt.'

They went off to their rooms presently and she got on with her cooking; presumably the professor would want his lunch when he got back. She laid the table, wondering if she should use the dining-room. She and the children had had all their meals in the kitchen and there didn't seem much point in using another room. She was hesitating about getting out the good china when he came wandering in.

'We've been eating in the kitchen—not just break-fast, but all the time. I expect you'd rather have lunch in the dining-room?'

'No, no. I find the kitchen very pleasant. Is lunch ready? We're going to Bulbarrow this afternoon, no great distance, but the children are bound to want their tea there. There's a nice little place—Dorset cream teas and so on.'

'I'll dish up while you have a drink, Professor.'

'We'll both have a drink. Lady Scobell at the Manor is charming, but I swear she gave us all cooking sherry.'

He went away and returned a few minutes later with two glasses of sherry. 'Something smells delicious,' he observed, and added, 'You'll come with us, of course.'

'I think not, Professor. The children are fond of you and want you to themselves.'

'Oh, I'm not sure about that.' He glanced at her. 'But if you prefer to stay here, please do. Have a quiet few hours free with a book.'

She assured him happily that she would do just that; she would also get the supper ready, do the last of the ironing and write home. She longed to go with him, but her enjoyment would be spoilt since the children would resent her being with them. It would spoil the afternoon for everyone.

Sherry had sent a little spurt of pleasure through her, so that she reminded herself not to wallow in self-pity. On a wave of sherry-induced cheerfulness she dished up and called the children to the table.

She was a good cook: the shoulder of lamb was just right, the roast potatoes were crisp on the outside and meltingly floury inside, and there were baby carrots and creamed spinach. She watched the professor carve and said apologetically, 'I'm sorry it's lamb again, but I didn't know that you were coming and Jimmy and Gloria like it best.'

'And so do I. You will make some lucky man a good wife, Miss Smith.'

He didn't see the children look down at their plates to hide their smiles, but Araminta did. She said airily, 'Yes, I shall enjoy being married and having a home of my own.'

She had the satisfaction of seeing their surprise. The professor looked surprised too, and rather thoughtful.

The professor insisted that everyone should help clear away the dishes and help with the washing-up before they left the house, and only when the last plate had been put away did he go out to the car.

'We should be back some time after five o'clock,' he told Araminta. 'Could we have supper around half-past seven? I'd like to leave at nine o'clock.'

He nodded a cheerful goodbye and she watched the car skim down the drive and into the lane, then she went back into the house and, since she had no wish to sit and think, got out her pastry board and made a batch of sausage rolls. She made a custard tart too, for afters. None of that took very long and the afternoon stretched emptily before her. The ironing could wait, she decided; she would find a book and get a jacket and sit in the garden for a while. It was a pleasant afternoon, still cool, but the sun shone and there were sheltered nooks where she could sit.

Tibs joined her, sitting beside her on the bench, and presently she closed her eyes and her book and allowed her thoughts to roam, and since there was no one to whom she could talk she talked to Tibs.

'This job has unsettled me,' she reflected. 'I dare say it's partly the children—naturally they don't like me, I'm all part and parcel of the upheaval, aren't I? And, to be honest, I do not like these jobs. I would like to do something worthwhile and be very good at it so that people said, "There's that clever Miss Smith," and I'd have enough money to buy lovely clothes...' She thought for a bit. 'And a different face!'

Tibs gave her a thoughtful glance and returned to her toilette; as far as she was concerned, her manner implied, Araminta could be cross-eyed and ten feet tall; she was the one who remembered to fill her saucer at the right times.

They both went indoors presently, to their respective teas, and shortly afterwards the others came back. Araminta, waging her usual obstinate battle over the hanging of garments on the hooks provided, hoped politely that they had enjoyed their afternoon, and was surprised to be answered just as politely, unaware that their uncle had expressed his displeasure at their casual treatment of her, and when they followed her into the kitchen and offered to help, she decided that the day hadn't been so bad after all.

He came into the house then, and they had their supper, and when the meal was over, obedient to their uncle's wish, they went upstairs to their rooms to play their loud music and watch the television.

As the first raucous notes floated down the stairs, Professor Lister asked, 'How can you bear it?'

'Well, actually, I can't, but it is their house, isn't it? And it's only for an hour or so in the evenings.'

'You enjoyed your few hours of peace?' He had sat down at the table. 'Please come and sit down, there are one or two matters...'

She sat. 'I've kept an account of the money I've spent,' she began.

'Yes, yes, don't bother with that. You'll need some more money—remind me before I go.' He stared at her across the table and she looked back at him enquiringly.

'Do you dislike me, Miss Smith?'

'Good heavens, no,' said Araminta. 'In fact I quite like you. Not that I know you, if you see what I mean. But that doesn't really matter, does it? I mean, we aren't likely to meet again once Mrs Gault comes home.'

He didn't answer that. 'You said that you were looking forward to getting married. Was that true?'

She looked at him in surprise, going rather red. 'No.'

'I am relieved to hear it. Have you no ambitions? Do you not wish to be a career girl?'

'Me?' She smiled. 'I don't look like one, do I? They are tall and thin, and wear those severe suits with very short skirts.'

He observed blandly, 'You have very nice legs, Miss Smith.' His eyes were on her face. Why, she wondered, had she ever thought that he was absent-minded? He was staring at her like a hawk. 'So your future is an open book...'

'Well, yes, until the next job turns up.' On an impulse she asked, 'Why do you call me Miss Smith? No one else ever does.'

He smiled then. 'It suits you!' He glanced at his watch. 'I should be going.' He fished in his pocket, took out his notecase and handed her some notes. 'That should keep you going for a few more days. Let me know how things are when I phone. I had better say goodbye to the children.'

The three of them watched him drive away, and Araminta, remembering their conversation, tried to make head or tail of it and couldn't.

Chapter 4

Later, in bed that night, Araminta thought about the professor. He had asked her some strange questions. Whatever difference did it make to him whether she liked him or not? And why should he be relieved to hear that she wasn't going to get married? Had he another job in mind for her and, if so, why hadn't he said so? He was really rather nice; indeed, if she allowed herself to do so, she could easily wish to see more of him, which was absurd, for they had very little to say to each other during their infrequent meetings. She knew nothing about him. For all she knew, he might be engaged...

He wasn't a young man...

She went to sleep at last and dreamed about him.

The professor didn't dream of her, but he found himself thinking about her as he drove back to his home. He knew considerably more about her than she did about him, and for some reason he found it difficult to dismiss her image from his mind. Perhaps because she was so unlike any of the women of his acquaintance. She had made no attempt to engage his attention; the reverse, in fact. He had found himself disappointed when she had refused to go with him and the children to Bulbarrow. She was refreshingly undemanding and he no longer found her plain. How pleasant, he considered, to be able to read and study in his library without the fear of phone calls begging him to dine or escort any of his women acquaintances, wasting hours of precious leisure listening to female chatter; a happy state which could be achieved if he were to marry a girl as undemanding as Araminta. He laughed aloud then, and dismissed the absurd idea.

There was little traffic; he was home soon after eleven o'clock, to be greeted by Buller with sandwiches and coffee and the dogs. He went straight into the garden with them, and then went to his study to sit back in his chair with a glass of whisky in his hand and the dogs at his feet—an hour of peaceful reading a pleasant prospect.

He had barely turned a page when the phone rang and he put his book down resignedly. At that hour it would be the hospital...

It wasn't the hospital. 'Jason,' screamed a voice, 'I've been phoning the whole evening. I'm at the Redvers'— it's her birthday, and you simply must come along. I suppose you've got your head in a book? Darling, you simply must come. It's ages since I've seen you.'

The professor frowned. 'I'm just home after a very long day, Vicky. And I've a very busy day tomorrow.'

'Oh, Jason, you are a staid old stick. You might just as well be married for all the fun you are!'

'Sorry, Vicky. There must be any number of young men falling over themselves to get at you.'

'Well, yes, there are. I'll leave you to your bed and book—there is a book there, I'll swear?'

He laughed. 'Yes. I dare say I'll see you some time.'

'Good. Marjorie had lunch with me the other day. She would love us to get married, you know.'

'Yes. I do know.'

It was a moment or two before she said, 'Oh, well, goodnight, Jason.'

'Goodnight, Vicky.' He put down the receiver with relief. Vicky was a dear girl, he had known her for years, since she had gone to the same school as his sister Marjorie and spent several holidays at his home, and later he had met her again from time to time. It had never entered his head to marry her; she was pretty and empty-headed and worked part-time in a boutique, and from time to time she phoned him, demanding to be taken to the theatre or out to dinner.

He picked up his book again, reflecting that if he were married... That nonsensical idea he had had driving up from Tisbury wasn't as silly as it seemed.

He didn't get back from the hospital until the early evening on the next day, intent on taking the dogs for a run in the park, but first he would have to phone Araminta. No need for a long talk, he told himself, just a routine enquiry as to the day, which was why he sounded impatient to Araminta when she picked up the phone.

It had been a typical Monday for her: several loads of washing, the ironing, shopping, Mutt to take for a walk, a meal to cook and the children, now that their mother was coming home, more boisterous than usual. Her 'hello' was decidedly snappy.

'Everything is all right?' he wanted to know.

She looked at the basket overflowing with school shirts and blouses, sports kit, sheets and pillowcases, endless towels… She said frostily. 'Yes, thank you.'

'Children behaving?'

'Yes, thank you. They are doing their homework.'

'Good. Goodbye, Miss Smith.'

He spent an hour in the park, dismissing from his mind the idea that Miss Smith had been decidedly cross. He went home presently and had his dinner, and then spent the evening by the fire, the dogs at his feet, reading the newspaper and dipping into Homer's *Iliad*, and presently going to his study to make notes for a lecture he was to give at the next seminar.

He spent the whole of the following morning in his consulting-rooms in Harley Street before going to the hospital for a ward round. He got home earlier than usual, to find Buller waiting for him in the hall.

'Mrs Gault telephoned, sir, not an hour ago. She's leaving in the morning and should be at Heathrow the day after tomorrow. She will ring again this evening.'

'Splendid, Buller. She isn't likely to ring for an hour or so, I should imagine. I'll take the dogs out straight away. If she should ring, ask her what time her plane gets in and say I'll meet it or arrange for her to be met.'

It was much later in the evening when Mrs Gault phoned again, which gave the professor time to adjust his appointments for Thursday as far as possible. Her flight would get in at six o'clock in the evening and, despite her eagerness to go home, she consented to spend the night at his house and be driven down early in the morning.

'But I shan't see the children—they'll be at school…'

'Suppose we drive down really early? In time for

breakfast? You can see them before they leave, spend the day unpacking and getting settled in, and be there when they get home at teatime.'

'Can you spare the time to take me home, Jason?'

'Yes, provided we leave here about half-past five. I must be back by one o'clock; I've several private patients to see.'

'You're an angel. Everything's all right, isn't it?' She sounded anxious.

'Perfectly, my dear.' He put down the phone and sat for a moment thinking. He could, of course, ring Araminta, but it was late evening by now; she might be in bed and asleep. If she wasn't, she might find it necessary to go around dusting and cleaning, anxious to have everything spick and span. He would have to explain about Patty and see what his sister wanted to do, and then he could leave everything to her. He went back to his medical journal with a sigh of relief.

Mrs Gault's plane was on time; he watched her hurrying through the crowds. She hadn't bothered with a trolley but lugged a case in each hand, and he went to meet her and take them from her.

'Jason.' She was bubbling over with excitement. 'Oh, it's marvellous to be home again—you've no idea—no proper loos and such strange food... Tom's fine, he's flying back next week.' She flung her arms round him and gave him a sisterly kiss. 'You're a darling to meet me. Has it been awful? The children, I mean, and no Patty. How have you managed?'

He had stowed her bags and urged her into the car before getting in beside her. 'I haven't—I found a treasure in Miss Smith, who's been looking after the children and running the house.'

'Oh, how clever of you. What's she like? I was too upset to notice.'

'Plain,' said the professor. 'Nicely plump, large dark eyes and a very direct manner.'

Mrs Gault stole a look at his profile and saw that he was smiling. She said mildly, 'She sounds just right. Do the children like her?'

'Not particularly. They resent her, you see—naturally enough—no Patty to let them do exactly as they like, so they treat her like a servant. Which doesn't appear to bother her in the least.'

'They can be tiresome,' said their fond mother. 'Teen-agers, you know.' She added, 'Well, I'm grateful to your treasure, but it will be nice when Patty can come back.'

'You can phone her this evening and see how she is. I'm sure Miss Smith will stay until Patty returns.' He stopped the car in front of his house. 'Mrs Buller has laid on a splendid dinner for us this evening—you're not too tired to enjoy it?'

'I'm tired, but I'm longing for something to eat. I was too excited on the plane.'

Presently, after the splendid dinner, they sat on either side of the fire in the drawing-room, Goldie and Nep-tune between them.

'Have you done anything interesting while I've been away?' asked Mrs Gault.

The professor said mildly, 'My dear Lydia, if by that you mean have I been out and about, wining and dining lady-friends and seeing the latest plays, then no, I have done nothing interesting. Vicky phoned and wanted me to go to some party or other, but I was only just back from Tisbury—oh, and Marjorie phoned, wanted to know when you would be back.'

Lydia said quickly, 'What an idiot I am. Of course, you've been going down to Tisbury as well as all the other things you do. You've not had a minute to yourself, have you? How's the hospital?'

'Bursting at the seams. I enjoyed keeping an eye on the children, my dear.' He glanced at his watch. 'If we're to leave early, I think you should go to bed.'

She yawned. 'I can't wait. What about you, Jason?'

'I'm going to the hospital. I shan't be long.' He walked with her to the stairs. 'Sleep well. It's splendid to have you home again and to know that Tom is well.'

She leaned up to kiss his cheek. 'I'm so grateful, Jason, and once I'm home I promise I'll leave you in peace. You can go back to your books and the dogs and your never-ending work. Are you never lonely?'

He smiled. 'I'm too busy.'

Which wasn't quite true, he reflected as he got into his car. He hadn't realised until just lately that he needed someone to talk to, someone who would listen. Someone, he had to admit, who would leave him in peace to read or to write during his hard-won leisure and not pester him to attend the various social functions he did his best to avoid.

'What you need,' his sister had said with sudden vigour, 'is a wife. You're fast becoming a crusty old bachelor.'

They left before it was light the next morning. It was a typical March day, with a fierce chilly wind and clouds scudding across a dark sky, but it was quite warm in the car and the dogs curled up and slept almost at once, leaving Lydia to talk excitedly as the professor drove through the almost empty streets and away from the city. Once away from it he drove steadily at the maximum speed; there was little traffic going west, and it was barely seven o'clock when he turned off the A303 and took the minor road to Tisbury.

There were lights shining from the village as he swept through its main street and presently turned off into the lane and in at his sister's gate. There were lights shining from the windows here too.

'I'd love a cup of tea,' said Mrs Gault in a shaky voice. 'I don't suppose they're up yet.'

'Perhaps not the children, but I imagine Miss Smith is going about her duties.'

As they got out of the car Lydia said, 'I hope she won't think that we're spying on her.'

He had turned away to let the dogs out. 'Most unlikely.'

'She has got another name, you know. You call her Miss Smith all the time?'

The professor took her arm. 'I think we had better knock...'

Araminta, trotting from room to room pulling back curtains and opening windows, went to open the door. The postman, she supposed, with something too large to go through the letter-box.

She flung the door wide. 'Mrs Gault—what a lovely surprise.' She smiled with delight. 'Won't the children...? You'd like a cup of tea while I get them up.' She rearranged her unassuming features into a polite and rather small smile. 'Good morning, Professor Lister. The kitchen's warm. I'll make the tea.'

The professor said deliberately, 'Good morning, Miss Smith. Tea would be delightful.' He took his sister's coat and tossed it on to a chair. It was barely half-past seven in the morning and Araminta looked as fresh as the proverbial daisy. No make-up, he noted, and her hair had been tied back with an elastic ribbon and, as far as he remembered, she was wearing the same sensible and dull clothes, and yet he had to admit she was pleasing to the eye.

Mrs Gault was sitting by the Aga weeping quietly. 'Don't mind me,' she told her brother, 'I'm so happy.'

'Of course you are,' he told her kindly. 'Shall you wait here until the children come down to breakfast?'

Mrs Gault looked at Araminta, who said in her matter-of-fact way, 'I'll call them about now—usually they have to be ready to leave by eight o'clock, but there's some kind of meeting for both schools today and they don't have to be there before half-past nine. Mrs Sloane takes them.'

The professor said easily, 'I'll drop them off as I go. Remind me to ring Mrs Sloane.'

Araminta said, 'Yes, Professor Lister,' and nipped upstairs to call the children; their mother could hear their indignant voices at being roused, followed by reassuring bumps and thumps as they got themselves out of their beds.

Araminta, already back in the kitchen, got out the frying-pan, bacon, eggs and mushrooms, and busied herself at the Aga, and when she would have collected plates and cutlery for Mrs Gault and the professor he got to his feet. 'I'll do that—do you want bread cut for toast?'

'Yes, please.' Araminta inspected her rashers and gave the mushrooms a prod, and Mrs Gault looked with astonishment at her brother, who, to the best of her knowledge, was the least domesticated of men.

'Perhaps you would fill the kettle,' said Araminta. 'The children will be down in a few minutes now.'

A sensible girl, reflected Lydia, no nonsense about her,

and she was making no effort to attract Jason's attention, although she was perfectly polite towards him. As for him—despite the coolness of his manner towards her, he was by no means indifferent… Interesting, thought Lydia, and turned a smiling face to the door as her children bounded in.

The meal was naturally enough a boisterous one, both children talking together and asking questions, wanting to know everything at once. If the professor noticed that they ignored Araminta almost entirely, he said nothing, and when Gloria said suddenly, 'I've torn my leotard, Araminta, and I have to have it for school,' and added, 'It's on my bed,' he watched Araminta slip away with a murmured excuse, unnoticed by the other three.

Presently Gloria, aware of his eyes upon her, looked across the table at him. He raised an eyebrow. 'Aren't you old enough to do your own sewing?' he mildly wanted to know, and she had the grace to blush.

'Araminta's here to look after us,' she muttered, 'she's paid…'

'Anyone who works gets paid,' observed her uncle blandly. 'I get paid too.'

Araminta came back presently, while they were sitting and talking at the table. 'Your leotard's on the bed,' she said, and began to clear the table. 'And will you both go and make your beds quickly? Your mother is tired and I've no doubt that she will want to rest today.'

'But you're here,' said Jimmy. 'You can do the beds…'

'Well, no. You see, now your mother is home there is no need for me to stay. I must get packed—I'd like to get an afternoon train.'

The children gaped at her. 'But you can't; Patty's not here.'

'I'm sure she'll be back very soon, and Mrs Pretty comes today.' Araminta looked at Mrs Gault. 'Everything's as you would like it, I hope. I'll do any shopping this morning, while Mrs Pretty is here. The arrangement was that I should stay until you returned.'

'Of course,' Mrs Gault agreed. 'I'm sure everything is in apple-pie order. I'll phone Patty and see when we can expect her back.' She smiled at Araminta. 'I am so grateful to you, especially as you've had to stay much longer than you had expected. Of course you can go this afternoon—you must be anxious to get home.'

The professor hadn't said a word, sitting in his chair listening. Now he spoke. 'Would you consider staying overnight, Miss Smith? That would be a great help to my sister. I'll come for you tomorrow morning—around nine o'clock, if that suits you?'

'That is very kind of you,' said Araminta 'but it's a long way to come just to fetch me, and there are plenty of trains.'

'Ah, but I need to see somebody at Odstock Hospital—the appointment is for eight o'clock, which gives me ample time to drive on here by nine.' He glanced at her. 'Not too early for you?'

'Me? No—no, of course not. Thank you very much, Professor Lister.'

'Oh, good,' said Mrs Gault. 'I must confess it will be nice to have you here until tomorrow.' She smiled at her brother. 'Thank you for bringing me home, Jason, and for taking such good care of everything while I was away—it was like a nightmare, you know.'

'Over now, my dear.' He stood up. 'If Jimmy and Gloria are ready, we'll be on our way. I'll see you both tomorrow.'

He collected the dogs, called to the children, kissed his sister's cheek, gave Araminta a brief nod and drove away.

Mrs Gault went upstairs to unpack while Araminta washed up and tidied the kitchen. Jason had been very carefully off-hand with Araminta and yet there was something...

'"Miss Smith", indeed!' She snorted. 'She's really rather sweet.'

Mrs Pretty came presently, delighted to be the first in the village to know that Mrs Gault was back, and lavish in her praise of Araminta's housekeeping. 'Proper little housewife she is, and looked after the kids too.'

She drank the strong tea and started on the kitchen, and Mrs Gault and Araminta took a tray of coffee into the sitting-room. 'I've kept accounts of what I've spent,' said Araminta, 'and the rest of the money Professor Lister gave me is in the dresser drawer.'

Mrs Gault wasn't interested in the household expenses. 'Tell me, my dear, were the children good at their uncle's? Poor man, he's used to a quiet life when he's not working. I'd better phone Patty.'

She came back into the room looking frankly relieved. 'Patty's mother died two days ago. I'm so sorry for Patty, but her mother was old and had Alzheimer's disease, so it was a happy release. Patty is coming back directly after the funeral—in three days' time.' She added apologetically, 'She's been with us for years—I'm lost without her.'

Araminta said, 'The children love her, don't they? It's nice that she has you to come back to and to know that she's wanted.'

'I'm eternally grateful to you, Araminta. I hope being here hasn't disrupted your life in any way?'

'No, not at all. Though I usually take jobs where I can go home each day...'

'You have parents, or do you live on your own?'

'I have a father and a younger sister.'

'My dear, you must ring them and tell them you'll be home tomorrow. I'm not sure when, though.' She frowned. 'Jason didn't say, did he?'

'Well, it doesn't matter. I'll be home round about noon, I expect—plenty of time to do the shopping and cook the supper.' She stood up. 'I'll just pop down to the butcher. What would you like for supper, Mrs Gault? And wouldn't you like to have a nap for an hour? I'll call you in good time for lunch. Mrs Pretty goes around one o'clock— would it do if I had lunch ready for just after that?'

'Something light. Don't go to a lot of trouble, my dear. You'll need some time to pack. There won't be much time in the morning; Jason is always so punctual.'

So Araminta took herself off to the village shops, buying with a prudent eye and saying her goodbyes with some reluctance; she had grown attached to the charming place during the two weeks she had been there. She had a mug of tea with Mrs Pretty when she got back, fending off that lady's searching questions as to her future with gentle vagueness.

There were several jobs to keep her busy for the rest of that day, and, supper over and cleared away, she excused herself with the plea that she still had to finish her packing and went to her room; the children hadn't had much of a chance to talk to their mother, nor she to them.

She washed her hair and then lay in a too-hot bath, thinking about the future. There would be quite a nice sum of money to collect from the agency, but most of it would have to go into the household purse. She only hoped that Alice hadn't been running up bills... She would have to take the next job she was offered, but it would have to be one where she could go to and fro each day. She felt no enthusiasm for that, and turned her thoughts to the drive back to London with Professor Lister. A strange man—reserved, wrapped up much too tightly in his work, and yet kind. She liked him, despite the fact that he didn't appear to like her—no, she had that wrong, he had never displayed any feelings towards her save gratitude, and that in an absent-minded fashion.

He arrived at nine o'clock, bade her good morning, made his unhurried farewells, assured his sister that he would be down to see her as soon as he could spare the time, popped Araminta into the car, got in and drove away. They had been driving for some time and were on the A303 before he spoke.

'Whereabouts is your agency?' And when she told him, he said, 'We'll call there on our way, shall we, and you can collect whatever is owing to you?'

'How kind, but there is no need. I can go this afternoon or tomorrow morning.'

His grunt left her uncertain as to whether he agreed with her. 'You will take a few days off?'

'Well, not if there's a job available where I can go home each day.'

'Perhaps if your sister has been sufficiently reassured by her doctor, she will find something to do.' His voice was dry.

'Well, I don't know what,' said Araminta forthrightly. 'She isn't trained for anything, you see.'

'Neither are you, Miss Smith.'

A remark which she felt put her neatly in her place.

She had no intention of replying to it but sat composedly, watching the scenery flash past.

As they neared Fleet service station, he asked, 'Coffee? Breakfast seems a long while ago,' and turned the car into the vast car-park.

The place was crowded but he found a small table for two, sat her down at it and went to fetch the coffee. They drank it in friendly silence and without waste of time, and as they got up to go he said easily, 'I'll be in the car—come when you're ready.'

Thankfully Araminta sped to the ladies'.

As they approached the outskirts of the city, she asked, 'Would it be more convenient for you to put me down at a bus-stop? I dare say you're busy and I have all day.'

'So have I until late this afternoon. I'll take you home, Araminta.'

The Rolls drew up soundlessly before her house and the professor got out, opened her door, and crossed the narrow pavement beside her, waiting while she got out her key and unlocked the door. The little house felt chilly and rather damp. It was quiet too.

'Alice,' called Araminta. 'Alice?' And she poked her head round the sitting-room door. The room was empty and extremely untidy and dusty. She withdrew her head and turned to the professor. 'There's no one at home. Would you like some coffee?' She hoped she didn't sound as unwilling as she felt to let him see the sitting-room— and the kitchen would be worse.

Professor Lister had taken in the air of neglect, the faint smell of a meal which hung in it, the film of dust on the small table in the hall. He was filled with a pitying concern—to come home to such a place—no welcome, and that didn't mean that there had to be someone there, but a cheerful and clean house, a few flowers, a nice feeling that someone would be back home soon. Araminta was making the best of it, although he suspected that once she was alone she would burst into tears...

He hadn't gone into the agency with her; she had come out looking cheerful, with the observation that there was a job waiting for her only a short bus-ride from her home. He had asked her to have lunch with him then, but she had declined quietly and he hadn't pressed her. He wished now that he had. He said, carefully casual, 'Well, since there is no one at home, I suggest you come with me and we'll find somewhere to eat.'

'You're very kind,' she told him, 'but if you don't mind I'd better stay here. I expect Alice is shopping; she might be home at any minute.' She smiled rather shyly. 'It was very kind of you to bring me home. I'm most grateful.'

He studied her quiet face for a moment. 'I'll get your bag,' he said.

Which he did, setting it down in the narrow hall, towering over her. 'I—my sister and I—are most grateful to you, Miss Smith. I hope that you will be able to take a few days off before you take another job.'

'Oh, I shall,' she told him earnestly, not meaning a word of it. She put out a hand and had it engulfed in his large, firm grip. 'I enjoyed it, you know—Tisbury was lovely; to open the door in the morning and see nothing but green fields outside.' Her eyes were on the row of identical red-brick houses opposite. She said too brightly, 'Goodbye, Professor Lister.'

To his astonishment he found himself wishing to kiss her, but he didn't, merely released her hand, smiled and got back into his car. He drove away without looking back.

'That's that,' said Araminta, and shut the door behind

her, took her bag upstairs and went down to the kitchen. It was a miserable little place in any case, now made much worse by the dirty dishes waiting to be washed, used pans on the grimy stove and a floor sadly in need of a good scrub, let alone a sweep. She was hungry, but she couldn't eat until she had cleared up the mess. She got her pinny from behind the kitchen door and set to work. There wasn't time to do all that needed to be done, but the dishes were washed, the stove wiped clean and the floor swept and mopped. She made herself some tea then, found bread and butter and cheese and sat down to eat it before going along to the sitting-room. She had restored it to a dusted and tidy state when Alice came back. She stood in the doorway, looking at Araminta. 'So you're back, and high time too. Living off the fat of the land, I suppose, while I slave away in this beastly place.'

'Hello, Alice. I didn't let you know I would be back because I wasn't sure what time we'd get here.'

'We? Who's we?'

'Professor Lister gave me a lift.'

Alice flung her coat and a plastic shopping-bag on to a chair. 'And I missed him. Is he coming again?'

'No, why should he? The job's finished. The agency has another one for me—mornings. Nine o'clock until noon. It's ten minutes from the bus.'

'Well, I hope you've got some money. There's the butcher and greengrocer to pay—I've been running up bills.'

'Surely Father gave you the housekeeping...'

'I spent most of it on a jacket—it looks just like leather, and I just had to have it.'

'Supposing I tell you that I haven't been paid,' said Araminta.

Alice shrugged. 'We'll just have to keep on running up bills. I'm glad you're back because you can do that.'

She's my sister and I must love her, thought Araminta desperately. 'Did you go to the doctor?'

'Yes, but only because that heavenly man told me to.'

'And what did he say?'

Alice said sulkily, 'He said that I should have gone months ago to see him.'

'So there's nothing wrong with you?'

'That's what he said, but I'm delicate—Father says so.'

'All the same, you'll have to find a job, Alice, with enough money so that you don't use the housekeeping. And this place was like a pigsty.'

Alice eyed her with astonishment. 'Good Lord, what's come over you? I shan't do anything of the sort; there's enough with you and Father working. I'll look after the house.'

'But you don't, do you, Alice?'

'Well, it's so boring, isn't it? What's for lunch?'

'I had a sandwich. What have you got for supper to-night?'

'Steak—Father fancied that—it's on the bill, so I didn't have to pay for it.'

Araminta bit back the words on her tongue. What would be the use of getting angry? 'I'm going to un-pack and do a load of washing and then the ironing.' She started for the door.

'There are a lot of Father's shirts,' began Alice.

'I shan't be long. You can put in a load after mine and do the ironing tomorrow morning while I'm at work.'

Alice stared at her. 'What's come over you, Araminta? You like housework; you've been doing it for years.'

'Yes, and I expect I shall go on doing it for years to

come, but I get paid from the agency—I've never been paid here, have I?' Araminta spoke in a matter-of-fact voice. 'Now I really must get ready for the morning—you'll see to supper?'

But, when she went downstairs with a load of washing for the machine, Alice had gone, leaving a note on the kitchen table. She had promised a friend that she would go to the cinema and she wouldn't be home until the evening.

So Araminta cooked the supper and greeted her father when he got home.

'You're back.' He kissed her cheek. 'I'm glad to see you, my dear. Alice really isn't up to running a house, you know. Did you get paid?'

Araminta was laying the table. 'Yes, Father. I'll go tomorrow afternoon and pay the bills, if you'll let me have them, and I shall need some housekeeping money.'

'Things are a bit tight—there have been one or two expenses... You've enough to tide us over?'

'I don't think so. I'll settle as many bills as I can. Father, now that Alice is as fit as you or I, she should get a job too and help out. Don't you agree?'

'Well, my dear, Alice isn't cut out for hard work. Surely between us we can manage to keep her at home? She's such a pretty girl she's sure to get a good husband, especially now she's going out and about quite a bit.'

Araminta dished up. She wanted to scream, throw something, break a few bits of china; she was back on the treadmill again with no hope of escaping. She could earn just enough from the agency to keep them solvent, and even when Alice married, as she was certain to do, she herself would have to stay at home to look after the house and her father. She said in a quiet little voice, 'Supper's ready, Father. Alice has gone out with friends.'

'She deserves a little jaunt. I must say, Araminta, that leaving us to fend for ourselves was rather unkind of you.'

There was no answer to that. Presently, after supper, she did the ironing while her father watched television, and then she went to bed, where she cried herself to sleep because she was unhappy. 'The unfairness of life,' she mumbled into her pillow. 'Being plain and poor and condemned to endless household chores and never going to see Professor Lister again.'

She was up early to cook the breakfast and then leave to catch her bus. Alice wasn't down yet and her father had hardly spoken to her, and that, she knew, was because she hadn't given him any of her earnings. She had added up the bills she had found stuffed in a drawer and the total shocked her; there was no question of giving him any money, although being a still-loving daughter she felt guilty about it, but if she had given way to his wishes no bills would have been paid, she was sure of that.

The address she had been given was in a quiet street in Bloomsbury, one of a terrace of tall Victorian houses with basements with barred widows. It looked well-cared-for, and that cheered her. The agency had told her that she was needed to assist the house-owner with her elderly mother, and the pay was quite good. She mounted the steps and rang the bell.

Chapter 5

The door was opened by a woman with a grubby apron and an even grubbier pair of hands. 'You're the new help?' She nodded her head over her shoulder. 'Come on in and good luck to you, ducks.'

She stood aside and Araminta went past her into a wide hall, handsomely papered and thickly carpeted. 'She's in 'ere,' said the woman, and opened a door.

It was a large room, made small by the amount of old-fashioned heavy furniture in it. The curtains were half drawn so that it was gloomy and, as the window was shut, Araminta was met by a wave of cold stuffy air.

The woman gave her a poke in the back. 'Mrs Taylor will be along, ducks,' and closed the door behind her.

Araminta walked into the centre of the room and peered around. There was a narrow bed pushed into the corner of the room, and she went towards it. Presumably the hump in it was a person. Araminta said 'Good morning,' and wondered if she should pull the curtains. The door opened and a youngish woman came in, crossed to the window, pulled back the curtains and turned to look at Araminta.

'I hope you're strong,' she said, and then added, 'You are from the agency?'

'Yes, good morning.' Araminta supposed that she should have added 'madam' but she wasn't going to; the woman was ill-mannered and Araminta, with enough to worry about, wasn't inclined to be meek.

The woman nodded towards the bed. 'My mother—she has to be got up, washed and dressed, and sat in her chair. You'll clean the room and make up the bed, light the fire and see that she has a hot drink. Mrs Loder goes at half-past eleven. If I'm not back, you'll have to wait until I get home.'

'The agency told me that the hours were nine o'clock until noon.'

'That's right. I hope you're not a clock-watcher. There's a cloakroom off the hall; you can wash Mrs Price there. You'll find all you need in the kitchen at the end of the hall. I'll see you when I get back.'

Not very satisfactory, reflected Araminta, and took a good look at the room before going to introduce herself to the occupant of the bed.

The furniture was good, even if too large, but it was dusty and dull from lack of polishing. There was ash in the fireplace behind the high fire-guard, and a pile of newspapers on one of the chairs. She advanced to the bed. Her 'Good morning, Mrs Price,' was greeted with a grunt, and an elderly, ill-tempered face peered at her from a tumbled bed.

'I've come to help you,' said Araminta. 'I will help you wash and dress and tidy up a bit.' She eyed the bed-linen. 'And put clean sheets on the bed.'

'I don't want to get up. I'm very comfortable as I am.'

'Well, if I'm going to make the bed I'm afraid you'll have to get out of it, and you'll feel much more the thing once you are in a chair.'

Araminta, wheedling the old lady to get from her bed, wondered why the agency hadn't told her that it was really a job for someone with nursing experience. It took the best part of an hour to get Mrs Price to walk to the cloakroom, get her washed and dressed, and then sitting in a chair while Araminta brushed her sparse white hair. 'I'm cold,' said Mrs Price.

Araminta rummaged in a drawer and found a shawl. 'I'll get the fire lighted,' she promised.

That took some time; Mrs Loder had to be found and asked where brushes and bucket, firewood and coals were kept, and the ashes had to be swept up and carted away. 'And I want clean sheets,' said Araminta firmly as she came back into the house from the back yard, 'and the vacuum cleaner and dusters.'

'New brooms sweep clean,' said Mrs Loder, 'and mind you remember that I'm off when me time's up and not a minute longer.'

Araminta lighted the fire, made a warm drink for Mrs Price, and began on the bed. She wondered when the sheets had last been changed, and got great satisfaction from the sight of the nicely made bed when she had finished it. She dumped the used linen in the cloakroom and set about vacuuming, and by then it was almost twelve o'clock. She flew round with a duster, tut-tutting at the dirt and at the same time engaging the old lady in conversation. 'Do you go out at all?'

'Me? No, Miss Nosy, I don't. I prefer to stay here in my own room, although my daughter can't find a sensible woman to clean the place and attend to my wants, and I don't know why.'

'We're hard to find,' said Araminta mildly, and longed for five minutes peace and a cup of coffee.

Twelve o'clock came and went and there was no sign of Mrs Taylor. It was half an hour later by the time she returned. She came into the room, nodded to her mother and observed, 'You found everything then.' Her eyes lighted on the bed. 'Clean sheets—surely not necessary…?'

'The bedlinen was filthy,' said Araminta, and had the satisfaction of seeing Mrs Taylor's face grow red.

'You put everything in the washing-machine, I hope? There'll be time for you to iron it tomorrow.'

'It's in the cloakroom, and I'll do the ironing if you wish me to, Mrs Taylor, but then I won't have time to do anything for Mrs Price.'

Mrs Taylor's ample bosom swelled visibly. 'Three hours is ample time to do the little there is to do for my mother. Since you are new to the job, I'll ask Mrs Loder to do the ironing. Be here punctually in the morning, Miss Smith.'

She went out of the room, which was as well, for Araminta was on the point of giving her employer the same advice.

There was no sign of Alice when she got home, although there were the remains of a snack lunch on the table. Araminta, feeling grubby after her morning's chores, washed and changed before sitting down to her own lunch. She didn't linger over it, but collected the bills, fetched her purse and shopping-bag, and walked to the row of small shops at the end of the street. She wouldn't be able to pay them all; she would need to keep some of the money back until such time as her father let her have more. She went in and out of the various shops, paying everyone something and buying food suitable to the household budget. Now that she was home each day there would be no need to buy the fast foods Alice had found so convenient.

Alice was still not home when she got back. She prepared a casserole, made a bread-and-butter pudding, and took her tea into the sitting-room, and while she drank it she wondered about Professor Lister. Would she ever see him again? she wondered. She began to dream, letting her tea get cold—appendicitis and rushed dramatically to hospital for immediate operation, and when she came round from the anaesthetic, there he would be, bending over her, reassuring her that she would recover, that she was a marvellous patient, that her courage in the face of pain had quite won his heart...

'Well, really,' declared Araminta loudly, 'I need my head examined—of all the nonsense.' She added with determined briskness, 'He'll have forgotten me completely by now.'

But he hadn't.

Her father came home presently. 'There you are, my dear,' he exclaimed, just as though he hadn't seen her at breakfast. 'Had a pleasant day? Alice has gone with friends down to Brighton—she needed a breath of sea air. She'll be back some time this evening. Something smells good...'

'Beef casserole, Father. Would you like it straight away?'

'Yes, yes, why not? And we must have a little chat. I'm sure you have enough money to keep us going for the time being? I find myself short of cash…'

Araminta sat down opposite him. 'No, Father, I haven't. I've paid some of the bills which were owing. Did you know how many there were? And there is no money left.' She crossed her fingers behind her back as she uttered the fib.

Her father blustered. 'Well, I must say that's very shabby of you, Araminta. Heaven knows how I struggle to keep you girls in comfort and pay our way.'

'Yes, Father, I'm sure you do. If Alice could find a small job, she could spend her money on clothes and out-ings and that would leave a great deal more housekeep-ing and you wouldn't need to worry.'

'You're hard, Araminta. I'm sorry to say it, but you lack a loving understanding. Alice and I are all the fam-ily you have—you should feel proud that you can help us to make life tolerable.'

Araminta cleared away the plates and fetched the pud-ding. There was no point in saying anything, for her fa-ther wasn't going to listen. *If I could save a little money,* she thought wildly, *I could leave home and find a job—anything to start with—and then get a training for some-thing worthwhile.*

Her father eyed her across the table. 'You look thought-ful, Araminta. I hope it is because you realise the sorrow your selfishness causes me.'

'Father, you sound like someone in a Victorian novel. Have some more pudding?'

'Thank you, no. Sufficient must be left for Alice; she

will probably be hungry after such a long day.' He got up from the table and stalked from the room, leaving her to clear the dishes and wash up. She stood at the sink, looking out of the window at the evening sky filled with scudding clouds through which the moon was doing its best to shine, and for no reason at all she started to think about Professor Lister again. He would be home by now, she reflected, sitting beside the fire with Goldie and Neptune crouched beside him. He would be wearing his reading-glasses and be deep in some interesting book, and presently Buller would come in to tell him that dinner was served...

The professor was indeed in his drawing-room, sitting, exactly as Araminta had imagined, beside his hearth, the dogs sprawled over his feet, a book in his hand. Only he wasn't reading; he was, if only she had known it, thinking of her. He was vaguely irritated that he seemed unable to get her out of his mind—after all, there was no reason why she should keep popping up in his thoughts. She was a very ordinary girl, hired to do a job which she had done with skill, and that was the end of it. On the other hand he had found her an ideal companion, making no effort to entertain him, making sensible conversation and with the gift of being silent—restfully so, without fidgeting or combing her hair, powdering her nose or fussing with lipstick. She wasn't a girl to demand attention either, but she was perfectly capable of holding her own in a no-nonsense fashion.

He got out of his chair as Buller appeared in the doorway. In a few days, when he had an hour or so to spare, he might look her up to see how she was getting on. The suspicion that she wasn't happy at home crossed his mind, and he frowned; it would be interesting to see her sister again and meet her father...

Araminta, optimistic by nature, arrived at Mrs Taylor's house exactly on time to be admitted by Mrs Loder.

'Back again, ducks. Plenty of work for you this morning.' She chuckled. 'Someone gave the old lady a box of chocs—she ate the lot.'

Araminta braced her small person and went into Mrs Price's room, pulled the curtains back and turned to survey the dire results of the chocolates. Mrs Price, her nightdress and the bed were liberally coated. Mrs Taylor would tear her cleverly tinted hair out by the roots when she saw the mess, although if Mrs Loder had told her about it she would quite likely, and very prudently, defer her visit until everything was cleaned up.

Araminta led the chocolate-covered old lady to the cloak room and washed her from top to toe, helped her to dress, and set her in a chair before tackling the bed. There was no help for it, it would have to be clean sheets again...

Mrs Taylor came during the morning, and by that time Araminta had the room and its occupant in a more or less clean state. Mrs Price, settled in her chair, had given endless orders and directions in a querulous voice, which Araminta had allowed to flow over her head while she bundled up sheets and pillow-cases. Mrs Taylor greeted her parent and then stopped short.

'Miss Smith, not another change of sheets, I hope.'

'Somebody gave Mrs Price a box of chocolates,' said Araminta and, since Mrs Taylor gave her an unbelieving look, she spread out a sheet for her inspection.

Mrs Taylor averted her eyes. 'Kindly take everything through to the kitchen. Someone will have to see to it.'

But not me, said Araminta silently, returning presently with Mrs Price's morning drink.

Mrs Taylor was still there. 'Really, I don't know what is to be done,' she declared.

'No more chocolates,' offered Araminta, and received a cutting glance. She ignored that. 'If someone were here while Mrs Price has her meals?' she suggested.

'Impossible. I have a very busy life.' Mrs Taylor narrowed her eyes. 'You could stay until one o'clock and see that my mother has her lunch.'

'I'm afraid I can't do that, Mrs Taylor. The arrangement was for three hours each morning.'

She waited for Mrs Taylor to say that in that case she would get someone else, but she didn't. All she said was, 'See that the fire is kept up—the room's not warm enough.' She glanced round. 'There is a window open.'

'Fresh air,' explained Araminta politely. 'The room wasn't smelling very nice when I got here.'

She wondered then who had brought the old lady's breakfast; surely they would have seen the mess? It didn't seem prudent to ask.

Mrs Taylor went away then and didn't come back until almost half-past twelve. Perhaps this was how it would be each day, thought Araminta, making good her escape.

The days dragged themselves to the end of the week: hard-working mornings and the chores to see to when she got home, for if Alice was there it was seldom, and then she would be sulking because Araminta didn't dare to let her do the shopping. Their heads were just above water, but only just; there was no knowing what Alice would see and buy if she had any money with her. And her father, sitting opposite her at supper each evening, darted reproachful glances at her and, when he caught her eye, smiled wistfully.

On Friday evening he was more cheerful. 'It's Saturday tomorrow—pay-day,' he said happily.

Araminta chose to misunderstand him. 'Father, didn't they pay your cheque in last week? Have you given the housekeeping to Alice?'

'Well, my dear, there were one or two bills—gas and electricity—and Alice needed one or two things. I quite forgot to let you have any money. You shall have it next week. I daresay you'll get paid from the agency tomorrow—you can use that, can't you? I'll pay you back.'

'I'm sorry to disappoint you, Father,' said Araminta, 'but Mrs Taylor doesn't intend to pay any fees until I'm not needed there. I believe there's a cousin coming to stay who'll take over from me, but I don't know when.'

Mr Smith was indignant. 'But that's absurd; you're entitled to your money each week. Still, I dare say there's still something left over from that other job of yours.' He smiled at her. 'I'm sure you've got something tucked away for a rainy day, my dear.'

It was no use, she thought wearily; she loved her father, despite the fact that he allowed money to trickle through his fingers like sand through a sieve. When her mother had been alive it hadn't been as bad, but now that Alice was grown up, wanting things...

'I've almost no money, Father,' she said gently, 'but I'll do the best I can. Perhaps you can persuade Alice to find a job—she won't listen to me...'

'Well, understandably, Araminta. You have hurt her feelings, you know—she's such a sensitive girl.'

* * *

At least it's Sunday tomorrow, thought Araminta as she dressed the next morning. She wondered what happened to Mrs Price on that day and what kind of a mess she would find on Monday morning. But first, Saturday.

Old Mrs Price was in a bad mood; she had never shown a sunny disposition but this morning she was more irascible than ever, and on top of that Mrs Taylor was coldly angry because Araminta regretted that she wouldn't be able to come on Sunday morning. 'The agency arranged for me to come from Monday until Saturday,' she pointed out quietly.

'Oh, I know that, but what are a couple of hours to you? You'll still have the rest of the day to yourself. I've a luncheon party I simply cannot miss.'

'Perhaps if you ring the agency, they will have someone who could take over tomorrow?' suggested Araminta.

'Don't be ridiculous, Miss Smith. Who would want to work on a Sunday?'

Who indeed? reflected Araminta.

'I shall be late back, I've things to do,' snapped Mrs Taylor. 'You'll have to wait until I return.'

'I will wait until half-past twelve, Mrs Taylor,' Araminta said reasonably, 'but then I shall go, for I have things to do. Indeed, I hoped to leave at noon today— that was the arrangement.'

'I shall replace you as soon as possible.' Mrs Taylor flounced away and presently left the house.

The morning was much as the other mornings had been. Mrs Price was cross and contrived to do everything twice as slowly as usual; the fire wouldn't burn briskly and the old lady spilt her elevenses all over the floor. Araminta mopped up and prayed for the morning to end.

Which it did, eventually, and, better than that, Mrs Taylor was only fifteen minutes late. 'Don't expect to get paid until you leave,' snapped Mrs Taylor. 'And mind you're here on Monday morning.'

Araminta nipped smartly through the door before Mrs Taylor could think of anything more unpleasant to say, took a breath of more or less fresh air and stood still on the pavement. Drawn up to the kerb was a dark grey Rolls Royce with Professor Lister sitting in it. He got out when he saw her, opened the door on the other side, scooped her neatly on to the seat and got in again. All without a word.

'Well, really,' said Araminta, at a loss for words. A silly remark, but she couldn't think of anything else.

He turned to look at her. 'Hello, Miss Smith—have you had a trying morning?' He sounded concerned, and she supposed that her appearance justified his enquiry.

'I have had a trying week,' she told him. 'Are you visiting a patient, Professor?'

'No. I thought we might have lunch together?'

'How did you know where I was?'

'I rang the agency.'

He began to drive away and she said quickly, 'It's kind of you to ask me to lunch, but I really should go home.'

'Why?'

'Well, there is the shopping to do, and if Father and Alice are at home they will expect lunch.'

'They won't worry if you are late back?'

'Worry? No, of course not, they'll think that I've had to stay at Mrs Taylor's for some reason or other.'

'That's all right, then. We can talk over lunch.'

'I'm not dressed for lunch,' said Araminta and pointed out in the most matter-of-fact way that she was very untidy.

'In that case we will go somewhere where you can tidy yourself and eat in quiet surroundings.'

'Why do you want to see me?' asked Araminta. 'If it's another job, I'm supposed to stay with Mrs Taylor until someone comes to take over.'

'That is easily remedied. As to why I want to see you, we will discuss that presently.'

He turned his head and smiled at her, and her heart gave a little skip of delight. She told herself sharply that that was quite enough of that; to get ideas about him would never do. She said primly, 'Very well, Professor,' and sat quietly until he turned into the forecourt of St Pancras station and parked the car.

She got out when he opened her door, and gave him a questioning look.

'We'll go to the restaurant, and then you can go and do whatever you need to do and join me there.'

The restaurant was large and, strangely enough, quiet. He led her to a table in a corner, said, 'Off you go, you know where I am,' and took out his reading-glasses to study the menu.

If I were looking for romance, I certainly wouldn't find it with Professor Lister, reflected Araminta, doing things to her face and repinning her abundant hair. Nothing could improve the cotton sweater and skirt under her jacket. It struck her then that that was why he had brought her here for lunch; she looked like hundreds of other women travelling to and from work, and had no need to worry about her appearance. The idea sent a little glow of pleasure through her person, that he should have thought of that and spared her any embarrassment.

He got up as she joined him. 'What would you like to drink? Sherry?'

'You can't drink, can you,' she asked him, 'since you're driving? So I won't either. I'd like a tonic water and lemon with ice.'

He ordered for her and picked up his menu. 'I don't know what the food's like, but choose whatever you would like.'

'A mushroom omelette and a salad, please.' And when he had ordered that, with a steak for himself, she said, 'You wanted to talk about something?'

He smiled a little, took off his glasses and put them in his pocket. 'Ah, yes, but might that wait until we have had our lunch? I should like you to tell me about this job of yours—from the look of you, I think it must not suit you.'

She went red and put her hands, roughened by a week of rendering Mrs Price and her room clean, in her lap, out of sight. If he noticed, he said nothing, but merely sat there, waiting for her to speak. She began carefully, 'Well, it is rather—well—messy, and Mrs Taylor...' She launched into an account of her work, careful not to exaggerate, and contrived to finish quite cheerfully. 'I don't expect I'll have to be there much longer, there's someone—a cousin, I think—coming to look after Mrs Price. The next job may be very much better.'

The waitress brought their lunch and the professor made no comment, but talked about a variety of subjects which only needed the briefest of replies. She ate her omelette with appetite, accepted his offer of applepie for dessert and, since he seemed to have lost all interest in her work, took care to follow his lead and talk about nothing much.

It was over coffee that he observed in his calm way,

'Of course you cannot go back to that dreadful woman. I'll see the agency and arrange for you to leave as from today.'

Araminta looked at him, aghast. 'Oh, please don't do that. I… We need the money…' She could have bitten her tongue the next instant for making such a revealing remark. 'What I mean is…' she began.

'I am aware of what you mean, Araminta.'

Diverted, she exclaimed, 'You called me Araminta.'

'And I hope I shall continue to do so,' he observed blandly. 'Now, I want you to listen to me, and pray do not interrupt.'

'Well, I'll try not to.' She poured their coffee and handed him a cup. 'But I might, you know, if you surprise or annoy me.'

'I may surprise you, but I hope that I shall not annoy you.'

Araminta took a sip of coffee. She was nicely full, the coffee was excellent, and she had to admit that she was very much enjoying the professor's company. She wondered briefly what he wanted to say to her, but, before she could begin to guess, he said in a conversational tone, 'I have decided to take a wife. Until recently I have found my life quite satisfactory; I have my work, my friends and a pleasant home, but I must admit I feel the need for a companion, a good friend, someone to come home to and who will listen to how my day has gone. I suppose that, like most men, I have hoped that one day I would meet a woman I would want to love and live with for the rest of my life, but it seems she has eluded me, so I must settle for second-best. After all, many love-matches come to grief, whereas a marriage founded on friendship and compatibility may well prove very successful.' He paused to look at her, sitting very much at her ease, smiling a little.

'Why are you telling me this?'

'I considered it right to explain my feelings before I ask you to marry me, Araminta.' She put her cup down very carefully in its saucer, and he added, 'I've surprised you, Araminta, but not, I hope, annoyed you.'

'Yes, you have, but I'm not annoyed. No one has ever asked me to marry them before; it's not something any girl would get annoyed about.'

She reflected that something had annoyed her, though; she was to be second-best, was she? If—and the idea was laughable, of course—she should marry him, she would make him eat those words, even if it took years. It was, in fact, a good reason for marrying him...

A fleeting vision of the professor kneeling at her feet begging forgiveness flashed through her head and was instantly sternly repulsed. She was aware that he was studying her face intently, and she met his gaze without coyness.

'I am serious,' he told her.

'Yes, I know that. You don't know anything about me.'

'I know all that is necessary; the rest I can learn later, can I not? But you are what I would hope to find in a wife, Araminta.'

She said honestly, 'Yes, maybe, but you don't love me, do you?'

'No, but I like to be with you. You are restful, and reasonable too; I believe that you could cope with being a medical man's wife very well—the late meals, the sudden calls away from home, the hours I like to spend in my study. All I ask of you is that, I think, for the time being at least, there need be no talk of love. Liking can grow into affection, and that is important in marriage.'

Araminta saw no point in contradicting him. Love, she considered, was what mattered in marriage—if you loved someone you put up with anything, just to be with him.

'I do not expect you to give me your answer now, only when you are ready. You may wish to talk it over with your father.'

She shook her head. 'No. I think not. You see, they would like to have me stay at home and keep house and look after things. When I have made up my mind, I'll tell him and Alice.'

He nodded. 'We will go to the agency and I will arrange for you to be replaced. Whether you decide to marry me or not, I cannot allow you to stay there with those unpleasant people.'

'But I—' she began, to be interrupted gently.

'No, Araminta, I must insist on it. Should you decide not to marry me, then I will see to it that you have more suitable work—away from home, if you prefer.'

She asked curiously, 'How will you do that?'

'I know very many people, and there are many possibilities for you.' He smiled gently. 'But I hope very much that you will consent to marry me.'

He signalled for the bill, and they went out into the station and then to the car. 'First the agency, and then I will take you home.' And, at her questioning look, 'No, I won't come in and meet your father, not until I have your answer.'

At the agency Araminta had to admit that the professor had impressive powers of persuasion. He had the austere owner agreeing to everything he said within ten minutes, he extracted the week's money from her, assured her that if ever he needed her assistance in finding an employee he would certainly call upon her, and ushered Araminta out of the bare little office, ignoring the sly glances she cast at them both. Araminta hadn't noticed; she had too much to think about.

He drove her home then, got out to open her door, and then got in the car again. She poked her head through the open window, inches from his face. 'Thank you for my lovely lunch, and thank you for proposing to me. Shall I write and let you know?'

He put a hand over hers where it clutched the window. 'How long will it take you to make up your mind?'

She thought for a minute. 'If I think about it for the rest of today and all tomorrow...'

'May I come and see you tomorrow evening? Whatever the answer is, we can have a meal together and discuss your future.'

'Very well, but I don't want to tell Father and Alice until it's settled.'

'I understand.'

She withdrew her head and watched him drive away.

There was no one at home; a note lay on the kitchen table asking her to do the shopping for the weekend. It was in Alice's handwriting but her father had added a PS: 'Sorry there's no money—but get everything put on account.'

There was no need for that; she bought what was necessary and wondered about the following week. If she married the professor, how would they manage at home? Alice would have to get a job, and what could she do? And even if she didn't marry him, she had no work for the following week. Would she be marrying him to escape from home and all its petty worries, or because she really wanted to be his wife?

She made a pot of tea then and thought about it. It was a pity there was no one to advise her. She thought with longing of her mother, a woman of strong character, who had passed on her good sense and plain face to Araminta, kept a guiding hand on the purse-strings and taken care that her husband didn't spoil Alice. There wasn't anyone… Yes, there was. She went to church on Sundays and the vicar of St John's was elderly, gentle and, she thought, wise. Her mind made up to go and see him the next day, she got on with preparing the supper; her father and Alice would be hungry when they got home.

Beyond remarking that she had been late coming home, they asked no questions; they only asked if she had done the shopping, fell to discussing the film Alice had been to see, and then switched on the television until it was time for bed.

In the morning Araminta took herself off to church and, after the service, lingered until she could speak to the Reverend Mr Thorn.

'If you could spare ten minutes?' she asked him. 'I need some advice.'

He led the way back into the church and they sat in one of the pews, and, conscious that he would be expected home for his dinner very shortly, she laid her problem before him in as few words as possible.

When she had finished, he asked simply, 'Do you love this man, Araminta?'

'No, but I like him very much. I like being with him, I'm easy with him and there are things we both like—I mean serious things. He's a serious man. I don't think he has asked me to marry him without thinking a great deal about it first.' She thought for a bit. 'I should like to marry him and I think we would be happy, even though we don't love each other. Is that possible?'

'Oh, yes, mutual trust and respect and liking would develop in time into true affection. You are concerned for your father and sister?'

She nodded. 'They aren't very good with money—since Mother died I've looked after them and the house.'

'Perhaps it would be a good thing if they were to take that responsibility upon themselves. Once they have got over the shock of fending for the two of them, it might open up an entirely new way of life.' He sat silently for a while and then said, 'I think you should marry this man. It is natural that he should want a wife and he has chosen you, and from the sound of him he seems a man who would not take decisions lightly.' They both got up and he took her hand. 'If and when you make up your mind, remember that you must keep to it steadfastly, Araminta.' He smiled. 'Now go home and dish up the lunch and let me know...'

'Yes, I will, and thank you, Mr Thorn—you didn't mind?'

'That's why I'm here.'

Chapter 6

'Why are you so late?' Alice wanted to know crossly. 'It's a good thing it's steak and kidney pudding, for I've no intention of cooking the dinner. It's something I hate doing.'

Their father, coming into the kitchen added, 'It would have been kind to have warned us that you would be so late, my dear.'

It seemed hardly the moment to tell them her news.

She decided that it was some kind of sign that neither her father nor Alice intended to go out that afternoon. They would be at home when the professor came, and she was thankful for that; she would never convince them that she was going to get married without some evidence. She got the tea a little earlier than usual and wondered when he would come. She was a sensible girl, but her nerves were positively jangling.

They didn't have to jangle for long, though; just after six o'clock the Rolls stopped before the house and the professor gave the doorknocker a resounding thump.

'The door, Araminta,' called Alice from her seat in front of the television. Her father, immersed in the Sunday papers, didn't look up.

Araminta went to open the door and the professor stood on the doorstep, looking down at her, wondering in his calm way if he was making the biggest mistake of his life. On the whole, he thought not; Araminta's ordinary face was lifted to his and held an expression which reassured him. She had beautiful eyes, he reflected, and a gentle mouth. He smiled then. 'Am I too early?'

She stood aside to let him come in. 'No. Do you want to know now?'

He smiled at her. 'Yes, please.'

'You haven't changed your mind?' She was quite serious. 'I mean, it's quite all right if you have—no harm done.'

'No, I haven't changed my mind, Araminta.' He bent and kissed her cheek. 'Shall we tell your father?'

She nodded. 'He'll be annoyed...'

He appeared unmoved at the idea. 'We will go back home presently and lay our plans.' He took her hand and went with her into the sitting-room.

Less than an hour later, sitting beside Jason in the car, Araminta relived the rather unpleasant half-hour with her father and Alice. They had stared in surprise as she and Jason had entered the room, and Alice had jumped to her feet. 'What a lovely surprise,' she had cried. 'I always hoped we'd meet again. Have you got another job for Araminta? Is that why you're here?'

Araminta had said quickly, 'Father, this is Professor Lister—my father, Jason.' She had seen Alice's look of surprise and her quick frown, and clutched his hand harder. It had been given a reassuring squeeze before the professor had shaken hands with her father.

'Araminta and I have a surprise for you, sir. We are to be married shortly.'

Her father had been too surprised to speak for a moment; it was Alice who had said, 'Marry Araminta? But that's ridiculous—I mean, she doesn't know how to dress decently, she's not even pretty, you'll be ashamed of her...'

She had stopped then because the look on the professor's face had frightened her. He had spoken very quietly. 'I'm sure you don't mean that, Alice.' He had turned to her father. 'I'm taking Araminta back with me now so that we can discuss the wedding. I have arranged for her to leave Mrs Taylor. I am sure you will be delighted at our news.'

Araminta had felt sorry for her father: he had looked as though he had been hit on the head and wasn't sure what was happening. He had said slowly, 'We shall have to manage as best as we can without you, Araminta,' a remark which had made her feel guilty, as he had intended.

But the professor had said briskly, 'I'm sure Alice will become as good a housewife as Araminta.'

Then he had suggested that Araminta should go and get her coat. She had no idea what had been said while she was upstairs, but she had a nasty feeling that when she got back that evening she would be met with reproaches and perhaps worse. But that was still hours away; she peeped at Jason and saw that he was smiling a little. She said, 'I'm sorry Father wasn't... That is, it was a great surprise to him.'

He gave her a quick sidelong glance. 'Yes, I could see that. Would you rather not go back home this evening, Araminta?'

'I expect when they've talked it over it will be all right, thank you.'

His grunt reassured her in some way.

When they reached his house she wondered what he had told Buller, for Mrs Buller came into the hall and she and Buller both wished her happy and shook the professor's hand with delighted smiles. When Mrs Buller had gone back to her kitchen and Buller had taken their coats and gone away too, Araminta asked, 'How did they know?'

He took her arm and urged her into the drawing-room. 'I told Buller that if we were here by eight o'clock he and Mrs Buller could congratulate me and wish you well.'

He sat her down, fended off the dogs, and sat in his chair opposite her, and after a few minutes Goldie and Neptune settled at his feet. It wasn't until Buller had come in with champagne in a silver bucket and gone soft-footed away that the professor said, 'I have a very full week ahead of me—if you would agree, we might decide upon a date for our wedding this evening.' He opened the champagne and handed her a glass. 'To you, Araminta.'

'To us both,' said Araminta. 'I'll marry you whenever you want me to, but I don't know anything about you— only that you are a surgeon and live here.'

He laughed. 'Supposing we get married first and take our time to get to know each other later? I don't want you to be at home for longer than is necessary. I'll get a special licence and we can be married as quickly as possible. Have you any preference? Your local vicar?'

'Yes, please. I asked his advice and he told me to

marry you—he said that mutual liking and respect were important and a foundation for...for...'

'Affection,' said the professor gently. 'He's quite right. Good. I'll arrange everything and let you know. Your father and sister will come?'

She gave him a troubled look. 'Perhaps they won't. Perhaps it might be better if we just got married—just the two of us.' She added, in a matter-of-fact voice which hid unease, 'I haven't anything suitable to wear—I hope you won't mind?'

'You will still be Araminta even in a potato-sack. You always look very nice.' He watched her as he spoke, aware that he might hurt her—the last thing he wanted to do. He sensed that she would refuse to take money from him until she was his wife, but he was aware that wedding clothes were important to a woman; after all, he had two sisters who had married with all the pomp expected of them. He would have to think of something. 'I don't think it matters, do you?' he asked. 'We shall be just the two of us...'

'As long as you don't mind.'

Over dinner they discussed the wedding with the impersonal interest of two people talking about a ceremony between mutual acquaintances. It was to be as soon as the professor could get the licence and arrange time in which to get married. 'I know it should be the bride who decides the day, but I shall have to rearrange my work so that I am free. I should like to see you as much as possible—may I ring you each day so that we can meet? You will be at home?' He saw her hesitate, and added quickly, 'You are thinking of taking another job—please don't. For one thing, this licence may take less time than I anticipate.'

'All right, I won't. Do you have a lot of friends? They might not like me.'

He smiled a little. 'When we are married you shall go shopping and buy some spectacular outfits and burst upon them in a blaze of high fashion. You will be a great success with my friends, Araminta.'

He began to talk about his sisters and then his work; casual remarks, some of which she stored away to think about later. As they sat by the fire presently, drinking coffee from paper-thin cups, she reflected that she must be out of her mind; how in heaven's name had she ever agreed to marry this rather remote man about whom she knew almost nothing? She could, of course, change her mind, and she knew without any doubt that he would accept her decision calmly. Only of course she had no intention of doing that; she had given her word. Besides, she liked him. She looked across at him and found his eyes upon her, and blushed, for all the world as if she had spoken her thoughts out loud.

She blurted out, 'I hope I'll be able to fit into your life, Jason.'

'I have no doubt of it. You may even find it rather dull. I suspect that you will be visited by my colleagues' wives and invited to join various committees and meet to gossip over coffee. Will you like that?'

'If that's what your wife is expected to do, then I'll like it.'

'I've a cottage in north Essex—we'll go there for the weekend and take the dogs. You like the country?'

'Yes—oh yes, I do. Is there a garden?'

'Quite a large one. There's a nice old man who comes from the village and keeps it in trim when I'm not there.

His daughter keeps the place clean and cooks, though I daresay we could manage the meals between us.'

'It sounds heavenly.' She saw the time and said, 'I think I'd better go home. It's been a lovely evening. I'm still not sure if I'm dreaming.'

He drove her home then, getting out of the car and waiting until she had gone inside before driving away. She had asked him hesitatingly if he would like to go in with her, but except for a glimmer of light in the hall there was no sign of life. They had agreed that, since it was almost midnight, her father and sister would already be in bed. 'I'll come tomorrow evening,' he assured her. 'Your father will be home then.'

Neither her father nor Alice was in bed; they were waiting for her in the sitting-room.

'I have been very disturbed by your news, Araminta,' began her father. 'This Professor Lister—who is he? How long have you known him? Will he be able to offer you the kind of life to which you are accustomed?'

Araminta sat down. Her father was talking like someone in a Victorian novel again. She said in her sensible way, 'No, it won't be at all the same, Father. He has a very nice home, and I shan't have to go out to work or do the washing-up or the ironing. I have known him for some time now; we saw a lot of each other while I was at Tisbury.' Which wasn't quite true, but it might allay any fears her father might have. She thought it unlikely that he had any fears about her anyway.

'You're sly,' said Alice in a furious voice, 'going behind our backs, leaving us in the lurch. How are we going to manage, I'd like to know?'

'Well, there'll only be two instead of three for a start, and if you get a job you'll manage very well. After all,

Father has quite a good salary. A part-time job will give you as much money as I earned; you can spend it on clothes and whatever you want; there'll be ample house-keeping then.'

'Don't think I'm coming to your wedding,' Alice raged. 'You've nothing to wear anyway—I suppose it'll be some hole-and-corner affair.'

'No,' said Araminta, 'just very quiet. Jason doesn't have much leisure.'

Her father shook his head. 'Well, you're old enough to know your own mind, Araminta. I only hope you're not making a big mistake.'

Araminta got up. 'Don't either of you want me to be happy?' she asked.

'Why should you have all the luck?' Alice asked angrily. 'You needn't come crawling home when he sees what a mistake he's made.'

'And you, Father?'

Mr Smith shook his head. 'Naturally I hope that you will be happy, my dear, but I doubt it. You're out of his class, for a start. He'll probably be ashamed of you among all his lofty friends.'

Araminta, accustomed to looking on the bright side of things, nevertheless cried herself to sleep. But, beyond a slightly pink nose, in the morning there was no sign of that. She cooked breakfast as usual, replied suitably to her father's comments about the weather and the busy day he had ahead of him, and wished him goodbye in her normal quiet fashion. He had barely answered her and she supposed that, while she was still at home and not working, he would present the same injured expression on his face. It was therefore a great surprise to her when he came home at his usual time and came into the kitchen where she was getting their supper.

He said in a warm voice, 'I'll come to your wedding, Araminta. I'll give you away, if you would like that.' He fished in his pocket. 'I daresay you would like a new dress.'

He put some notes on the table. 'It's the best I can do.'

'Father—how kind of you. I'd love a dress to wear, and I had hoped that you would come to our wedding. Thank you very much. I hope you haven't had to borrow—'

He said hastily, 'No, no. A small overdraft which I can settle next month. Where is Alice?'

'She went out about an hour ago, but she'll be back for supper.' Araminta came round the table and kissed her father's cheek. 'Father, it is most kind of you and I'm so grateful.'

He shrugged his shoulders. 'Must make an effort. Is the fire lighted in the sitting-room? I'll run through the paper while you're getting supper.'

He went and sat down in his chair and picked up the paper, but he didn't read it. He felt smug and pleased with himself, as though it were his money he had given to Araminta and not Professor Lister's—sent to him by special messenger, together with a courteous letter requesting his presence at his daughter's wedding. It had been more than the hundred pounds he had given to her, but Alice had just as much right to it as Araminta. It should have been his pretty Alice who was marrying a well-to-do man; what had Araminta ever done to deserve such an assured future?

He was immersed in the news when the phone rang.

Araminta lifted the receiver, and the professor's voice wished her good evening, said he would be with her in half an hour and that they would go back to his house for dinner. His goodbye was brief.

Araminta put the cottage pie in the oven and went to tell her father. 'Supper will be ready in about half an hour. I expect Alice will be back by then.'

Her father lowered his newspaper. 'I suppose we must expect this until you leave us. We'll manage, I dare say— I've had a hard day's work…'

'But Alice hasn't,' said Araminta with a snap, and then contritely, 'Sorry, I didn't mean that, but it would make things much easier if she would tackle the housekeeping.'

Her father didn't answer, and she went to her room and got into her suit, did her face and her hair, and was waiting when the Rolls came to a quiet halt before the door.

She answered the professor's thump at once and said, 'Hello,' then, 'Would you like to come in?'

She was surprised when he smiled and said, 'Yes,' but she led him into the sitting-room and sat quietly while the two men exchanged small-talk. It was as Jason got up to go that he observed, 'You will be giving Araminta away, of course, Mr Smith?'

'Of course. It is too early to fix a date, I suppose?'

'We will let you know as soon as it is arranged.' He put a hand on Araminta's arm. 'Shall we go, my dear? We have a good deal to discuss still.'

He swept her out of the house and into the car, where Goldie and Neptune were mounting guard from the back seat. 'I shall have the licence in a few days,' Jason told her as he eased the car into the evening traffic. 'I'm rather heavily booked for the next few weeks—would you mind very much if we marry at a moment's notice? You will come back with me to our home but you may not see much of me for a few days. We could wait, of course, but

I want you out of your father's house as soon as possible. What have they been saying to you to make you cry?'

'I haven't…' she began, and started again; if they were to have a good marriage, telling lies wouldn't be a good start. 'I thought it didn't show. Father and Alice are upset because I won't be there…'

'To work and clean and cook for the pair of them. I do not mean to be unjust, Araminta, but they are rapidly turning you into a doormat. You deserve better than that. I don't promise you an exciting life, but I shall do my best to make you happy.'

'Yes, I know. Father said that we're not in the same class and he's right, you know.'

'If you're going to talk like that, I shall beat you,' said the professor placidly, so that she laughed, suddenly at ease and happy.

Over Mrs Buller's delicious dinner—orange and tomato soup, then cassoulet of duckling followed by syllabub—Araminta told Jason of the unexpected gift her father had given her. 'Now I can buy a dress,' she told him happily, 'and he said he would give me away, although last night he said he wouldn't come to the wedding.'

'Now that is good news indeed,' agreed the professor, suitably surprised, while he wondered silently how much of the money he had sent Mr Smith had been held back from Araminta. Just as soon as he could, he would arrange for her to go shopping and buy anything and everything she wanted.

They went into the drawing-room for their coffee and sat by the fire talking like old friends, and when there was a phone call from the hospital asking him to go there urgently, she made no demur but agreed to be driven back by Buller.

'I do hope you won't have to stay up half the night,' she told him, 'and do take care how you go, won't you?'

He dropped a kiss on her cheek and went away. Really, he had chosen well, he reflected. Araminta would fit into his life very well—the kind of wife he had wished for, reflecting his moods, a quiet and intelligent companion. He smiled; it was most agreeable to be told to take care, and for someone to mind if he was kept out of his bed for half the night.

Buller drove Araminta back presently and waited until she entered the silent house. He had asked her if she drove a car as they went through the city. 'The professor will see that you have lessons, miss. You could manage this Rover easily, even here in London. It would be handy if you could drive yourself, him being away so much.'

She had agreed pleasantly; she liked Buller and his wife. It was a contented household, run on oiled wheels. For a moment she wondered what she was going to do with her days. Of course, learning to drive would keep her busy for several weeks, and there were the dogs to walk, and in the evenings there would be Jason...

The supper dishes had been left by the sink. She took off her jacket, tied an apron round her small waist, and turned on the taps. While she washed up, she thought about how she would spend her hundred pounds.

She spent every penny of it the following day, leaving home soon after breakfast while Alice was still strolling around in the kitchen in her dressing-gown, and for the next few hours she went slowly along Oxford Street, comparing prices, deciding what she could afford. She saw quickly enough that a hundred pounds wasn't going to go far; an elegant little suit with a boxy jacket and a pleated skirt left her with thirty pounds, which she laid out on a pretty blouse and plain court shoes—cheap, but a good imitation of more expensive footwear. Since she had some money over from the job at Mrs Taylor's, she browsed through the undies department of a large store and bought a modicum of lacy trifles, feeling guilty since the money could have been spent on meals for the rest of the week. She was walking down Oxford Street, feeling pleased with her purchases, when she stopped to look in a hat-shop window. Her suit was a dark green and burgundy plaid with a little velvet collar, and the hat in one corner of the window was exactly the right colour of burgundy. Moreover, it was marked half-price. Araminta bought it; it sat charmingly on her neat head—not a white tulle wedding veil, but the next best thing…

She bore her purchases home and found Alice lying on the sofa.

'You're back,' said Alice in a wispy voice. 'I feel rotten—you'll have to get the supper. I'd like a cup of tea and some lunch…'

Araminta put down her parcels and went to look at her sister. She looked the same as usual, only rather more cross. 'It's a bit late for lunch,' she pointed out. 'I'm going to make myself a cup of tea. I haven't had lunch either—I'll make toast.'

She went up to her room with her purchases and stowed them away in the bottom of the wardrobe; tonight, when she went to bed, she would try everything on. Now she went down to the kitchen, made tea and a plate of buttered toast and took the tray into the sitting-room.

'I'll have it here,' said Alice peevishly.

'Why not?' agreed Araminta cheerfully, as she poured tea for herself and began on the toast.

Alice watched her for a few moments. 'What about me?' she asked.

'I've made enough toast for both of us,' said Araminta. 'Alice, dear, I think you must stop pretending that you're not strong, that you can't get a job like everyone else. I'm sure you'd enjoy it once you got started. Think of the money!'

Alice got off the sofa and started on the toast. 'Why should I, when Father lets me buy what I want? It's all very well for you to talk. You'll live like a lady while I'm stuck here...'

'If you had a job you'd meet people.'

Alice took the last piece of toast and poured her tea. 'You're such a prig. You'll see, he'll get fed up with you in no time at all—you're plain and dull and your clothes are awful. I shall laugh myself sick.' She burst into easy tears. 'You always took such care of me, I never had to do anything.'

'That was because I thought you were ill. But you're as well as I am, love, and you surely don't want to sit about for the rest of your life?'

Alice tossed her head. 'I don't—I've plenty of friends— we have a grand time.' She went back to the sofa and lolled back on it. 'I hope there's something decent for supper.'

Araminta went to the kitchen, disappointed that Alice hadn't wanted to see what she had bought. She was at the sink with the taps running when the telephone rang. She didn't hear it, nor did she hear Alice answering it.

'She's not here. I don't know where she is—out for the evening, I dare say.'

She had slammed down the phone before the professor could reply.

* * *

Jason had got home earlier than he had expected and, rather to his own surprise, the first thing he had done was to telephone Araminta. A quiet evening over dinner and then an hour's talk would be pleasant. He replaced the receiver unhurriedly. He didn't believe Alice; if Araminta had been going out, she would have left a message. He whistled to the dogs, shrugged on his coat and went out to his car.

'I'm going to fetch Miss Smith,' he told Buller. 'I dare say we'll be back within the hour.'

The rush-hour wasn't quite over; it took him some time to reach her home, and it was already dusk when he got out of the car and banged the knocker.

Araminta came to the door, her gentle mouth curling into a delighted smile. She said, 'Hello, Jason,' and waited for him to speak.

'Get your coat,' he told her. 'We'll go back home for dinner—we still have a lot to say to each other, haven't we?' His smile was so kind that she felt the urge to burst into tears and bury her head on his shoulder.

'Come in,' she invited. 'I won't be a minute. I didn't expect you.'

'Telephoned half an hour ago and was told you'd gone out, probably for the evening.'

'Oh! Oh, dear. I was in the kitchen. I expect Alice…' She looked up at him worriedly. 'So sorry…'

'Run and get your coat, my dear, and stop apologising for your sister.'

'Yes… Well, would you like to go into the sitting-room?'

He shook his head. 'Just fetch your coat; you can do whatever else you want to do when we get back.' He bent suddenly and kissed her, and she flew upstairs with the delightful feeling that perhaps she wasn't as dull and plain as Alice had said.

Coming down again, she poked her head round the sitting-room door. Alice had the television on and Araminta raised her calm voice above the din. 'I'm going out, Alice. Supper's ready to cook.'

She whisked herself out again before Alice had answered.

'She's a bit cross,' she explained as they drove away. 'I'm sure she didn't mean to mislead you.'

To which remark Jason made no reply.

It was during dinner that he told her that he would have to go to Birmingham on the following day. 'I shall spend the night there and, if all goes well, get back some time during the next day. I'll ring you tomorrow evening around nine o'clock and let you know. Oh, and we may marry on Saturday. Will you see your Mr Thorn tomorrow? It's very short notice, but I dare say he can fit us in. I'll come for you on Thursday evening and we'll go and see him together, shall we?'

'Yes, very well, Jason.' She spoke in her usual sensible way, but her insides felt peculiar, as though she had taken a step that wasn't there; it was almost panic...

The professor, watching her without appearing to do so, said comfortably, 'Now tell me what you've been doing with yourself all day.'

It seemed a perfectly normal thing to do—to tell him about the suit she had found and the perfectly matching hat that so luckily was half-price.

'I look forward to seeing it,' he told her. 'Pack your things on Friday, will you? I'll collect them in the evening.'

'I've not got very much,' she told him seriously. 'Two cases—they'll go in the boot?'

He assured her that they would.

The evening was as pleasant as the previous ones had been. It was surprising, she reflected, how completely at ease she felt with him; it was as though she had known him all her life. The thought of not seeing him on the following day made her feel quite sad, but at least she would have things to do—pack her things and go and see Mr Thorn. Jason didn't try to delay her when she said after an hour or so that she would like to go home, but he drove her back, saw her into the house and drove off again.

She went to see Mr Thorn the next morning. 'A wise decision,' he told her. 'I believe that you will make the marriage a success, Araminta, and be a good wife. I should like to have met Professor Lister before you marry.'

'Tomorrow evening,' Araminta told him. 'He's in Birmingham today and doesn't get back until tomorrow, but he'll come in the evening. May we come and see you then?'

'Of course. The ceremony is to be a quiet one?'

'Just us. Father says he will give me away. Could it be some time in the morning?'

'You are going away afterwards?'

'No. No, I don't think so. Jason's not free. I was thinking of Father—he wants to take Alice out for lunch. Could it be about half-past ten or eleven o'clock?'

'You will be having a family lunch?'

'No,' she said soberly, 'Alice isn't coming to the wedding. Just Jason's registrar and your wife—we have to have two witnesses, don't we?'

'Shall we say half-past ten?' Mr Thorn's voice was

gentle. 'Then, if the professor is free, you will have the rest of the day together.'

She did the shopping next, since Alice had dressed and gone out early and declared that she didn't know when she would be back, then went home and tidied the house and, after a sandwich and coffee, went to her room and began to pack. She had nothing suitable for an eminent professor's wife to wear, she reflected. She hoped he wouldn't feel ashamed of her, and she supposed that he would give her some money to get the right kind of clothes. She hoped he would think of that, for she didn't think she could ask him. She might have to, she thought; he hadn't struck her as being very observant. She was, of course, quite mistaken.

It was quite early in the afternoon of the next day when the professor arrived. Alice was out again, and Araminta was on the point of washing her hair. She opened the door at his knock.

'You're back,' she observed. 'How nice. Did all go well? Come in, do. I was going to wash my hair…'

He smiled down at the pleased face. 'We're going out first. Wedding-rings—I had almost forgotten.' He bent and kissed her cheek. 'Get a coat and we'll go now.'

'I can't go like this.' She looked down at her tweed skirt and woolly jumper. 'Would you wait for five minutes? I'll be quick.'

'Five minutes then.' He strolled into the sitting-room and stood looking out of the window at the street. As soon as he could spare the time, he would take her to the cottage…

He took her to a Bond Street jeweller and waited patiently while she tried on various rings, choosing in the end a plain gold band, and when they were alone for a minute he said, 'Will you give me a ring, Araminta? You can pay for it out of your allowance later on.'

'Oh, yes, please. I thought of it, but I haven't any money. If you don't mind lending it to me…'

'Not in the least. I am, after all, going to endow you with all my worldly goods on Saturday.'

So she chose a ring for him too, as plain as hers. As they left the shop, he said, 'I have to go back to my consulting-rooms in an hour or so, but there's time for tea.'

He took her to a small and elegant tea-room and gave her Earl Grey tea and delicious cream cakes, and watched her ordinary face glow with pleasure. He didn't care for tea-rooms himself, but it was rather like taking a child out for a treat and he felt unexpected pleasure from that.

He drove her back presently, waiting only until she had let herself into the house before driving away for his appointment. 'I'll be here as near seven o'clock as I can manage, and we'll go home for dinner afterwards,' he told her.

Alice was at home, in the sitting-room doing her nails. She looked up as Araminta went in. 'You're back—what's for supper?' And when Araminta told her, she said, 'You'll see to it, won't you? I don't feel like cooking.'

'I'll get everything ready, but I'm going to see Mr Thorn at seven o'clock and I won't be back until later this evening.'

'Then Father will have to take me out. I don't feel up to cooking.'

Araminta, on her way out of the room, turned to ask, 'Alice, are you going to find a job? If you did, you could afford to pay someone to do the housework once a week.'

Alice shrugged her shoulders. 'I might think about

it, I suppose. It won't be any of your business anyway, will it?'

Araminta, in the kitchen making a fish pie, clashed the saucepans and their lids in an attempt to work off her ill-humour. It was fully dispelled at the sight of the professor, though. Pausing only to wish her father a pleasant good evening and warn Alice that the pie was in the oven, she skipped through the door and into the Rolls. It was surprising, she reflected, how quickly one could become accustomed to the good things in life.

Mr Thorn liked the professor, she could see that at once. They sat in the comfortable shabby sitting-room at the Vicarage and drank the coffee his wife offered them, and the two men discussed the chances of England against Australia during the next tour. It surprised her that Jason knew so much about cricket. The actual arrangements about the wedding were disposed of in no time at all; indeed, while they were being discussed, the professor's manner was that of a man who was talking of someone else's marriage, not his own.

'That's settled,' he observed placidly as they got into the car. 'We'll have dinner, shall we?' He gave her a sideways glance. 'Cold feet?'

'Certainly not,' said Araminta, who had.

Not for long, however; the evening was as comfortable as the previous ones had been. Curled up in her bed later that night, she thought sleepily that the future was everything she could wish for.

She hadn't expected flowers in the church when she arrived with her father, but there they were: glowing bunches on either side of the altar and a wrought-iron stand of roses and lilies and carnations near the pulpit, and there was a little posy of lilies of the valley and rosebuds for her—the vicar's wife had handed it to her in the porch, and then followed them into the church. Jason was there; for one dreadful moment she had imagined that he hadn't come, but there he was, enormous and calm, his best man, his registrar, beside him. She tucked her hand in her father's arm and walked steadily down the aisle.

Chapter 7

As any girl would, Araminta had dreamed of bridal veils and white satin and bridesmaids, but now none of these mattered. Mr Thorn had a splendid voice; the words of the service rolled off his tongue in all their splendour and she listened to every one of them, standing beside Jason, small and straight in her new suit, making her responses in a steady voice.

The service was quite short; they went out of the church arm in arm and her father and the best man came behind them with the vicar and his wife, and in the porch they stood for a few minutes, being congratulated. The professor was quite at his ease, his hand holding Araminta's in a secure clasp. He didn't let it go when her father said, 'Well, I'll be off. I'm taking Alice out to lunch—mustn't be late.' He pecked Araminta on the cheek and went away with a brief word to Jason, who wished him goodbye with a bland face which gave away nothing of his feelings.

'You'll come back for half an hour and drink to our health?' he asked Mr Thorn. 'Peter will wait while you take off your cassock, Vicar, and bring you and Mrs Thorn to our house.' He smiled down at Araminta. 'We'll go on ahead, my dear.'

He popped her into the car and drove away, beginning at once on a casual rambling conversation so that Araminta, who had suddenly found herself tongue-tied, began to feel normal again.

'I like the outfit,' said Jason. 'You look very nice, Araminta. You have good taste in clothes. Next week you shall go shopping and, if I can spare the time, I'll come with you.'

'I'd like that, for I've no idea what to buy.'

'I find that remark, coming from a woman, very hard to swallow.' He gave her a brief smile. 'I can see that I'll have to lend a hand.'

The Bullers were waiting in the hall, beaming their congratulations, while the dogs pranced around getting in everyone's way.

'I should have carried you over the threshold,' observed the professor. 'I quite forgot. Remind me to do so at some time.'

They had gone into the drawing-room and there was no time to talk, for a moment later the others arrived and Buller came in with champagne and a tray of tiny smoked salmon sandwiches. The talk was cheerful and of nothing much, and Araminta, drinking her second glass of champagne, thought how delightful it was among these friendly people who seemed to like her. The future, considerably enhanced by the champagne, bade fair to be rosy, and presently, when everyone had gone, they would spend a pleasant day together; there was a great deal she had to learn about Jason—his likes and dislikes, his work, what he liked to eat, how he spent his leisure...

Their guests went and they had lunch together, a festive meal at which Mrs Buller had excelled herself. They talked comfortably about the wedding, and he told her about Peter, his registrar, and a little—a very little—of his work at the hospital. Not just one hospital: he went wherever he was needed, frequently abroad.

Araminta sat quietly, not interrupting, listening carefully, storing away odds and ends of information. Later, she hoped, he would tell her about his family. After lunch, perhaps, since they had the rest of the day together.

She was to be disappointed; over their coffee he suggested that she might like to see her room and go with Mrs Buller round the house. 'I've some phoning I must do—I'll be in my study.'

So she went with Mrs Buller up the stairs and into a large room, furnished in a cunning mixture of pastel colours which showed the beautiful mahogany bed and dressing-table to the best advantage. There were little easy chairs and a *chaise-longue*, delicate bedside tables with porcelain lamp-stands and a vast tallboy. The clothes-cupboard along one wall was vast too; she could never fill it, she reflected, peering into the bathroom, and then, with Mrs Buller sailing in front of her, through another door into another bedroom, smaller, and furnished without any of the delicate colours and lovely fabrics of her own room.

'The professor's room,' said Mrs Buller. 'Well, his dressing-room, as one might say, ma'am.'

Araminta, momentarily diverted at being called 'ma'am', wasn't really listening.

They toured the house right up to the top floor, where the Bullers had their small flat, and it was all quite perfect. 'Would you wish to unpack now, ma'am, or shall I show you downstairs?'

'Oh, downstairs, please, Mrs Buller. I haven't much to unpack.'

The small sitting-room behind the dining-room was not grand like the drawing-room but very comfortable, with small Regency furniture and two high-backed armchairs, one each side of the fireplace. It would be nice to have tea there, thought Araminta, one each side of the fireplace like the married couple they now were, while Jason told her about his day...

There was another room too, a small library, with shelves of books and leather chairs beside the centre table. Araminta drew a blissful sigh and went back to the drawing-room.

There was no one there, but presently Buller brought in the tea-tray. 'Shall I let the professor know, ma'am?' he asked.

She jumped up. 'I'll go, thank you, Buller.' She tapped on the study door and was answered by a grunt. When she went in, Jason looked at her over his spectacles as though he had never seen her before. She faltered for a moment, then asked, 'Would you like your tea here?'

'Is it already that time? No, no, I'll join you.' His smile reassured her; she must have imagined that look of complete indifference...

They had their tea, making comfortable conversation the while, and later they had dinner together and it seemed to Araminta as though they had known each other for ever, talking at their ease, lapsing into silence without the feeling that there was need to talk.

It was while they were drinking their coffee that the phone rang. Buller answered it. 'The hospital, sir,' he said from the door, 'in your study.'

The professor went unhurriedly and didn't come back for several minutes, and when he did it was to tell her that he was needed urgently. 'I expect to be gone for some time,' he told her. 'I'll say goodnight now and see you at breakfast. Sleep well!'

Araminta reminded herself that she was a surgeon's wife now, and that this was the way it would be for the rest of her life: she would be shut out of the greater part of his life. She wasn't even sure if he wanted her to know about it. He had said that he wished for someone to be at home when he got there at the end of the day, but he had told her to go to bed. The pleasant picture she had had in her head of waiting up for him with a hot drink and a sympathetic ear she now dismissed as sentimental nonsense. She finished her coffee and, with Goldie and Neptune keeping her company, she embarked on a slow tour of the portraits and pictures on the drawing-room walls. Family, she supposed, and ancestors, some delightful miniatures, and a group of pencil sketches of a child's head. She wondered if they were of Jason, and fell to wondering about him as a small boy. Perhaps, when she got to know his sisters, she would be able to find out.

Since by eleven o'clock there was no sign of Jason, she went to bed. She fell asleep at once, waking in the small hours, her head very clear as it so often was at that time. Jason had married her for companionship, for someone to come home to. He had been honest about that: love wasn't going to enter into it, although later perhaps his liking might develop into affection. So she would be a good companion. She went back to sleep.

He was reading some papers when she got down in the morning, but put them down as she went into the dining-room, asked if she had slept well and if she had all she wanted.

'Like a log,' she told him cheerfully. 'How about you? Were you kept at the hospital?' An unnecessary question—she could see he was tired. 'It was something urgent? I do hope you were able to sort it out.'

They had sat down at the table and Araminta poured his coffee as Buller came in with several covered dishes. The professor got up, asked her if she would like eggs and bacon, scrambled eggs or boiled, served her and then himself, and sat down again. 'Yes, I hope the man will recover,' he told her, 'but shall I not put you off your breakfast if I talk about it?'

'I'll tell you when to stop,' she suggested, and began on her scrambled eggs.

She listened intelligently, although she didn't understand all that he was saying, and she did not interrupt; it was obvious to her that he was mulling over his night's work—thinking out loud, getting it off his chest. When he finished she said, 'It must be very satisfying to be a surgeon, to be able to do something when everyone else just has to stand around feeling helpless.'

'I quite often feel helpless, Araminta.'

'Well, yes, I can understand that, but you still go on doing your best, don't you? Will you be able to go to bed now for a few hours?'

She passed the toast-rack and poured him more coffee.

'No, I'm afraid not. I must go back to the hospital, but

I should be home by six o'clock. I'll give myself a morning off in a few days and we'll go shopping.' He smiled. 'At least, you will shop. I shall sit on one of those uncomfortable little gilt chairs and admire what you buy.'

He got up, gathering his papers. 'And before you argue about it, I wish my wife to have everything she wants, within reason. We can't possibly buy all you need in one morning, but we can make a start.'

He dropped a friendly hand on her shoulder as he passed her chair.

'Shall I walk Neptune and Goldie in the park?' she asked.

'Would you? Buller will tell you where he usually goes. We might take them again this evening before dinner.'

He had gone, leaving her to sit at the table, wondering what to do with the greater part of her day.

The problem was solved for her within a few minutes. Buller, coming in to clear, enquired of her in a fatherly manner if she would care to step into the kitchen and have a little talk with Mrs Buller. 'You'll be wanting to know how the house is run, ma'am—the shopping and so on—and you'll wish to inspect the household linen.'

So Araminta went along to the kitchen and sat down at the scrubbed table and paid attention to Mrs Buller's motherly titbits of information. She would, it appeared, be expected to see Mrs Buller each morning to discuss the day's meals with her. As to shopping, Fortnum & Mason delivered a weekly order, which she would make out, but there were, naturally, items needed from time to time which she might care to purchase for herself. The household expenses were handed to the professor at the end of each month, but no doubt he would be glad if those could be dealt with by ma'am.

Mrs Buller beamed across the table. 'If you've the time to spare, ma'am, we might take a look at the cupboards, and if you want anything altered I'd be happy to oblige.'

'Mrs Buller,' said Araminta earnestly, 'please don't alter anything. I'm sure the professor likes the way his home is run by you and Buller. I know very little about running a house such as this one; I've always done the housework and cooking and my home was small. I'll have to learn a great deal from you and I hope you will help me.'

'Don't you worry, ma'am, me and Buller will do all we can to make things easy for you. You'll soon find your feet—such a nice young lady as you are, you can't fail to get into the way of it. Now, shall we check the linen-cupboards first? You'll be wanting to take the dogs out presently—we might go through the china and the silver in the pantry when you come back before lunch.'

'That sounds fine.' Araminta got to her feet and they went upstairs to a vast cupboard at the end of a passage leading from the landing, and spent the next hour examining damask tablecloths, napkins by the dozen, piles of linen sheets and pillow-cases, blankets as soft and light as thistledown, and satin-covered quilts.

Mrs Buller answered her unspoken thought. 'The professor's parents lived here; his mother bought only the best.' She chuckled. 'I doubt if he knows the half of what's here. It's a pleasure to check everything with you, ma'am. Men just don't want to know.'

When they got back downstairs Buller had coffee waiting, and stayed a moment to offer advice as to the best way to get to the park. 'And I was to remind you to keep to the main paths, ma'am. The dogs are obedient, they'll come when you call them. They like a good run.'

It was a blustery day. Araminta found her way easily enough and, once in the park, let the dogs loose for half an hour. They rushed around happily, coming back to her every so often and racing away again. They came at once when she called, to her secret relief, and they walked briskly back home to find Buller waiting to dry paws and lead the dogs away for the biscuit they were allowed before settling down in front of the drawing-room fire.

As for Araminta, she was served a delicious lunch in the cosy room at the back of the hall and, still feeling like a guest in the house, she joined Goldie and Neptune by the fire to read the newspapers and then, wishing to know something of Jason's world, to search the bookshelves for something which might give her an insight into it.

She was struggling to understand a heavy tome on haematology when Buller brought in the tea, and she still had her nose buried in it when Jason came home.

He greeted her cheerfully, refused tea, and took a look at the book. She answered his raised eyebrows rather tartly. 'Well, I have to begin somewhere…'

He sat down in his chair and the dogs fell on his feet. 'Of course you do,' he agreed placidly. 'I'm delighted that you're interested. Will you allow me to choose the books which will teach you quickly and easily?'

She nodded, and he asked, 'What exactly do you want to know?'

'I want to be able to understand when you tell me things—the names of operations and illnesses, what goes on in hospitals, what sort of anaesthetics are used, the different treatments…'

'Supposing you start with the hospital? The different

departments, the operating theatres, the intensive care unit, Casualty. I'll bring some books with me tomorrow, and when you have read them I'll take you round so that you can see everything for yourself. Then you can work your way through the basics.'

'Thank you. It's so that I can understand a bit… You don't mind?'

'Of course not. I'm delighted. Now tell me, what have you done with your day?'

She told him, and then asked him about his.

He told her briefly and added, 'What about that walk? I could do with some fresh air.'

She got her coat and, with the dogs on their leads, went with him up to the park. It was a chilly evening and the wind was still blustery. They walked briskly, Araminta skipping a few steps now and then in order to keep up, and as they walked they talked—about nothing much and with comfortable silences from time to time. They might have been an old married couple, thought Araminta, peeping at his calm face. This must be how it would be when one had been married for half a life-time or more, walking companionably together, not having to make conversation, at ease with each other. Was that being in love? she wondered. In that case, was she in love with Jason? If so, it wasn't in the least as she had imagined it would be. Where were the excitement and the thrill, the galloping pulse, the caught breaths? But she liked him; she liked him very much.

They went back presently and, after a pleasant dinner, Jason excused himself and went away to his study, taking the dogs with him. Araminta, struggling once more with haematology, decided to find the nearest wool-shop in the morning and buy wool and knitting-needles and the most complicated pattern she could find.

She gave up her reading presently and sat thinking about her father and Alice. They knew where she lived now and she had given them her phone number, and she had half expected to hear from her father. She would wait a few days, she decided, and then go and see them. Jason had told her that she was to have an allowance; she could give some of it to Alice...

There was no sign of Jason, so presently she went to bed, not sure if he would expect her still to be there when he eventually came back into the drawing-room.

It was past midnight when he came into the room, opened the doors for the dogs, and stood looking out at the quiet garden. He was still mulling over the lecture he was to give on the following day and, to tell the truth, he had forgotten Araminta.

However, he felt pleasure at the sight of her at the breakfast-table in the morning, smiling and cheerful and as neat as a new pin. 'I've rather a busy day,' he told her, 'a lecture this afternoon to first-year students and one or two things to clear up afterwards. I'll probably be home rather later than usual.'

'I'll ask Mrs Buller to get dinner—when? Eight o'clock? We'll have something that won't spoil, so it won't matter when you come home.'

'Will you do that? I'll phone if I get held up.' He got up to go. 'I've given myself the morning off tomorrow; we'll do that shopping.'

She conferred with Mrs Buller after he had gone. 'He'll be tired,' said that lady. 'A nice fricassee of chicken and one of my cheese soufflés—he'll need to sit a while

with a drink—and what about a nice queen of puddings
to follow?'

'That sounds ideal, Mrs Buller. Do you want me to
do any shopping? I'll take the dogs first, but there will
be plenty of time after that.'

'There's a few good shops ten minutes' walk away,
ma'am. Buller will show you where. I could do with
some fresh thyme and marjoram and basil, if there is any.
There's a good greengrocer there—sells good fresh stuff.'

So Araminta took herself off after walking the dogs,
carefully primed as to how she should go by Buller. It
was pleasant walking through the quiet streets lined with
dignified houses, and the shops, when she reached them,
tucked away discreetly down a narrow lane, were delightful: the greengrocer, a delicatessen, a very up-market
newsagent, a chic boutique and, right at the end, a tiny
shop selling wools and embroidery silks.

She had a little money in her purse. She went in and
poked around under the friendly eye of the elderly owner.
She had intended to buy wool and needles; instead she
purchased a fine canvas with a complicated pattern of
flowers suitable for a chair-seat or a firescreen. She
bought the silks to work it, reflecting that she need never
sit idle again.

'You'll need a frame,' said the elderly lady; she found
one and demonstrated how to stretch the canvas taut between the hoops.

Araminta bore her parcel away, bought the herbs, and
then loitered outside the boutique. There wasn't much in
its small window, but she coveted everything there. Tomorrow, she reminded herself, she was to go shopping;
she had no idea what Jason would want her to buy, but
certainly she would need more clothes if she were to go

anywhere with him. The wedding outfit was all right but it wouldn't do for his wife; she had the good sense to know that.

She spent the afternoon getting started on the embroidery. She had never done tapestry before, but she was handy with her needle and not impatient. After tea she told Buller that she would take the dogs into the park, since otherwise they would have to wait until Jason came home, which might be late.

'The professor wouldn't wish you to go into the park alone in the evening.' Buller was deferentially fatherly. 'They will be quite happy in the garden, ma'am, and if the professor is late home, I will exercise them myself.'

So she went upstairs and changed her blouse, her only possible concession to dressing for the evening, and when she came downstairs Buller told her that the professor had telephoned to say that he would be kept late at the hospital. 'Eight o'clock at the earliest, ma'am, and what would you wish Mrs Buller to do?'

'Would she mind keeping dinner back? I'm sure the professor will be hungry. And please have your own meal at the usual time—I don't know when that is, but it's only just gone six o'clock.'

He replied suitably and went back to the kitchen, where he told his wife that the new missus was a very nice young lady. 'Very thoughtful,' he added. 'She'll suit the professor a treat. Won't get in the way of his work...'

Mrs Buller looked thoughtful and said nothing.

When the professor got home just after eight o'clock, Araminta greeted him without fuss. 'Would you like ten minutes or so before dinner, or are you ravenous?'

'Ravenous, but I'd like ten minutes first.'

'Well, sit down. I'll get you a whisky.' Which she did without waiting for his answer.

When she took it to him he said, 'I believe that I have been missing something before I took a wife.'

She smiled and went to sit down again. He wouldn't want to talk, she could see that. He was tired; perhaps after he had had a meal he would tell her about his day.

However, although he talked of this and that while they ate, he didn't speak of his work, and afterwards he whistled to the dogs, told her he would take them for a quick run, and left the house. She went back to the drawing-room, having agreed pleasantly, and presently, when he came back, he sat in his chair with the dogs beside him and, after a few casual remarks, put on his glasses and buried his handsome nose in the day's newspapers.

Araminta stitched busily, her thoughts just as busy. Did she bore him? He had said that he enjoyed her company, that he liked her, but was that enough to satisfy him? Would he have been happier married to a girl who expected to be entertained, talked to, admired, someone to break down his self-contained way of life? Perhaps I have made a colossal mistake, she reflected, and, for all I know, he's discovered that too. She looked up and found his eyes on her.

'You must not think that because I sit here with my nose buried in the newspapers that I am not aware and content to have you sitting there like a friendly mouse. You are filling an empty space in my life, and I think that when we have had time to get to know each other, we shall have a successful marriage.' He smiled. 'You agree, I hope?'

'Yes, I do,' she told him; anything else she might have said was cut short by the phone. It was a lengthy conversation, mostly yeses and noes on his part, and then a stream of instructions of which she understood very little. He went back to his reading then, and she sat for another half-hour or so, and then wished him a quiet goodnight and took herself off to bed.

He got up when she did and opened the door for her, touching her shoulder briefly as she went past him. 'Sleep well,' he said very kindly.

He hadn't said any more about their morning shopping, she thought as she got ready for bed. Perhaps he had forgotten about it, and she hadn't liked to remind him. She counted the money in her purse—there was almost nothing in it—and she wondered what she should do. Her clothes were quite inadequate but he didn't seem to be aware of that, and to ask him for money was something she couldn't do. She lay wakeful for a time until she decided with her usual good sense that worrying wouldn't help in the least; she might as well go to sleep. Which she did.

At breakfast he asked her if she had any preference as to which shops they should go to.

'Oh, we're going…?'

He stared at her. 'Of course—did I not say so?'

'Yes, yes, you did, but I thought that you might be too busy.' And, as he still looked at her with questioning eyebrows, 'I don't know about shops. I mean, I've always gone to Marks & Spencer or C & A, and just once or twice when there's been a sale to Country Casuals.'

He said smoothly, 'Then I think it had better be Harrods. I imagine there will be plenty of choice there.'

She said on an excited breath, 'What do you want me to buy?'

He was carefully casual. 'Oh, everything. Outdoor

clothes, dresses—you will get drawn into the consultants' wives' coffee-mornings and tea-parties—something for the evenings. I'm not very socially minded but I do have several close friends…'

Araminta's eyes had grown round, her head already agreeably filled with the picture of new clothes. 'Will you please tell me how much I may spend?'

'I can't do that, for I don't know what you intend to buy. You shall choose what you like, and if it costs too much I'll say so.'

'Promise?'

'Promise.'

On their way up to the first floor of Harrods Jason observed, 'You'll need things for the country—we'll go to the cottage next weekend. Get a Burberry.'

It was hard to know where to start, but once the saleswoman had grasped the fact that madam needed an entire wardrobe and that her husband was there, sitting on one of the fragile chairs, apparently agreeable to the entire shop-floor being purchased if his wife wished, there was neither let nor hindrance. Before an hour was out Araminta had acquired a tweed coat and skirt, two knitted suits, a short jacket, a number of pleated skirts with the necessary blouses and sweaters, a Burberry, and several pretty dresses. She had tried everything on and stood before Jason for his approval and, once or twice when the saleswoman wasn't there, had hissed at him in an urgent tone that he was spending an awful lot of money.

He had only smiled a little and told her to leave that to him. Bearing this remark in mind, she allowed the saleswoman to lead her to the footwear department, where she bought boots, several pairs of wildly expensive shoes, and stockings to match. Back again with the professor, she was reminded that she would need a hat for church, so she was whisked away to look at hats and, since she couldn't decide between a felt with a brim, which seemed to do miracles for her profile, and a jaunty little velvet affair, she had them both.

They were well into the second hour now, and she remembered that Jason had said that he had some patients in the afternoon. She sat down beside him, her cheeks pink, her eyes sparkling. 'I've bought simply masses of clothes. I expect you want to go home—it's almost lunchtime and you have patients later.'

He smiled a little. 'I'm glad you have found what you liked. I think that tomorrow you must come and get the rest.'

'Oh, undies? Well, yes, I would like some new things, but I could go to—'

He cut her short. 'No, will you come here, Araminta? I have an account and you will get everything you want. You might see a couple of frocks to wear when we dine out…'

She nodded wordlessly. She hadn't dared to look at any of the price-tags, but he must have spent a great deal of money. The clothes were good, though; she consoled herself with the thought that they would last for a long time.

The saleswoman came with the bill and he paid with a credit card, asked for everything to be delivered to his home, and swept Araminta out of the shop and into a taxi. He was a man who did things without fuss, she reflected: a lifted finger, a nod, and the doorman had a taxi at the kerb within moments.

Back in the house, sitting down to lunch, she tried to

thank him. 'I hope you don't think that I married you for money,' she said worriedly, 'because I didn't.'

'I know that, Araminta. You married me, did you not, for the same reasons as my own: friendship, pleasure in each other's company, a mutual liking? What is mine is now yours also, my dear.'

He left the house presently, with the warning that he might not be back until six o'clock. She longed to ask him where he was going after he had seen his patients—the hospital, she supposed. She wished once again that she knew more of his life. Patience, she told herself, there was plenty of time.

The Harrods van arrived then and Buller bore the boxes up to her room and she set about unpacking them. She tried everything on again, fearful that it would look different away from the luxurious showrooms, but the clothes looked even better, she decided, and hung everything away in the closet. Tomorrow she would buy undies...

After her solitary tea, with the dogs for company, she went back to her room and showered and got into one of the pretty dresses—nut-brown crêpe-de-Chine with a wide Quaker collar and cuffs of cream silk—and it became her very well. Pleased with her appearance, she went down to the drawing-room and sat down to work at her tapestry, and while she sat there she tried to decide what to do about her father and Alice. Did they want nothing more to do with her? she wondered. Should she go and see them, or wait and see if they phoned or wrote to her? She would ask Jason's advice when he got home.

He came presently, and she went into the hall to meet him. He said, 'Hello,' briskly, and then added, 'I've some work to do before dinner—you won't mind?'

Her 'Of course not' was uttered in her usual sensible way, but she wondered what he would have said if she had told him that she did mind. 'You're a busy man's wife,' she muttered, going to sit by the fire again. Perhaps it would be better if she didn't go to meet him in the evenings when he got home? That way, if he wanted to go at once to his study, he could do so without having to apologise. She picked up the tapestry and stitched busily, concentrating on the pattern, and presently Buller came to ask whether dinner was to be served at the usual time, or would the professor wish for a later hour?

'I'll go and see,' said Araminta. She tapped on the study door and went in in answer to his quiet 'Come'. He was at his desk, his glasses on his nose, a book in his hand. Just as he had previously done, he looked at her as though he was surprised to see her there. Indeed, she had the impression that he wasn't really looking at her; his thoughts were miles away.

'Dinner,' she said briskly. 'Mrs Buller would like to know when you would like it—it can easily be put back for a while.'

He took off his glasses. 'No need. I had rather forgotten the time.' His finger was marking the page in his book, and he withdrew it reluctantly. He glanced at his watch. 'I've five minutes? I'll be with you.' He got up to open the door for her. 'Make that ten—time for a quick drink.'

He spent the rest of the evening with her, talking about the cottage, telling her where it was, and then suggesting that as soon as he could manage it they might go to Tisbury and see how Lydia was getting on. 'And you must meet Marjorie,' he told her. 'I believe she intends to give a dinner party so that you can meet as many people as possible.'

Araminta said placidly, 'That will be nice,' and inwardly quailed at the prospect. She would have liked to ask about visiting her father and Alice, but Jason had picked up the medical journal from the table beside him and was leafing through it. She tidied away her work, said cheerfully, 'I'm quite tired after such an exciting day. Goodnight, Jason, and thank you for all my lovely clothes.'

Surely that might remind him to look at her and see the new dress? It didn't. He got up and went to the door with her, wishing her goodnight, smiling as she passed him, and going back to his chair to immerse himself in a long article concerning jaundice in the new-born.

As for Araminta, she gained her room, hung the dress in the closet and got ready for bed, all the while weeping quietly. She wasn't sure why; she only knew that she felt sad about something and unhappy.

It was silly to cry for no reason, she told herself sharply. She had had a lovely morning and tomorrow she would go shopping again; she had more clothes now than she had had in her entire grown-up life, so what had she to cry about?

She went to the windows and pulled back the curtains and looked out on to the garden below. It was very quiet at the back of the house; it might almost be country. As she looked, the outside light by the French windows of the drawing-room was switched on and the dogs, followed by the professor, came into the garden. The dogs raced off into the dimness beyond the circle of light, but he stood in its brightness, his hands in his pockets, looking up at the sky. She stared down at him, knowing now why she was crying. She had fallen in love with him. Perhaps it had happened weeks ago, when they first met, and she hadn't known it, only that she liked to be with him. So love wasn't always like a bolt from the blue; it could come gradually as well, sneaking up on one without warning. Now this was a pretty kettle of fish, since he had shown no sign of even a mild romantic thought about her.

The obvious answer was to get him to fall in love with her. Araminta, a practical girl and used to making the best of things, took one last loving look at the professor and jumped into bed, fired with the laudable purpose of doing just that. On the face of things it seemed unlikely, but with patience, and the help of a good hairdresser and products from the cosmetic counter at Harrods, and never forgetting to present him with a cheerful friendly manner with no hint of romance, she could at least have a good try.

Chapter 8

Araminta went down to breakfast the next morning wearing one of the new skirts, a silk blouse and a cashmere cardigan. The blouse and skirt were sand-colour, the cardigan duck-egg blue, and she had put on a pair of Italian shoes. Very suitable, she considered, turning this way and that before the enormous looking-glass behind the clothes-closet door. Perhaps Jason would notice…

He did indeed look up as she went into the room. He took off his glasses too, put down the letter he was reading and stood up with a pleasant, 'Good morning, Araminta,' but as soon as she sat, he resumed his own seat, gave her an absent-minded smile and picked up his letter.

Buller, hovering, murmured, 'Bacon and egg, ma'am, or perhaps a poached egg?'

She shook her head; she would have choked on either, but, since Buller was looking worried, she took a piece of toast and nibbled at it and poured herself a cup of coffee. Buller went away and she filled Jason's cup too and, since he had finished his letter, enquired if he would be home late or not.

'Round teatime, if I'm lucky. We'll take the dogs for a run. There's a letter for us both from Marjorie—she wants us to go over for dinner on Friday. There will be one or two friends there—a chance for you to meet them.'

She agreed quietly and, seizing the opportunity, asked, 'Jason, would you mind if I phoned Father? I'm not sure… That is, they may not want to have anything to do with me just at the moment, but perhaps once they're used to me being married to you…'

'You'd like to go and see them? Or have them here, by all means.'

She said awkwardly, 'I don't want them to think that I'm—I'm flaunting being married to you, if you see what I mean.'

He was putting his spectacles away in his pocket and didn't look at her. 'Yes, I see what you mean, Araminta. Perhaps it would be best if you phoned—that would give you some idea of how they feel.' He gathered up his papers and presently left the house.

She went to the kitchen for her morning's chat with Mrs Buller and, that done, went into the park with the dogs. After lunch she put on her new suede jacket and took herself off to Harrods. She felt a little uncertain without Jason; supposing they queried her right to charge everything to his account?

She need not have worried. Wandering around looking for underwear, she encountered yesterday's saleswoman, who, when Araminta confided her doubts, assured her that there was no problem and took it upon herself to

take her to the lingerie department and hand her over to
a friendly young woman who produced a tempting col-
lection of silk and lace garments. Araminta, shocked at
their price but carried away with their sheer prettiness,
allowed herself to be coaxed into buying nighties to go
with them and a pink quilted dressing-gown with matching slippers. She hadn't looked at their price-tags; Jason
had told her not to, hadn't he? She consoled herself with
the thought that everything she had bought was so well-
made and of such fine materials that she would be able
to wear them for years. She went back the way she had
come, and her friendly saleswoman stopped her to suggest that she might like to see a couple of dresses which
had just come in that morning.

That reminded Araminta that they were to dine with
Jason's sister. Perhaps a suitable dress? 'Something right
for a dinner party?' she asked, and was shown the very
thing: pale grey chiffon over a pink slip, its full sleeves
gathered into satin cuffs, the modest neckline bordered
with the same satin. Standing before the mirror, Araminta saw that it suited her very well. 'The thing is,' she
explained, 'I'm not sure if it's long skirts...'

'No problem, madam—if you would prefer a short
dress, then bring this one back and we will exchange it.'

The matter happily settled, Araminta took herself
home again to have her tea in the sitting-room she found
so cosy, the dogs beside her. The professor, coming home
earlier than he had anticipated, found her there, her nose
buried in a medical journal.

Her heart gave a happy leap at the sight of him, but
she said sedately, 'You're home early—how nice. Would
you like tea?'

'I had tea with Theatre Sister. Shall we take the dogs for their run?'

She got up at once. 'I'll fetch a coat...'

'Have you phoned your father?'

'No. Not yet.' She paused at the door, looking up at him. 'But I will.'

'Shall we do it now?' he suggested quietly, and picked up the phone on a side-table, dialled the number and handed the phone to her.

Her father answered.

'It's Araminta,' she told him, and flinched at his 'Tired of being a rich man's wife already, my dear? Just my joke. We're getting along very nicely. I could do with a small loan if you can spare it. Mustn't forget your old father, must you?'

Before she could answer, Alice's voice cut in. 'He's not tired of you yet? Early days, I suppose. Don't come back here, we're doing very nicely. Maybe I'll come and visit you one day.' She hung up, and Araminta put the receiver down slowly.

'They don't want to see you, but they expect you to send them money,' said the professor.

'Yes—how did you know?'

'My dear, I have met your father and sister. You have been a dutiful daughter and sister, and they're banking on that.'

'You make me sound a prig.'

'No, no, never that. Don't send them any money, Araminta, I'll deal with that side of things. I may be able to help your father in some way. Will you leave it to me?'

'You're kind. You have enough to do without bothering with my family.'

He put an arm round her shoulders. 'Allow me to be the best judge of that.'

They walked for an hour in the park with the dogs, comfortable in each other's company. Araminta could have walked forever, but they went back presently and dined in a leisurely fashion before the professor went to his study, leaving her to her needlework. This, she perceived, was to be the pattern of their evenings when they were at home—but not forever. Something must be done about that.

She went back to Harrods the next morning and had her hair washed and trimmed and dressed in an artful knot which made the most of its gentle brown. She had a manicure too. A facial was unnecessary, she was told; her skin was perfect, her eyebrows silky arches, her lashes long and curling. A little discreet lipstick, mascara of a suitable colour to enhance the lashes were all that was needed. She went back home well pleased with the beautician's efforts and hoped that she would be able to cope with the hair…

The professor, coming home rather later than usual, paused in the doorway to look at her. She was wearing the same pretty dress she had so hopefully worn after they had gone shopping together, and this time he noticed it. There was something different about Araminta too. He had always found her pleasant to look at but now he took a second look, uncertain what the difference was.

As she put down her work and got up to greet him, he said, 'That's a pretty dress…'

It wasn't much, but it was a start…

The following evening, getting ready for Marjorie's dinner party, Araminta paused to look in the looking-glass. She would never be pretty, but it was surprising what powder and lipstick and a professional hair-do did for one. She had worried over the right dress, but now, studying herself, she decided that she had made the right choice. The pink silk gleamed faintly through the grey chiffon and the dress was a perfect fit. As for the shoes— she had never had anything so elegant in her life before: grey satin with high, slender heels. She collected the evening bag which went with them, picked up the gossamer wool wrap and went downstairs.

Jason was in the drawing-room, standing by the open doors to the garden, watching the dogs romping together. He turned to look at her as she went in, and she thought how magnificent he looked in his dinner-jacket.

'Charming,' he told her in a voice which, to her anxious ears, sounded merely friendly, 'and will you wear these with it? A belated wedding-gift.'

Pearl drop ear-rings set in diamonds. 'They're beautiful,' she exclaimed. 'Thank you, Jason.' She crossed to the big mirror over the fireplace and hooked them in and stood admiring them.

'This too,' said the professor. 'I should have given it to you before we married, but it slipped my mind.'

He slipped the ring over her wedding-ring: sapphires ringed with diamonds and set in gold.

'Oh,' said Araminta, and then added, 'It fits…'

'I remembered the size when we bought the wedding-rings.'

She stretched up and kissed his cheek. 'Thank you, Jason. I'll take great care of it and wear it constantly.' Were her efforts paying off already? She doubted it. She wondered if any other girl had been given an engagement-ring with the observation that it had slipped the giver's memory.

It wasn't until she was sitting beside him in the car on the way to Marjorie's house that she had the unwelcome thought that he had given the ear-rings and ring to her because his sister might have commented on her lack of jewellery. It was a sobering thought.

Marjorie lived in a rather splendid house in Richmond with her husband and four children. Araminta wondered if she was as nice as her sister and tried not to feel nervous. There was no need for that; she was welcomed warmly, kissed and embraced and laughed over, and swept upstairs to see the children: three boys and a girl. 'Twins, my dear,' explained Marjorie. 'The boys— they're seven—then there's Piers, who is five, and our little Rosie—she's three.'

Marjorie was younger than Lydia but just as nice, thought Araminta, admiring all the children under the rather stern eye of an elderly nanny. She was whisked back downstairs then, and led into a room full of people.

'Old friends,' said Marjorie. 'They're all longing to meet Jason's wife!'

Jason took Araminta's arm and led her from one to the other of the guests, and his firm hand gave her confidence so that she lost her initial shyness and began to enjoy herself. She thought she was going to like everyone there, although she had her doubts about a pretty redhead, older than herself and strikingly dressed. 'This is Vicky,' Jason told her. 'We've known each other for a good many years now.'

Vicky kissed his cheek. 'Darling Jason, going behind my back like this and getting married—my heart's broken!' She smiled at Araminta. 'I do hope you'll be able to mend it, Araminta.'

Araminta smiled. 'I wouldn't have married him if I hadn't been sure of doing that!' she said lightly. She added mendaciously, 'Since you're an old friend of Jason's, I hope we'll be friends too.'

Vicky for once was uncertain. 'Oh, of course—we must have coffee some time. Or lunch. Jason used to take me to a delightful little restaurant—we might go there.'

Someone else joined them then, and presently she wandered off, leaving Jason faintly amused and Araminta at boiling-point. It rather suited her, for it gave her a pretty colour in her cheeks and added a decided sparkle to her dark eyes. When she was in a temper, he had noticed, they became almost black.

It was late by the time they got home, and Araminta wished Jason goodnight as they entered the hall.

'You enjoyed the evening?' he wanted to know.

'Yes, very much, thank you. I like Marjorie and your friends. I—I hope I did all the right things. I wouldn't like to let you down.'

He crossed the hall and took her hands in his. 'My dear Araminta, you were delightful—they all found you charming.'

It would be nice, reflected Araminta, if Jason found me charming too. Love, if this was love, wasn't at all what she had expected; any charms his friends might have seen in her were clearly not visible to him. She withdrew her hands gently, wished him goodnight once more and went upstairs.

Something would have to be done, and quickly, before that wretched Vicky got her elegant little claws into him.

How, she wondered, did one get a man to fall in love with one—even show an interest…?

Something which the professor was doing, if only she could have known. There had been something about Araminta which had caused him to look at her thoughtfully during the evening. There had been something different about her; it was as though she had made a discovery of some sort. Whatever it was, she was keeping it to herself. He smiled a little; her goodnights had been friendly but brisk. That was what he liked about her, he decided, her lack of coyness, her matter-of-fact way of looking at things. He went to his study with the dogs and sat down to make some notes for his next lecture, dismissing her comfortably from his mind. All the same, as he went to his room later he reminded himself that they would go to the cottage the next weekend—Araminta was good company and she had the gift of making herself invisible when he needed to work or read.

They left London the following Friday morning and, since they hoped to spend the weekend walking and pottering in the garden, Araminta wore the suede jacket and one of her new skirts with a silk shirt and cashmere sweater. She wore sensible shoes too, prudently added her Burberry and a headscarf, and added a plain jersey dress which the saleswoman had assured her would be most useful for countless occasions. One never knew, thought Araminta.

She hadn't seen much of Jason during the last day or so; he had been operating each day as well as seeing his private patients, and in the evenings she had sat quietly, saying little at their meal but listening while he talked.

'I don't bore you?' he had asked.

'No, I like to hear about your work. I don't always understand what you are saying but I can always look it up later on.'

He had laughed then. 'I really must arrange for you to come to the hospital.' He was kind and considerate to her. He had effortless good manners even when he was absorbed in his work, asking her how she had spent her day, suggesting things they might do together when he was free. Well, he's free now, she reflected as they drove through London, through its suburbs, and on to the Bishop's Stortford road.

The professor took the road to Saffron Walden from Bishops Stortford, and on reaching that small town turned into a narrow country road. He hadn't said much on their journey, but now he told her that they were only a mile or two from the village. 'It's rather charming,' he said. 'Ashdon lies in a valley with its church on a hill above it. Our cottage is on the other side of the village—ten minutes' walk away. It isn't isolated, but our nearest neighbours are a couple of fields away. I hope you'll like it.'

'I'm sure I shall.' Araminta found the countryside charming. 'Do you come here for your holidays as well as weekends?'

'The odd week, specially in the summer, but if you would prefer it we can go abroad.'

'I've never been out of England,' said Araminta cheerfully, 'and I don't know much of it. I shall be quite happy going wherever you want to go.'

'I go away fairly frequently,' he observed. 'Seminars, examining students—that kind of thing—and of course consultations, and to operate.' He added, 'On my own, of course.'

'Of course,' she agreed, and felt disquiet at the idea of

his being in some foreign country surrounded by charming women. Would he have taken her with him, she wondered, if he had loved her? Only time would tell her that.

Ashdon was charming, with the Rose and Crown pub overlooking a stream. The houses were old, its few shops looked as though they had been there for a very long time, and at the end of the village, halfway to the church, Jason turned into a roughly surfaced lane, passed a house or two and then, after a short distance, came to a halt before a wide gate. He got out and opened it and drove through to stop the car before the cottage door. It was a solid door, rather narrow and low, with a porch and seats on either side of it. The dogs were uttering happy barks and he said, 'Don't get out for a moment and I'll shut the gates—they always go a little mad when we get here.'

Not surprising, thought Araminta; the cottage was charming. It was whitewashed and thatched, with a great many small windows, and, as far as she could see, the garden stretched on all sides. She was as impatient as the dogs to get out and look around, and she skipped out when Jason opened her door.

It was a splendid day and, although the wind was fresh and chilly, there were white clouds scudding across a blue sky. She took a deep breath and looked with pleasure at the flowerbeds crowded with daffodils, early tulips and great cushions of polyanthus.

'What a beautiful garden—Jason, it's lovely…'

He unlocked the cottage door. The dogs pushed and jostled to get in first, and she stood just inside the narrow hall and looked around her. There were doors on either side and another facing her which Jason opened, revealing a small kitchen. She peered over his shoulder and saw that it had a tiled floor, plastered walls and an old-fashioned white porcelain sink. There were red enamelled saucepans on a shelf and a small fridge beside a gas stove.

She nodded her neat head in approval. 'It wouldn't be right to modernise it too much.' She went past him to the door and opened it, anxious to see more of the garden.

There was a small, bedraggled cat on the step, almost skeletal in its thinness. It made no effort to run away but mewed soundlessly as she bent to pick it up. The dogs crowded round, and she tucked it securely in her arms and said urgently, 'Jason…'

He had been turning on the gas, but something in her voice made him go to her. 'Look,' said Araminta, 'she was on the doorstep—she's starving and I think she's going to have kittens. Oh, Jason…'

He took the little beast and laid it gently on the table.

'There should be milk in the fridge—can you warm a little?' He was examining the pathetic bundle with careful hands. When she brought the milk, he said, 'I don't think there's anything broken or damaged. She's certainly starved. Will you give her the milk, just a little at a time, while I find a box and papers? She's very cold. I'll light the fire in the sitting-room and we can keep an eye on her.'

'Goldie and Neptune?'

'They'll not harm her.' He went away and came back presently with a box lined with newspaper. The cat had taken the milk eagerly, and he lifted her into the box and left it on the table.

'She needs more food,' said Araminta. 'Shall I give her more milk?'

'Yes, and see if there's anything in the cupboard—tinned milk?—just a little.'

Araminta went to look; the cupboard was well-stocked. 'There's a tin of sago.'

'Splendid. Will you warm it while I bring in the bags and see to the dogs?'

Half an hour later, as they sat with the cat before the fire and the dogs on either side of the box and mugs of instant coffee in their hands, the professor observed, 'Rather a disrupted start to our weekend, I'm afraid.'

'I'm glad we came and I hope she'll be all right. How lucky you were here.' At his questioning look, she added, 'You knew what to do…'

He didn't answer her but said presently, 'I expect you would like to look round the cottage—Mrs Lott keeps it clean and the cupboard stocked.'

The sitting-room was small, with a couple of armchairs, a table or two, an alcove with its shelves lined with books, and a corner cupboard. There were several watercolours on its cream-painted walls, and the open fire. A cosy place, thought Araminta, getting up and following him from room to room. The other one held a round table with straight-backed rush-bottomed chairs, a sideboard and a smaller table under the lattice windows. Jason opened a door beside the fireplace and mounted the narrow twisting stairs, and Araminta, quite enchanted, skipped up behind him. There were two rooms leading off a tiny landing with a bathroom between. Both were simply furnished, but the curtains and coverlets were chintz and the rugs on the polished floors were pale and silky. Someone had furnished the little place with great care, and surely Jason wouldn't have known how to choose the pretty lampshades and the wall-sconces in every room? A woman's touch, thought Araminta, and I wonder whose. She asked guilelessly, 'I expect you have your friends to stay? It must be quite beautiful in the summer.'

The professor, who had put his spectacles on so that he might examine the books on one of the bedside tables, took them off to look at her. After a moment he said blandly, 'From time to time,' and watched her cheeks grow pink. She looked pretty, and for some reason he found that disturbing. 'I think you may prefer this room,' he added. 'There's a marvellous view. Shall we go down and see how our visitor is getting on?'

The cat was asleep; she looked pathetic but the professor pronounced her to be better. 'A week's good food and cosseting and she'll be splendid.'

'We can keep her?'

'Of course, isn't that what you want?'

'Yes, oh yes. Oh, Jason...' Araminta went bright red, mumbled about lunch and fled to the kitchen. She wasn't sure what she had been about to say, but whatever it was would have been disastrous; she would have to pull herself together. She began to poke around the cupboards and presently looked out of the window and saw him walking down the garden with a spade and the two dogs. She stared at his enormous back; wearing a sweater and wellies, he looked years younger. 'I must stop drooling,' Araminta told herself. 'If he wants a companion and a friend, he has me; if he'd wanted to fall in love he'd have chosen someone like Vicky.'

So over the entire weekend she maintained a determinedly friendly manner which, while it might have concealed her true feelings, caused an awkwardness which the professor was quick to notice and wonder about. He had to admit to himself that in the short time in which he had known her she had become a part of his life which was becoming increasingly important to him, but he was aware that she was keeping him at arm's length. They were still on excellent terms; they tended the cat together, dug the garden, went walking with the dogs and went to church on Sunday morning, but Araminta had retreated and he couldn't think why.

As they drove back on Sunday evening, the dogs on either side of the cat's basket on the back seat, he asked casually, 'You enjoyed our weekend? You are quite happy, Araminta?'

She said rather too quickly, 'Oh, yes, I'm very happy, Jason. It was a lovely weekend and your cottage is beautiful…'

'Our cottage,' he corrected her. 'If you would like to look round the hospital, I've an outpatients' clinic in the afternoon on Tuesday; you could spend an hour or so there and pick me up at the end of the clinic.'

'I'd like that very much. I won't be in the way?'

'No, no. Theatre's closed on Tuesday afternoons. I'll speak to Sister.' Another step in the right direction, thought Araminta—to know something of his day at the hospital. Perhaps Theatre Sister would give her a few clues…

Buller welcomed them back with dignity, received the information that a cat had been added to the household, and took the dogs away for their meal, the cat in her basket in his hand. He assured them that Mrs Buller would feed the little beast and wait for the professor's wishes as to its future.

'Mrs Buller won't mind?' asked Araminta anxiously.

'Not in the least. Come down and we'll have a drink before dinner.'

There were messages for him on the side-table in

the hall; usually he took them straight to the study, but now he went into the drawing-room and sat down in his chair, holding them unopened in his hand. The weekend had been delightful; he had gone frequently to the cottage on his own, but with Araminta for company he had felt contented and relaxed. She had been happy, cooking their meals and making beds, helping in the garden, caring for the cat. All the same, there was something... She had looked charming at the cottage, wrapped in a pinny, bending over the stove; washing dishes was something he was quite unaccustomed to, but he had enjoyed the chore with her, drying the plates while they planned their day. He frowned. She had fitted into his life like a hand in a glove.

He took his spectacles from a pocket and began to read the first of the messages. He was interrupted by a slightly flustered Buller, swept aside by Vicky as she came into the room.

'Darling Jason, say you're glad to see me. I've had the dullest weekend and I'm bored to death, so I've come to share your dinner.' She glanced around her. 'Where's Araminta? She won't mind, will she?'

The professor put down his notes with a sigh. 'We are just back from the cottage,' he said as he got up. 'I'm sure Araminta will be delighted to invite you to dinner—she will be down in a minute.'

Vicky pouted. 'You don't sound very pleased to see me. Have you turned into a dreary old married man already?'

He smiled thinly. 'Here is Araminta.'

Araminta had changed into one of her pretty dresses and put on a pair of high-heeled shoes, something she was glad of when she saw Vicky. Her greeting wasn't to be faulted, and when Jason said that Vicky would like to stay for dinner, she said at once, 'Oh, how nice, of course she must. I'll tell Mrs Buller.' She smiled widely at them both and took herself off to the kitchen to discuss with Mrs Buller how dinner cooked for two could be stretched to three. When she went back to the drawing-room, Vicky was sitting close to Jason, chattering in her high voice and laughing a great deal.

He got up as Araminta joined them. 'Time for a drink before we eat—what will you have, Vicky?'

'Have you forgotten already? Gin and tonic, of course—unless there's champagne.'

He handed her the drink and turned to Araminta. 'Sherry for you, my dear?'

'Please, Jason.' She sat quietly, not attempting to compete with Vicky's light-hearted gossip, for the most part about people she had never heard of, mutual acquaintances of Jason and Vicky.

It was brought to an end by Jason's quiet, 'What a chatterbox you are, Vicky.' He glanced across at Araminta. 'Is our little cat quite comfortable?'

'Yes, she's asleep by the Aga.' Araminta turned to Vicky. 'We found a cat at the cottage—the poor thing was half starved and going to have kittens—we brought her back here to live with us.'

Vicky wrinkled her pretty nose. 'Darling, are you one of those dreadful do-gooders who go around rescuing animals and giving money to beggars? How absolutely dire.' She turned a laughing face to the professor. 'Jason, did you know Araminta was so—so worthy when you married her?'

The professor's mouth was a thin line but he spoke quite quietly. 'What a peculiar remark to make, Vicky, and I'm afraid you must consider me worthy too, for I also rescue animals and give money to beggars—Araminta and I are completely in accord over that.'

He had spoken without seeming to look at Araminta, who had gone an unhappy pink; now he smiled across at her. 'Isn't that so, darling?'

The 'darling' was a surprise and took her breath, but she nodded and smiled. He didn't mean it, of course, he was saying it to squash Vicky's spite. She lifted her chin and said to Vicky, 'I expect you have any number of friends?'

'Hundreds.' She sounded sulky. 'I scarcely have a moment to myself. Life's too short not to get as much fun out of it as possible.'

There was no need to answer that, for Buller came to say that dinner was served, and they went into the dining-room and ate the garlic mushrooms, rack of lamb and peach pavlova. The professor kept the talk general, which gave their guest no chance to get personal.

Over coffee Vicky said, 'You'll drive me home, won't you, Jason? I had a taxi here—there's never anywhere to park a car...'

'It will have to be a taxi back,' he told her. 'I'm on call and must stay at home, I'm afraid. Buller shall get you a taxi.'

She was in no hurry to leave, however, and when the door finally closed behind her Jason collected up his notes. 'I'll have to see to these,' he told Araminta, 'if you'll forgive me. A wasted evening...'

Araminta wasn't sure if he meant that Vicky had wasted his evening or if he had intended to spend it in his study. She murmured a nothing and said that she would go to bed. Her goodnight was cheerful, and she added, 'It was a lovely weekend—thank you for taking me, Jason.'

He came to the foot of the stairs. 'Thank me?' He sounded harsh. 'Why should you thank me? I found every moment of it delightful.'

He turned away and closed the study door after him and she went on upstairs, thinking over his words. It was early days, but was he at least noticing her? Although I can quite see why he married me, she reflected, to escape from women like Vicky; I'm a buffer, aren't I? The thing is to make the buffer attractive.

She laid her head on her pillow and slept at once, sure that she had at least one foot in the door, as it were.

The professor came home at lunchtime on Tuesday and drove Araminta to the hospital, where he handed her over to Theatre Sister, a tall, stout lady with iron-grey hair, small, twinkling blue eyes and an extremely brisk manner.

'Take care of her,' he said to Sister Weekes. 'I'll be finished around five o'clock if you'll send her down to OPD.'

He went away and Araminta started on her tour. Sister Weekes was a good guide and she was willing to answer Araminta's questions. In reply to the query as to how long she had worked with Jason she laughed. 'Years, my dear. I can remember him when he was a houseman here; always had his nose in a book, very studious, although he played rugger for the hospital. There was no holding him back, of course—got the best brain I've ever come across and knows how to use it. Glad he's married; the girls have been after him for ten years and, since he spends his leisure with his nose in a book, he might easily have found himself married to one of them without realising it. He'll be happy with you, though.'

Araminta said faintly, 'I do hope so,' and then, more strongly, 'But he did know he was marrying me, if you see what I mean.'

'Never did a better thing in his life,' declared her companion. 'Shall we go to the children's wards?'

By the time they reached OPD the vast hall was almost empty. 'Still at it?' asked Sister Weekes. 'Sit down here, my dear, he won't be long now. I'll have to go, I'm afraid. A pleasure meeting you—come again whenever you want to. I'll probably be in Theatre, but there's no reason why you shouldn't poke around on your own.'

She sailed away and Araminta sat on one of the benches and watched as the last handful of patients went one by one through the doors at the end of the hall. Presently Jason came out, looking quite different in a long white coat with a stethoscope hanging round his neck. He had a sister with him and an arm full of folders, and when he saw her he called, 'I'll be with you in a moment, Araminta,' and disappeared through another door.

'You haven't been waiting long?' he asked as he returned presently and, when she said no, asked if she had enjoyed herself.

'Yes, oh, yes. I had no idea. I wish I were a nurse so that I could work with you.' She had spoken without thinking, and blushed at the silliness of her remark.

'So do I,' said Jason softly. 'On the other hand, I'd rather have you to come home to, Araminta.'

He was staring at her so intently that she looked down at her person. 'Is something wrong?' she asked him.

'No, no, something is very right and I've only just discovered it.'

'Oh, good. I expect you are pleased when things go right. Do you want to go home now?' She stood up, admired her shoes for a moment, and then looked up at him. 'I like your Sister Weekes.'

'So do I. She's a martinet in Theatre but she has a heart of gold.'

Back at the house, Araminta went off to see how the cat was faring.

'Two kittens,' Mrs Buller told her. 'Little dears, and she's fine, ma'am. But she needs a bit of feeding up.'

'The professor will be pleased.' She hurried to tell him and he went back to the kitchen with her, bending over the box, his arm round Araminta's shoulder.

'She'll do. Do you feel like a quick walk when we've had tea?'

The rest of the evening they spent together, and Araminta went to bed almost happy. Jason didn't just like her, he was actually enjoying being with her. She lay awake for a while, deciding what she should wear the next day—it was very important to make herself as attractive as possible. She couldn't compete with someone like Vicky, but bread and butter made a nice change from cream cakes, and she didn't think Jason was partial to too many cakes...

Chapter 9

Araminta got up early so that she had plenty of time to arrange her hair just so, do her face carefully and get into a knitted two-piece in a pleasing shade of brown. It had been very expensive but worth every penny, she decided, surveying her person before going down to breakfast.

Indeed Jason gave her a second and lingering glance as she sat down. He wondered why he hadn't seen that she was really rather pretty. Also so restful, he concluded, as he opened his letters.

Araminta had seen the second look and felt satisfaction. Given a month or so and no interference from Vicky, another weekend at the cottage, and regular visits to the hairdresser, there might be real progress. She had no great opinion of her powers to attract, but love had given her a strong determination. She ate her breakfast, leaving him to read his post in peace.

She was in the kitchen just before teatime, feeding the

cat, when Buller came to find her. 'Miss Alice Smith has called, ma'am. I've put her in the drawing-room.'

'My sister? Oh, thank you, Buller. Could we have tea presently, please?'

Alice was fingering the small silver ornaments set out on a small ebony side-table. She turned round as Araminta went in. 'Landed on your feet, haven't you?'

'Hello,' said Araminta. 'It's nice to see you, Alice. You'll stay for tea?'

'That's why I came—well, partly. I wanted to see where you were living before we go.'

'Go where?'

'Father's being transferred to Bournemouth—promotion. More money too.'

'He's pleased?'

'You bet he is. What's more, he's had an offer for the house. You're not the only one to live on easy street.' Alice abandoned her restless wandering and sat down near the fire. She gave a little laugh. 'Been shopping too...'

'Yes. Will you like living in Bournemouth, Alice?'

'Rather. Plenty going on there. I might even get some sort of job—a boutique or something like that.'

'When is Father going? Is he coming to say goodbye?'

Alice shrugged. 'I don't know—he's fed up with you leaving us in the lurch.'

It was a good thing that Buller brought in the tea then, for Araminta was on the point of answering that. She stayed silent and poured their tea and handed scones and tiny sandwiches and a rich chocolate cake, while Alice talked of the new clothes she was going to buy.

'You'll miss your friends,' said Araminta.

'No, I shan't. I'll soon have new friends and plenty of

men to take me out. They like a pretty face. I could have got your old professor if I'd wanted him.'

'Presumably you didn't want him!' said Jason from the doorway. 'Welcome to our home, Alice.' He crossed the room and bent to kiss Araminta. 'I'm home early,' he told her, 'and I hope it won't upset your arrangements if an old friend of mine and his wife come to dinner?'

Buller came in with fresh tea and Jason sat down with the dogs beside him. It was Araminta who spoke. 'Alice came to tell me that Father has got promotion—they're going to live in Bournemouth.'

'Indeed? Will you like that, Alice?'

'Yes, and so will Father. We're going quite soon, as soon as the house is sold.'

'Perhaps a little difficult in these times?' he suggested blandly.

'We've got a buyer.'

'Splendid. Perhaps before you go you will be our guests for dinner?'

'At a restaurant? Will you phone Father and fix a date? It'll have to be soon.'

'Tomorrow evening? I'll book a table in the hope that it suits him. Would you ask him to give me a ring this evening?'

'Where are we going?'

'What about the Gay Hussar?' He turned to Araminta. 'You'd like that, my dear?'

'It sounds delightful.'

Alice got to her feet. 'I bought a new dress the other day, and now I can wear it. It's a dressy sort of place, isn't it? I must get my bus.'

'Short and pretty, I should think,' said Araminta.

'Buller will get you a taxi,' said the professor, and submitted to Alice's kiss.

She didn't kiss Araminta but waved her fingers at her with a 'See you tomorrow evening, thanks for the tea.'

Araminta stood at the door with Jason and watched the taxi drive away. In the hall she said, 'That was very kind of you to invite Father and Alice to dinner. I—I was a bit surprised to see her but it's such good news that Father has promotion. I think they'll be very happy at Bournemouth and he's sold the house—it seems like a miracle.'

She glanced at him and found him looking at her with a half-smile.

'It wasn't a miracle,' she said slowly. 'You've done it all, haven't you? You said "Leave it to me" and I did, but I never thought… Why did you go to so much trouble?'

'I wanted to make you happy, Araminta.' He was standing very close to her, looking down on to her enquiring face.

'You have, oh, you have, Jason. Thank you very much indeed. I can't thank you enough. Was it very difficult?'

'No, no. I do know a number of people and they know other people, so sooner or later one gets in touch with the right person.'

'Father doesn't know it was you…?'

'Certainly not, nor must he be told. You agree?'

'Yes, of course I do. Is the Gay Hussar the kind of place where you dress up?'

'A pretty dress will do.'

'I wouldn't want to outshine Alice—well, I can't do that, she's so pretty, but you know what I mean.'

'I'm sure you will wear exactly the right frock,' he assured her solemnly.

* * *

Her choice, it seemed, was just right—silk jersey, very plainly cut; its colour was stone, the height of fashion and, mindful of Alice's feelings, she didn't wear the diamond ear-rings, only her ring. She and Jason made an elegant pair as they went into the restaurant and were shown to their table. Jason had arranged for a taxi to bring Alice and her father, and barely a minute later they arrived. Her father looked very much at his ease; he was a good-looking man and well-dressed, and Alice walked beside him, aware that she was gathering admiring looks, smiling radiantly, knowing that her pale blue dress became her. The professor stood up to welcome them and Araminta's father stooped to kiss her cheek. There was no warmth in his greeting but he shook hands with Jason, fussed over Alice and then looked around him. It was obvious that he had no intention of saying much to Araminta, and after a brief silence the professor took affairs into his own hands, ordering drinks, making conversation, drawing Araminta into it with effortless ease.

Once the meal was started it became easier, and when Alice had had a glass of wine after her sherry, she started to talk about her plans for Bournemouth. She was full of ideas and certain that life there would be exactly as she planned and presently her father joined in. The professor, listening gravely to what they had to say, knowing most of it already, encouraged them to talk so that, after those first few awkward moments, the dinner party was a success.

Only as they stood in the foyer, waiting for the taxi and saying goodbye, did Mr Smith say suddenly to Araminta, 'Of course, you treated us very badly, my dear. I am surprised that any daughter of mine could be so cold-hearted and ungenerous, leaving us to manage on our own. However, I shall say no more about it; Alice and I will do very well at Bournemouth, but I find it hard to forget your selfishness even if I can forgive.'

Araminta was thankful that Jason and Alice were standing a little apart and hadn't heard this. She said quietly, 'Goodbye, Father. I'm glad you have such a promising future,' and saw with relief that the taxi had arrived.

It wasn't until they were driving back home that Jason asked, 'What did your father say to upset you, Araminta?'

'Oh, nothing much, I'm sure he didn't mean it.' She turned her head away, fighting a wish to weep. 'They did enjoy themselves. Thank you for inviting them, Jason.'

He said harshly, 'Unless you wish to do so, you do not have to see your father or Alice again. They have treated you badly, used you as a housekeeper and bread-winner, and shown not one jot of gratitude. They do not deserve to have their circumstances improved but it was the only way I could think of that would set you free.'

He had set her free when he married her but she didn't say so and, before she could even speak, he went on in his usual calm way. 'Would you like to come to my rooms tomorrow afternoon? I've several patients to see but I should be through by four o'clock. I'd like you to meet Mrs Wells and Mrs Dunn—they have been with me for years and they're dying of curiosity about you.'

'I'd like that. Are your rooms close by? Can I walk there?'

'Easily, but I'll be home for lunch. I'll drive you there and we can come home together.'

'Oh, good. I won't be in the way?'

'No, Araminta.' The certainty in his voice left her content.

* * *

When she went down to breakfast the next morning it was to find him already gone. 'Needed at the hospital,' Buller told her. 'Left the house soon after I was up, ma'am. I was to tell you that he'll be home for lunch but to make it one o'clock.'

There was plenty to keep her busy during the morning: the dogs to walk, flowers to arrange, Mrs Buller to see, the cat and kittens to attend to. All the same, the hours dragged before she would see Jason again.

'Just remember why he married you, my girl,' she reminded her reflection as she tidied her hair and checked her make-up. 'Companionship, friendship, and someone to talk to…'

He was a little late for lunch, but nothing in his manner betrayed that he had been operating since before eight o'clock that morning. 'A nasty road accident,' he told her. 'Teenagers in a stolen car.'

'Tell me about it.'

Since she obviously wanted to know, he told her and, when he had finished, he said, 'What a good listener you are, Araminta,' and smiled as he added, 'But that is partly why I married you, isn't it?'

He spoke casually but he watched her from under his lids as he spoke.

'That's right. But you see, I am really interested—I want to know about your work.' That sounded a bit too enthusiastic. 'I think perhaps I would have liked to have trained as a nurse.'

Jason's rooms were in Wigmore Street, in a tall red-brick house with a dignified entrance and well-polished brass plates beside the door. He led her up a flight of stairs and opened a door on the landing. The waiting-room, comfortably furnished with flowers here and there, was light and airy, the windows curtained in a pretty flowery chintz. Reassuring, thought Araminta, and soothing to a nervous patient. Mrs Wells was there, and so was Mrs Dunn, both cosily shaped, with kind faces and severe hair-styles. It wasn't until Araminta was shaking hands with them that she acknowledged the fear that they might have been willowy young women with beautiful legs and lovely faces.

They carried her off to a small room behind the waiting-room and sat her down. 'You'll have a cup of tea, Mrs Lister? We are so very glad to meet you. I must just pop back and see if the professor wants anything and show in the first patient, then I'll be back and Dolly will have to go into the consulting-room.' Mrs Wells beamed at Araminta. 'We have been so anxious for the dear professor to marry— a family man at heart despite his books, we have always said, and that lovely house, just right for little children.'

There was more than enough room for half a dozen, thought Araminta, three of each, and the little girls would be blue-eyed and fair-haired and beautiful...

'Such a joy, I always think,' Mrs Wells was saying, 'and in such a pretty village.' She was looking rather anxiously at Araminta, who made haste to agree although she wasn't sure what she was agreeing about.

Mrs Dunn nodded her head in a pleased way as Mrs Wells went away, to return presently so that Mrs Dunn could take her place. 'We'll have a cup of tea now, shall we? Dolly will be some time with the patient— she's rather elderly.' She poured the tea. 'How do you like being a doctor's wife? Well, I should say surgeon, shouldn't I? And a busy one too—such a shame that you don't see more of each other. My hubby was a chemist so he had regular hours.' Just for a moment she looked wistful. 'There's nothing like a happy marriage. Me and Dolly, we've been lucky and still are, for the professor is so considerate. There's nothing we wouldn't do for him.'

Araminta accepted more tea. She had wanted to know as much as possible about Jason; here were rich pickings. She asked, 'Have you both been working for him for a long time?'

Mrs Wells was only too glad to gossip and, when she was at her desk, Mrs Dunn was in and out. Araminta learned a good deal about Jason, things that she thought he might not tell her himself: hours on end at a railway crash, lying under the wreckage of a huge transporter, amputating a leg so that the driver might be freed, being lowered from a helicopter on to a giant wheel at a fun-fair to deal with a child's head injuries. There were countless incidents about which he had never spoken except, of necessity, to his two faithful helpers.

Later, when the last patient had gone, he came to fetch her, and she had such a strong urge to fling her arms round his neck and tell him how much she loved him that she could only nod and smile when he asked her if she had enjoyed meeting Mrs Wells and Mrs Dunn.

A week went by, during which Araminta had ample time to realise that concealing her true feelings from Jason while at the same time doing her best to make him fall in love with her was going to be fraught with hazardous moments. Once or twice she had caught him looking at her in a thoughtful manner, rather like a doctor not quite sure of his diagnosis, but not, to her regret, in the least lover-like. On the other hand, he had taken to sitting with her after dinner in the evenings, immersed in a book, it was true. She took pains with her appearance, taking care to sit so that the gentle rose-coloured light from the lamp on her table shone on to whichever of the new dresses she was wearing. Not that he would notice, she reflected.

The professor did notice. Immersed in the newspapers or the poems of Juvenal—in the original of course— he yet found the opportunity to watch Araminta sitting there, the picture of tranquillity, stitching away at her tapestry. It was a pity she never looked up, for then she would have seen that his manner wasn't in the least thoughtful, so they sat, the pair of them, each concealing their true feelings, entirely at cross-purposes.

All the same, they were the best of friends, exchanging their day's news each evening, and Araminta, primed by the books he had found for her, was beginning to understand what he was talking about while he listened with inward amusement to her accounts of coffee-mornings and afternoon teas with his colleagues' wives. They were kind to her, she told him, although some of the older wives were a little overpowering.

'We'll give a dinner party,' he told her, 'but not just yet. I thought we might go to the cottage again...'

'I'd like that—when?'

'This weekend, if that suits you? I'll be free on Saturday and Sunday.'

The weather began to worsen towards the weekend but they decided to go just the same. They left on Friday evening in pouring rain and a fierce wind, which seemed fiercer once they had left the city behind them and were driving through the flat Essex countryside. They reached the cottage without mishap to find that Mrs Lott had left a meal ready to be warmed up, the fire laid and the central heating on. They had brought the dogs with them, but Blossom the cat and her kittens had been left in Mrs Buller's care. Araminta went from room to room turning the lights on, while Jason lit the fire and then took the dogs for a run while she got the supper. The three of them came back presently, wringing wet.

'It's turning nasty,' observed Jason. 'Let's see what the weather forecast is.'

'A rapid deterioration in the weather,' said a serious forecaster. 'Storm-force winds likely to sweep across the country within the next twenty-four hours.' There would probably be damage to buildings; people were advised to secure their homes and avoid travelling unless it was necessary.

'We had better go home tomorrow morning,' said Jason as they sat at supper. 'I'm going to make everything secure here and we can leave as soon as possible.' He spoke easily. 'I think it best if we return early. I've a list on Monday morning.'

Araminta hid disappointment. She had been looking forward to a day or two with him away from phone calls and emergencies, to say nothing of the hours he spent in his study. He would have time to talk to her. What about, she had no idea, but if there was nothing else to attract his attention he might take rather more interest in her as a person. 'That seems sensible,' she observed. 'I've not unpacked the bags yet. What a good thing.'

After their meal the professor went out again with the remark that he would be back presently, but it was half an hour before he returned, very wet.

'Where have you been? You're wringing wet again.' Araminta sounded so like a nagging wife that he smiled. 'I've battened down the garden shed and the coal-shed, and moved everything which can be moved into the lean-to. I went down to the village and saw Mrs Lott, and told her that I would shut off everything before we go so that she won't need to come here until the weather improves.'

'The cottage will be all right? The roof...?'

'Thatch, my dear. Pretty safe, and the walls are thick. The weather's worsening, though. Suppose we leave after breakfast—nine o'clock suit you?'

She bade him goodnight and went upstairs to her bed, leaving everything ready for their breakfast in the morning. She would get up early and empty the fridge and pack away the tins and packets—things which would come to no harm if they were stored for some time. The wind was howling round the cottage as she got into bed, and she had expected that it would keep her awake, but she was asleep within five minutes, her last thoughts of Jason, as they always were.

A hand on her shoulder brought her upright in the dark room, lighted by the torch the professor held. 'My dear, I'm sorry to wake you. We have to go back as soon as possible. Lydia phoned—how the lines are still working is a miracle—Jimmy is missing. The river has broken its banks and parts of Tisbury are under water. He's been staying with a friend on the other side and the friend's parents phoned her to say that their boy came back a few hours ago and Jimmy wasn't with him. Lydia is distraught. I must go and see what I can do...'

Araminta tossed her hair over her shoulder. 'Of course you must. What's the time?'

'Five o'clock. I'll make tea while you dress.' He went away and she shot out of bed and into her clothes, tied back her hair with a handy piece of string and hurried downstairs. Jason was in the kitchen, pouring hot water into the teapot. 'Thank heaven we've got gas.' He put their mugs on the table and put down water for the dogs. 'Can you be ready in ten minutes?'

'Yes.' She opened the fridge door and began to load its contents into the box they had brought with them. She was as good as her word. She was ready, her Burberry closely belted, a scarf tied over her head and the dogs beside her when he came in, closing the door against the gale.

He loaded their bags and the box and came back for the dogs, clipping on their leads. 'In case we need to get out of the car,' he explained in his unhurried way. 'Stay there and I'll come for you.'

It was dark in the cottage for there was no electricity. It seemed like hours instead of minutes before Jason came back with the torch, and Araminta had her teeth clenched on a scream, but his unworried, 'Ready? Don't let go of me once we're outside or you'll be blown over,' reassured her.

She had no intention of letting go; she clung like a limpet as they went outside. The car was very close; he opened the door and tossed her in as though she had been a feather, made his way round the bonnet and got in beside her, fastened her seatbelt and switched on.

'Did you turn off the gas and electricity?' asked Araminta and he laughed.

'What's so funny?' she asked edgily.

'No, no, not funny, I find it so reassuring that you should think of it—as though we were going on holiday and you were having last-minute doubts about leaving the family home. I am delighted to see that you are not prone to hysterics when things go a little wrong.'

'I was about to scream when you came back,' said Araminta, ever truthful.

The professor turned to look at her. The scarf tied

tightly over unbrushed hair did nothing to enhance her ordinary face, pale with fright. He thought that she looked beautiful. He sent the big car forward carefully, but not before he had bent to kiss her.

She sat like a mouse, not moving a muscle as he drove through the lane, already flooded in places, and when the headlights revealed a fallen tree only yards ahead she made no sign as he reversed back up the narrow road until he reached a crossroads. 'Look at the map,' he told her. 'The signpost says Little Mitchford—can we work round through there back to the Bishop's Stortford road?'

'Yes.' She was peering at the map with the aid of a torch. 'At Little Mitchford you'll have to turn left to Great Winley…'

'If I can. We'll have a go!'

It was lighter now, as light as it would get for some time, the sky leaden and menacing, and Jason switched on the radio.

'Severe storms,' said a cheerful voice, 'increasing in the west of the country, causing severe flooding; minor roads blocked by fallen trees; drivers are urged to stay at home unless their journey is absolutely necessary.'

'Could we go by train?' began Araminta.

The voice continued, 'Train services to the south and west of the country are seriously disrupted.'

'I'll take the car, Araminta,' said the professor, and added, 'I shall go alone.'

Araminta, who had no intention of allowing him to do any such thing, said, 'Yes, Jason,' and then, 'We turn off here to Great Winley.'

They finally gained the main road, almost empty of traffic, but they were driving into the wind now and it slowed their progress; nonetheless Jason drew up before their front door soon after eight o'clock.

'A hot bath for you, Araminta and a few hours in bed. But we'll have breakfast first, shall we?'

'I'll tell Buller. You're going to Tisbury?'

'Of course, but breakfast first.'

A worried Buller came into the hall as they went in with the dogs. He said, 'Good morning, ma'am, professor. We were a little worried. You'll be needing a good breakfast. Very nasty weather outside.'

'Very nasty,' agreed his master. He looked at Araminta. 'Breakfast in twenty minutes, my dear?'

Araminta, the picture of wifely acqiescence, said yes, and watched him throw off his wet raincoat and go into the drawing-room to let the dogs out into the garden. Upstairs she tore out of her clothes, showered in less than no time and dressed again, this time in tartan trousers and a thick pullover. Buller had taken their Burberrys to dry, and her wellies were still in the car. She unpacked her shoulder-bag and packed it again with spare undies, toothbrush, comb and a torch, bundled her hair into a plait and found a thick woollen scarf and gloves. With five minutes to spare she was downstairs again, leaving the bag, scarf and gloves in her room.

Jason had changed too. He glanced up as she joined him in the drawing-room and they went to have breakfast. 'You need not have dressed again—a dressing-gown would have done well enough. In fact, you could have had breakfast in bed—I should have thought of that.'

'It's nice to feel warm again,' said Araminta chattily, 'and I'm famished.' She applied herself to breakfast and made no effort to talk. Jason was looking thoughtful, probably deciding the best way to get to Tisbury.

They didn't linger over their meal. As they left the dining-room he said, 'I'll be off now. Don't worry if you don't hear anything, probably the phone won't be working, but I'll keep in touch as soon as I can from the car.'

He had stopped to fondle the dogs, and started to get into his Burberry.

Araminta said nothing but skipped upstairs, to appear in no time at all clad for the journey.

His frown might have intimidated anyone less determined than Araminta. 'I'm coming with you,' she told him.

'Indeed you are not…' His voice was icy.

'You'll need someone to hold the torch and open the car doors—and go for help. I'm coming. I'm sorry if it annoys you. I won't say a word in the car and I'm not a bit frightened when you're driving.'

'You have no need to butter me up.' He sounded outraged.

'Don't be silly,' said Araminta. 'I'm sensible and strong and another pair of hands, which I'm sure you will need when we get there. I'm coming.'

'I don't want you with me, Araminta.'

'I know that, but you'll just have to put up with me!'

'It will probably be dangerous.'

She gave him a long look. 'That's why I'm coming,' she told him quietly. 'We're wasting time…'

He wrapped her round with his great arms. 'If anything should happen…' he said half-angrily, but she didn't care; it was like being held close by a very solid tree. In a Burberry, she reflected absurdly.

'Nothing will happen,' she muttered into his shoulder.

He ran a gentle finger down her cheek. 'Let's go,' he said.

It wasn't until they were clear of London and its suburbs that the full force of the storm made itself felt. The rain beat relentlessly against the windscreen and they could see the flooded fields on either side of the motorway. There were trees lying uprooted, and several times Jason had to brake to avoid falling branches, but the car held the road well and, since Jason appeared unperturbed, Araminta did her best to imitate him. They didn't talk; it was hardly a situation where conversation was required, and they had said all that there was to say for the moment.

After what seemed to her to be a lifetime, they reached the Tisbury turn-off and found the road for the most part under water. It was strewn with debris from the storm as well, and twice Jason stopped the car to get out and haul aside branches lying across the road. It was noon by now and there were no signs of the storm's dying down; it was still raining as hard as ever and the sky hung like a dark grey blanket over their heads. Araminta, peering from her window, just hoped that Jason knew the way, for there were narrow roads every mile or so and lanes running off in all directions, all awash. It was with relief that she glimpsed a glimmer of light and saw that they were passing scattered houses, most of them with candles in their windows. 'Tisbury,' said Jason, and looked at the car clock. 'Almost one o'clock.'

Araminta, practical and hungry, observed that it was lunchtime, and he laughed. 'You have hidden depths which continue to astonish me, my dear.' He drove slowly now as they neared the village, and she sat wondering just what he had meant. Obviously he wasn't going to tell her then. The road was fairly clear of water but, as they reached the top of the hill leading down to the shops and station, she could see that the flood-water was deep there. He turned the car up the hill and presently stopped before Lydia's door.

Lydia flung the door open as he got out and went to

open Araminta's door. 'Jason, oh, Jason. The phone's out of order and Jimmy's gone—I know he is.' She burst into tears. 'I don't know what to do…'

'Stop crying, Lydia, and tell us just what has happened, then we can go and look for Jimmy.'

They had all gone into the kitchen, where the table was littered with plates and mugs and something was boiling dry on the gas stove. Araminta turned it off. 'Shall I make us all a cup of tea while you tell Jason what happened?'

Lydia sat down at the table. 'I haven't been able to do anything—I'd love a cup of tea. Dear Araminta, so sensible…'

Jason had taken off his Burberry and helped Araminta with hers. 'A quick meal?' he suggested softly. 'We can eat and talk at the same time—we can't rush off until we have some idea of where to go.'

Araminta put eggs on to boil, made toast, cleared the dishes off the table and washed the mugs. 'Where is Gloria?' she asked.

'Thank heaven, she's staying with friends in Bath. Jimmy was spending the weekend with the Dempsters—you know—on the other side of the river.' Lydia mopped her eyes and blew her nose. 'He and Philip Dempster went off for a hike after school yesterday afternoon, although the Dempsters tried to stop them, but you know what boys are… Philip didn't get back until late in the evening. He said Jimmy had fallen and hurt his leg—somewhere—oh, miles away and no roads—you know where I mean: woods and rough fields and the river running through the middle.' She paused and gulped and Araminta put a mug of tea in her hand, passed one to Jason, and dished up the eggs.

'I couldn't eat,' said Lydia, weeping again.

'I dare say there'll be a lot for you to do when we bring Jimmy back,' said Araminta in a sensible voice. 'You will feel more like getting his room ready and planning a meal if you've eaten something yourself.'

Lydia smiled at her. 'I think you must be Jason's treasure,' she said, and took a piece of toast.

'We'll need to cross the river,' said Jason.

'The bridge is down; the Dempsters phoned just before the line went dead. They said it may have caved in and they didn't dare to take the car across.'

'Had Philip any idea how far away they were when Jimmy hurt himself?'

'He thought about two miles, but he was ages getting back—he had to go round the worst of the floods.'

'I'll take the car as far as the bridge and take a look…' He caught Araminta's eye and smiled a little. 'All right, we'll take a look. The sooner the better.'

They had to drive down into the village before they could turn off towards the bridge, and the river and the floods were deep here. Araminta curled her toes in her wellies in speechless terror as they reached the bridge and Jason stopped the car in the swirling water. 'I'll cast an eye on the damage before we go over,' he told her cheerfully, and got out of the car.

It was a narrow bridge built of stone, and the flood-water was fast enveloping it. She watched Jason go to the end and then turn and come slowly back. He got into the car again. 'I think we might risk it. There's that piece of higher ground on the other side; we can park there and walk.'

Araminta closed her eyes as they went over the bridge, her teeth clenched so tightly that her jaws ached. 'You can look now,' said Jason, and parked the car on a rough bit of ground away from the worst of the flood.

It was like a nightmare. If it hadn't been for Jason's large hand holding hers firmly she would have turned and run. The wind seemed to strike at her from all sides and she couldn't see for the blinding rain. At least she could cry without its being noticed, the tears streaming down her cheeks to mingle with the rain. Presently she began to feel better. Jason seemed to know where he was going, forging ahead in the teeth of the wind, taking her with him. She supposed that there was a path, but since there was water all over the place it wasn't visible. There was no point in asking where they were going either; she would never be able to make herself heard above the wind. She squelched along, her feet sopping inside the wellies because the water had splashed over them, and she discovered that she was really rather happy.

What would happen, she wondered, if she were to stand still and tell Jason that she loved him? Only of course it wasn't possible; the wind would sweep her off her feet and, even if it quietened down long enough for her to tell him, she would still have to shout—one should declare one's love in a shy whisper, preferably in a pretty dress, with soft lighting. A tug on her arm brought her back to the realities of life. Jason was changing course, going towards a copse beside the river, which was bedraggled and a foot deep in muddy water.

They hadn't struggled halfway through when Araminta gave a small shriek. 'There he is—look. Wedged between that fallen tree and those bushes.'

He was conscious too, cold and wet and in pain, but alive. One leg was doubled up under him, though, and the professor squatted down beside him to take a look. First he took a flask from his pocket and poured some of its contents down Jimmy's throat before handing it to Araminta.

She took a mouthful and caught her breath and gave him a reproachful look, which he ignored, before he took a pull himself. 'Now to work,' he said cheerfully. 'Jimmy, we will have to hurt you before we can get you out of here...'

'Shall I go back and get a stretcher and some people?' suggested Araminta.

Jason glanced at the swollen river racing past, carrying trees and wooden boxes, a hen-coop, and a mass of debris besides, and then he looked at her. She gulped— of course, the river was rising all the time, and before help could reach them, even if she could get back on her own, the flood would be upon them. She said, 'What do you want me to do?' and glowed at his smile.

He told her. Jimmy fainted when Jason took out a knife and cut off his shoe, which was fortunate for him, and Araminta, holding his leg steady while Jason straightened it until she heard the bones grate together, felt queasy. 'Don't leave go,' she was warned, as he took a plastic pack from somewhere under his Burberry, eased it on to the leg and inflated it, strapped it firmly, and stood up. He helped her to her numbed feet and just for a moment held her close. He kissed the tip of her nose. 'You will have to hang on to my coattails,' he shouted above the storm, and bent to heave the still-unconscious Jimmy on to his shoulders.

Getting there had been awful; getting back was far worse, even though they had the wind behind them. She slithered and stumbled along behind Jason's enormous back, thankful when he paused for a rest, clinging to his mac with numb hands. If she had had the breath she would have cheered when they reached the car. Instead she opened doors and laid out rugs and, when told to do so, got in beside Jimmy, who was reviving nicely, and held him steady while Jason took the car over the bridge once more, through the flooded village and finally home.

It was all rather a blur after that; it was only hours later, when Jason had driven away with Jimmy and his mother, bound for Odstock Hospital, that Araminta mulled over the day. Alone in the house, and uncertain when they would get back, she had tidied up, laid the table for a meal, put soup to simmer on the stove, fed the animals and made up the beds. Jason had told her to go to bed if they weren't back by eleven o'clock, but it was warm in the kitchen and the noise of the storm wasn't so loud. She put her head on the table and went to sleep.

When she woke it was one o'clock, and it seemed to her that the storm wasn't as fierce. She went upstairs and tumbled into bed, to wake to a thankfully quiet morning. The rain had stopped and the wind was a mere breeze. She crept downstairs and found Jason in the kitchen, making tea.

She blinked at him from a sleepy face. 'I went to bed. When did you get back? How is Jimmy?'

'Two o'clock and he's in his bed. His leg's in plaster and no harm done otherwise.'

She fetched mugs and milk and sugar and they sat together at the table and drank their tea. 'We'll go home today—after tea. Patty is spending a couple of days in Shaftesbury with friends—I'll fetch her later. Tom will be home this week, and I'll warn Dr Sloane.' He smiled from a tired face. 'Thank you, Araminta, I couldn't have managed without you!'

'I'll start getting breakfast,' said Araminta, not meeting his eye in case she said something she might regret later.

Their journey back wasn't easy; there were frequent halts where roads had been blocked, although on the main roads the floods were draining away already, so that it took twice as long as usual. Araminta heaved a great sigh of relief as they stopped in front of the house and Jason came to help her out. They hadn't talked much on the journey, but there had been no need. Now he said, 'I hope Mrs Buller has a meal ready.' He opened the front door and found Buller in the hall, hurrying to meet them.

'A very anxious time,' he observed. 'Me and Mrs Buller have been worried. There's some dinner ready when you would like it, ma'am.'

'Ten minutes? We're very hungry...'

'Perhaps you would like a tray in bed,' suggested the professor.

She looked astonished. 'Me? Oh, no, thank you, that is, unless...'

Jason was watching her, knowing what she was about to say. 'Good—may we have it in ten minutes or so, Buller?' And to Araminta he added, 'Time for a drink, my dear.'

All the same she went to bed early. There was a pile of letters by Jason's chair and a sheaf of messages he must be impatient to read. She wished him goodnight, expressed her pleasure at being home again, and went upstairs.

It was during the night that she woke and decided that something would have to be done. It wasn't honest to go on as they were; she would tell him that she had fallen in love with him and leave him to decide what to do. She had never been good at pretending... She went to sleep again, and when she woke it was morning. She remembered that he had a list, which meant that he would be up already.

She pulled on her dressing-gown, stuck her feet in slippers and flew downstairs. He was in the drawing-room, standing by the garden door while the dogs raced around on the little lawn. He had his post in one hand, and as she went in he turned to look at her over his spectacles.

'Jason,' said Araminta. 'Jason—there's something I must tell you. Can you spare a minute?'

He put the letters down, took his spectacles off and put them in his pocket, and crossed the room. 'I can spare a whole lifetime for you, my own dear heart.'

She gave a great gulp, peering up at him through an untidy head of hair.

'You—what? I'm your own…?'

'Dear heart.' He nodded. 'Indeed you are, Araminta. I have been waiting for you all my life and when I found you I didn't know it—not at first.'

'Oh, Jason—you mean you love me too? I was going to tell you…'

He had taken her in his arms. 'Darling girl, a moment.' He bent to kiss her, gently at first and then with a fierce enjoyment which took her breath.

Perhaps there was no need to tell him, she thought dreamily, he seemed to know already. All the same she said firmly, 'I must tell you, my dear Jason, I love you too.' Then, when he had kissed her again, she added in a wifely voice, 'You'll be late for work, Jason.'

Buller, coming into the hall, heard the professor's shout of laughter and trod back to the kitchen. 'Happy ever after, that's what—didn't I tell you?' He beamed at his wife. 'Happy ever after and about time too!'

* * * * *

*When Jed Dalloway started over, ranching a
mountain plot for his recluse boss is what saved him.
So when hometown girl April Reed offers a deal
to develop the land, Jed tells her no sale.
But his heart doesn't get the message...*

*Read on for a sneak preview of
the next book in* New York Times *bestselling author
Allison Leigh's Return to the Double C miniseries,*
A Promise to Keep.

"Don't look at me like that, April."

She raised her gaze to his. "Like what?"

His fingers tightened in her hair and her mouth ran dry.
She swallowed. Moistened her lips.

She wasn't sure if she moved first. Or if it was him.

But then his mouth was on hers and like everything
else about him, she felt engulfed by an inferno. Or maybe
the burning was coming from inside her.

There was no way to know.

No reason to care.

Her hands slid up the granite chest, behind his neck,
where his skin felt even hotter beneath her fingertips, and
slipped through his thick hair, which was not hot, but
instead felt cool and unexpectedly silky.

His arm around her tightened, his hand pressing her
closer while his kiss deepened. Consuming. Exhilarating.

Her head was whirling, sounds roaring.

It was only a kiss.

But she was melting.

She was flying.

And then she realized the sounds weren't just inside her head.

Someone was laying on a horn.

She jerked back, her gaze skittering over Jed's as they both turned to peer through the curtain of white light shining over them.

"Mind getting at least one of these vehicles out of the way?" The shout was male and obviously amused.

"Oh for cryin'—" She exhaled. "That's my uncle Matthew," she told Jed, pushing him away. "And I'm sorry to say, but we are probably never going to live this down."

Don't miss
A Promise to Keep *by Allison Leigh,*
available March 2020 wherever
Harlequin Special Edition books and ebooks are sold.

Harlequin.com